HEARTBREAK AT HARPERS

ROSIE CLARKE

Boldwood

First published in Great Britain in 2024 by Boldwood Books Ltd.

Copyright © Rosie Clarke, 2024

Cover Design by Colin Thomas

Cover Photography: Colin Thomas

A CIP catalogue record for this book is available from the British Library.

Paperback ISBN 978-1-78513-119-6

Large Print ISBN 978-1-78513-120-2

Hardback ISBN 978-1-78513-118-9

Ebook ISBN 978-1-78513-121-9

Kindle ISBN 978-1-78513-122-6

Audio CD ISBN 978-1-78513-113-4

MP3 CD ISBN 978-1-78513-114-1

Digital audio download ISBN 978-1-78513-116-5

Boldwood Books Ltd
23 Bowerdean Street
London SW6 3TN
www.boldwoodbooks.com

PROLOGUE

'What do you think of this, Beth?' Sally Harper placed some photographs and a few lines of explanatory script on the desk in her office at Harpers Emporium. 'I was asked by *Tatler* magazine to provide them with some copy for a feature they want to do on Harpers – do you think they will like these?'

Sally had made a collection of photographs of the various windows Harpers had presented through the years since they had first opened in 1911, right through the war until today, which was a Thursday at the end of February 1926. She'd dug out some pictures of members of her staff, some of whom had not returned from the war, together with images of some rather special items that were currently on sale in the prestigious London store.

'Look at this one of me when I was first employed here,' Beth Burrows remarked with a laugh as she picked it up. The picture had faded over the years, but she could still see the high-necked dress she'd worn for her first day at work; she'd worked in the office at first before becoming a supervisor in the hats and bags department. 'I had forgotten these were taken...'

'Yes, so had I until I found them in Ben's desk,' Sally said. 'I shan't be including these very early ones, but I thought you would like to see them. I doubt the magazine will use more than half a dozen and they will probably feature the windows to highlight the changing times since Harpers opened.'

'Yes, I imagine that is what they will be more interested in,' Beth agreed. She sipped her coffee, looking fondly at her friend, who was wearing a soft, low-waisted dress in a dark blue with a neat white collar. 'Fashions have certainly changed a lot!'

'Haven't they?' Sally said and laughed as she held up a faded black and white picture of herself. 'Not quite what appears in their fashion pages these days.'

'No, I should say not. What did you do to get the *Tatler* interested?'

'Nothing really,' Sally laughed at the disbelief on Beth's face. 'Ben took me to a reception at the Savoy some months ago, before last Christmas. It was to honour some war heroes and I got talking to a young man. He was very interested in Harpers, because he'd been told that I more or less kept it going throughout the war. I didn't think anything of it at the time, but then he came to the office and asked to see me. He said he was doing a series of articles for the magazine about the way life had changed in Britain since the war – the roaring twenties and all that – and he'd been told that I'd kept most of my female staff on when the men returned home. He was intrigued and wanted to know more. What I thought about women's role in business and society and a whole lot of other stuff.'

'What does Ben think about it?' Beth asked. 'Or have you not been able to ask him?'

'It was a few days before he left for America when I was approached. He thought it should be good publicity for the store and I suppose it will.'

Beth nodded. 'I read the *Tatler* and they are pretty fair in their reporting, but be careful what you tell them, Sally. I wouldn't let them have any personal stuff if I were you.'

'That is what Ben said,' Sally smiled but looked thoughtful. 'During the war, there was a picture of me in one of the papers – and that's how my mother found me...' Sally sighed because for so many years she hadn't even known her mother was alive. Brought up in a convent, an illegitimate child, apparently abandoned by her mother at birth, she had not known the true story. Her mother had been forced to give her up at the time, but when she tried to reclaim her, the nuns would not tell her where Sally was because they did not consider her a fit mother.

'Yes, I know.' Beth nodded. 'She looks very well these days and your stepfather, too. I think the years since she came to live near to you have treated them well, Sally.'

'How is your father-in-law and Vera?' Sally asked. Bert Burrows had married for the second time to a widow he'd met a few years back, something that had surprised them all at the time.

'Well, I think,' Beth replied. 'I see them most days – but often only for a few minutes. The children go there after school sometimes if I am here – or out with a friend.'

Beth came in to Harpers two mornings a week for her meetings with Sally and did her walk about the store; it was her role to take note of anything untoward and report it and also to give her opinions on what might be changed to improve sales or conditions. It was just an interesting thing to do and her viewpoint was important to Sally, who liked to talk things over. Ben oversaw the store in general, making decisions about renovations, new departments, expansions, and he did the buying for a few departments. He was actually on a buying trip at the moment. He'd gone to America to try to source some new suppliers but was expected home in a couple of weeks or so. Sally still did the buying for certain departments and kept a general eye on the store, though, these days, they had several buyers as well as the store manager and all the department supervisors as well as a larger office staff. Harpers was a thriving concern and very different to the way it had been during the war.

'Well, I shall keep my information all very much on the business side,' Sally said decisively. 'It can't hurt to remind people of the way it was – even though I think some of the younger ones are doing their best to forget.' The papers were always reporting some wild party or kick-up that the 'Bright Young Things' had been involved in; treasure hunts were the rage and often involved a group of intoxicated young men and women driving round town looking for things on the treasure list. They didn't much care whose property they appropriated, including policemen's helmets and even chimney pots.

Beth nodded. 'I shall look forward to the issue featuring Harpers. You will let me know when it is coming out?'

'Yes, of course,' Sally said as Beth prepared to leave. 'I was wondering if you could come in full-time for a week next month, Beth. We will be doing the stocktaking in the fashion departments before our spring sale and the supervisor there is new – not quite on top of things yet. If you wouldn't mind giving her a hand?'

'Oh, I'd love to,' Beth told her at once. 'The boys can go to Dad and Vera for their tea and I enjoy anything like that, as you know.'

'Good.' Sally stood up and collected her bits and pieces. 'I'll talk to you soon – and thanks for your advice. I know it is good, as always.'

'We've been friends a long time,' Beth said as they touched hands for a moment. 'Nearly fifteen years since we first met—' She laughed. 'Oh, that makes me feel old.'

'Well, you're not – you're in the prime of life,' Sally retorted, eyes sparkling. 'We are both very lucky, Beth. We have good husbands and children and friends. I don't see Mick O'Sullivan and Andrea much these days since they went over to Ireland to live – and I do miss Maggie, when she doesn't come up to town, but you and I – we go on forever.' Mick had been a good friend of Sally's for many years. He'd married one of Harpers' supervisors, and after Andrea's son left school, they all went over to his home in Ireland to live.

'Let's hope so,' Beth said and laughed. 'I'd best get on. Don't forget you are bringing the children to tea on Saturday and they're all going to watch a football match with Jack first.'

'I am not sure Jenny will go to the match,' Sally said, 'but she can stay and help with getting their tea if she wants.'

'I bet she decides to go to the match.' Beth quipped as she left and Sally nodded as the door closed behind her. Her daughter Jenny had not yet reached her teens but was a rather opinionated young girl of nearly twelve. She liked to have her own way and was sometimes mutinous with her mother, though Ben had only to look at her to have her grinning and wanting to please him.

Sally smiled to herself. Her son, Peter, was a loving boy, two years younger than his sister, but easy-going and gentle – unless fighting with Jenny. She wouldn't change either of them or her life.

Clearing her thoughts of home and family, Sally reached for the latest account sheets. She liked to keep her eye on them each week, to watch out for dips or surges in takings so she could understand the position the store was in financially. She didn't check the accounts; they had office staff for that and an accountant at the end of the year, but she watched the sales figures and, of late, they had been showing a definite downturn.

The accounts had gone up steadily for the first few years after the war and Harpers had done very well. The whole country had been buzzing after the end of hostilities; the age, one of prosperity. It was also the era of the Flapper, of cocktail parties and a feeling of throwing caution to the wind. The Jazz Age had the young women showing their legs, driving cars and throwing off the inhibitions of their parents. It was a good time to be alive.

However, lately, Sally had noticed a drop in Harpers' sales and she cast her eye over the latest figures to see if there was an obvious pattern. Yes, this week was slightly down on last week, so the trend was continuing. She frowned slightly. As yet, it was nothing to worry her – and, as she'd said to Beth, the years at Harpers had been good for them all. She could only hope that this was a glitch and not a sign that the good times were gradually coming to an end.

1

Harpers was thronged with customers that March morning, several ladies browsing the dress rails, and others in the fitting rooms, as the spring sunshine brought out the crowds after a dull few weeks. Life was brighter, the war almost forgotten in this new golden age that had been promised. Time to have fun, to dance and party. Time to make up for all the heartache that had gone before.

'Mrs Burrows, please...' Beth turned as the young salesgirl approached her.

'Yes, Miss Wilson, how can I help you?'

'I know you told me, but I can't remember – where should I enter the spoiled and damaged items in the book?'

Beth sighed inwardly, as she once again showed her the column listing stock that would be placed in the next sale. Kitty Wilson was a pretty young girl, but whether she was up to being a sales assistant at Harpers Emporium was debatable in Beth's opinion. Sally Harper had asked Beth if she would come in to help out in the dress department this week, since its manageress, Mrs Phillips, had recently left due to ill health. Another senior assistant, Marion Jones, was temporarily in charge but had confessed she didn't feel entirely confident coping with customers and the quarterly stocktaking.

'I don't want to let you down, Mrs Harper,' Marion had told Sally. 'I feel a bit lost since Mrs Phillips left. While I can manage the sales side, I don't feel able to oversee the stock accounting at the same time.'

Sally had perfectly understood the young woman's reticence and that was why Beth had agreed to come in daily during the stocktaking and it was as well she had, because Miss Jones had all she could manage with a continuous stream of customers. Harpers was very busy that morning.

'Mrs Burrows...?' Kitty Wilson's voice broke into Beth's thoughts once more and she turned with an expensive gown in her hands.

'Yes, Miss Wilson?' she asked. 'What is worrying you now?'

'It's just this dress,' the younger woman replied, looking anxious. 'Someone must have tried it on and got lip rouge on it, I think – but it is such an expensive dress. The ticket says six guineas and I think the mark might come off if I took it home and washed it...' She looked even more anxious as Beth was silent. 'Is that wrong?'

'The sentiment is laudable, Miss Wilson,' Beth said and was pleased to see the girl's anxiety fade away. 'I don't think we can do that, but the dress will be reduced to half-price and whoever buys it will be able to wash it themselves. I have just found a similar mark on this dress – and it came from Miss Susie, an exclusive designer, and was twice the price of the one you have there.'

'It was very careless of whoever did it, Mrs Burrows,' Kitty said, shaking her head.

'Both dresses have adequate openings and should be easy to get on and off, so it shouldn't have happened, which makes me wonder if it was deliberate.'

'But why?' Kitty's eyes opened wide.

'Either as a malicious act – if someone has a grudge against the store or its owners, or if they want to buy the dresses in the sale, because everyone knows that Harpers has a sale of slightly damaged goods three times a year. Mrs Harper says it clears old stock and that people like a bargain – and, as you say, these small marks would come out with washing.'

'Shall I make a note of any others that have been damaged in the same way?' Kitty asked and Beth revised her earlier opinion of the girl. She was thinking in exactly the same way as herself.

'Yes, if you can manage to do that as well as the normal stocktaking,' Beth said. 'Am I right in thinking both these dresses are a size 36?'

'Mine is,' Kitty told her. 'I'll check that as well, Mrs Burrows.'

'Yes, that would be helpful,' Beth replied. 'To make it easier, put all of them onto one rail as you find them. I should like to know if it is merely a coincidence or deliberate.'

Kitty nodded. 'Shall I take that one, Mrs Burrows?'

Beth held it out to her and she carried it away, placing both damaged dresses on the rail indicated.

Beth returned to checking the expensive rails, many of the exclusive gowns had come from the much in-demand Miss Susie in Dressmakers' Alley in the East End of London. Sally Harper was friendly with the designer, who was – rumour had it – a lady of some consequence. Sally had told Beth that the actual designer was a society lady, though for the moment her identity was a closely guarded secret, and the establishment was run by Miss Susie, who was a personal friend of the lady and had once been her dresser. Of course, Beth hadn't told anyone of Sally's confidences, but she was sure in her own mind that it must be Lady Diane Cooper. She'd met the lady once, coming from Sally's house when she'd taken the children on the Underground to Hampstead to visit the Harpers. Sally had introduced her as a friend, but Beth had glimpsed a folder of exquisite designs.

Beth examined the garments closely but found no more traces of lip rouge. Most of them were recent stock and nothing else would be placed on the sale rail. However, as she finished her task, Kitty Wilson came up to her carrying two further garments. One was a pretty afternoon dress and the second a silk blouse.

'Both of these have just a trace of the same colour lip rouge – and they are both the same size,' Kitty told her. 'It does seem that your suspicions are right, Mrs Burrows. I don't believe so much damage could be accidental, do you?'

'I very much doubt it,' Beth replied. 'Thank you for drawing my attention to this, Miss Wilson. I shall mention it to Miss Jones – and to Mrs Harper. When we have the sale, it will be interesting to see if one person buys all four items at the reduced price.'

'That is like stealing!' Kitty exclaimed. 'It isn't right.'

'No, it certainly isn't,' Beth agreed. 'I will check with Miss Jones and see if any more items have been similarly damaged.'

'Whoever did it should be ashamed of themselves.' Kitty was indignant.

'Unfortunately, some people have no shame,' Beth said. 'I remember we had a thief working in the bag and jewellery department once. She stole several items from all the departments.'

Kitty looked horrified. 'One thing my dad doesn't hold with is thieving. He'd have the skin off my back if I ever stole one penny.'

'How is your father, Miss Wilson? I believe Mrs Harper told me he hadn't been well?'

'He had an accident at work,' Kitty said, looking sad for a moment. 'He is a builder, Mrs Burrows, and he fell from a ladder. The doctor said he was lucky he came off so lightly, but he had a broken leg and damaged his spine. I think he is in a lot of pain, though he doesn't say much.'

'I am so sorry to hear that,' Beth replied. 'Was that why you applied for a job at Harpers?'

Kitty nodded. 'My mother never wanted me to work. She was a seamstress before she married and I helped her at home. She still makes clothes for ladies she used to work for and I can sew quite well.'

'Why didn't you find work as a seamstress?'

'Because Mum says it is poorly paid work and ruins your eyes. Dad said I didn't need to work, but then he fell and they cut his wages to less than half until he recovers. It is barely enough to pay the rent and coal—'

'Oh, that was unkind,' Beth sympathised, but she knew that many employers would simply refuse to pay employees who could not work; instead they dismissed them on the slightest pretext.

'Dad says his boss can't afford to pay him if he doesn't work. The accident was his own fault – and he wants his job back when he is better.' Kitty beamed at her. 'I don't mind working, Mrs Burrows. I love it here at Harpers. Everyone is friendly and it's nice being amongst beautiful things.' For a moment, her smile dimmed. 'I wanted to be a secretary, but Mum needed me at home – and Dad says girls from decent families don't have to work. He thinks I should just stay home until I get married...'

'I was once in a similar situation. My aunt didn't think shop work was the right thing for a "properly brought up" girl, either.'

Kitty's smile came back instantly. 'Thank you, Mrs Burrows—' She seemed as though she wanted to say more, but just then Miss Jones approached them.

'It is time for your break, Miss Wilson. Mrs Burrows – may I have a word, please?'

Beth turned to her with a smile. 'How can I help, Miss Jones?'

'A customer has asked for some embroidery on one of our gowns as an extra. I wasn't sure if we still did that?'

'Mrs Stockbridge does wonderful embroidery. It makes such a difference to plain gowns, but not everyone wants it these days. However, I am sure she would take it on if we asked her. Do you know what the customer wants?'

'I said I would speak to you – if you could just have a word.'

Beth agreed. Minnie Stockbridge didn't do as much as she had before her marriage, but she was a lovely person and Beth was certain she would be happy to embroider a gown for their customer if asked. When she talked to the lady who had enquired about the embroidery, she discovered that she'd had a gown embroidered by Mrs Stockbridge at the beginning of the war and still wore it.

After a few minutes' discussion, Beth was able to send the customer away happy and Marion looked at her in awe. 'Thank you. I wasn't sure what to do, Mrs Burrows. You were so sure Mrs Stockbridge would oblige.'

'I know her well,' Beth smiled. 'We are old friends. You may leave it to me to arrange.'

Beth smiled as the young woman went off to serve another customer. It was just like old times, when she'd been supervisor in the bag, hat and jewellery department, and she was enjoying herself.

* * *

'So, you think those items were deliberately soiled?' Sally Harper frowned as Beth joined her for coffee at their regular meeting in her office. 'That is annoying. We accept a certain amount of damage to stock; it is only to be expected, but if done deliberately... and one of them was a Miss Susie design?' She shook her head in disbelief.

'Yes, I'm afraid so,' Beth said. 'At the moment it is with the other damaged items in the stockroom. We normally mark them down when you have the spring sale in April, but... I believe you said none of Miss Susie's designs were to be sold cheaply?'

'Yes, I did,' Sally agreed. 'I promised their designer, because she is keen to keep her designs exclusive. What size is it?'

'All the items are the same size – 36-inch hip.'

Sally's gaze narrowed. 'That is rather suspicious. You informed Marion Jones, of course. We need to watch for this sort of thing if it is deliberate.'

'She was shocked, too, and promised to watch carefully.' Beth nodded her agreement. 'It is unpleasant if it is deliberate and rather too much of a coincidence to be accidental, I think.'

'Someone wants to buy themselves some nice things at a reduced price,' Sally remarked. 'Well, we shan't oblige them.' She thought for a moment. 'I think we will offer the slightly damaged goods you've picked out to our girls. They can have them at the reduced price, plus their staff discount.' Sally's eyes sparkled with mischief. 'I am sure some of Harpers' girls would be happy to have something pretty at less than half the shop price.'

'I'll speak to Marion Jones,' Beth said, amused at Sally's reaction. 'Tell her that those four items are only for staff. I know Kitty Wilson admired the day dress. She offered to wash it for us, said she could easily get the mark out.'

'Yes, I rather like Kitty,' Sally smiled. 'I hope she can afford to buy it, but I think she has to give most of her money to her mother.'

'Yes, I expect so. She told you her mother only allowed her to work because they badly needed money?'

'Yes. Her father is laid up after his accident...' Sally looked thoughtful. 'I think all the girls in the dress department should get a small bonus for their hard work with the stocktaking. I'll inform Mr Stockbridge. An extra five shillings this week.'

'Lucky girls,' Beth said with a smile. 'You are such a good employer, Sally – you and Ben.'

'We like to be fair to our young ladies,' Sally said, a hint of mischief in her bright eyes. 'After all, I was one of them a few years ago and I know most of them are stony broke half the time.'

Beth nodded. 'I remember the feeling, Sally. We've both been very lucky in our lives and it is right that we do what we can for others. I would buy that Miss Susie dress in a heartbeat, but I need a larger size now. I do hope one of the girls can buy it.'

'Yes, let's hope so. I'll tell Marion they can pay by instalments if they wish.' She smiled fondly at Beth. 'You haven't forgotten you are coming to lunch Sunday week – you and Jack and the children? I'm hoping Ben will be back by then, but in his wire, he said he couldn't be certain and would let me know if he managed to get a passage. I haven't heard anything more, so perhaps he was too late. He'd been told there was a berth going, but he might have missed it.'

'I suppose the passenger ships are busy again now. Everyone wants to do all the things we couldn't in the war.' Beth smiled. 'No, of course we haven't forgotten we're lunching with you. We all love coming to visit you, Sally.'

'Yes. I think it is why Harpers is so busy at the moment. It is as if those who survived the war feel they have to live hard because they are on borrowed time.'

Beth gave a little shiver. 'Please don't, Sally. It makes me wonder what can go wrong next – but I think you are right. The papers are filled with photographs of bright young women and dashing men dancing the night away and the outrageous clothes some of them wear... I think it is almost as if they are determined to party until they drop.'

'Yes, that is absolutely true,' Sally replied seriously. 'Some of the young girls are becoming quite wild... drinking and dashing from one nightclub to another.'

Beth nodded. The papers often had headline stories about young debutantes and their escorts behaving in a shocking manner. Young men had always been high-spirited, yet somehow that was expected, but now the young ladies were behaving similarly. It was a sign of the age, so they said – or a reaction to the dreadful war. 'Yes, I suppose they do,' Beth agreed. 'I can't understand it myself, Sally. Even if I was free to go out every evening, I wouldn't behave like some of them do.' She laughed. 'With my two boys, chance would be a fine thing.'

'I've always had help with the children,' Sally said. 'I couldn't manage without Mrs Hills – but Mum looks after mine a lot of the time now. She adores Peter and Jenny; says she's making up for not being able to look after me when I was little.'

'The children love their granny, don't they?'

'Yes, they do, and I don't worry when Mum is there. I know she will look after them while I am working.' She was thoughtful for a moment. 'Have you seen the window displays this week?'

'I caught a glimpse as I came in this morning. Why?'

'Have a look when you leave this evening.' Sally frowned. 'Something is missing but I don't know what...'

'Yes, of course I will.' Beth looked at her. 'You haven't heard from Mr Marco, I suppose?'

'I haven't and Ben has been abroad. It was supposed to be a few weeks Mr Marco would be away, but he wrote and extended his stay yet again...' Their talented window dresser – and one of Ben's closet friends – had suddenly decided to go off to France after Christmas. They'd thought it would be a quick visit, but he'd written to Ben and asked for extended leave. 'Oh well, I suppose he will come back when he's ready.'

'I am sure he will.' Beth nodded and glanced at the clock. 'I'd better go, Sally. I have some more checking to do and I want to leave by three as Vera has a doctor's appointment at four, which means I need to collect the boys from school.'

'Oh, nothing too serious I hope?'

'I certainly hope not,' Beth replied with a frown. 'She and Bert are so comfortable together. It would be a shame if anything were to cut their time short.'

'Let's hope not,' Sally said instantly. Bert had been the store manager at Harpers for years and she thought a lot of him; it would be sad if anything happened to his wife.

'I'm sure it's nothing much,' Beth said.

2

Kitty Wilson walked the last few yards to her home in the street of back-to-back terraces. Before her father injured himself, they'd lived in a much nicer area with a back garden and neighbours who were friends, but they hadn't been able to afford the rent after he'd had to stop work, and, just a few weeks previously, they'd had to move to Kettle's Yard. It was so called because the three rows of terraced homes formed a kind of square, at the bottom of which was a junkyard with a big board advertising Kettle's Yard. Sometimes, a smell hung in the air, emanating from the yard, and Kitty's mother complained that she'd seen rats at the back of the house. She was sure they had come from the junkyard.

'I can't imagine what goes on there,' she'd complained with a shudder of horror. 'I never expected I would end up in a place like this...'

Kitty's mother was at the big black range, stirring a pot, when Kitty entered and looked up but didn't say anything.

Kitty put down her handbag, took off her coat and turned to her. 'Is there anything I can do, Mum?'

'Well, I'm glad someone wants to help.' Annie Wilson cast a look of disgust at her husband as he sat slumped in his chair, nursing a mug of hot tea. 'My poor mother would turn in her grave if she saw what I'd been reduced to...' Her sniff was audible, but Kitty looked at her and couldn't see any tears.

'Dad can't help it, Mum,' she said, defending him. 'It's only until he gets back on his feet again.'

'If he ever does—'

'Mum!' Kitty glanced at her father, but he didn't appear to have heard. His head was back, his eyes closed; she noticed he hadn't shaved and it looked as if he was wearing the clothes he'd been wearing for days now. Kitty's heart sank. Her father had been a proud, upright man and the change in him was disheartening. He seemed as if he'd just given up. She went to his chair and touched his hand. 'Are you all right, Dad? Is there anything I can get you?'

He looked up at her words and smiled. 'Kitty, you're back. Did you have a good day?'

'Yes, thank you. It is lovely working at Harpers.'

'Good. I'm glad you're happy, lass.'

Something in his tone told Kitty that he had heard her mother's complaints but had chosen to ignore them. She wondered how much more he'd had to listen to since his accident. She glanced at her mother, who was still stirring something on the range. Her face wore a look of discontent and Kitty's stomach plummeted. It was obvious her mother was in one of her moods. She'd suffered from them all her life, though never as much as now.

'Shall I set the table, Mum?'

'It's your job,' her mother replied coldly. 'Or do I have to do everything around here?'

Kitty didn't answer, because whatever she said would be wrong. Instead she fetched a cloth from the dresser drawer and spread it over the pine table; then she set cutlery and plates for three people.

'What are we having this evening? It smells lovely.' Kitty hoped a compliment would ease her mother's sullen anger.

'Stew again and more vegetables than meat,' came the reply, but Kitty's mother didn't turn.

'Oh, I forgot,' Kitty said brightly. 'I've been told to expect another five shillings in my pay packet this week – because of the extra work we've all done stocktaking.'

'Well, that is something. I will be able to pay the rent man when he comes next Monday.' Kitty's mother turned with a saucepan in her hand. 'Not that I approve of you working in that place – but beggars can't be choosers.'

'Oh, Mum, it is lovely there,' Kitty exclaimed, stung by the tone of her voice. 'I really enjoy helping ladies choose their new clothes – and Mrs Burrows has been there all this week. She is very nice and Miss Jones is, too. I think I was lucky to get the job there.'

'In my family, girls didn't go out to work. They stayed home and helped their mother until they married.' Annie Wilson frowned at her. 'I dare say you do your best, Kitty, but we barely get by on your wage... It would be much better if you encouraged that nice Mr Miller to call on you. He would look after us if you married him.'

Kitty swallowed hard. She couldn't meet her mother's eyes as she gave her head a little shake. Joshua Miller owned a big gentlemen's clothing store in Commercial Road and drove a smart car. His elderly mother had lived two doors away from them before they'd moved and he'd stopped by on his frequent visits to her, bringing small gifts of flowers or fruit from his garden. Kitty's mother had insisted that he was sweet on her, but he was in his forties, a widower with two children. He was also a rotund man with close-set eyes and thinning hair. The thought of being married to him sent shivers down Kitty's spine. 'Oh, Mum, please don't,' she begged as the fragrant stew was ladled onto plates. 'I couldn't – I just couldn't...'

'Well, you always were a selfish girl. I suppose that is what comes from your father spoiling you all these years.' Kitty's mother made a tutting sound.

'For goodness' sake, stop bullying the girl, Annie.' Kitty's father's voice cracked like a whip, startling them both. 'You never stop complaining. It isn't her fault we've had to move to this dump – and yes, I do know it isn't what you're used to. I don't like it either, but there's not much I can do about it at the moment. If I can return to work, I'll find us somewhere better to live.'

'What do you mean, *if*?' Annie's look was slaying. 'How do you imagine we'll live if you don't, Robert?'

'Oh, I'll work the minute I can,' he replied bitterly. 'The sooner I can get away from your scolding tongue, the better, woman.' He hauled himself to his feet, using his wooden crutch to steady himself.

'Your meal is on the table,' Annie snapped as he hobbled towards the door. 'Where are you going?'

'Out – to the pub if I can get there,' he replied without turning his head. 'I'm not hungry and I prefer to be with blokes I can trust than sit here and listen to your misery.'

'Well!' Annie glared at Kitty. 'That's the first and last time he speaks to me like that or he'll be sorry.' Her eyes narrowed. 'It's your fault, girl. If you did your duty by us, it needn't have happened.'

Kitty didn't answer. She ate her portion of the stew because she was hungry, but it seemed to stick in her throat. Tears burned behind her eyes, but she held them back. She wouldn't let her mother see how her unkind words hurt her.

'Do you think Dad will be all right?' she said after a few moments of silence. 'Should I go after him?'

'If he falls and hurts himself, it will be his own fault,' Annie declared. 'For all the good he is to this family, he would be better out of the way.'

'You don't mean that,' Kitty cried, horrified. She pushed her plate away, the food unfinished, and jumped up. 'He is my dad and I love him.' She grabbed her coat and rushed out of the kitchen, her cheeks wet with the tears she could no longer hold back.

* * *

Kitty saw her father leaning against one of the houses further down the lane. His face looked white in the gaslight and his eyes were closed, but he opened them as she approached and smiled. 'You shouldn't have come after me, Kitty. I'm all right. I just needed to get away.'

'From Mum's nagging?' Kitty asked and he sighed.

'From sitting in the house all day and staring at a bleak future, Kitty.'

Kitty nodded, because the future did look bleak for him unless he could return to work. 'Surely your leg will mend, Dad? You will be able to work again.'

His eyes met hers. 'The doctor thinks I'm unlikely to go back to my old job...' He hesitated, then, 'It seems the reason I fell was due to a spell of dizziness and... the doctor says it may be something bad in my head...'

'Oh Dad...' Kitty stared at him in distress. She'd believed the fall was due to an accident and he would get better in a few months. 'Does Mum know?'

'Not that I might have something wrong in my head,' he told her. 'But I told her this morning that the doctor thinks I was too severely injured to do what I've always done. I can't carry a hod up a ladder or lay bricks all day. I'll have to let Mr Harding know I won't be back and I'm not sure what else I'll be able to do. It wouldn't suit me to sit in an office all day, but what else is there? I might get a caretaker's job, but the pay wouldn't be as much as I was earning before.'

'Oh, Dad, I'm so sorry,' Kitty said, recognising the blow to his pride. 'But have you been dizzy, again? Does the doctor know what is wrong with you?'

'He says it may be a brain tumour, or a blood clot caused by a seizure, but isn't certain. I'd need to have all sorts of tests at the hospital – and we don't have the money for that, Kitty. Besides, if they discovered something nasty, it would hang over me like a shadow. They probably wouldn't be able to operate, too dangerous – so it's just a case of wait and see whether things get worse.'

Kitty nodded, knowing that what her father said was true. There were many things the doctors didn't truly understand and if her father did have a brain tumour or a blood clot in his head, he was unlikely to receive much relief. Even if they could do it, the operation and care would be far more than they could afford. Her stomach spasmed with sudden fear for him.

'Would you have the tests done if you had the money?' she asked, but he shook his head.

'We don't have it, Kitty, so I haven't considered it.'

Kitty drew a deep breath, then, 'I could ask Mr Miller to lend it to me and pay him back. It would take a long time, but perhaps he wouldn't mind—'

'You are not that naïve, Kitty,' her father said sharply. 'You know he would want something in return. I'll not have you sacrifice yourself for my sake – besides, the doctor may be wrong. The dizzy fit only happened a few times...'

She swallowed hard, forcing herself to say, 'I would do it for your sake, Dad.' She would for him, even though it would make her wretched.

He gave a shake of the head. 'I forbid it. I don't like that man. You stay clear of him, Kitty. You're all I have to brighten my day. We'll manage. You bring in a wage now and I'll find work of some kind – even if it is sweeping up at the jam factory.'

'You shouldn't have to work until you're fit,' Kitty said, but her father was on his feet again. 'Are you coming home?'

'Not yet,' her father replied. 'I was just resting. I may need to rest a few times before I get to the pub, but that's where I'm going. I'll see Mr Harding there and tell him I won't be back to work, not as a bricklayer anyway.'

'Shall I walk with you?' Kitty asked, but again there was a negative gesture.

She stood watching as her father made slow progress down the lane towards the main road and the tears ran down her cheeks. She couldn't imagine life without her father. He was a strict, honest man with high principles and he hadn't spoiled Kitty as her mother claimed, but he had shown her love and he'd taught her to laugh. He'd played with her as a child and been kind but firm as she grew into a young woman. She loved him and it hurt to see him humbled and uncertain.

Kitty loved her mother too. Annie Wilson had a sharp tongue, but she'd been a good enough mother and wife in her own way, and until the move to Kettle's Yard, she'd seemed content – though she'd always grumbled over small things. Kitty knew that it was her mother's pride that was hurt because they'd been brought so low, but she and her father had been able to make the best of what they had – and, of course, Kitty was at Harpers every day and that was a pleasure.

'A penny for them?' A deep voice startled Kitty and she spun round, looking at the man who stood under the gaslight. Lost in her thoughts, she hadn't notice him approach.

'Mr Norton...' she said, catching her breath. He was tall and had broad shoulders, but she didn't know him well and, even though he seemed pleasant, she felt a bit nervous of him. He was, she thought, good-looking, with his light blond hair and blue eyes. 'I didn't see you.'

'You've been crying,' he said, 'and my name is Larry. What's upsettin' you, lass?'

Kitty shook her head. She didn't know this man – had only seen him passing down the street on his horse and cart. 'I must go...' she said and turned, but he reached out and caught her by the arm.

'You're Kitty Wilson. Your family moved into that empty house after your dad had his accident.'

'Yes, we did,' she acknowledged. 'Your dad owns the junkyard.'

'Yes, worse luck,' he said with a big grin. 'I wanted to work on the ships, but he wanted me in the business with him. I've got a sister, but I'm the only son.'

She nodded. 'I must go in. My mother will wonder where I am. I'm not allowed to speak to men.'

'That's a shame. I was going to ask if I could take you for a walk on Sunday afternoon.'

Kitty's cheeks flushed, because he was smiling at her in a way that told her he liked her. 'She wouldn't let me go with you...' she said and discovered that she was a little breathless. 'I'm sorry. I must go in or she will be angry.'

'Why were you crying?' he asked, but she shook her head and pulled away from him. He let her go, but she knew he was watching her as she ran to her house. 'I'm always around if you need help,' he called after her, but Kitty didn't turn her head.

She went into the kitchen to find her mother had cleared the dishes.

Annie turned to look at her, a frown on her face. 'What have you been crying for?'

'Dad's not well,' she answered and then wished she hadn't when her mother scowled.

'Do you think I don't know that. It's me that has to help him. He can't even shave or dress himself properly these days, though I'm sure his leg must be mending by now.' She sniffed. 'It's shame that's what it is – shame for bringing us so low.'

'He couldn't help what happened, Mum. We should be glad he is still alive.'

Annie sniffed. 'I suppose you're right and I've been hard on your dad –

but I hate living here. I had a nice house where we lived before and now look at this place. My parents would be horrified. They were decent folk, never owed a penny in their lives.'

'It isn't so bad...' Kitty said, but as she looked around the kitchen, the words died on her lips. The walls were whitewashed, but dark patches in the corners told of damp, despite the range that was kept going all day and night – and the window was small, making the room dark. The parlour at the back had been wallpapered in a horrible purple and cream stripe, and the bedrooms were cold and a little damp, too. 'Perhaps we can move again when Dad is better.'

'When or if he does get better,' her mother said. 'The doctor told him he won't carry a hod up a ladder again. His trade is bricklaying, so what can he do? From what I can see of things, he'll sit in that chair for the rest of his life. It's no use you crying, Kitty. Don't you think I want to cry? I've told you the only way out for us, but you refuse to do your duty by your parents.'

'Dad wouldn't want me to do that, he said so...' Kitty shook her head at her and then ran upstairs. Her mother was blaming her for their situation – but perhaps she was right and Kitty was selfish to refuse to marry Mr Miller. A shiver went through her. She couldn't bear the thought of being that man's wife – and her father had told her he didn't want it either. If he'd asked her, then she would force herself to accept, though she would rather be dead.

No, she wasn't going to give into her mother's bullying. She would work hard at Harpers and perhaps she would earn enough to help her parents move back to a nicer area.

3

Later that week, Beth called in at her father-in-law's home to collect the children. Vera was sitting in the large kitchen, her knitting at her side, a kettle boiling on the old range beside her. She'd been staring into space, lost in thought, but looked up as she heard Beth enter and smiled.

'I was miles away,' she said and smiled. 'Would you like a cup of tea, love?'

'Thanks, Vera,' Beth replied and watched as the elderly woman moved about, preparing their drink. 'How are you? What did the doctor say?'

'Nothing much,' Vera answered without looking at her. 'The lads are in the garden with your father. He loves playing with them and they love him.'

'Yes, I know,' Beth said, watching as Vera's hand trembled slightly as she passed her a cup of tea. She had the distinct feeling that Vera wasn't telling her something but she hesitated to pry. 'It isn't too much having them here, is it? You would tell me—?'

'Lawks alive, they keep us laughing the whole time,' Vera said and sat down with her tea. 'Besides, it is only this week you're working full-time, isn't it?'

'Yes, but—' Beth was about to ask if there was anything worrying her when the garden door opened and her boys came rushing in, followed by Bert. Their faces were glowing from the fresh air, their eyes shone and their happy looks lifted her heart as they ran to her and she embraced them. 'You've had a lovely time with Grandad?'

'We went to see Grandad's friend. He has greyhounds and the bitch has six puppies,' Jack told her. 'They're lovely, aren't they, Grandad?'

'Aye, they are,' Bert agreed. 'Beautiful little pups and worth a bit. Their father was a champion courser and their mother comes from a line of coursers, too. George reckons he's got a winner or two there.'

'Greyhound coursing!' Vera scoffed, but her gaze was warm as it rested on the boys and her husband. 'It's a cruel sport – and they only do it for gambling.'

Bert grinned at her. 'You won't catch me wasting my money on the dogs, Vera. I've got better things to do with it.'

'I should think so too,' she said, but she was smiling. 'I don't grudge you the odd bet on the horses, Bert, if you fancy it.'

'That's more in my line,' he agreed. 'George reckons he's got a sure-fire winner for this Saturday at Newmarket. I don't think any race can be certain – unless it is fixed, and I don't hold with that – but I'd enjoy a visit to Hampstead Heath one evening to watch the dogs coursing, if you fancy it? George says they mostly chase lures attached to the back of a van anyway, because there aren't always rabbits about – and there's talk they are thinking about some kind of mechanical thing for the greyhounds to chase on a track. If they open one in London, would you fancy a trip out one fine night?'

'Me? Stand there watching some daft dogs run after a lure while a lot of even dafter men yell their heads off?' Vera scoffed. 'You go, Bert. I'll stay home with my knitting and you can tell me all about it.'

'We'll see,' he muttered and accepted a cup of tea. Beth noticed the anxious look that flitted across his face and was swiftly hidden. 'There's a good musical show on at the Haymarket. It's your birthday soon, Vera. You'll have to decide what you want to do for your treat...'

'That sounds lovely,' she agreed and looked at Beth. 'What are you doing this weekend, love?'

'Jack has heard about a circus on Hampstead Heath,' Beth replied. 'He is going to take the children on Saturday afternoon. He will be working in the evening – but if Dad wants to go to Newmarket – or the heath – with his friend I could come and keep you company for a few hours, Vera. I know someone who will look after Jack and Timmy for me.' She frowned, then, 'I think Jack is taking us all for a drive out on Sunday. We'll go to Richmond Park, have a walk, and then have lunch somewhere nice. Jack has to work again in the evening, of course.'

'Doesn't that son of mine ever get an evening off?' Bert asked gruffly. 'The lad never seems to stop working.'

'The restaurant is busy, Dad,' Beth replied. 'He has one Saturday evening off a month and takes me somewhere nice, but I am quite content with my life. I have friends and I meet them sometimes or they come over and have a chat and we have sandwiches and coffee or a light meal if I feel like cooking. Sally Harper invites me over, too. I don't miss out and Jack wants the restaurant to be a success.'

'Of course he does,' Bert said. 'But I hope he won't sacrifice his family on the altar of work.'

'As I said, he is taking the boys out on Saturday and we'll all go out together on Sunday. It is only the evenings he feels he needs to be there. Although, most days, he is at the restaurant for both lunch and dinner service.'

Bert nodded, but he was still frowning. Beth thought it was probably more to do with Vera than the fact that his son worked most evenings. Jack was the manager of Harpers Restaurant in Oxford Street. He and Ben Harper were partners in the venture; they'd opened it just after the war and it had become as prestigious as the store, patronised by a good clientele. When they were first married, he'd been away from home for long periods at sea, and then he'd served in the Merchant Navy during the war. Nowadays, she saw far more of him than in the past, and so did the children. So Bert couldn't be upset by that – no, it had to be Vera. Beth had a niggly feeling in her tummy, but they were obviously not ready to tell her, so she couldn't press for details.

'Well, I'll get home then,' she said, though there was no rush. Jack would still be at the restaurant. Beth had no plans that evening, other than to bathe the children, feed them a light supper and read stories until they fell asleep.

'Yes,' Bert agreed. 'We'll see you tomorrow, Beth love.'

'Thanks, Dad.' Beth kissed his cheek, bidding the children to do the same. She then kissed Vera on the cheek and received a little hug. The boys clambered on Vera's knee and Beth heard a sharp intake of breath. 'Everything all right, Vera?' she asked, feeling anxious.

'Yes, just a knee in the wrong place.' Vera smiled at her and kissed both boys on their pink faces. She told them to be good for their mum and promised treacle tart when they came the next day.

Beth was certain both Bert and Vera were hiding something from her but kept her tongue in check. She would have a quiet word with Bert when she could get him alone. He would tell her what was bothering him, but perhaps Vera didn't want to talk about whatever was wrong with her yet.

* * *

Beth took the Underground line to Hampstead from Euston with the boys, stopping to buy some fruit from a barrow boy who was just packing up his stall.

'Got anything nice for me this evening, Jerry?' she asked and he grinned. They often had a chat when Beth visited his stall. Now and then he gave her a peach or an apple for the boys, refusing to take money for them. He was a friendly lad in his late teens and Beth liked him. She always asked after his family and he told her about his mother, whom he looked after at home.

'Saved some of them grapes for you,' he said and handed her a brown paper bag. She'd seen them on her way to work earlier that day and bought some for herself and the children. 'Thought you'd like a few more?'

'Yes, I would; they were delicious,' Beth answered with a smile and paid him. 'Has it been a good day for you?'

'Yeah, I reckon, sold most of me stuff – get fresh in the mornin'. Wot yer fancy for them lads termorrer?'

'Oh, perhaps oranges?' Beth asked. 'See what is available at the wholesalers' market, Jerry.' She hesitated then, 'How is your mum now?'

'Her foot don't get no better,' he said, his cheerful grin disappearing. 'Them toes of hers are just rottin' away, missus. Doctors reckon nothin' they can do but cut 'em orf.'

'Oh, Jerry, that sounds awful,' Beth murmured sympathetically. 'Is there anything I can do to help you?'

'Nah. I've saved the money for her to have it done,' he replied with a shrug. 'It's just gettin' the old bat to let 'em.' He gave a shrug of his shoulders. 'I've told her they'll go gangrene if she don't, but she won't listen...'

'Well, if you did need extra money, just ask,' Beth said impulsively. 'You can pay me back when you're ready.'

A glimmer of tears appeared in his eyes. 'You're a good 'un, missus,' he said. 'You're the only 'un that asks. If the daft old girl makes up 'er mind to it and I run short, I'll ask.'

'Good. Please do,' Beth said and walked on. Jerry had his pride and probably would rather do three jobs, working all hours, than ask for help, but she knew how much he cared for his mother and wanted him to know help was there if needed.

Beth continued on her way home. Their house, which was about fifteen minutes' walking distance from Sally Harper's in a quiet but more modest residential area, was a fair distance from the station, but they were happy and chattered as they walked. Timmy walked close beside her, but Jack strode out sturdily by her side. The gas lamps were lit and most of the houses in the streets they passed along were showing lights through heavy curtains; there was a smell of smoke in the air as people lit their fires to keep out the chill of the frosty evening air.

Beth was just a few yards from her home when she heard the loud bang. It made her jump and she looked round as she heard three more in quick succession.

That was gunfire! Beth dropped the grapes and grabbed Jack by the hand, rushing the boys the last few feet to her house and unlocking the front door, pushing them inside and locking it after them. She heard shouting and running feet and one more shot, and then it went quiet. Timmy was crying, but Jack looked at her with big frightened eyes.

'Was that shooting, Mum?' he asked.

'Yes, I think it must have been,' she replied honestly. She was utterly shocked and felt a bit trembly inside. 'I think whoever it was has gone now.' She breathed deeply, fighting her own fear because of the children.

'Was it the Germans?' Jack asked and she looked down at his anxious face. 'They won't shoot Dad and Grandad and Grandma, will they?'

'Oh no, darling, they won't,' Beth said and bent to kiss the top of his head. At nearly twelve, he was very grown-up, but still a child in some ways. 'It wasn't the Germans. The war is over, Jack. I think it must have been gangsters – though I would never have expected them around here...'

'Are we safe, Mummy?' Jack asked as Beth switched on every light, leading them into the big kitchen. He never called her Mummy, only Mum, and she understood he was frightened but trying not to show it.

'Yes, of course we are, darling,' Beth assured him; she had to remain calm for their sakes, and they were safe enough. All the doors were solid and locked, and the garden had a high wall all the way round, so she didn't fear any intruders. 'What would you like to eat before bed? A ham sandwich or egg on toast?'

'Can I have a ham sandwich please?' Jack asked and wandered off to sit by the range, which Beth's husband had made up before he left for the restaurant.

'Timmy, stop crying. It's all right now,' Beth told him. 'Are you hungry, love? What would you like to eat?'

'Chocolate cake,' Timmy said promptly. 'Big piece.'

'You can have a tiny piece after you have one little sandwich,' Beth promised. She went over to the automaton that Jack had bought for them the previous Christmas and wound it up. As it played a tune, the stuffed figures shaped to look like monkeys seemed to play their instruments while a little dog twirled at their feet.

'Want doggie,' Timothy said and Jack looked up eagerly.

'Those puppies Grandad showed us were lovely, Mum,' he said. 'Can we have a dog – please?' His little face was strained and anxious and Beth felt herself giving way to his plea. She'd felt they were a bit too young still, especially Timmy, but perhaps it was time.

'Dogs need feeding and walking every day,' she warned.

'I'll do it, Mum. I promise,' Jack said quickly.

'I'll talk to your dad,' she replied. 'We'll see what he says—'

'Thanks, Mum.' Young Jack's face lit up. He knew if his mum said yes, his dad would get them a puppy.

* * *

After the boys had eaten their supper, Beth took them upstairs and gave them a bath in the lovely shining white tub. She knew she was so lucky to have such a luxury in her home, because so many people still went to the toilet in an outside shed and used a tin bath once a week in front of the kitchen fire. Jack had insisted on having one installed when they got their house and it meant she could bathe her sons each evening, which was a time they all enjoyed.

When the boys were dry and warm in bed, Beth read to them from their favourite book of *Grimm's Fairytales*, until they fell asleep. She kissed them softly and went back down to the kitchen to wash the plates and cups they'd used for supper. She had just finished stacking them on the huge oak dresser when she heard a scratching sound at her back door.

Beth stopped, an icy trickle running down her back. Could this have anything to do with the shooting she'd heard earlier? Cautiously, she approached the door. There was frosted glass in the top half with some coloured panels. She could vaguely see the dark shape of a man.

'Help. Please help. I'm hurt bad... You said you would—'

Instinctively, she recognised the voice making the plea for help. 'Jerry? Is that you?' she asked and when the affirmative came, she unlocked the door.

Jerry stumbled in and collapsed on the floor. Beth locked the door behind him and then bent down. His eyes flickered open. 'Sorry...' he whispered. 'Didn't know where else to go... said you would help...' His eyes closed and his breath expelled on a whimper of pain.

'Yes, I will help,' Beth told him and knelt by his side. She felt for a pulse and found one, but also discovered the blood trickling down his arm from a wound to his shoulder. On further examination, she found the burnt cloth and the hole where the bullet had entered. There was no doubt, he had been shot – through the shoulder. 'Hold on, Jerry.'

Beth sat back on her heels. She wasn't a nurse or a doctor and all she might be able to do was temporarily stop the bleeding. She decided to do that and fetched a towel and the scarf she'd been wearing earlier. She pressed the towel inside his thin coat and then bound him across the chest and shoulder as tightly as she could. Whether that would help she wasn't sure, but after placing a cushion under his head and a car rug that usually hung over the big chair in the corner over him, she left him and went to the telephone in the hall. Bert had thought it extravagant when Jack had it installed, but Beth thanked God for it now. She knew the number of their family doctor and asked for it when the operator came on the line. Within a short time, she was talking to Doctor Rolph and rather breathlessly explaining what had happened.

'And you know this man – he wasn't one of the gangsters?'

'No. He is a respectable barrow boy and always polite and pleasant. I think he was just an innocent bystander.'

'Very well, I will be there as swiftly as I can.'

Beth walked back to the young man lying on her floor and knelt beside him. His face was deathly pale, but thankfully he was still breathing. She said a little prayer of thanks and waited for the doctor to arrive.

* * *

Doctor Rolph was there within ten minutes, frowning in concern as he saw the patient lying on her kitchen floor.

'How do you think he is, doctor?' Beth asked, anxious for the young man she liked. 'He won't die, will he?'

'I will do what I can, though you seem to have halted the bleeding. I have summoned my driver and he will be here shortly with the ambulance we keep for emergencies.' He shook his head. 'I thought when we invested in it that I should scarcely need it, but between the six of us doctors, it is used at least thirty times a week.' He looked at Beth and all kinds of questions sprang to mind.

Doctor Rolph and his colleagues ran both their own private surgeries as well as a clinic for the poor and needy of the district, which was largely free. The doctors gave their time for nothing, but the nurses were paid, as were the porters and the ambulance driver. The ambulance was an ex-army vehicle and had been used in the war. However, after the clinic acquired it, it had been painted white and now bore a red cross proudly on its sides. Well known in the district, everyone saw it on its journeys back and forth and nodded with pride. It wasn't every district that had their own ambulance to take away those in desperate need.

Bent over his patient, Doctor Rolph grunted as he tightened the crude bandage Beth had applied, after examining the wound. He looked up at her. 'This is Jerry Woods, isn't it? His mother needs her toes amputated and I've told him to bring her to the clinic, but she refuses to come. She lives with him...'

'Yes, he was telling me about her this evening,' Beth said. 'I'm not sure if she'll manage with him in hospital.'

'I can give you her address if you want to call in on her. I'll go round myself and tell her what has happened after I see him off to the clinic. He'll need an operation to remove the bullet, but he was lucky. A fraction lower and he could have lost a lung or been killed outright.'

'So he will be all right?'

'Yes, but he won't be selling fruit for a while. He's lucky to be alive. If you hadn't taken him in, he could have bled to death before he got help.'

Beth nodded, feeling a little sick. 'I can hardly believe it happened – here? It is still light and this isn't a rough area...' She looked at him anxiously.

'No, but these gangsters often live in respectable areas. You would never know them from decent folk; they don't look like thieves or murderers. It's only when they are in their clubs and dives that you see them for what they are. Not all of them are violent either. Some crimes are unseen and tolerated when they should be stamped out.' Doctor Rolph's voice rose a little in indignation, but when Beth looked at him, he shook his head. 'You don't need to know, Mrs Burrows. Just be aware that wealth doesn't always come honestly. You'd be surprised at some of what goes on...'

Beth wanted to press him but decided against it. She would ask Jack when he got home. He would be shocked and angry too – angry that a shooting could happen in their street.

'Have you heard – was anyone else killed or hurt?' Beth asked.

'Not that I've been told about,' he replied. 'I'm not on call to the local police station, so I wouldn't be asked to deal with it. One of my colleagues does that...' He frowned. 'Besides, these gangsters have their own doctors. Any wounded would be taken off and treated in secret for fear of reprisals

for the crimes they commit. Their victim may be dead – but sometimes
they take the body and dump it elsewhere to confuse things.' Doctor Rolph
seemed to know a lot about it, particularly as he wasn't on call to the police
himself. 'My colleague keeps me informed,' he added, almost as if he could
read her thoughts.

'Yes, I suppose he would,' Beth said, and then, because she didn't know
what else to say, 'Would you like a cup of tea while we wait for the
ambulance?'

'And the police,' he said, surprising her. 'Yes, that would be nice, thank
you.' He smiled as he saw her look of shock. 'It is my duty to let them know.
Besides, it would be best if they searched your garden and the surrounding
area, don't you think? Don't want your neighbours stumbling over a body in
the early hours.'

'No. That would be awful,' Beth replied. She wasn't sure how many of
her neighbours had telephones or whether they would ring the police after
hearing shots. She hadn't even thought of it, though she did now open her
door and retrieve the grapes she'd dropped earlier, rushing back inside
again quickly, and closing the door after her, as a shiver went down her
spine. Yet surely whoever had shot Jerry had gone long ago?

She went to the front parlour window as she heard a bell ringing and
saw the ambulance pull up outside her house. Doctor Rolph opened the
front door and she heard them talking in hushed voices and then two men
entered and took Jerry away on a stretcher. His eyelids fluttered and he
muttered something. Beth thought he said his mother's name; she knew he
was very fond of her and went quickly to him and touched his hand.

'I will see she is all right,' she told him, though she wasn't sure he could
hear her.

No sooner had the ambulance driven off than a police constable
arrived. He was young and keen and he asked a lot of questions, looking
Beth over as she told her story, and apparently deciding to accept it.

'You took a big risk, Mrs Burrows,' he told her. 'Have you thought it
might have been the villains asking for help?'

'I buy fruit from Jerry often. I knew his voice.'

'Right you are – still, it was a bit of a risk. If the gangsters had come after
him, they could have burst into your home.'

'Why would they?' Beth asked. 'He was just an innocent bystander.'

'I think Mrs Burrows is right, officer,' Doctor Rolph said. 'I know the lad and his mother – both decent folk. I believe you ought to search the area, make sure there are no bodies lying on the street.'

'We've got men doing that,' Constable Watkins confirmed. 'I'll just have a look out the back, shall I?'

Beth agreed and he did, returning a few minutes later to tell her it was all clear.

'I won't detain either of you further – but please don't leave town without letting us know. We may need to speak to you again.' With which dire comment, he left.

Doctor Rolph looked at Beth after the door closed and laughed. 'Well, that told us,' he said, evidently amused. 'I think young and eager describes our Constable Watkins, wouldn't you say?'

'I think he half-thought either you or I had shot poor Jerry,' Beth said and smiled. 'If it were not so serious, it would be funny.'

The doctor's smile vanished. 'As you say, Mrs Burrows, it is serious, because we do not yet know what was behind it – or if it is likely to happen again.'

'I do hope not,' Beth replied and shuddered.

'How long will your husband be?' Doctor Rolph asked and when she told him some hours yet, he shook his head. 'Will you be all right here alone? Is there someone I can call for you?'

'Thank you, but I am quite calm now,' Beth told him. She was still a little shaky but didn't wish to worry Bert or Vera – and Sally would be at home with her children, because Ben wasn't expected back home for a few days yet. There wasn't anyone else Beth would wish to call, apart from Jack, and she couldn't take him from his work. There was no point in worrying him for nothing.

'Then I shall take my leave,' the doctor said and offered his hand. 'You are a brave lady, Mrs Burrows. You did a good thing taking Jerry in and calling me. Never hesitate to call me if you need me – and there will be no charge for my services this evening.'

'Are you sure? I am willing to pay.'

'Quite sure. Goodnight – and make sure you lock your door after me.'

'Yes, I shall,' Beth said and did so.

After he'd gone, she went upstairs to check on her children. They were both sleeping peacefully and she returned to the kitchen. There was a large bloodstain on the floor. She would clean it and then go upstairs and have a bath. Perhaps soaking in some warm water would get rid of the unease in her stomach, because now that it was all over, she did feel quite wobbly and upset over what had happened.

4

Jack stared at Beth in disbelief when she told him what had happened. For a moment, he was silent, dumbfounded, but then he looked angry.

'Why on earth did you open the door?' he demanded. 'If the gangsters had been after him... My God! You could all have been dead. That was stupid, Beth. Stupid!'

She flinched, then, 'I knew it was Jerry. What was I supposed to do, just leave him there to bleed to death when he came to me for help? He is a decent young bloke. It isn't his fault he got in the way of some gang fight – if that's what it is, and Doctor Rolph thought it must be. He said I was brave and so did the police officer.'

'You're not their wife and those boys upstairs are not their sons.' Jack glared at her. He reached out and gripped her shoulders. 'Don't you realise what could have happened to you, Beth?'

Beth burst into tears, overcome as she gave way to her feelings at last. She'd been holding it in, but now she was shaking as the real horror of it hit her. 'I'm sorry—' she burbled as the shock and horror of it and what might have happened tumbled out of her. 'I didn't think and— You're hurting me, Jack.'

'What? Sorry...' Jack's anger suddenly dissolved and he pulled her into a fierce hug. 'I didn't mean to hurt you, Beth. Of course I think you're brave and wonderful – but I've met some of these gangster types and I know how ruthless they can be.' He held her pressed to his shoulder while she sobbed, letting go of her fear and the shock of seeing Jerry bleeding on her kitchen floor. 'I love you, Beth. I couldn't bear to lose you or the boys. You know that...'

She looked up at him, forlorn and weeping. 'I know and I'm sorry – but I like Jerry. I thought only of helping him. I think he was just a bystander and whoever did it cleared off as soon as they could.'

Jack looked down at her and nodded. 'Yes, I expect so. It was the shock of hearing what had happened. I thought this was a safe area...' He let her go and sat down, staring at her in a daze.

'Doctor Rolph says there are criminals living in the area – but not the sort you would suspect of crime. I'm not sure what he meant...'

'I am,' Jack said. 'When I was working on the ships, I met all sorts. I've seen them with their smart suits and their bulging wallets. You'd take them for gentlemen, but they are rotten to the core.' He ran his fingers through the dark hair that rippled back from his brow in short waves. His eyes were strange and made Beth shiver. 'There are a couple of men I know – who are mixed up in some nasty stuff – who come to the restaurant. They bring women with them – actresses, and some rich young ladies who spring from good families. They drink a lot and go off to a nightclub and I wonder what happens to those girls, Beth. We had them in this evening...' He shook his head. 'It makes me sick when I see things – but I have to give them the best tables and serve them...'

Beth stared at him in astonishment. She had never heard Jack talk this way before. He loved the restaurant and was always telling her about how wonderful their customers were. All the famous and rich people who came in were noted and recalled to her. 'Who are they, Jack? What do they do that you hate so much?'

He looked at her sombrely. 'I can't prove they do anything, but I've caught snatches of conversation... when they laugh behind the girls' backs. I know one of them owns a nightclub. Everyone goes there – including royalty – but I think— I suspect that unpleasant things go on in a part of the place that most of the public don't see.'

'Do you mean prostitution?' Beth asked and he nodded.

'Amongst other things. I've heard a whisper that opium is given to the girls and young men – rich young men. Men so young that they didn't get to fight in the war. Some of them feel guilty that their older brothers and fathers were killed, others just want to forget – and these men help them do it; they also help them to lose their fortunes in back rooms where they gamble illegally.'

'They lure them into using drugs so that they can control them... is that what you think?' Beth was horrified as Jack inclined his head. 'Does Ben know about these men and what you suspect?'

'Yes.' Jack frowned. 'He says keep out of it. As long as they pay their bills and don't use the drugs in the restaurant, it isn't our business – and he is right in a way.'

But Beth knew what he wouldn't say, that he didn't like such people in his restaurant but couldn't go against his partner. 'Perhaps Ben doesn't realise – he doesn't witness these men and what they do, in the way you do.'

'He only knows what I tell him, but we are doing well at the restaurant, Beth, and some of our important customers might think we were stepping out of our place, if we got the police in. I suppose some of them might take the odd recreational drug themselves... a little opium occasionally perhaps.' He was silent for a moment. 'Some of the girls have wealthy – even titled – fathers.'

'How can opium be for fun?' Beth demanded. 'It should be to help people in pain, nothing else.'

'Why do folk get drunk?' Jack asked rhetorically. 'Maybe it's to let go of pain – the kind that dwells inside and won't let go...'

'The kind you had after Tim died?' Beth said softly and he nodded. The loss of his brother during the war had hit Jack hard and it had taken him a while to recover.

'I tried drinking,' Jack admitted. 'It didn't work and I had a war to fight. I wanted to get even – but these youngsters only have themselves to please. Some do know what the war was like; they were survivors, and they do it to forget, others just seem to need something to shake off their boredom...' He hesitated then, 'I heard something odd this evening...' He paused, looking at her oddly. 'Do you know if any expensive clothes were spoiled at Harpers recently?'

'Yes, I told you – don't you remember?'

He nodded. 'Vaguely. Tell me again!'

Beth did so and he nodded as if it confirmed his thoughts.

'I heard two young women discussing it. They were giggling, saying they would be there at the head of the queue when Harpers had their sale.'

'They will be out of luck. We've let the soiled garments go cheaply to Harpers staff.' Beth clicked her tongue. 'Were they poor girls or rich ones?'

'One was titled, but I don't think the family has a lot of money these days – but I didn't know the other. Anyway, they probably just do it for the heck of it – to see what they can get away with. It's as if life isn't fast enough for them – as if they think they have to live hard...' He breathed deeply. 'In a way, I understand. They lost brothers, fathers, lovers, husband, sons... it means life can't be the same, so why not just go out and do as you damn well please? A whole generation was decimated and it left a lot of guilt behind – those who didn't get to fight and those who survived when many didn't.'

Beth nodded. There was an undercurrent of wildness in society these days, especially the rich young things and flapper girls. They played hard but didn't work so had endless time and they got bored. It was quite a regular thing to see the names of young men and women of good families in the society columns as having been arrested for cutting a lark – which could mean anything from knocking a policeman's helmet off to driving a car into the river when drunk, or causing an affray by running amok at a respectable restaurant. It was always hushed up, brushed off as young people having fun, while their wealthy parents paid the bills, and they were let off with a warning.

Jack yawned and smiled. 'I can't put the world to rights, Beth, and I'm sorry I was angry with you. You did the noble thing – but just be careful. You are very precious to me and to your sons.'

'I know,' she said and went into his arms as he stood. 'I love you, Jack, and you're right. You can't fight the rottenness in society single-handed. I don't suppose the police can do much either.'

'Just be careful. We don't want to attract the wrong kind of attention, Beth.'

'No, we don't,' she agreed. 'Shall we go to bed – do you want a warm drink?'

'I'll have a small whisky,' he said. 'What about you?'

'No, I don't think so, thanks,' she answered. 'I'm going up – are you coming?'

'Yes...' He went through into the dining room and she heard the clink of glass as she walked upstairs.

Jack joined her as she was undressing. 'The boys are sound asleep.'

'Yes, I know,' Beth said as he sat on the edge of the bed. 'I nearly forgot after all that... I'm a bit worried about Vera...'

* * *

'She doesn't want a fuss made,' Bert said when he arrived to fetch the boys that Saturday; he was taking them out to see some friends and to a football match that morning. He would have them back for their trip to the circus with their dad later that afternoon. 'Practically pushed me out of the house...'

'I sensed something was wrong,' Beth nodded in understanding. 'What did the doctor say?'

'She has a lump under her right arm,' Bert replied with a worried shake of his head. 'Doctor Wright says he doesn't know what it is, whether it is something that might be a problem or just some fatty tissue. He wants her to make an appointment with the hospital to have some tests done... not sure what they are yet, but Vera doesn't want to go.'

'She must,' Beth said instantly. 'She needs to find out what is wrong, Bert. Otherwise she will just keep worrying.'

'That's what I told her, but she said I was making too much fuss and she doesn't want to be messed around at her age.'

'No wonder you both looked so worried.' Beth placed her hand on his. 'Don't worry, Dad. I will talk her into it. I'll go with her and listen to what the doctors say.'

'Maybe she will, if you go with her,' Bert agreed and his expression lightened. 'I heard you had some excitement round this way the other night – gunshots and the police all over, searching and knocking on people's doors?'

'Yes,' Beth nodded and then told him all about the barrow boy she'd helped. His eyes widened and then he frowned, tutting a little.

'You took a big risk there, Beth love. Supposing one of the gangsters had been outside your door?'

'I recognised Jerry's voice,' Beth said. 'He wouldn't have led them to my door, Bert. I like him and he needed help.' She could tell her father-in-law felt much as Jack had when she'd told him the story, though he hid it better. 'Jack was cross with me. He said it might have been a trick, but I just wanted to help.'

'I know, Beth love, but, if anything happened to you or the boys, we'd none of us know what to do – so just be careful.'

'Yes, I know,' Beth smiled and gave him a hug. 'And try not to worry too much about Vera. We'll get her to the hospital and have those tests...'

* * *

'You did take a bit of a risk,' Sally Harper said later that day; they were in her office, having coffee together. 'But, if I'd known who it was, I think I would have done the same as you.'

Beth sighed and made a wry face. 'Jack was angry at first but only because it frightened him. He said the gangsters who probably did the shooting are ruthless and... he said something interesting that concerns Harpers...' She paused as Sally stared at her. 'You remember those spoiled garments?' Sally nodded. 'One of the girls, who was with some men Jack reckoned were up to no good, was laughing about it – telling her friend she would be at the head of the queue when you have your sale.'

'So it was deliberate,' Sally nodded her satisfaction. 'Well, at least we know – and the salesgirls are aware to keep an eye out for that kind of thing now. It is annoying, but we can't do very much about it. And it is nothing when you think what happened to that young man.' She frowned. 'Is Jack sure these men are gangsters?'

'He thinks they run illegal gambling clubs, along with other unpleasant practices,' Beth told her. 'They are customers at the restaurant and some of the girls are from good families – one of them has a title, apparently. Ben didn't think they should report what they'd overheard as other customers might take it as interference. I suppose it could affect trade but—'

'You think it should be reported,' Sally interrupted, adding: 'and I agree. I wonder at Ben. I think most people would think you'd done your duty by alerting the authorities.'

'After what he undertook in the war, it doesn't quite seem like him,' Beth suggested and Sally nodded her agreement.

'I'll talk to him when he comes home...' She smiled then and changed the subject. 'The first order he made for us in France has arrived. There are some wonderful things, Beth – clothes and perfumes. We have a whole new range of them. I'm really excited by them. I can't wait to see what will arrive next. It is wonderful to be able to buy all these lovely things for the store again. We had a lot of beautiful Murano glass in just yesterday – the colours are amazing.' She handed Beth a small sample tester of their new French perfume to try.

Beth held it to her nose and sniffed. 'Oh, Sally, that is gorgeous. I love it... Oh, it's by that fashion designer, Chanel...'

'Yes, it first came out in 1921, but we have only just got the concession. I have been trying to get it for ages, but Ben persuaded them to let us sell it here. It is so exciting.'

'Is it expensive?'

Sally nodded.

'Then I'll ask Jack to buy me a big bottle for my birthday.' Beth glanced at her wrist watch. It was Art Decco in design and a previous gift from her husband. 'I had better get back to the department if we want to finish the stocktaking in time. I hope to have the finished list on your desk before I leave this afternoon, Sally.'

'That would be great...' Sally sighed. 'I shall miss our little chat every day, Beth – but then, next week I shan't be in every day either.'

'It will be back to normal – and you must come over with the children and have tea one day soon.'

Beth left the office to return to the dress department. The stocktaking was nearly done. She had enjoyed working this week, but two days a week was enough mostly, because she had other things she needed to do. She needed to visit Jerry's mother and see how she was faring, enquire after his health at the hospital, and her most pressing mission was to persuade Vera that she must visit the hospital and have those tests...

5

Kitty felt tired but happy as she walked home after leaving her bus at the corner of the street. The stocktaking had been busy all week, but she'd enjoyed it. She loved working with Mrs Burrows, who had such a calm air and made all the girls feel easy in her presence. Miss Jones was fair-minded but usually looked a bit anxious, as if the job of supervisor was a little too much for her.

The five-shilling bonus was in Kitty's purse, which would make things easier for her mother this week – and, to Kitty's great surprise, she had been given one of the items that had been soiled with lipstick. Mrs Burrows had handed it to her that lunch break.

'As you said, the mark will be easy to wash out,' she'd told her. 'It is a pretty blouse and I thought you deserved something special for all your hard work this week. I expect your bonus will be needed at home?' Kitty had nodded, too overcome to speak. 'So I bought this for you from the sale goods.'

'Oh, Mrs Burrows...' Kitty had looked at the blouse. 'It is so beautiful, thank you – but I'm not sure I ought...'

'Yes, you should,' Mrs Burrows had said firmly. 'You deserve it, so no more about it, Kitty.'

Kitty had been close to tears but managed to hold them in check. Even when her father had been working full-time, she could never have hoped for such a beautiful thing. Her mother had made Kitty's clothes until she was old enough to use the machine and do it for herself. Kitty was actually much better at dressmaking than her mother, because she had an eye for style and took her time over it. The dresses she alternated each day for work at Harpers were her own work. She could have had one dress as her uniform or an allowance for the material and she'd chosen the allowance, knowing that she could make three smart dresses for the price of one. Kitty's mother had sniffed over it, saying that she thought two would have been sufficient and she could use some of the money, but Kitty had reminded her that it wasn't easy to wash and dry clothes during the winter. Besides, she had chosen varying weights of material so that she had one for warm days, one for cold days, and a third that would get her through all but the hottest or coldest of days.

Annie Wilson had looked displeased but in this, at least, Kitty had her way. She had one Sunday dress, which she'd made when her father gave her six shillings one birthday, but she was very careful to take it off whenever she came home and she sponged it to keep it fresh and clean. She had a couple of skirts and some blouses and two cardigans her mother had knitted for her, and one decent pair of shoes. For work, she wore sensible ones that laced and were not very attractive, but they complied with the dress code and were comfortable. Never, had she had such a beautiful blouse as the silk one Mrs Burrows had given her. It was cream with a heavy lace collar and ruff at the front and neat sleeves that finished in a plain cuff at the wrist, so it looked elegant and expensive, which it had been before it was marked down. Kitty couldn't wait to try it on, but she was also a little apprehensive of her mother's comments when she saw it. There was no way she could hide it, because it needed a gentle wash and iron to get the lipstick mark off.

* * *

Her mother was watching the vegetables simmering when Kitty got in. She looked up and nodded expectantly as Kitty put her wage packet on the table but didn't smile. Annie Wilson counted out the money and gave

Kitty back the four shillings a week she allowed her. Kitty was expected to pay for her shoe repairs and her stockings from that four shillings, as well as her bus fare to work, which was why she walked home if it was fine.

'I suppose they haven't said anything about a permanent rise?' Annie Wilson said as she scooped up the money and put it in her housekeeping pot on the shelf.

'No, that was just a very generous bonus from Mrs Harper for all the hard work the girls put in over stocktaking week.'

'Pity...' Her mother gave her a sour look as Kitty took the distinctive black bag from her basket. 'What is that – it looks expensive...?'

'Mrs Burrows – she is a friend of Mrs Harper and she oversaw the stock-taking – she gave it to me. It was marked down in the sale because someone had smeared lipstick on it, and the staff were allowed to buy the damaged items cheaply. Mrs Burrows bought it for me.'

Her mother's eyes widened as Kitty took it out. 'That must be real silk, Kitty!'

'Yes, I am sure it is,' Kitty said. 'Isn't it beautiful, Mum?'

'Yes, it is... and worth a few bob, especially once that smear is washed out.'

Kitty looked at her in alarm knowing what she meant. 'It was a present, Mum. The only chance I'll ever have to own something this pretty.'

For a moment, her mother stared at her in silence. 'If you were a thoughtful girl, Kitty, you would do it without my asking, but you can be very selfish.' She sighed heavily. 'I suppose I can't force you to give it up...' She paused and then nodded. 'You can wear it when Mr Miller calls for tea on Sunday.'

'Mr Miller is coming for tea?' Kitty gasped in dismay.

'Don't look at me like that, girl,' Annie Wilson snapped. 'You say you don't like him, Kitty, but you don't know him. He is actually a very kind man. He called here earlier today and he has offered your father a job in his office doing the accounts for the shops.' She looked very pleased with herself. 'It is an easy job and your dad was always good with figures. I said yes, of course, even though your father wasn't here.' She took a deep breath. 'Anyway, I asked him to tea and he wants to take you for a walk afterwards.

Once you get to know him, I am sure you will see it is right and proper that you should be his wife.'

Kitty shook her head, her face pale. 'Where is Dad?' she asked, because his chair by the fire was empty. She'd thought he might have gone out to the back yard but could see from her mother's face that it wasn't so.

'He'd gone to look for work. He didn't find anything, of course. His precious mates and so-called friends aren't interested in a cripple. I told him I'd found a job for him and...' She paused and something flashed in her eyes. It might have been regret or anger. Kitty wasn't sure because it was gone in an instant as her mother's mouth hardened. 'He said he wouldn't do it – wouldn't work for that man – and went off in a temper. I suppose he'll come back, unless he can find someone to buy him a drink...' The scorn in her voice was like a whip and Kitty flinched.

'Dad needs something in his life – and he makes a half of bitter last all night. He doesn't get drunk.'

'Only because he hasn't got the money.' Annie Wilson's face was twisted with bitterness. 'Don't you think I need something, too? No one buys me a drink at the pub – or buys me a silk blouse.'

Kitty turned away. Her mother's bitterness would spoil her pleasure if she let it, but she was determined not to let it and picked up the blouse, heading for the scullery.

'Where are you going? Your dinner is nearly ready.'

'I am just going to rinse this through,' Kitty replied. 'I'll come when you call me.'

'And what about setting the table, miss?' her mother demanded.

Kitty paused, undecided, and then someone knocked at the kitchen door. Her mother jerked her head and Kitty went to investigate. She recognised the man at once; it was Larry Norton.

'Forgive me for disturbing you, but I must speak to Annie Wilson,' he said and followed her into the kitchen as Kitty moved back to allow him to enter. He was in his working clothes and a faint smell of horses followed him. Kitty's mother's face registered her disgust as she looked him up and down, but even as she opened her mouth to deny him, he raised his hands, palms up. 'I know you don't approve of us, Annie Wilson, but I had to bring the news – your man was taken ill in the street. I took him up in the cart and he's in the infirmary. I think he may be very ill...' As she stared at him in stunned silence, he took a step back. 'That's all – but if you wanted, I could take you there in my van. It's not used for work; it doesn't stink of the yard or the horse.'

'Thank you,' Kitty said and dumped the blouse on the nearest chair. 'I'd like to go, please.'

'Your dinner is ready,' her mother protested.

'I don't want it. Dad is ill,' Kitty replied. 'Are you coming, Mum?'

Her mother shook her head. 'I'll go tomorrow sometime. If you're so worried, you'd best go with him – but behave yourself.'

Kitty threw her a look of disbelief. No word of thanks to the man who had taken her husband to the infirmary. Just a warning to behave, as if she was going dancing or to the pub with a boyfriend.

She was silent as she went out, but as Larry Norton held the passenger door of his van open, she looked at him, tears glimmering. 'I can't thank you enough for what you've done, Mr Norton. I am so grateful – and sorry for my mother's manner just now. I am sure it is just the shock...'

He allowed her to settle in the seat, closed the door, and then got into the driving seat. He gave her a friendly smile. 'We Nortons know what folk think of us,' he said cheerfully. 'Your ma isn't the only one round here who thinks we lower the tone of the place.'

Kitty bit her lip. She could apologise again, but that wouldn't change anything. 'Well, *I* am grateful,' she said and looked at him as he started the engine and drove away from the kerb.

*　*　*

There wasn't much traffic about just now, but she could see he was a careful driver and felt safe with him, even though she'd never in her life been so close to a man, other than her father. In the intimacy of his van, she could not help noticing the smell of horse and something else that clung to his clothes but decided it was a small price to pay for his kindness.

'Dad told me something was wrong but—' She caught back a sob. 'We — I hoped it wasn't anything nasty.' Her mother didn't care or she would have come to the hospital with them.

'Mebbe he'll be all right, lass, but... he was in a bad way when I found him.' There was sympathy in his voice, which made her throat catch.

She needed to stop herself thinking about her father, so she said, 'I didn't know you had a van. I haven't seen you in it before.'

'Nay, you wouldn't have. I don't use it for Dad's business. I've got a bit of a sideline going on for myself. Dad doesn't much like it, but he can't order me not to, so he doesn't try.'

Kitty nodded but didn't comment; it wasn't her business to pry.

'I cart stuff for other people,' he told her after a small silence. 'There are a lot of small businesses round here and the owners can't drive or afford to buy a van, so they ask me to fetch stuff for them – or take it somewhere else. It's a regular job and Dad's isn't. We sometimes don't get a call out from the yard for days – so I took another job on for myself. 'Course, we get small stuff brought into the yard often, but Dad can see to that. I'm around when he needs me.'

'Do you get on well with him?' Kitty asked and then blushed because she'd been betrayed into asking a personal question by his friendly, informative manner. 'Sorry, that isn't my business...'

He laughed, a deep throaty sound. 'It's a good question, lass. He's a funny old bugger – excuse the expression, but it suits him. You'd think him sour and gruff if you met him in the yard. He's hard in business – made a fair bit over the years – but show him a child in tears and there's a threepence in his hand to make the tears go away. He ought to have had a big family, but my mother couldn't manage it – she died in childbirth a few years after I was born. I reckon that's when he turned sour...'

He glanced at her before pulling into a big open space before the infirmary.

'Shall I wait here for you, lass? I can't rightly come in like this...'

'You could,' she said, but then shook her head. 'I'll be all right, thank you, Mr Norton. I can get the bus home. You must have other things to do.'

'Nothing that can't wait,' he replied. 'I doubt they will let you stay long with him, lass. I'll just sit here and wait. It is nearly dark and I'd be uneasy if you had to make your own way home.'

Kitty hesitated, then nodded and thanked him. She got out of the van and walked across the courtyard to the door of the infirmary. It opened into a small, poorly lit reception area. No one was there, so, after waiting for a few minutes for someone to come, she rang the bell on the desk. After another minute or two, a man came through a door to the right. He approached the desk and looked at her.

'Sorry, miss. We just had another emergency brought in – that's three in the past hour. How can I help you?'

'My father – Mr Wilson – was brought in here a little while ago. I wondered if I could see him, please?'

'Wilson?' He checked through his book. 'Ah yes – barely conscious on arrival...' He hesitated, then, 'Well, we don't always allow visitors at night – but in this case... I'll show you the way, Miss Wilson. Your father is in a room on his own.'

Kitty swallowed hard and followed him through the door. They walked down a long, dark passage and then up a flight of stairs to another narrow landing. Here, there were nurses moving from ward to ward and one of them frowned and came towards them.

'Not at this hour, Stan. You know the rules.'

'It is Miss Wilson – her father is in Room D...'

'Oh...' The nurse looked at Kitty and her expression became sympathetic. 'Very well. I'll take her. You get back to reception, Stan.'

He nodded, looked at Kitty. 'Good luck, miss,' he said and walked away.

Kitty's heart was banging with fright. It was so obvious that her father was gravely ill. She swallowed hard as the nurse paused outside a closed door.

'Is he conscious now? Will... Will he know me?'

'Who can say? The doctor who examined him said he didn't think there was much we could do. I am very sorry – but it's best you understand, Miss Wilson. Your father is dying. It is just a matter of time. Now don't cry. It won't help him and I don't want my patients upset. You can cry when you leave.'

Kitty nodded and blinked hard. The nurse sounded harsh but she knew she was right.

'You can go in but only for ten minutes. I'm sorry, but we are breaking the rules as it is.'

'Yes, I know, thank you.'

Kitty opened the door and entered, the nurse walked away. She stood for a moment just inside the tiny room, in which there was a bed, a chair and a small trolley beside the window. Walking softly forward, she looked down at her father's pale face. His eyes were closed, his arms lying straight by his sides. She bent to kiss his cheek and he stirred, his eyes opening.

'Ker... itty...' he mumbled in a thick voice. His hand groped for hers and she held it.

'Dad,' she said chokily. 'I came as soon as Mr Norton told me where you were. Mum said she will come tomorrow...'

He moved his head negatively and tried to speak, but the words were too jumbled to make sense. 'Ly Ker... itty...' he managed at last and she blinked hard as the tears stung, because he was trying to tell her that he only wanted her to visit. 'I... sorry...'

'You don't need to be. I love you.' Kitty sniffed hard, holding back the choking tears.

'Not your ma...' he struggled to say the words, and then his fingers gripped hers tightly. 'Mustn't... Miller... bad man...'

'I know, Dad. I won't marry him whatever Mum says.'

'She... no right to make... ahh...' He closed his eyes, his hands futtering in agitation as he couldn't form the words.

Kitty held his hand gently, stroking it with one finger. 'All right, Dad, I'll tell her not to come until you're better and I won't marry him,' she said and smiled at him. 'You will get better, because I love you.'

'Know...' the word was hardly distinguishable, but she understood: he knew she loved him. He struggled as he tried to say more but couldn't, closing his eyes in exhaustion.

'I know you love me, Dad,' she said, stroking his hand gently with her fingers. 'You've been the best dad ever...'

A little smile touched his lips, but he didn't try to reply and he didn't open his eyes. Kitty sat beside him for much longer than the ten minutes she'd been allowed, even when she believed he was sleeping. Then a nurse came and beckoned to her. She got up reluctantly and bent to kiss her father. There was no reaction.

'I love you and I'll come again,' she said and then turned and walked to the door. There she paused and looked back. He looked peaceful, but she wasn't sure he was aware of anything any more. Choking back her tears, she followed the nurse out.

'I'm sorry. I know I stayed too long.'

'Sister will have my guts for garters if she sees you still here,' the nurse said, 'but I hadn't the heart to make you leave. If I had my way, I'd let you stay longer.'

'Thank you,' Kitty said. 'Goodnight.'

* * *

Kitty walked quickly to the stairs, down, through the long dark passage and out into the reception area. Stan was busy with some people who had brought in a woman who seemed to be in the throes of giving birth. She glanced at him and smiled and he nodded. Then she was out in the night air. She stood for a moment as the tears ran down her face, overwhelmed and disorientated. Forgetting everything but her grief, she stumbled away, and then someone took hold of her arm, steadying her.

'All right, lass. I'll get you home.'

For a moment, Kitty just looked at the man, hardly knowing who he was or where she was, her grief too intense to speak. She just nodded dumbly and let Larry Norton lead her to his van. He opened the door, helped her inside and closed the door, then got in beside her. He didn't speak all the way home, but she could feel his sympathy as she sobbed into her hands.

When he pulled up outside her house, she just sat where she was for a few moments. 'Thank you...' she whispered. 'I don't know...'

His hand touched hers briefly, and then he got out and went to open her door for her. 'You'll be all right, lass. It's hard to bear, but you'll manage – and anything you need, just ask. I mean it.'

'Thank you...' she managed and then moved away to the house, opening the door to go in. She knew he watched her enter before he went back to his van.

Her mother was sitting at the kitchen table, staring at the wall. She glanced at Kitty, then, 'Is he dead?'

'No but... they told me it won't be long. The doctor said there was nothing they could do for him.'

'He always was a quitter,' Annie Wilson said bitterly. 'Just like him to go and leave us.'

'Mum!' Kitty's fractured nerves gave way as she screamed the words. 'How could you? That's wicked. Wicked and hateful!'

Her mother stared at her and then she inclined her head. 'Yes, it was,' she said, looking shamed. 'He wasn't a bad man, did his best for us – but he gave up too soon. He should've fought for his life... for us.' Her head came up as she met her daughter's accusing stare. 'I know I'm bitter and I never gave him any peace – but it was too hard coming here, Kitty. I was taught to expect better. I came from a good family and a decent home.' Kitty didn't answer and her mother stood up, an air of defiance about her now. 'Yes, I'm sorry he's dying – but I'm sorry for myself, too. Even this dump will be too expensive for us on what you earn once the last of his savings have gone, and that won't be long. We'll be living in digs before you know it – one room between the pair of us. See how you feel then, miss...' She walked to the bottom of the stairs that led up to the bedrooms, paused and looked back. 'When you're faced with reality, Kitty, perhaps you'll see that I was trying to give you a better life. Mr Miller would make you a good husband – and he'd look after me, too.'

With that, she went out, leaving Kitty to sit at the table and weep. She cried until the tears dried up and her chest hurt, then she rose and went into the scullery. The blouse she'd brought home was hanging up and the stain of lipstick had been washed out carefully. Her mother had done it for her.

Kitty blew her nose hard. When the blouse was dry, she would iron it and give it to her mother to sell. She couldn't keep it now, because she knew her mother was right. It would take every penny she earned to keep them from now on.

'He shouldn't have told you!' Vera cried when Beth asked her if she'd booked her hospital tests yet, the following week. 'I'm sure it's nothing – and I don't want to make a fuss.'

'You aren't,' Beth said. 'Dad is worried and so am I. Won't you let me take you to the hospital and stay with you while you see the doctors?'

'Would you?' Vera looked at her for a moment and then smiled, a hint of tears in her eyes. 'Perhaps I could face it if you came with me, Beth...' She took a deep breath. 'The truth is, I'm a bit scared of what they will say – and I'm not sure I'll understand it. Doctors talk in their own language.'

Beth laughed. 'Yes, they do rather. I'm not sure if it is to confuse us or reassure us that they are clever and know what they're doing. You might be worrying for nothing, Vera. Isn't it better to find out, one way or the other?'

'I suppose so, but if they say it's... you know...' She lifted frightened eyes to Beth's. 'Your father had a hard time with his first wife being ill and now me. It isn't fair on him if— I don't want to be a burden.'

'You wouldn't be. Dad cares about you, Vera. We all do. You are part of our family. Besides, Dad will only fret until he knows the truth – but if it is the worst, he will want to look after you, just as we all will.'

'Yes, I know. I was very lucky when I met Bert, but I don't want to cause him a lot of pain and misery.'

'You won't. If you have a nasty illness, it isn't your fault. You can't blame yourself if we worry for you, but perhaps the doctors can help; it might be something much less serious than your fears.'

Vera was silent for a moment and then nodded. 'I'll go back to my doctor and ask him to make the arrangements,' she said and smiled. 'You're a good girl, Beth, and I love having the children, so don't stop me just because I have a little problem, will you?'

'No, I shan't,' Beth said and, as Vera had changed the subject, went on, 'Dad told you about poor Jerry, didn't he?' Vera nodded, looking anxious. 'Well, I rang the hospital and they told me he is making satisfactory progress and his mother can visit now. I'm going to visit her after I leave you, ask if she would like me to take her to the hospital.'

'That is so nice of you, Beth.' Vera hesitated, then, 'It must be so nice to be able to drive a car. Do you enjoy it, Beth?'

Beth had only recently learned and didn't have a car of her own, as Sally Harper now did, but she was able to borrow Jack's, though Jack often drove himself to work. However, Sally wasn't using hers and had offered it to Beth for the day.

'I wouldn't say I enjoy driving,' Beth replied thoughtfully. 'Sally loves it, especially if she can get out into the country for a few hours, but it is useful and it gives one a little independence – though in town there are plenty of buses and the Underground.'

'I always take the bus if I can. I don't like the underground trains,' Vera said. 'What if they go wrong and you're stuck down there for ages?'

'Yes, I wouldn't like to be stuck down there for a long time, but they are convenient,' Beth replied, making a mental note to make sure she had access to a car when the time came for Vera's hospital visits.

'Well, I am glad you can drive, Beth. You should ask Jack to buy you a little car of your own.'

'Oh no, that would be too extravagant, Vera. I consider I am very lucky to have a beautiful house and so much already. I never expected half of what I have now. Money was tight when I was a girl – though we weren't really poor...' Beth sighed. 'I hate to see children on the streets with dirty faces, ragged clothes and sometimes no shoes.'

Vera nodded. 'It pulls at your heartstrings,' she agreed. 'I worked all my life so I was never that destitute, but there were times when I didn't know if I could bear to open the door to the rent man. I dare say there are quite a few have that worry every week – especially if they have a drinker for a husband.' She gave a little laugh. 'I have to push Bert off to have a drink with his mates at the pub and then he only ever has a half of bitter.'

'Bert is lovely,' Beth said. 'He isn't bothered about going to the pub now, because he has you, Vera. Is he going to the greyhound coursing this week?'

'I've told him I want him to go, but whether he will or not I don't know...'

'Supposing, I fetch you to ours for the evening? Bert can come and collect you when he's ready.'

'That's sweet of you, Beth, but to be honest, I'd rather just stay home and knit while I listen to a bit of music on the wireless – if I can get the daft thing to work. If not, I'll just sit by the fire and doze.' She smiled. 'I'll be fine, love. I used to spend all day and all night alone, remember. Now I have Bert to look after me, but I want him to see his mates sometimes – he mustn't lose touch with them for my sake.'

Beth nodded. She understood what Vera meant. If she should be very ill and then pass away, Bert would be lonely again, and more so if he gave up seeing his old friends. 'Yes, he should have his friends,' she agreed. 'Tell him you've agreed to have the hospital tests but you want him to have an evening out. He'll be so pleased; he will go off as happy as a sandboy.'

'That's a good idea,' Vera said with a laugh. 'Now you'd best be off, Beth. You've got a lot to do today.'

* * *

Beth felt relieved that Vera had agreed to speak to her doctor again. She left her quite content, preparing lunch for herself and Bert for when he returned from helping one of their elderly neighbours with his garden. Bert enjoyed his gardening now he had more time for it and often helped folk out with little jobs, though he was reluctant to leave Vera for long these days.

Settling into the smart little car she'd borrowed from Sally, Beth checked the directions she'd looked up on a map. It should be easy enough to find the house she was looking for, though she'd never been to the area before. She started the car and set off feeling optimistic.

However, Beth became a little uneasy when she drove into the street of dilapidated terraced houses close by Kettle's Yard half an hour or so later. The house that Jerry's mother lived in wasn't in Kettle's Yard itself, but close enough to make Beth wonder if she would have done better to come in a taxi. It might be unwise to leave a car unattended in this area. She got out and stood pondering if it was safe to leave Sally Harper's car, when, to her surprise, she saw someone she knew.

'Kitty...' she called, wondering why the girl wasn't at work. 'Can you spare me a few minutes?'

Kitty turned and Beth saw her eyes were red from weeping.

She went to her instantly, forgetting the car for a moment. 'What is wrong, Kitty love?'

'Oh, Mrs Burrows...' Kitty looked at her and suppressed a sob. 'I couldn't come to work today – my father died in the night. We had the news from the infirmary this morning.'

'I'm so sorry,' Beth said. 'Come and sit in the car with me for a minute, and tell me what happened. I thought he was getting better after his accident?'

Kitty got into the car and Beth sat with her, listening as she haltingly told her story. It came out between the sobs and tears, the story of their move here, her mother's bitterness, her insistence that Kitty could save them by marrying a rich old man she didn't like, and then finally, her father's last illness.

'I am so sorry, Kitty. It is awful to lose your father and just when you'd believed he was getting better. Is there anything I can do to help you?'

'Oh no, of course not. I shouldn't have poured it all out like that but—' She swallowed a sob. 'I've been so miserable.' She gulped back more tears and dabbed at her eyes.

Beth offered her a handkerchief and she took it gratefully, wiping her face and blowing her nose. 'I want to help if I can,' Beth said. 'I am not sure what I can do just yet but I will think about it... Would it help if your mother had a little job as well? Just a few hours a week perhaps?'

'I expect it would, if she would accept it,' Kitty replied hesitantly. 'I am not sure she has ever worked outside the home. Her people were better off and women didn't work in their circle.'

'Well, I might be able to think of something,' Beth told her. 'Look, I need to go into that house just here – and I shall probably take the old lady to the hospital with me. Her son is allowed visitors now.'

'You mean Mrs Woods?' Kitty said. 'I heard her son was shot. How do you know Bella?' Kitty looked surprised and Beth smiled.

'I often buy fruit from Jerry. He has his barrow near an Underground station I use quite often. He told me his mother isn't well and can't get about much, so I've come to see how she is and take her to visit him if she wants to go.'

'She can't walk far, because of her poor feet,' Kitty told her. 'I sometimes pop in on Sunday or my afternoon off – that is where I was going, just now, but I couldn't stop crying.' She sniffed and wiped her eyes on Beth's hand-kerchief again.

Beth nodded. 'Could you sit in this car for a little while, see the kids don't do anything to it, please? It belongs to Mrs Harper and I don't want to leave it unattended just in case.'

'It is lovely...' Kitty said, stroking the leather armrest. 'Yes, I'll do that for you, Mrs Burrows.'

'Unless we're working, my name is Beth to you, Kitty – and I won't forget about your mum or you...' She smiled and got out, leaving Kitty to guard her borrowed car.

* * *

Beth knocked at the door of number nine. A voice called out that she should go in and she entered, catching the sour odour of urine. Once her eyes were accustomed to the gloom, she saw it must come from a pail near where Jerry's mother sat in her armchair. There were used mugs, plates with scraps of food on them lying about the place, and it was obvious that the woman in the chair was unable to do much to clean or tidy.

She glared at Beth. 'What yer want then?' she grunted. 'If yer one of them do-gooders come nosing, I ain't goin' into no home – bloody workhouse that's what it is, no matter what yer call it. My Jerry will look after his ma when he gets 'ome.'

'It's Jerry I've called about,' Beth told her and saw the way her eyes narrowed, suddenly eager. 'I've spoken to a nurse at the hospital. He is making good progress and can have a visitor now. I've come to see if you will let me take you. I have a car waiting outside.'

'How do I know it ain't a trick ter get me out and into that place – the ruddy workhouse?' Jerry's mother demanded.

'Well, I suppose you don't,' Beth replied. 'You will have to trust me – but you can ask Kitty about me if you wish. She is watching my car for me.'

'You know Kitty Wilson?' the elderly lady's eyes sparked with interest.

'Yes, we work together sometimes. Would you like to visit Jerry, Mrs Woods?'

'You'll 'ave ter wait while I get me coat...' Mrs Woods' eyes narrowed suddenly. 'I stink. I ain't 'ad a wash since Jerry never come 'ome. Can yer bear it in yer posh car?'

'I can – but I have time to give you a little wash and tidy up a bit before we go, Mrs Woods – if you'd like me to?'

The woman's eyes met Beth's and she saw the hesitation in them, the pride that didn't want to admit she needed help, and then the resignation. 'I ought ter be clean afore I sees my Jerry in the 'ospital. Don't want ter shame 'im.'

'I doubt you'd do that,' Beth said. 'I'll boil a kettle, shall I?'

'You'll need a shillin' fer the gas,' Mrs Woods said. 'I used all Jerry left.'

'Well, I think I can do that,' Beth said and took out her purse from her coat pocket. She spotted the meter in a corner of the room and fed it with three shillings, which was all the suitable coins she had; then she went through to the tiny back kitchen and filled a kettle, setting it on the gas ring and lighting it.

Despite the run-down look of the area and the house being old, Jerry had made the kitchen clean and smart with a new cooker and a small scrubbed pine table with three assorted chairs, also a cupboard, which probably stored food.

Opening the cupboard, Beth found a tea caddy with a fair amount of loose tea, also a large blue bag containing sugar. There were still some clean mugs, but she couldn't find any milk – and then she saw an unopened tin of condensed milk. She would ask Mrs Woods if she wanted a cup of tea after she'd washed her.

The water in the kettle was warm enough now for washing and Beth turned off the gas and poured the warm water into the enamel bowl resting in the sink. She found soap on the drainer and there were some cloths piled up on a little chest and a towel. She tucked the cloths under her arm and carried the basin into the kitchen.

'Now, Mrs Woods,' she said. 'Shall we do hands and face – or will you take your clothes off and let me give you a proper wash?'

* * *

It was more than an hour later when Beth managed to help Mrs Woods hobble out to the car. Kitty was still sitting there, but she got out when she saw them and held the door for the elderly lady.

'I was just coming to see you, Bella,' she said. 'Is there anything I can pop in and do for you?'

'This un's done it all,' Bella told her with a grin. 'But there's two half-crowns in me pot on the shelf. Yer can go and get me a bit of bread and marge – and some shrimp paste if yer will.'

'Yes, of course I will,' Kitty said. 'I'll pop in and make you some toast later if you like.'

'Yer a good lass, not like yer ma,' Bella said. 'I was sorry ter hear about yer father, Kitty. He were all right... often come in ter see I was OK if Jerry were at work.'

Kitty nodded and swallowed hard.

Beth looked at her and smiled. 'I'll come and see you another day. When will you be up to returning to work?'

'Next Monday. I can't afford to be off work, though I'll take a day off for the funeral.'

'I will see you at Harpers then,' Beth said, got into the car and drove off.

'You work at that Harpers too?' Mrs Woods said as the car moved off down the street. 'You must earn a lot ter 'ave a motor like this.'

'I work part-time – and the car is only borrowed from a friend,' Beth replied. 'How will you manage for money while Jerry is in the hospital, Mrs Woods? Can I help you? I can let you have a pound or two. Jerry will repay me when he can, of course.'

'I'll ask 'im,' she said. 'Yer can call me Bella if yer like – most do.'

'Thank you, I shall,' Beth said, smiling inwardly. It had been a struggle getting Bella to have a proper wash and let her clear up, before having a cup of tea with her, but she felt a quiet pleasure in her success.

'I like Kitty. She's a lovely girl, like her dad, honest and kind – her mother's a bitter one, though. She gives poor Kitty a rough time,' Bella went on. 'She'll miss 'er dad proper bad.'

'Do you know Annie Wilson well?' Beth asked.

'Nah. No one does round 'ere. Keeps 'erself to 'erself – but folk talk. Me neighbours pop in fer a chat now and then. Someone would've cleared up later – more than likely Kitty. She comes most days just fer a few minutes – but 'er mother wouldn't lift a finger ter 'elp me.'

'Perhaps she doesn't like to interfere,' Beth suggested. She didn't know Kitty's mother so couldn't truly have an opinion, but from all she'd heard it was hard to think well of her. 'She might think you would tell her to go away?'

'Aye and I might,' Bella muttered. 'Snooty one she is – thinks she's come down in the world. What I say is, don't matter what yer've got as long as yer mean well. My Jerry don't earn a fortune, but 'e does what 'e can and we manage. He never owes a penny if 'e can help it – and I reckon 'e's got a bit saved but 'e don't tell me where, thinks I might run off and spend it!' Bella cackled with mirth.

Beth laughed. 'I don't think there's much chance of that...' She'd seen the sores on Bella's legs as she washed her. It was an opportunity, though she wasn't sure if she ought to take it, then Beth suddenly made up her mind – *in for a penny...* 'Do you ever consider going to the infirmary to have your leg and feet treated, Bella?'

Bella didn't answer at once, then, 'I might not come out – then what 'appens to my Jerry?'

'Surely you would? They can do lots of things now.'

'Couldn't save Kitty's father, could they?' Bella retorted. 'They'd 'ave me leg orf and then I'd be more work fer 'im.'

'He worries about you, Bella. Perhaps you should think about seeing a doctor for his sake.'

'I ain't got money fer doctors.'

'There is the free clinic,' Beth said. 'I could take you there and see what they say – if you like?'

Bella was silent for a long time. It was only as they drew up outside the hospital that she broke her silence. 'Take me in this, would yer?'

'Yes, if I can borrow it – if not, in my husband's car.' Beth looked at her as she put her hand on the door. 'Would you come if I could manage it?'

'I'll think about it,' Bella said. 'I want ter see my boy first.'

7

'So where do you think you've been, miss?' Annie Wilson demanded when Kitty returned from delivering Bella's shopping. 'Leaving me alone to face everything—'

'I just went to get some food for Bella from the corner shop.' Kitty didn't look at her as she spoke.

'You look as if you've been crying your eyes out,' her mother said. 'There's no point in making yourself sick over it, Kitty. He's gone and we can't bring him back.' Her mother shook her head. 'No good you looking at me like that, girl. We have to face facts. There's just the two of us and I don't know how we'll manage.'

'Supposing you could find a little job...?' Kitty's voice tailed off as she saw anger and shock in her mother's eyes.

'So now I am supposed to work as well as cook and clean, to say nothing of the washing and ironing. It takes me all day on a Monday just to wash, starch and iron the sheets and your father's—' Annie Wilson broke off as she remembered she would no longer have to wash her husband's shirts. For a moment, she glared at Kitty and then she burst into tears. 'I know I nagged him since the accident, but it was this place and the worry...' she blubbered, dabbing at her nose as the tears and mucus merged. She scrabbled in her pocket and brought out a large man's handkerchief and blew her nose. 'Stupid girl, making me cry. He never expected me to work... would never let me...'

'I know; it was his pride that you didn't have to, Mum,' Kitty said. 'It was just a thought – because I know you hate living here...'

Annie gave a little shudder and then looked at her. 'What do you suppose I could do, Kitty? I can cook but not well enough to hire myself out – I'm not a fancy chef. I can wash and iron or scrub floors...'

'I don't want you to do that kind of work,' Kitty said. 'I wasn't thinking – of course you mustn't look for work, Mum. We'll manage.'

'There is a way and you know it,' her mother said and now her gaze was flinty. 'If I send word to Mr Miller and ask for his help with the funeral, he will call round to see us. You only have to smile and speak to him pleasantly, Kitty, and he'll be asking you to marry him within the week. He's hinted to me enough how much he admires you.'

Kitty's heart sank. While her father lived, she'd had his support in resisting her mother's demands; there had been hope that things might get better – but now that hope had gone.

'Let me see if I can find another job – something I can do in the evenings,' Kitty said. 'If I can, we might manage to stay here until...' She drew a deep breath. 'I might meet someone I *could* love, Mum, and he would support us both.' Her eyes pleaded with her mother to understand. 'Please let me try...'

Annie Wilson hesitated, then, 'You can try, but the minute you realise how hard it is going to be, you will realise that I want what is best for us both.' She gave her daughter a hard look. 'I can't see what you dislike about him so much. He is a kind man.'

'Or he pretends to be,' Kitty said and shuddered. There was just something about that man that sent a shiver down her spine. Every time he looked at her, it was as if he were stripping her with his eyes. She couldn't help it; she just didn't like him – and her father hadn't liked him either. He'd told her she mustn't marry Mr Miller, so she wouldn't.

* * *

Kitty returned home from work on the following Monday to discover they had a visitor. Mr Miller was sitting in the Windsor chair by the range – her father's chair – and it was clear from the way her mother was smiling that she was quite content to see him there.

'Ah, there you are, my love,' Annie Wilson said in a soft tone that Kitty had not heard in a long time. 'Here is Mr Miller come to visit us and ask if he can do anything to help in our time of grief...'

'Now you know I've told you to call me Joshua, Annie,' Mr Miller said in a chiding tone. 'I hope that both you and Kitty will think of me as a good friend – and I intend to do all that a friend should do in the sad circumstances you find yourselves in, my dears.' He beamed at her expectantly, and then looked at Kitty.

Kitty felt her stomach clench. She found it difficult to speak, but managed, 'You are most kind, sir.'

'Joshua has insisted that he will pay all the expenses for your father's funeral, Kitty. Isn't that kind of him? You know that we would have found it difficult, if not impossible, to find the money, with your father off work so many weeks.'

'It is my honour and my pleasure to do it for you – both of you,' he said and his gaze dwelled on Kitty. 'You look tired, Kitty. Won't you come and sit by the fire, dear?' He stood up and offered her his chair.

Kitty's nails curled into the palm of her hand as she fought to stop herself showing the revulsion she felt. How could her mother do this to her?

'You— you are very good, sir, but I will find the money somehow...'

'Nonsense, Kitty!' Annie Wilson's voice carried its normal whiplash. 'I will not have you working yourself into the grave when Joshua is so generous – and to refuse his kind offer is an insult.'

'I meant no offence, sir...'

'Of course you didn't, Kitty,' he said and smiled at her. 'Please, you must call me Joshua. I want us to be good friends – all of us.' His look embraced her mother. 'Kitty, Annie, and my children – we must all be friends. I am only too happy to do this little thing for you, but if you wish to please me, you must let me hold the reception at my home. So much more comfortable for you – and you can meet my children. It will be so nice for them...

they have been without a mother too long.' He looked at Kitty. 'You've only seen them once I know – but Hannah adores you and so does young John.'

'They are nice children,' Kitty managed, for it was true. She'd seen them once at their grandmother's home before she'd died. It was before they moved here to Kettle's Yard and she'd often stopped to speak to the old lady, who lived nearby, and whom she'd liked. Kitty had visited her to ask if she could help her – and that was when she'd first met Joshua Miller. He'd seemed pleasant enough, still grieving his wife and concerned for his mother. It was only when he'd started calling at their home, and turning his unwanted attentions to Kitty that she had become uncomfortable in his company. 'I don't know what to say to you, sir.' She didn't want him to arrange the funeral but could do nothing to stop it since her mother had accepted his offer.

'You may say, "thank you, Joshua. I should be content for you to help my mother and me, because I know you are a friend." Do you think you could do that, Kitty? Because I am, you know.'

She lifted her head and looked at him. 'I thank you as a friend... Joshua. You are very kind to do this for us.'

'Now that is sensible, Kitty. I am glad that you have—' Whatever Annie Wilson was about to say was quelled by a look from Joshua Miller. 'Besides, the offer was made before you came home and I accepted it.' She flashed a defiant look at Kitty.

'Well, I shall set it all in train, Annie,' he said and held out his hand to her. She took it gratefully and he offered his other hand to Kitty. Reluctantly, she let him take her hand and hold it. His hand felt too warm and a little moist. Kitty had to fight herself not to snatch her hand back, but she allowed him to press it. 'Do not worry about anything, Kitty. I intend to look after you in future – both of you...' he added, but she saw by the look in his eyes what he meant. By allowing him to do them this service, she was letting him into her life and she knew what he wanted. It was there in his face. 'Farewell for now, Kitty, Annie – I shall be in touch very soon, my dears.'

Picking up his hat, he turned and left the kitchen, leaving only silence behind him.

* * *

Once he had gone, Kitty took a final look at her mother and then went up the stairs to her own room. She sat on the edge of the bed and buried her face in her hands. No tears came. She'd cried all her tears for her father. There were none left for herself.

'Kitty...' She didn't immediately look up as her mother came to the bedroom door and then entered. 'I know what you're thinking, but I didn't ask him to call. He heard about your father and just came and made his offer. What did you expect me to do? How could I refuse when I hardly know how we shall pay our rent?'

'I thought Dad had an insurance for his funeral?' Kitty said, looking up. 'I am certain I heard him speak of it...'

'That was before his accident, before he let it lapse. Why can't you get it into your head that we have no choice. We have nothing, not a penny over what you earn – and we can't afford to bury your father.' Her mother's tone was harsh once more. 'Either we accept Joshua's offer or your father will be buried in a pauper's grave. Is that what you want? Answer me, Kitty. Do you want your father buried decently or not?'

'Of course I do,' Kitty said. All hope had drained from her. She knew that she was trapped. She would struggle against it, but realised that between them her mother and Joshua would do everything they could to push her into a marriage she would hate. Blinking away her tears, she said, 'Why do you never call Dad by his name? It's always "your father", never Robert or my husband?'

Her mother looked at her in silence for a few moments and Kitty sensed she was hiding something. 'I loved him when we married,' she said at last, 'but he let me down when he brought me to this wretched place. Don't blame me for the situation we're in, Kitty – blame the father you think was so wonderful...'

With that, she turned and stalked out of the bedroom, leaving Kitty to stare into space as she struggled to come to terms with the reality of her situation. All her hopes and dreams were fading into nothingness. She would be expected to leave Harpers if she married Joshua Miller – to be his wife and a mother to his children – to lie in his bed...

Her throat tightened and tears burned behind her eyes. It was impossible! She couldn't do it! Somehow she would find a way to repay him and refuse the offer of marriage when it came.

* * *

Kitty was walking home from work two days later when she saw Larry Norton waving at her. He was dressed in his stained working clothes and standing outside her house. She hesitated and then walked up to him, smiling as she saw him looking at her with concern.

'I've been away for a few days,' he told her. 'I heard your dad had died – I'm so sorry, Miss Wilson...' His hand moved towards her but fell to his side. He wiped the palm on his breeches, as if aware it was dirty. 'If there is anything I can do for you, please ask.'

'You are very kind,' Kitty said, blinking to shut off the foolish tears. 'I don't think there is anything you can do, Mr Norton.'

'The funeral,' he said and hesitated as he saw her flinch. 'If you need help or money, I can help and I should be pleased to do it for you – and your ma.'

'Thank you, that is so kind.' Kitty swallowed hard. If only he'd offered two days earlier, but even as the thought occurred, she knew her mother would not have accepted help from him. 'My mother has accepted help from Mr Joshua Miller.' A tear slid down from the corner of her eye and she flicked it away with the back of her hand.

'Oh, well, if there is nothing I can do?' He looked uncomfortable and somehow hurt and, impulsively, Kitty moved forward and touched his arm.

'I wish it were you instead of him,' she said and her throat caught with tears. 'I don't like him. He... frightens me...'

'Kitty...' Her name was on his lips and his hand reached for hers, holding it in a firm cool clasp that made her feel better immediately. 'Forgive me, but I don't like to see you so upset – and if anyone frightens or hurts you, let me know and I'll sort him.'

Kitty lifted her eyes to his briefly. 'He doesn't want to hurt me, he wants to marry me,' she whispered, 'and I won't.'

'You can't marry him – you mustn't...' he cried, a note of alarm in his voice.

'I don't want to – I hate him.' With that, she broke away from him, shocked at revealing so much of her inner self to a man she scarcely knew. She went inside quickly, closing the door behind her and leaning against it for a moment with her eyes closed as the heat of embarrassment washed over her. How could she have told him? He must think her so forward.

'Kitty... trust me...'

She thought she heard the words just before the door closed but the next moment, her mother spoke.

'You wicked girl,' her mother's voice was accusing. 'I saw you talking to that common fellow through the window – letting him hold your hand. And you almost a married woman. If Mr Miller saw you behave in such a way, he would change his mind about wanting to marry you!'

Kitty raised her head and looked her mother squarely in the eyes. 'If that is so, I am glad,' she said. 'I've told you before, Mum, I am not going to marry him. I don't like him – I couldn't bear him to touch me... You don't know... You don't understand...'

Her mother glared at her. 'You don't have a choice any longer. He has gone to a lot of trouble and expense for us and you have to repay that the only way you can, Kitty.'

'No, I won't.' Kitty's gaze challenged her. Suddenly, she had found her courage and was determined to refuse the offer when it came. 'If you think he is so wonderful, you marry him yourself.'

'I'd have him like a shot if he'd take me instead of you,' Annie Wilson said. 'Just remember that he could put us out on the street if he chose.'

'What do you mean?' Kitty was surprised by the statement.

'Don't you know that he owns most of Kettle's Yard?' Annie said. 'He told us about this place when your father had his accident and he knew we had to move. He apologised to me for the state of the place and assured me it was only temporary and that he would see us right.'

'Mr Miller owns this house?' Kitty was shocked. 'He should be ashamed of himself for allowing it to get into such a state.'

'He says it is not worth renovating while the Nortons own that junkyard. If he could get rid of them, he would smarten all his property up here.'

Annie nodded. 'They are a thorn in his side, because they own the yard and the three houses nearest to it. He's offered them a good price to move on – but they are stubborn and refused his offer.'

'Why should they move their business just because he wants their property?'

'You call that junkyard a business?' Annie stared at her in disgust. 'You just be careful, my girl. You will end up getting dragged into something that will see you shamed and brought low. Just because he has a handsome face doesn't mean he can look after you.' Her mouth twisted bitterly. 'I found that out to my cost. My father warned me against marrying your father, but I would have my way – and look where that got me.'

'We had a good life until Dad was ill,' Kitty told her. 'You know we did – and I don't care what you say, I would rather marry a man who lives in a junkyard than your precious Mr Miller!'

Her mother's hand snaked out and slapped her across the face. Kitty gasped, stared at her, and then walked past her and up the stairs to her room.

'You will marry who I tell you to,' Annie Wilson called after her. 'You can't marry without my permission and I would never allow you to demean yourself by marrying beneath you.'

Kitty ignored her and closed her bedroom door. She didn't know why she'd said such a thing to her mother – or why she had told Larry Norton about her troubles. There was nothing he could do to help her – and just because he had been kind, taking her to the infirmary to see her father, it didn't mean he cared for her...

Yet, somehow, she sensed that he did care about her, and she realised with a little shock, she had not been so far from the truth when she'd told her mother she would prefer to be his wife than Mr Miller's.

Kitty's face flushed hot, because she knew she was reading too much into a little kindness from a stranger. He was a good person, she knew that instinctively, and she'd wanted him to put his arms about her and protect her – but that was only because she needed someone to look after her. Of course it was. She didn't really know him, so she couldn't have any deeper feelings for him and... and it was all so hopeless...

Flinging herself down on the bed and burying her face in the pillow,

Kitty wept. She wept for her lost father, for her situation and for the little ache in her heart that she did not understand.

8

'Do you have any small jobs at the restaurant?' Beth asked Jack when they were having lunch together some days after her trip to Kettle's Yard. 'What with arranging for Bella's trip to the clinic and Vera's hospital tests, I had forgotten about it for a while, but I promised to ask if there were any jobs going that a woman with no experience of work – other than in the home – might do. Perhaps washing up?'

'Not at the moment,' Jack said. 'I could possibly give her a few hours cleaning – if you think she would want it, but it is hard work, Beth, and the journey would make it difficult for her, if not impossible. Fares and working hours… I doubt she would want late-night shifts washing up, and the wage is hardly worthwhile, unless you are young and can put in enough hours.'

'No, she probably wouldn't,' Beth said with a little sigh. 'I looked in today's evening paper for possible jobs for her, but everyone wants experience and Kitty's mother doesn't have any. It would have to be domestic work – and the only one I saw was an advertisement for a parlourmaid.'

'They are usually expected to be young, because they are on their feet for long hours,' Jack said. He raised his eyebrows. 'Is it really your place to be looking for work for a woman you don't even know?'

'No – but I do like Kitty so much and I feel sorry for her,' Beth said. 'I suppose I could offer her a couple of hours a week doing housework?'

'If you wish for help in the house, get someone pleasant and helpful,' Jack said. 'From what you told me of Kitty's story, I don't think you would enjoy having her mother around.'

'No, I don't think I would,' Beth admitted. 'It's just that I wanted to help Kitty.'

'You could offer her a little part-time work in the evenings, looking after the children sometimes,' Jack said but smiled as he saw her face. 'I know we don't go out that often – but I don't see what else you can do. It isn't really your problem, Beth. You have Vera to think about – and this other one... Bella. I think you've taken on as much as you can manage with her, love.'

'Yes, she is a bit of a handful,' Beth admitted with a laugh. 'I do like her, though, Jack. She is full of courage. If you saw what she has to put up with – and yet she doesn't buckle under. She comes over as being a grumpy old thing, but underneath she is brave and funny too.'

Jack leaned across the table and touched her hand. 'I wonder why I love you so much,' he said and then raised her hand to kiss it. 'Now, tell me, has Vera got her appointment yet?'

'No – but she has told the doctor that she will go for tests. He thinks it will be a couple of weeks or so before he can arrange it.'

* * *

Beth couldn't put Kitty's troubles out of her mind. She knew Jack was right. It wasn't her place to find work for Kitty's mother, but the girl needed help. Feeling frustrated, she decided to deliver little Jack to his school and then take her youngest, Timmy, who, because of some building inspections, had no school that day, to see Sally and tell her what was on her mind.

She found her at home. Peter went to the same school as Timmy so they were both off for the day, and they welcomed their guests, inviting them to stay for coffee and cake, which Beth accepted. It was lovely to spend time with Sally when they were not at work and could really chat.

'Jack was correct in saying it isn't your job to find Annie Wilson work,' Sally said as they drank coffee and the two young boys played together. 'But I do know how you feel. I'm not sure what we can do, Beth.' Sally looked thoughtful. 'I don't have a supervisor's position free at the moment or I would offer it to Kitty. She is a responsible girl and pleasant. I would like to help her.'

Beth sighed and nodded. So often Sally seemed to have the answer to problems, but perhaps not this time.

'Have you taken Bella to the clinic for treatment again yet?' Sally asked and Beth shook her head, still pondering Kitty's problems. 'You don't think Annie Wilson would like a few hours a week looking after her neighbour? If she would cook and clean for Bella, it would be better for them – and you. You could pay her a few shillings a week to do it. I know it isn't much – but anything helps when you're short of money.'

Sally hadn't always been the wife of a successful businessman and had known hard times herself. Beth sat and looked at her. 'That is an excellent suggestion, Sally – if she would do it, and if she won't, I could offer the same terms to Kitty.' Beth nodded to herself. 'Kitty already tries to help Bella. If I made it a job she can do at weekends or even a half an hour or so in the evenings, that would reward her for her kindness. I must make sure Bella is all right for money too, though she says she can manage.'

'There you are then—' Sally broke off to grab Peter as he tried to punch Timmy, who was patiently setting up the skittles again. 'No, Peter! You do not hit your friends, because if you do, you won't have any.' He looked at her mutinously for a moment and then smiled, saying sorry. Sally stroked his dark hair back from his forehead. 'So when are you and Jack coming for lunch again, Beth, and the children, naturally? I thought perhaps Sunday next week, if you're free?'

Beth smiled, because she had reached the best solution she could to Kitty's problem for the moment. 'We would love to,' she said. 'Jack will be home all day that Sunday; it's his free day that week.' She looked at Sally. 'Is everything all right? I've been so wrapped up with my problems – but I can see you have something on your mind. Is it anything you can tell me?'

'Oh, I wish I could,' Sally said with a little grimace. 'Ben told me something in the strictest confidence and so I can't – but I want to...' She laughed and shook her head. 'I mustn't because I promised Ben.'

'Well then, don't,' Beth said. 'A promise is a promise, Sally. I haven't seen Ben since he got back from his buying trip – how is he?'

'Ben is fine – a bit worried about something, but fine in himself. He did very well in selecting the merchandise and I approve of almost everything he ordered. However, he says he won't do it alone again. He thinks I could have done better – and he missed us. So I imagine I shall be going with him next time.'

'That will be exciting,' Beth exclaimed. 'How will you manage with the children – or will you leave them here with your mother and Mrs Hills?'

'That is something I shall have to decide on next year. It depends on many things – on her health and Trevor's too. He has seemed a bit better since he gave up his work and they moved to be near us, so I am hoping he will continue to improve.'

'Good for him,' Beth replied. 'If you do take the children with you, you will need a nanny again.' She laughed as she saw Sally's face. 'I know the last one didn't work out too well, but Winnie was just a mixed-up girl. You need an older woman you can rely on.'

Sally inclined her head in agreement. 'Yes, though Winnie is doing very well in her new job. She is working as a receptionist at Miss Susie and I understand she is both reliable and honest these days.'

'She just went through a bad time,' Beth replied. 'It can happen to anyone, Sally.'

'Yes, I know, and I have forgiven her and forgotten that she tried to ruin my marriage, as well as stealing from me.'

'I know it was a bad thing to do, but I felt sorry for the girl when I heard what a rotten home life she had,' Beth said and then frowned. 'I feel sorry for Kitty too.'

'You've settled what you're going to do for her,' Sally said firmly. 'Now, tell me what you think to all this nonsense in the papers – do you think there will be a general strike, as they say?'

'Surely not?' Beth was shocked at the idea. 'Whatever would happen if everyone went on strike? We'd have no milk or food in the shops before long – and if the buses stopped running...' She shook her head. 'It can't happen, Sally. People must see that...'

'The miners are already saying they will strike,' Sally replied, 'and the other trades are saying they will support them – and Ben thinks it is going to happen.'

'It will bring everything to a standstill...' Beth said in horror.

'Ben says he will join a committee to help keep things moving – they are talking of volunteers keeping the trains running so the milk can be brought into London as usual, buses and the docks too. We need to unload the ships or the country will run out of food.'

Beth stared at her. 'If they break the strike like that there may be trouble, especially on the docks; they are a tough lot of men...'

'I agree. However, Ben says they are prepared for that; there is certain to be fighting if they try to cross the picket lines – as they will. It has to be done – and he says they will need canteens set up for the strike breakers. He wants me to be on a committee for that and, of course, I said yes. If you have time, you could help – and you could ask Kitty and Annie Wilson if they want to, though they may be on the side of the workers.'

'I think they would be, so I won't ask them,' Beth said, hesitated, then, 'Is that what Ben told you not to tell me?'

'No. No, it isn't,' Sally said. 'It is something even more worrying – but I just can't tell you. Beth, I'm sorry. I should not even have mentioned it...'

'You don't have to. I understand,' Beth assured her. 'I don't like to see you looking worried, but whatever it is, have faith. Ben normally knows what he is doing.'

'Yes...' Sally shook her head again. 'I shall not deny that I am worried, but it is best if you don't know. Now, tell me, how is Vera?' Her change of subject was deliberate and Beth accepted it.

'She is as well as can be expected in the circumstances, a little anxious about her condition – afraid it is something nasty. Fortunately, I believe she will soon have her appointment for those tests and then we shall know. I am not sure what happens if it is what she fears – but I pray it isn't.'

Sally nodded. 'No one mentions that word, but I did hear of someone who had a lump removed from under her arm recently. It was a big operation but she seems to be getting over it.'

'Do you still do your hospital visiting?' Beth asked.

'Yes.' Sally looked thoughtful. 'I started it because of all the badly injured men in the war – but now I visit the wards where elderly patients are treated. I take papers, magazines, fruit and sweets – just one afternoon a week. They are so pleased to see me and to talk.'

'I suppose some of them have no one to visit them,' Beth said, nodding.

Sally's reference to hospitals made her think of their mutual friend, who had been a nurse in the war. 'I had a letter from Maggie yesterday. She is doing much the same thing down there in the country. The home she began for the war wounded is now taking in elderly folk who can't look after themselves.' Maggie had volunteered to be a nurse during the war and it was at a hospital where she was recuperating from a nasty illness that she'd met her husband, Colin. Colin had been wounded and was permanently in a wheelchair, but despite that, they were happy running the estate that had been his father's.

'Yes, I know...' Sally sighed. 'She and Colin spend most of their time in the country since his father died. I miss seeing her – but she says she may come up for a couple of weeks this summer.'

'I hope she will, but she has Colin and the children to look after, as well as her home, and her duties as the lady of the manor.' Beth laughed. 'It seems strange to think of our Maggie living in a big country house, doing so many things – charity committees, tea with the Vicar and all the rest!'

'She is happy and she deserves it because of what she went through during the war and after,' Sally said. 'If she hadn't met Colin and married him – and if her first love, Tim, hadn't been killed, she would've been your sister-in-law, Beth.'

'Yes. I often think that and wish things had been different – but, as you say, she is happy. She loves Colin and she fills her life with the children they adopted and her charity work. I doubt she has time to think about the past or what she experienced during the war.'

'We were all shop girls at Harpers once,' Sally said and laughed. 'How things change, Beth – but I don't regret any of it, do you?'

'No – some things might have been better, but we came through and we're all happy now, aren't we?'

'Yes, even Rachel,' Sally said, smiling reminiscently. 'Since she took over the buying for Jenni's shop, she has been as happy as I've ever known her.'

Rachel had been their first supervisor when they had worked on the counters together at Harpers. She had married a man quite a bit older than herself and been obliged to retire to the Sussex countryside with him when his health failed. However, after Jenni – Ben's half-sister – had died of a haemorrhage in her brain, Jenni's husband had been unable to cope with the buying for the fashion shop Jenni had started and loved during her last years. He was a brilliant surgeon, specialising in treating burns and had no time for the business, but Rachel had offered to take over the buying for him and now practically ran the whole thing, with the help of a manager and some supervisors to look after the staff. It meant she had to take regular trips up north and she quite often broke her journey in London to visit Sally and Harpers.

'Yes, she writes now and then, but I think she contacts you more often?'

'I help her with anything she is unsure of, but that isn't much these days. She often knows more about new merchandise than I do.' Sally laughed as Beth shook her head. 'Rachel always was very efficient and she soon learns.'

'How is William and the little girl she adopted?' Rachel lived with her husband, William, and the child, and her mother-in-law from her first marriage had become her friend and lived nearby, always at hand to help if needed.

'Both well, I understand,' Sally replied. 'The country air suits them – as it does Maggie.'

Beth agreed but sighed. She was happy in her life but talking of old friends made her realise how much she missed them, and she decided to write letters to both Maggie and Rachel when she got home. 'Do you hear from Mick O'Sullivan these days?' she asked. There was a time when Mick was always around, a great friend to Sally, but she hadn't heard much from him recently.

'I had a letter from Andrea two weeks ago,' Sally replied with a frown. 'She says Mick has been unwell since Christmas, but thinks he is on the mend now.'

'Does she say anything about coming over for a visit?'

'No, not a word. Goodness, is that the time?' Sally said. 'Excuse me, Beth, but I have an appointment in half an hour. I am meeting a representative for a new toy firm and I am hoping for some quality goods.' She smiled. 'Do you remember in the war that injured soldier who made me some wooden toys when I couldn't buy any for Harpers?' Beth nodded. 'He has his own company now and they are making wonderful toys – and every one of his employees is an old soldier...'

'That is fantastic,' Beth said and stood to leave. 'I must go anyway. I want to pop in to see Vera before I go home...'

They kissed and hugged and Beth took Timmy off to see his granny, while Sally hastily got ready to meet her travelling salesman.

* * *

Beth told Jack about her visit with Sally when he came home that evening. He listened and looked grave when she told him that Ben thought there would be a general strike.

'Yes, it looks increasingly possible,' he agreed. 'I'm not sure how it will affect the restaurant, but if the chefs and waiters decide to strike, I suppose we shall have to close for a while.'

'Oh, Jack, that is a shame – and you're doing so well,' Beth cried in sympathy, because she could see he was worried. 'Has Ben discussed it with you?'

'Yes, we discuss most things when he pops in,' Jack replied and frowned. 'Yet I get the feeling there's something he isn't telling me. I don't know what it is – they haven't quarrelled, I suppose?'

'I don't think so,' Beth said thoughtfully. 'If it was that, I am sure Sally would've told me. She said Ben had told her something in strictest confidence and she wouldn't tell me what it was – even though I knew she wanted to.'

Jack frowned. 'That is strange – I wonder if it has something to do with the restaurant...'

'Surely he would tell you if it had?'

'Unless he isn't satisfied with it and is thinking of getting out...'

'He wouldn't!' Beth looked at him in distress. 'I know he would discuss it with you. Besides, it is doing well, so why would he want to sell?'

'No idea,' Jack replied with a shrug. 'I don't intend to worry about it, Beth. Let's have a nice lunch out somewhere with the children tomorrow – and then I shall have to get back to the restaurant. We have a full house tomorrow evening, every table is booked.'

9

'Had a good day?' Ben asked that evening and kissed Sally, before turning his attention to his son Peter, who clawed at his arm, demanding attention. Jenny had been reading one of her books about ballet, a new passion since she'd seen pictures in a glossy magazine, but seeing her brother being tossed up in her father's arms, she jumped up and went to demand her share of his notice. Lulu, their little brown dog, joined in the general hulla-baloo and it was several minutes before Mrs Hills came to take the children off to the nursery and Sally was able to answer.

'Beth came over to see me and we had coffee... She thought I was looking worried about something...'

'You didn't tell her?' Ben frowned.

'No, of course, I didn't,' Sally said. 'You particularly asked me not to.'

'I know it is difficult for you to keep secrets from Beth – and I don't find it easy keeping Jack in the dark, especially as he knows there is a problem. I was told in confidence myself and I agreed to the plan – but if Jack knew, he might give our strategy away. Not that he'd do it on purpose, but he might make a slip of the tongue.'

'And Jack really has no idea that his new head waiter is a secret agent for the American government?'

'None at all. The man is very good at his job. No one would ever guess he was there to trap a very dangerous individual – and I understand our government is eager to oblige the Americans in this. The person they are after is wanted on several counts of murder, and they think he is behind illegal alcohol running, as well as other criminal activities in New York and Chicago.'

'Prohibition was a drastic measure for the Americans to take,' Sally said, looking at her husband thoughtfully as he poured himself a small whisky. Something he did most days when he came home. 'It was always bound to ferment trouble and criminals take advantage of people's desire for something they are forbidden to have – but why would someone like that come here? We don't have such strict laws on the sale of alcohol.'

The Temperance Movement in America had been stronger throughout the late nineteenth century than its counterpart in Britain and it was because of their lobbying that it had become law there.

'Thank goodness for that,' Ben remarked as he sipped his whisky. 'It is just one of the things I love about your country, Sally; the tolerance.' Ben was himself an American but had settled here when Harpers was first opened and during the war he'd worked tirelessly for the British government. 'I don't know the answer to your question, Sally. I was told it was believed the person was here, possibly using another name, and he was reported as being seen in our restaurant. I was asked if I would allow a government agent to work secretly in the restaurant and I agreed.' He shrugged and poured himself another small measure of whisky, looking thoughtful. 'I would guess that things might have got too hot for their quarry over there – the authorities haven't been able to get near him, but I heard something when I was over there...' He paused and Sally looked at him expectantly.

'Are you going to tell me?' she asked after some moments of silence, and raised her eyebrows.

'It was only a whisper. Someone said that Al Capone had a rival who had annoyed him, and he'd put a hit man on to him... Capone is one of the most notorious and feared gangsters over there, Sally. I don't know much about him – but there was a street fight between two rival gangs when I was in Chicago for a couple of days. I saw them shooting at a restaurant... They gunned down everyone sitting there, except a few who managed to crawl under a table, fortunately I was across the street.'

'Oh my God!' Sally was shocked and horrified as she looked at Ben. 'That couldn't happen here – could it?' She felt the ice at her nape and colour drained from her face. 'Something happened not far from Beth's house recently. Someone she knew was shot...'

'It could well be connected,' Ben said. 'If the man they think is here is looking to muscle in on the gangs in London, they will fight him – and he has money, I imagine, so he might live anywhere in London.' He twirled his glass. 'I think he must be a really vicious type for the American government to send their agent to find him.'

'I think I'll have a whisky too,' Sally said and Ben poured one for her. She sipped it thoughtfully.

'Perhaps I shouldn't tell you these things,' Ben said, looking at her anxiously. 'I thought it better you should know – we've always shared everything.'

'Of course I want to know,' Sally replied. 'It was just so shocking – what you said about the attack on the restaurant...'

'I was told that it was probably Capone's men, but no one knew for certain – there are quite a few gangs and they normally stick to their own rackets and leave the others to get on with theirs, but if someone gets greedy, they have to be taught a lesson – or that's what I heard.' Ben stared moodily into his glass. 'We can do without that sort here. Obviously, we already have criminals of our own, but if the Americans move in... it could happen here.'

'At our restaurant?'

Reluctantly, Ben nodded. 'At any restaurant the men involved happen to frequent. We've been lucky so far that no one has demanded protection money.'

'Does that happen often?'

'I think a lot of the smaller places pay. It could happen to us.'

'Would you pay?'

'We might have to – so if this American can be removed...'

Sally nodded and then frowned. 'Don't you think you should tell Jack who his head waiter really is?' Sally said. 'He ought to be aware of what could happen, Ben.'

Ben replied sombrely, 'I've been hoping this man will be arrested before anything happens.' He sighed. 'I was told not to inform Jack because he might give the agent away by accident – but I don't feel comfortable with it, Sally. He has the right to know—'

'Then tell him,' Sally urged. 'I am certain you can trust him – and he did tell you there were some rowdy customers he suspected of being involved in unpleasant business.'

'Yes...' Ben gave her a rueful look. 'I suppose that is why I told you, Sally. I knew you would put me right. After all, Jack and the restaurant mean more to us than whether or not they catch an American criminal. I would prefer it if they went home... this person, whoever he is and his gang.'

'I suppose that depends on whether or not there is enough money here to make it worth his while.'

'Or if the police make it too uncomfortable for him,' Ben replied. He stretched and put down his glass, shrugging his shoulders. 'I'll tell Jack tomorrow then. So what is for dinner?'

Sally laughed. 'Mrs Hills has prepared a beef pie for us – and there is a lemon meringue for afters.'

'Good, I'm hungry,' Ben said, sliding an arm about her waist, still slim despite giving birth to two children. 'You always help me to settle my problems, Sally. I've no idea what I would do without you.'

'Come, let's eat,' she said and kissed him. 'And thank you for telling me. I should hate it if you had secrets from me – and I know Jack would feel the same. Once he knows, he will be more alert.'

'As long as he doesn't try playing the hero,' Ben said and the smile left his eyes. 'Beth would never forgive me if anything happened.'

* * *

'So I was right,' Jack said when Ben told him what was going on the next day. He'd listened in silence and growing frustration. 'I know the man they're after, Ben. I noticed his accent the first time they came to the restaurant; he's a big brute of a man with a dark complexion and greying hair. He looks like a brawler despite his smart suit and gold watch on his waistcoat – but there was an Englishman with him. He is a gentleman by birth, but I wouldn't trust him an inch. They were obviously in cahoots and I heard them send the girls off for a while when they wanted to talk privately. Any waiter who tried to approach was waved away. I'll certainly keep my eyes and ears open in future.'

'Be on your guard, Jack. These men are dangerous. If they suspected you were listening in to their private business, they wouldn't hesitate to kill you. You have to be careful not to give Lucas away, because they would kill him without a thought. It might not be here in the restaurant, but he could be followed late at night and so could you. They probably know all about you already. I think they're smart enough to want to investigate the private lives of the people who run the places they frequent.'

Jack's face drained of colour. 'Beth and the boys...?' Ben nodded and Jack's hands clenched. 'My God – they could be at risk...'

'Only if these men suspect you are a danger to them,' Ben said. 'So be careful, Jack. Some of these criminal bosses have nasty minds. Let them come and go; don't interfere. They are trying to remain in the shadows here in London. Lucas will discover their other haunts. He and others will follow them, discover where they live – and then, when they're sure it's the man they are after, they will move in.'

Jack nodded. 'I wondered where Lucas disappeared to three nights ago. One of the men – not the American – was here then. Lucas slipped out for a while when he left. I told him off for not doing his job.'

'Do so again, but not if our suspects are here, as we don't want to draw attention to him,' Ben said. 'I don't want him to know you're aware who he is – and you shouldn't let anyone else see anything is different regarding his position. Treat him as you would any waiter, but don't sack him – unless I tell you to. I'll only do that if that's what the American government wants.'

'Unless the man who has been paid to kill this American gangster turns up and guns him down in a restaurant full of diners...' Jack frowned. 'I know you've allowed him to work here, Ben, but I don't like it.'

'Nor do I,' Ben admitted. 'I was approached by someone I trusted and I agreed, but I've had second thoughts since. However, if I tell Lucas to find somewhere else to track his prey, and then there is an incident here...' He shook his head. 'I feel as if I am between the devil and the deep blue sea, Jack. We can't stop these dangerous men coming here – so what's the answer?'

'I would not have agreed,' Jack said stubbornly, but then he shook his head. 'No, that's not fair. If our police had wanted to set a watch here, I would've agreed – it's just got me jumpy.' He looked worried. 'It was bad enough when Beth took that fellow who was shot into our kitchen and bound him up until the doctor came – but this...' He shuddered. 'I like an enemy I can see and fight – not shadows...'

Ben nodded his agreement. 'I feel the same, Jack, but I'm not here all the time. If it was happening at the store, I would be most uncomfortable.'

'Well, some of the girls who come with them shop there,' Jack said. 'Let's hope their friends don't start doing the same.'

'God forbid,' Ben said looking stern. 'I think they are more into alcohol, prostitution and gambling – but if they ever come making me an offer for Harpers, I'll be in the proverbial...' He grimaced. 'These criminals are dangerous and a nuisance, but when they move their money into legitimate businesses, they will be harder to stop, because they will just disappear and no one will know what they do in the shadows.'

10

The funeral and the reception were over. Kitty had barely managed to get through it, standing in a bitterly cold churchyard in a fine drizzle, even though it was almost April now. Her grief for her father was pain enough without the revulsion she felt at the gleam of triumph in Joshua Miller's eyes. He thought she belonged to him now, his certainty was there in his eyes and in the way his hand lingered on her arm as he helped her from the car that had taken them to the church and then brought them to his house.

It was still considered proper for women to remain at home while a funeral took place, but Kitty had insisted on attending her father's funeral and, because she had friends who would have gladly taken her, it had been grudgingly allowed.

'I suppose I must come too,' her mother had said sourly when Kitty told her she would go no matter what anyone thought of her. 'You are a wilful girl, Kitty Wilson, and you'll see us both in the workhouse I make no doubt.'

'I have no intention of going to the workhouse. Besides, most of them are now infirmaries for the sick and elderly,' Kitty had replied. 'Mrs Burrows is paying me ten shillings a week to do a bit of cleaning and caring for Bella. It will enable us to stay here for the time being – and I will find a way of paying Mr Miller for Father's funeral costs.'

'Stubborn girl,' Annie had muttered. 'You have a comfortable life with a good man offered on a plate and you turn your nose up.'

'I don't like him. He makes my skin crawl,' Kitty's reply had been true then and it was still true now.

She saw him returning to the parlour after he had seen the last of his guests to the door. Throughout the ceremony and the reception, Joshua had been everything proper, a kind considerate host and benefactor, but Kitty saw the glint in his eyes as he found her alone, her mother in his kitchen offering to help his housekeeper wash up and thank her for providing an excellent tea for all the guests. A few had been Kitty's father's friends, but most were unknown to Kitty, though Joshua had punctiliously introduced her to them as his 'dear friends, Mrs and Miss Wilson.'

'Ah, my dear Kitty,' he said and reached for her hand, trying to take it, but she moved away, turning her face aside. 'Yes, I understand your grief, my dear, but it is over now. We should be thinking of the future.'

Kitty stood as stone, refusing to look at him.

'Come, Kitty, you must know how much I care for you – and your mother, naturally.' Annie Wilson at that moment re-entered the parlour. 'I have made no secret of my hopes and intentions. You must know that I wish you to be my wife so that I can care for you both.'

Kitty waited a moment longer, then turned to face him, her manner proud and cold. 'You have been kind to us,' she said and her eyes flashed with sudden fire. 'Yet I cannot – I will not! – marry you. Please do not persist or you will cause us all distress, sir.'

'Kitty, you unnatural girl!' her mother said in tones of anger. 'After all Joshua has done for us both—'

'I am aware of my debt,' Kitty said and her hands trembled, but she hid them behind her. 'I will repay whatever you have spent for us, sir – but I shall never marry you. I would rather be dead...' She raised her head to look into his eyes and saw the suppressed fury there. It was a stupid thing to say and she knew it, wished it unsaid, but it was too late.

His face went deathly pale and his hands clenched. For a moment, she thought that he would strike her, but he controlled himself and merely inclined his head. 'Is that so, Miss Wilson? Then I suggest that you consider ways of paying me back –I will be generous and charge nothing for the receptions. Flowers, cars, and expenses may be in the region of seventy pounds. I will let you know the total in a few days – and give you... shall we say six months to repay, but, of course, the longer it takes, the more interest will accrue...' His eyes flicked to Kitty's mother. 'Such a shame you deceived me into thinking she was a biddable girl, Mrs Wilson. I will say good day now and leave you to make your own way home. Please excuse me. I have two young children who will be most disappointed that the new mother they longed for does not love them.'

With that he left the parlour. In the silence that followed as they retrieved their coats from the hall and left his house to begin their walk home, Kitty's thoughts tumbled in her mind. How could she find seventy pounds in six months – and how much would her debt grow if she did not repay him in that time? She had never dreamed it could cost so much, nor had she ever seen such a large amount of money in her life and the enormity of it terrified her.

Kitty's mother glared at her when she directed an anxious look towards her, her face tight with anger, but she said nothing as they walked through the streets to their home.

* * *

Only when the door of their terraced house was closed did Annie Wilson look at Kitty.

'Well, are you proud of yourself, girl?' she asked. 'Seventy pounds – and more if he has his interest. How do you intend to pay? Even the money you get for being a skivvy for that wretched old woman down the road won't help you pay that. If we gave him every penny you earn, we'd still be in debt.'

'I thought I could pay him a little bit at a time,' Kitty said, but her knees wobbled and she felt tears on her cheeks. She shook her head. It was her mother who had insisted on letting him arrange the funeral, but now it was Kitty who must find the money to pay him, and it seemed an impossible task. 'Are you certain my father didn't pay into an insurance to cover such things?'

Her mother gave one sharp shake of her head. Kitty gulped. She'd thought her father would have done that while he was at work. He was usually careful about such things.

Her mother grunted. 'I told you we would not get a penny – you should've listened to me.'

'I know, but Dad had a few savings and his boss paid him a little until he told him he would not return to the building – I thought he would have kept an insurance up, especially as he knew he was so ill.'

'How many times do I have to tell you? It lapsed.'

'I was just asking,' Kitty said and looked up. 'I will offer Mr Miller five shillings a week until the debt is paid. I refuse to be blackmailed and he won't get a penny interest. He insisted on paying for the funeral and you agreed with him.'

'Because we both imagined you were a grateful girl who would repay him by becoming his wife and caring for his motherless children.'

'You make me sound wicked,' Kitty said and stared at her mother proudly. 'I would gladly have looked after his children for a wage – but I could never wed him. He disgusts me...'

'You made that abundantly clear,' her mother said in a cold voice. 'Had you asked for time, pleaded your grief, he might not have demanded his money back. Did you not realise that you wounded his pride?'

Kitty hung her head. 'I should not have done that – but it was the look in his eyes. He was gloating.' She looked up at her mother then. 'He isn't a good man, surely you can see that? Why would you want me to marry a man I cannot like? If you loved me...' She left the rest unsaid, her heart sinking as her mother's cold stare did not falter.

'You were a fool, Kitty. You've antagonised him now. I doubt he'd want you even if I told him you were sorry and begged him to forgive you...'

'Please do not,' Kitty said. 'I am sorry if I hurt him – but it is only injured pride. He doesn't love me. He just lusts after me like a—'

'Kitty!' her mother's furious voice interrupted. 'Do not speak in such a way. I forbid it.'

Kitty fixed her with a look of grief. 'You don't love me either, Mother. You would have sold me to him for a life of ease and not cared one bit how I felt or suffered.'

Annie Wilson looked at her and then inclined her head. 'You are my daughter and I care for you in my way – as I did your father – but I need a decent roof over my head and a soft bed to sleep in. I need food and clothes and a little comfort.' There was defiance in her now. 'When Joshua comes, I shall plead with him. I shall tell him how disappointed I am in you, and offer myself as a nurse to his children. I will ask him if he will let me repay the debt by being their nursemaid – but if I do, I shall live in his house and this one will be given up.'

'What shall I do if you give the house up?' Kitty stared at her in shock.

'That is for you to decide. You've made your bed, Kitty. Now you can lie on it. You will find a room somewhere, I dare say.'

Kitty met her mother's cold gaze and nodded. 'As you wish. Have you thought what you will do if he refuses?'

A flicker of fear passed across Annie Wilson's face. 'I shall pray that he will not – in fact, I shall write him a conciliatory letter giving him my proposal and hope that out of the kindness of his heart he accepts.'

'You will beg him to become his servant,' Kitty said with a note of scorn and then she sank onto a hard wooden chair. 'I am sorry, Mum, that was unkind of me. I hope for your sake that he accepts – if it is what you want.'

'I think it is my only chance of a decent life. It is not what I might have had – but there is no sense crying over spilt milk. I am sure he would not have you now after you insulted him.'

Kitty just shook her head, repressing the shudder that went through her. The way Joshua Miller had looked at her when she'd given her final answer told her that she had made an enemy. He hated her now and she sensed that beneath the polite veneer was a cold, ruthless nature. She could not imagine what he would do to her if he had the chance – humiliate her at the very least. Could he have her arrested for debt? She did not know, but she would have to find out – because unless he accepted her mother's offer, the day would come when she would have to face the consequences of her actions.

* * *

'I am not certain of the law on debt,' Beth told Kitty when she asked her the question some days later during a break at Harpers. 'I know that once upon a time there was such a thing as a debtor's prison and people were put there until the debt was paid – but how one can pay off a debt inside prison, I fail to see. I suppose the family had to find the money somehow.' She looked at Kitty. 'You had best tell me the whole, my dear – did your father leave a lot of debts?'

'No. It was just the cost of the funeral...' They were in the canteen at Harpers, having their lunch, and Kitty poured out her story in halting phrases. 'I told him I would rather die than wed him...' she said, sniffing to hold back the tears. 'That is when he told me he would give me six months to repay the debt...' Kitty blew her nose. 'Of course he knows I can't. It would take me ages to repay seventy pounds – and that is without the reception.'

'It must have been an expensive funeral – with cars and flowers?'

'It was. He insisted on arranging it and paying for it. I would never have dreamed of spending so much money. I told him that we wished for a simple ceremony and would do it ourselves, but he just took over and my mother agreed with him. In the end I reluctantly went along with it – but I knew at once that he thought he had got me. Mum said it was my duty to be his wife, but I just couldn't... the touch of his hand revolts me. I know it is wicked of me...'

'Nonsense! He and indeed your mother are at fault here,' Beth told her. 'He is an unscrupulous man who has taken advantage of your grief to push you into an impossible situation. Leave it to me to deal with him.'

Kitty stared at her in astonishment. 'But you can't, Mrs Burrows. I couldn't let you.'

Beth's eyes sparkled with the light of battle. 'I refuse to see that awful man force his will on you. Seventy pounds is a lot of money and I would need to see all the receipts before he was paid one penny. However, if need be, I would do so. I have the money saved. Just tell me where to find this man and I will make him wish he had not acted so shabbily towards you. And I'll get a letter to say that the debt is paid.'

Kitty felt the tears slide down her cheeks. 'You are so kind to me – I will repay you in time, I promise.'

'Let us see what I can do first. I would much prefer that you did not pay him one penny, Kitty, but if he will not be moved, then I shall see the debt settled.' Beth hesitated, then, 'I am sorry I have not been able to find work for your mother.'

Kitty gulped back her tears. 'She says she intends to hire herself out to Mr Miller as a nursemaid for his children. It was to repay the debt – but if that were paid, she might stay at home with me and perhaps seek some work herself...'

'Well, let me deal with this awful man for you, Kitty, and then your mother can make up her own mind what she wants to do.'

Kitty nodded. 'Thank you so much, Mrs Burrows. I will repay you one day – and when Jerry comes home and Bella no longer needs me, I will find another job in the evenings and pay you the whole of the seventy pounds.'

'If that is your wish,' Beth said and smiled at her. 'You had best go and wash your face before you return to your department, Kitty. Now stop worrying and I will sort this out for you. I promise.'

'Thank you. I shall never forget your kindness,' Kitty said. She smiled at Beth, got up and went off to wash her face and hands before returning to the dress department.

Beth sat and watched her go. Her nest egg that she used for treats for herself and the children would be much depleted by this act of generosity, but she was glad she had made the offer. She would seek out Mr Joshua Miller that very afternoon and tell him exactly what she thought of him. Only if he threatened to bring the law on Kitty and her mother would she pay him. If she had her way, he would be the one paying by languishing in prison!

* * *

Kitty was just leaving work the following day when Beth came up to her. It was warmer now that the nights were pulling out and it had felt like a spring day. She handed Kitty an envelope.

'There you are, Kitty – all paid, and done.'

Kitty stared at her in delight. 'He accepted your money? I feared he would refuse and make me pay...'

'He had no choice,' Beth replied, a little satisfied smile about her mouth. 'I do not say he was pleased by it – but I told him that if he did not, I should bring the law to bear – and I asked to see the receipts. He pretended he could not find them, but I told him he would only be offered the money once and, if he attempted to blackmail you into marrying him again, I should go to the police.' Beth smiled as Kitty gasped at her boldness. 'I told him I was friendly with a chief constable and he went pale. You were perfectly right to refuse him, Kitty. I disliked him intensely and I believe he has something to hide. He fetched out a few receipts then. They totalled thirty pounds, not seventy, and that is the amount I paid. I made him sign to say you owed him nothing more and that it was his idea to pay for the funeral. He is fortunate to get anything, for as I told him, having offered to pay he could be held to have become liable for the debt.'

'Oh, Mrs Burrows – Beth – I am so grateful,' Kitty choked on a sob of relief and took the envelope, holding it close to her chest. 'I shall pay you as soon as I am able. I promise.'

'You need not, but I know that you will.' Beth smiled at her. 'Now go home and tell your mother to stop worrying over it.'

Kitty thanked her again. They left Harpers together but then parted as Beth was going to the restaurant to meet her husband and Kitty walked home, feeling as if a dark cloud had been lifted from her.

* * *

Her mother was sitting at the kitchen table when she entered, wearing her coat and hat. A carpet bag was on the table beside her. She looked at Kitty, a spark of triumph in her eyes.

'Joshua has been to see me – you just missed him. He has forgiven me and asked me to move in and look after his children. I am leaving now that you are back. You will have to find somewhere else to live – unless you can pay ten shillings a week rent.'

'That is twice what it was,' Kitty exclaimed in dismay. 'You know I can't.'

'Those were his terms,' her mother said. 'I told him you would leave – and you will have to find another place to live. I dare say one room will be enough, if you can find someone to take you.' She stood up, prepared to leave.

'You don't have to do this,' Kitty said. 'Mrs Burrows paid the debt. We don't owe him anything.'

'I know. He told me that one of your friends had paid him a visit and the debt was settled – and he will pay me a pound a week, plus my room and board. It will be a better life for me. I like him; I like his house – and I like his children.'

'He told you...' Kitty stared at her. 'The debt is paid and still he wants twice the rent.'

'Did you imagine he would not take some form of revenge?' her mother asked. 'When you hurt a man's pride, expect him to hurt you back. Well, Kitty, I doubt we shall meet again. I do not know what you will do – but perhaps your posh friends will help you again.'

With that last taunt, Annie Wilson walked from the house and out of her daughter's life.

* * *

Kitty sat down feeling stunned. Had her mother truly just walked off, leaving her alone? She shook her head, stunned and unbelieving. She hadn't expected gratitude for having found someone to lend her the money to pay their debt, for it was as much her mother's as hers – but this...? It was shocking.

So what could she do now? Kitty counted the money in her purse. She had two shillings to keep herself until Friday, four days away. Getting up, she went to look in the pantry. There was half a loaf of bread, a little butter in the dish and two eggs. Kitty's mother hadn't done any shopping that day, or if she had, she'd taken it with her.

She would have to leave this house and find lodgings. Feeling hungry, she used the bread to make toast and poached the eggs. In the morning, she would have to go hungry. She couldn't ask Mrs Burrows for more help, nor would she see her the next day. Somehow, she would have to manage until she got her wages, even if it meant going without food – and she would need to find a room. Somewhere not too far away.

Having eaten and washed her dishes, Kitty decided to visit Bella and do her usual chores for her. It was as she was reaching for her coat that someone knocked at her door. She opened it to discover Larry Norton standing there. He was holding a little posy of flowers and a box with a velvet bow.

'I hope you like mint creams?' he said as he handed her his gifts with a shy smile.

'Mr Norton...' Kitty said. She hesitated for a moment, then, 'Won't you please come in? I am going down to Bella's in a few minutes, but I have time to offer you a cup of tea.'

He entered, looked about him, and nodded. 'It's true then. Your ma has gone off and left you on your own.'

Kitty filled the kettle and placed it on the hob. 'Who told you?' she asked as she turned to face him.

'I popped in to see Bella myself. She'd heard it from a neighbour – Jerry is back. She asked me to tell you.'

Kitty nodded. 'Mum has gone to be a nursemaid to his children... Joshua Miller. My friend Mrs Burrows paid our debt to him. Mum knew that but she still went...' Kitty was fighting her tears, hardly knowing what she said, 'She doesn't care about me.'

'Bella told me about the debt. She was up in arms over it. We all know his sort. He's not the kind of man you want to deal with, Kitty.' Larry was still standing. He looked at her, compassion in his eyes. 'What will you do now? You can't stay here?'

'He doubled my rent – so no, I can't stay here,' Kitty said, spooning tea into the warmed pot. 'I shall find a room somewhere.'

'My sister says there is a room at her house,' Larry said, his eyes never leaving her face. 'She gets lonely of an evening now I don't live there – and she says she won't charge you. If you'd like to give a hand with the chores when you have time, that's payment enough. She'll be glad of the company.'

Kitty stared at him in astonishment. 'Stay in your father's house?'

Larry frowned. 'I know it might not look much of a place from the outside, but it's comfortable inside, Kitty. Mariah would look after you and it would only be until— you sort yourself out.' He cleared his throat. 'I know there's a bit of an odour in the yard sometimes, though we do our best to keep it clean, but rags and old stuff always smell a bit, and there's the horse of course – but the smell doesn't get in the house much.'

'I wasn't worried about that,' Kitty replied swiftly. 'I just thought how kind it was of your sister to ask – we've hardly met. I think we spoke once in the corner shop.'

'Mariah doesn't go out that much,' Larry said and smiled. 'You'll understand that she's a bit shy of company. You've seen she walks badly, I know.'

'Yes, I asked her if she'd hurt her leg, but she shook her head.'

'She was born with one leg shorter than the other,' he said, looking sad. 'What with that and where we live – and looking after the old man, she hasn't had much chance for friendship. I'd be grateful if you'd take her offer, at least for a while.'

Tears of gratitude filled Kitty's eyes and spilled over. 'Thank you so much – so very much,' she said. 'I need to find a room and if helping with the chores would pay my rent, I would be grateful. I want to repay Mrs Burrows the money she loaned me to pay Mr Miller for the funeral – and I was going to do it for a while with the money from helping Bella, but she won't need me now Jerry is home.'

'She says she does,' Larry said and grinned. 'She says you look after her better – and he agrees and says he will pay you twelve and sixpence if you will continue to do it for them.'

Kitty lowered her head. The kindness of her friends overwhelmed her. The extra money plus not having to pay rent would enable her to save and help her repay Mrs Burrows. 'Then, thank you,' she said. 'When can I come, please?'

'Why not tonight?' he suggested. 'I'll go and tell Mariah that you are coming while you pack your things.'

Kitty stood up; the tea forgotten. She looked around her at the furniture. 'What shall I do with all this? It can't be worth much.'

'Some of it will fetch a bit,' Larry said. 'You leave it to me. I'll clear it and sell it and give you what it makes.'

'Thank you,' Kitty said and smiled at him. 'I was close to despair until you came – but I am lucky to have such good friends.'

His cheeks turned pink and he shook his head. 'Make haste and get ready then,' he said. 'I'll have this lot cleared tomorrow and the key back to Mr Miller – and if he tries to charge you a penny in rent, he'll have me to deal with.'

11

Mariah Norton was a dark-haired woman with strong features that made her appear stern when seen at a glance, but her smile was warm and friendly, as was the fire burning in the grate of the huge kitchen. She took Kitty's hands in hers, held them firmly and kissed her cheek. 'Come in by the fire,' she said. 'It's turned chilly tonight, even though it's spring and should be warmer. I've some hot soup simmering if you're hungry and a pot of tea on the go.' She looked at the old man sitting by the open fire as she busied herself at the range where a pot of delicious-smelling soup burbled and the kettle whistled loudly as it let off steam. 'Now then, Father, here's Miss Wilson – say hello to her.'

'What— who?' he grunted and peered at Kitty from rheumy eyes that had once been a piercing blue. 'Oh, the lass what's ma went off and left her. Oh, aye, she's welcome to stay – if she can stick it...' He gave a harsh cackle of laughter and muttered to himself, drifting back into his own thoughts.

'Don't mind Father,' Mariah said with a little snort, but there was affection in her grey eyes. 'Some folk are frightened of his bark, but underneath he's as soft as a puppy. He thinks folks look down on us, because of the junkyard, and it's true, they do – but it's our living and we do better than most.'

Kitty's eyes moved about the room, noting its spaciousness and its comfort. At one end was a large Welsh dresser, its shelves lined with a collection of beautiful pieces of china and pottery, too many to take in at a glance. A large sofa stood against the wall beneath the small windows; it was covered with a rich shawl that was red in colour and embroidered with silks of blue and gold. It looked exotic and strange but somehow suited the old house. Around a large scrubbed-pine table were arranged six chairs. Two were what Kitty would describe as wheel-backed, because their spokes formed a circle; they looked old, as did the four single chairs that sort of matched them but not quite. In the middle of the table was an exquisite cut-glass bowl with an arrangement of ever-lasting flowers. There were small chests and tables here and there and every surface had bits and pieces crammed on top – figurines, silver pots, and bowls, and one huge urn that looked like brass turned black, that Kitty was later to learn was Chinese bronze and hundreds of years old, and pistols. She counted at least three just lying around. It was a house of curiosities.

'It's a treasure trove,' she breathed and then blushed as Mariah's sharp eyes looked at her. 'Oh, I beg your pardon. I spoke my thoughts aloud – but it is rather wonderful, a bit like Aladdin's Cave.'

The old man gave a crack of laughter. 'At least she appreciates my treasures!' His eyes gleamed suddenly. 'I'll tell yer all about them one day, girl, if yer want to learn the trade.'

'Of course she doesn't, Father,' Mariah said. 'She has just come until she finds somewhere better to live.'

'I don't think I could,' Kitty said in awe. 'I can't thank you enough for letting me come to your wonderful home, Mariah – Mr Norton. I have never seen such a marvellous room.'

'You'll suit Father,' Mariah said with a wry glance at him as he got up and beckoned Kitty to take his chair.

'Oh, I couldn't, sir, that's your chair,' Kitty said, blushing faintly as he took her hand and led her to it.

'Sit you there and get warm,' he told her, nodding. 'I've something to do in the yard. You women want to talk fer a while. I will be back for some of that soup later, Daughter.'

'Yes, Father,' she said and smiled as he shrugged on a tattered jacket and went out into the yard.

'Will he be able to see?' Kitty asked. 'It must be dark out by now.'

'There's a storm lantern in the hall,' Mariah replied as she pushed a thick mug of strong sweet tea into Kitty's hands. 'Father can see in the dark, he reckons, but he'll take his lantern, I dare say.'

'Are you certain it is all right for me to stay here?' Kitty asked. 'I know it is an extra burden for you – and you must have so much to do in this big house.' She hadn't dreamed their house was so large, because little could be seen of it, tucked behind the mountains of junk in the yard in front.

'You can help me with some of it,' Mariah said. 'I can't abide ironing so that will be your job. You can make your own bed and help with the dishes – and there's a pile of mending if you can bear to do it.' She glanced at an old-fashioned treadle sewing machine. 'I've never been able to use that thing, but Father won't buy a new one.'

'I can use them,' Kitty said. 'My paternal grandmother showed me how. She died four years ago. She left her bits and pieces to me, but Mum wouldn't let me keep her machine; it was just like yours...'

'Then you can mend and help me make some new curtains.' Mariah chuckled. 'I think that's enough to be going on with or you'll think me a slave driver.'

'Oh no, I don't think that. I like to be busy—' She broke off as Larry entered the kitchen. He had met her and brought her here in his van, then carried her possessions up to the bedroom she was to use. She smiled at him and he nodded.

'Everything is in your room,' he told her. 'Mariah will look after you now, Kitty – and if you need anything, I'm here most days.'

'Thank you so much for helping me,' Kitty said. 'You are all so kind.'

'Nay, lass,' he looked embarrassed, 'it's little enough – and this place isn't fitting for you, but it's all I could offer for now.'

'Oh, but I love it here,' Kitty exclaimed. 'This room is filled with interesting things – and it smells of baking and something sweet.'

'That's the rose petals,' Larry said. 'Mariah makes her own pot pourri to keep the house sweet. As for all Father's stuff – well, you'll find it wherever you go in the house. Some rooms are stuffed so full you can't get into them. Mariah doesn't even bother to clean in there.'

'Not the bedrooms, though,' Mariah said. 'Mother forbade that and I've kept him to his promise to her. You'll find your room comfortable, Kitty – and I'll take you up once we've had supper so you can get some rest.'

Kitty's eyes stung with tears, but she held them back. She could hardly believe that her luck had changed so much so quickly. To be here in this warm, comfortable kitchen with people who didn't criticise and were welcoming filled her heart.

'Will you stop for a bite to eat, Brother?' Mariah asked, but Larry shook his head.

'Thank you, Mariah, but I won't this evening,' he replied. 'I am meeting someone on a bit of business – but I will call in the morning to see if you need anything.'

'Thank you, Brother,' she said and nodded to him as he moved towards the door. As he reached it, he turned back to look at Kitty. 'You know you have only to ask if you need my help,' he said. 'You'll be safe here with Mariah.'

'She knows that – now off with you and if you see Father, tell him I am about to serve supper.'

Larry nodded and went out without another word.

Mariah looked at Kitty. 'Will you set the table, Kitty? You'll find a cloth in the middle drawer of the dresser – and the knives and spoons in the drawer next to it. We'll use the blue and white bowls from the dresser tonight.'

Kitty rose and went to the dresser. She found a starched white table-cloth in the drawer, brought it back and covered the table, before returning for the soup bowls, plates, spoons and knives.

Mariah had taken a large crusty loaf from a cupboard and was slicing it with a sharp knife when the door opened to admit her father. He took off his jacket and hung it up and then walked towards Kitty and presented her with a blackened kettle and a stand.

'What do you think of that, girl?' he demanded. 'Bought that today fer a shillin'…'

Kitty looked at it for a moment and then smiled. 'It's real silver, isn't it? Once it is cleaned, it will look beautiful.'

'Aye, it will lass – do yer fancy the job?'

'Yes, I'll do it for you gladly. It's beautiful.'

'Georgian, I reckon. It's a spirit kettle – and if yer like it and yer make it look good, I'll give it to yer as a welcome gift.'

'I'll *clean* it for you, but I can't accept it,' Kitty said, alarmed by such generosity. 'It must be worth a lot of money.'

'Who cares what it's worth?' the old man said his eyes fierce. 'It's the beauty of the thing that matters – you see that, don't yer?'

'Yes, yes, I do,' Kitty stuttered, afraid she had offended him. 'But... you hardly know me.'

'Aye, it's true, but my son brought yer here and I like yer – it's a gift. Do yer want it or not?' he demanded.

Kitty smiled and stroked the curve of the kettle with her hand. 'Yes, please, sir. It will look beautiful when it is clean and I shall treasure it.'

He nodded, satisfied with her answer. 'Yer can call me Alf,' he said and took his seat by the fire. 'Is that supper ready yet, Daughter?'

'Yes, Father,' Mariah smiled. 'Come on both of you and sit. The soup is just right.'

* * *

The bedroom was so comfortable. A large room with dark-stained wooden floors covered here and there with beautiful rugs in rich colours, some wearing a little thin, but all of them good quality with wonderful patterns. Kitty thought they must have been expensive when new. The bedhead was polished brass, the soft mattress piled with pillows and warm covers. There was a washstand of mahogany with a pink jug, basin, soap dish and a slop bucket inside the cabinet. Mariah had put out fresh towels and soap. There was cold water in the jug, but Kitty had brought a can of warm water up with her so that she could wash before bed.

She'd unpacked her clothes and they were hanging in a wardrobe that was a completely different style to the washstand and tallboy. Each was a beautiful piece of furniture but individual in style. Obviously, they had all been purchased through the scrapyard at different times. Mr Norton – or Alf, as he'd told her to call him – had good taste and he kept only the best things.

Kitty shook her head as she sat and brushed her hair on the edge of the bed. Her wardrobe had a mirror inset so that she could check she looked tidy before she went to work. What would her mother have said if she'd seen these things? She'd scorned the family who lived here, thinking them beneath her, but they lived far more comfortably than Kitty and her parents ever had even when her father had work.

'There's always something good to be had in this job, if you know what you're doing,' Alf had told her after they'd eaten. He'd showed her some of his treasures, amazing her with his knowledge. Amongst the clutter there were Chinese bronzes, centuries-old jade carvings, silver pots and candlesticks, beautiful fans, clocks – and a wonderful automaton that had a collection of mechanical monkeys that played a tune while the monkeys appeared to fiddle and play their flutes.

'I never dreamed you had so many wonderful things here,' Kitty had said, admiring them all in turn. 'How did you learn so much?'

'By experience,' he'd told her with a gleeful look. 'I made plenty of mistakes – let some good things slip through my fingers. I took something to the museum once and discovered it was ancient Egyptian. I'd sensed it was good but had no idea of its true worth. Once they showed me a few more pieces, I haunted the place whenever I had time, learning as much as I could. There was a curator there – a chap about the age I am now – and I was young. He liked airing his knowledge.' Alf had chuckled. 'And I gave the museum the Egyptian piece – gold it was and from one of them rich tombs. They had a passion for digging up them things back in the last century. It probably wasn't come by honest. I bought it for next to nothing, so I made the museum a present of it – and they made me an honoured guest, allowing me to come and go as I pleased. That's how I recognised the bronzes as genuine and the jade. As for the furniture, well, you've either got an eye for it or you haven't.'

'You are amazing,' Kitty had said awed by his knowledge. She saw the gleam in his eyes. 'This house is full of wonderful things.'

'Listen to the girl, Daughter,' he'd addressed Mariah with a rallying tone. 'She knows what's good...' He'd winked at Kitty. 'That one would have me sell it all, move to the seaside and buy everything new.'

'So I would, Father,' Mariah had said but didn't seem annoyed or upset by his teasing. 'Mebbe then I'd find a husband, which I shan't do here in this place.'

'And what about Arnie Walker then – he's forever sniffing around, but you won't look at him.'

Mariah had given a snort of disgust. 'I don't get on with his ma. I've told you, the minute you're gone, me and Larry will sell this lot and be off to enjoy life in the sunshine – somewhere warm...' She'd winked at Kitty, not meaning one word of it.

'Heathen,' her father had grunted, but his eyes had sparkled with mischief. Kitty had looked from one to the other, realising that they enjoyed baiting one another and that Mariah's words held no malice. It was their little joke. Despite the way they spoke at times, they were deeply fond of one another. Kitty had envied their friendship then. She'd never had that kind of relationship, even with the father she had loved so much.

She'd been so lucky to be offered a home here. Kitty felt warm and secure as she went to sleep that night. It seemed all her troubles were over, at least for the time being. Of course she couldn't stay here forever, but once she'd found her way and settled her debt to Mrs Burrows, she would think about her future. Perhaps if she did well in her job, she would be promoted to supervisor at Harpers and then she might be able to afford her own house – though nothing like the comfort she'd been shown here.

It would be tempting, she thought as she slid into a peaceful rest, to stay here for the rest of her life, but of course she couldn't. She would have to stand on her own feet one day, but for now she was content to be here with this family.

12

'So Kitty's problems are settled then,' Sally nodded and smiled, as some days later, Beth told her that the girl had found a comfortable home. 'Well, that is good. You can stop worrying about her.'

'Yes, I can,' Beth agreed. 'Vera has her appointment for next Tuesday afternoon, so I'll be taking her – and keeping my fingers crossed for the results.'

'Yes, that is a worry,' Sally said. 'If there is anything I can do – would you like to borrow my car?'

'I think we shall take a taxi,' Beth said thoughtfully. 'I don't want to be fussing about where I can park, so we'll just arrange to be taken. Bert wanted to come with us, but Vera says no. She thinks he worries too much – and, it's true, he does.'

Sally leaned forward and poured them both coffee. They were in her office and had been checking the sales goods most of the morning. 'So the sale starts on Monday. I always enjoy the atmosphere when we have our sales, Beth. Of course we have the big one in January, but these seasonal ones are just as much fun.'

Beth nodded, but made no comment.

Sally looked at her. 'Something wrong? Is it Bella?'

'Goodness no, she is no trouble,' Beth said and laughed. 'I popped in yesterday and everything is as neat as a new pin. Jerry wasn't there, but she said he wants to come and see me – to thank me for what I did for him and her.'

'So what is wrong?' Sally prompted. 'I know something is on your mind, Beth.'

'It's nothing I can put my finger on,' Beth answered hesitantly. 'I just get the feeling that Jack is not telling me something. He's been a bit odd recently – moody isn't the right word. He plays with the children and he brought me some lovely red roses home yesterday. It was a lovely surprise but I know something is on his mind...' She frowned. 'He normally tells me most things.'

Sally picked up a chocolate biscuit and nibbled it. 'Ben is like that sometimes,' she said. 'He'll worry at something – and then, all of a sudden, he'll come out with what he's been fretting over.'

'Yes. Ben likes to get your opinion,' Beth agreed. 'Jack does keep things inside sometimes – he worries and won't tell me why.'

'I suppose he doesn't want *you* to worry,' Sally said. 'I'm sure it is nothing, Beth. He might be planning to surprise you with a nice trip to the theatre or something.'

Beth shook her head. 'We always discuss things like that – no, he's anxious about us – me and the children – for some reason. I've seen a look in his eyes when he watches them play.'

'If you are really concerned, Beth, ask him.'

'Yes, I will,' Beth said and stood up. 'I've just got a couple of things to check – and then I must get home. Jack said he might get back this afternoon and take the boys out to the heath for an hour or so. They want a dog like your Lulu, but I'm not quite sure. I still think they are too young...'

'Lulu is a little love, the children adore her,' Sally said. 'I said no at first. but Ben thought it would be a good thing – and it has been.'

'I shall probably have to let them then.'

They smiled at each other as Beth left. But as soon as her friend had closed the door behind her, Sally's smile left her face. She had a good idea of what was on Jack's mind...

* * *

Beth spent half an hour chatting with Vera and Bert, before taking the children home on the Underground. They both loved going on the little trains that rushed from one part of London to another and spent their time giggling and staring out of the window at the various stations. When they got off, Beth held tight to their hands and guided them up the stairs out into the fresh air of Hampstead. She saw almost at once that Jerry was back at his pitch and stopped by his barrow. He was serving another customer and she waited, looking at the assortment of fruit and vegetables on his stall.

'Mrs Burrows,' Jerry said with a big grin on his face. 'I am coming to see you later when I pack up this evening.'

'Well, now I've saved you the trouble,' Beth said. 'I am glad to see you looking well – are you feeling better?'

'All healed – bar a bit of soreness,' Jerry told her. 'I'll pop round later, missus. I've got somethin' for you – just a thank you for helping Ma. She's taken to you proper. Don't usually get on wiv strangers, but she says you've got guts.'

'I like her too,' Beth said and saw the smile in his eyes. 'You really don't need to give me anything, Jerry – but thank you. If it is some of your lovely asparagus, I'd love to have it.'

'It's the first of the season.' He nodded. 'I remembered you liked it. I'll be round later.'

Beth thanked him and moved away as another customer approached. She crossed the road and, keeping a tight hold of the children's hands, walked them through the streets towards their house. It was just as she was about to cross the road to her home that she noticed a car hovering nearby. She looked at it uncertainly – was the driver about to move off or...? She hesitated, not wanting to be caught in the middle of the road if it suddenly shot forward.

The driver wound down his window. A man she'd never seen before leaned forward. Beth took a step towards him, thinking that he wanted directions, and then she saw he had a gun and it was pointing at Timmy.

'Tell your husband to keep out of my business,' a voice with a strange accent said. 'If he wants you and the kids safe, he should get rid of the stooge.'

'I don't understand,' Beth said, pushing the children behind her. 'Who are you – what do you want?'

'Just tell him,' the voice said and then the car revved and shot off down the road, leaving Beth standing there, clutching the boys' hands so tightly that Timmy squealed and cried out that she'd hurt him.

Beth crossed the road, hurrying the children inside the house. She locked her door and leaned against it, her heart pounding. Surely she'd heard wrong or imagined it. This was England, not America, but she'd been threatened by a man with a gun... No, he'd threatened Timmy and that was even worse...

* * *

Beth's nerves were on edge and she kept herself busy, making the children's tea, but her mind was tumbling, her thoughts jumbled like a kaleidoscope. Just what was Jack involved in to endanger all their lives? She wanted to talk to Jack, but hesitated because he would come rushing home if she rang him and told him what had happened. Beth felt as jumpy as a kitten, but reluctant to call Jack from his work. Not sure what to do for the best, she flinched when someone knocked at the door. She peeped out of a side window, and when she saw it was Jerry, she scolded herself for giving into her nerves.

'Come in, Jerry,' she invited as she saw he was carrying a small wooden crate packed full of vegetables and fruit, with a large bunch of fresh asparagus on the top. 'Will you put it on the kitchen table, please?'

He did so, and then looked at her. 'Is there somethin' wrong, Mrs Burrows? You were as white as a sheet when you opened the door just now.'

She took a shaky breath, then, 'I— or, rather, my son – was threatened by a man in a car with a gun as I arrived home... It made me feel uneasy.'

'I should bloody well think it did!' Jerry looked fit to explode. 'I got shot because I was in the wrong place at the wrong time. I saw something – or they thought I did – so they shot me. Whether they meant to kill me or it was just a warning, I don't know – but you were just minding your own business...' His gaze narrowed. 'It wasn't 'cos you 'elped me?'

'No – something to do with the restaurant, I think,' Beth said. 'You know my husband and Mr Harper own the restaurant in Oxford Street?'

'Yeah, I sometimes supply them and a few others with fresh veg.' Jerry nodded. 'I reckon some of the crooks go there – take their women, make out they're big shots because they've got money to throw around,' he said. 'That's what was wrong that night I was shot, Mrs Burrows. One of the girls belonged to someone else – a powerful man who has most of the rackets in London in his grip. The American has been muscling in on his territory and they tried to kill him, but he was too quick and too sharp. He killed the hit man—' Jerry caught back whatever else he'd been going to say as he saw the look on Beth's face; he'd said too much and was scaring her.

'How do you know all this, Jerry?' she asked in a hoarse whisper. 'You're not mixed up with criminals, are you?'

'I have to pay them for the privilege of working my stall,' Jerry told her. 'If I had my way, most of 'em would be behind bars – but I reckon they either have the cops on their payroll or they're too scared to move against the big man.' He hesitated as Beth nodded, accepting his word. 'I hear things, Mrs Burrows. I'm a Londoner and an East End boy. They know all about the big man on the streets. He's one of us for all he's a crook – but that American... We don't know him and don't want to. He's trouble.'

'I've never heard anything about all this... but I'm glad you're not involved, Jerry.'

'There was a police constable,' Jerry went on. 'He was around after my dad died and he helped us. I think he might have been sweet on Ma – and he was honest and brave. Too brave for his own good. He discovered a lot of the small traders were being forced to pay protection money to the big man and... he went after him. He took him down the station and charged him.' Jerry's face twisted in disgust. 'His fancy lawyer had him out on bail within half an hour.'

'What happened to your friend?'

A flash of grief showed in Jerry's face, but then it was gone. 'He got reprimanded and lost his chance of promotion – and he hung himself because he was disillusioned and shamed. Or that was the story the police put in the papers.'

'You didn't believe it?'

'I know it for a lie,' Jerry said. 'He'd come to ours earlier that day and he was angry, but he wasn't ashamed or disillusioned. He said he wasn't giving up and he'd get his man another time – and he promised to take me to the cricket match that weekend. Bernie wouldn't have done that if he'd planned to kill himself. It was made to look that way – but it was *him,* the big man who controls it all. He lets others run the various scams, but they have to give him half what they make, and if they try to cheat him...' Jerry drew a line across his throat. 'He killed Bernie, but you'd never convict him of it – because he just gets others to do his dirty work and they're too scared, or too well-paid, to tell the truth.'

Beth looked at him in dawning horror. 'Do you think this American works for him?'

Jerry hesitated, then shook his head. 'Nah, he's a newcomer and he's testing his strength. He's a rival to the local men. He may have come to an arrangement to run some of the stuff. I only know the word on the street – and that was that the American would be eliminated when the big man is ready.' He shook his head. 'The big boss may come from hereabouts, but he's a bad man... no one messes with him or takes what is his.'

'Do you know the name of the man who controls the criminal world in London?' Beth asked curiously. Jerry nodded, but wouldn't answer. 'Why won't you tell me – have you been threatened?'

'Nah. I'm just a barrow boy who pays his five bob a week. I don't cheek them when they take the money. I'm nothing. It wasn't his man who shot me – no, that was the American lot. They were running scared. Shot at anyone they saw on the street, I reckon.' He paused, then, 'It's best you don't know, Mrs Burrows. Just keep quiet – don't even tell your husband what I told you. I reckon the American will be dealt with afore long.'

'Is that the word on the street?'

Jerry nodded. 'I've mebbe said too much already, Mrs Burrows. Don't you get involved – leave it to others. I'm not one of them, but I know men who are. I've heard that someone is coming to get our cuckoo and take him back where he belongs.'

Beth heard screaming from the boys' bedroom and sighed. 'I shall have to see what they are up to – but thank you for your gift, and what you've told me. I shan't say anything to anyone. It is best I don't. If something I repeated was learned by this gang, it might lead to trouble for you – and us.'

'Very wise, missus,' Jerry said and grinned. 'I'll put the word out that you're to be watched over. I've done a few favours for a couple of them, some of 'em ain't that bad... Mebbe they'll keep an eye out in this district.'

Beth didn't answer. She was thoughtful as she saw Jerry out. Much as she liked him, he seemed to know a little too much about the criminal element prevailing in London. He might not actively be involved in what they did, but that he knew some of them – perhaps minor crooks – and was their friend, was certain.

Sighing, Beth went up to the children and stopped an escalating pillow fight. It would be late when Jack got home that evening, but she intended to sit up for him.

* * *

'Beth, I'm sorry I didn't tell you,' Jack said, after she'd told him her story, leaving out the bit Jerry had asked her to keep secret. 'Yes, something has been going on in the restaurant. We know about this American and his criminal activities – but it was supposed to be a secret, so I thought it best not to tell you. Besides, I knew you would worry if you thought I might be in danger...'

'He said I was to tell you to get rid of the stooge – whatever that means,' Beth said looking at him, half angry, half frightened.

'One of our waiters is an agent working for the American government. They want their criminal back – and they are not the only ones after him. He has upset a man named Al Capone. Capone is a powerful gangster over there and he wants this gangster dead because he knows too much. The American government want him alive. Ben reckons they think he might spill the beans concerning Capone's dirty little empire.'

'Oh, Jack, that sounds so dangerous,' Beth cried. 'Why did Ben agree to have this stooge at the restaurant and without asking you?'

'Goodness knows!' Jack's mouth tightened. 'He had no right to. We are partners – and he has apologised. However, I would probably have agreed if he'd asked, Beth. The truth is, I don't like our restaurant being used by these men for their dirty little meetings. I don't like what they do and I would rather they were all arrested, but this agent is supposed to be working in secret, because if the Americans can corner their man and kidnap him, take him back to America – perhaps he will give them the information they need.' He frowned. 'However, it seems he knows there is someone after him, someone working for us, but isn't sure who it is...'

Beth nodded, a coldness at her nape. 'I wish they would hurry up and do it then,' she said. 'After what happened today...' A shudder went through her. 'He could have shot us and driven away before anyone knew what was happening.'

Jack reached out, drawing her into his arms and holding her close. 'I know. I think you should go away somewhere, Beth. Take the children. Rent a cottage at the seaside for the spring and summer.'

'You mean run away and leave you here to face all this alone?' Beth shook her head. 'No. I won't do that, Jack. Tell Ben to get rid of this man he's foisted on you. We don't need to be involved. Let them alone, these crimi-nals. They will move on somewhere else – or perhaps the American secret service will grab them or whatever they need to do...'

'I shall,' Jack said and there was a decisive glint in his eyes. 'I'll sack him myself. He can continue his work elsewhere.'

Or perhaps the big man who controlled London's criminals would act first and rid himself of a rival. Beth shuddered as she allowed the thought. It was wicked to wish anyone dead, but she would be very glad if someone managed to persuade this unpleasant American to leave their shores and their restaurant – one way or another.

13

Kitty was smiling as she worked, gently brushing the stock on the rails, as she did once a week, and checking for any marks or faults on the beautiful clothes.

'We are ready to open the doors,' Miss Jones said as she came up to Kitty. 'Leave the rest for another day, Miss Wilson. Had you forgotten our sale starts today?'

'No, I hadn't,' Kitty replied. 'I just thought I would get some of the tidying done before we start. Some customers buy the full-price goods, even though there is a sale on.'

'Yes, I know – but I shall be dealing with them. You and Miss Shelly and Miss Harris will look after the sale side.'

'Yes, Miss Jones.' Kitty watched as her supervisor walked away. Marion Jones was all right to work with, but she tended to get nervous if the department became too busy. Kitty thought she worried too much, felt her responsibility like a weight on her shoulders rather than as a privilege. Kitty would love to have charge of the department and thought that she would enjoy making some changes – but that wasn't likely to happen.

Miss Jones had unlocked the door and allowed the first customers in the queue to stream in, moving out of the way as they all rushed to the sales rails to look for bargains. Harpers was known for the quality of its sales.

During the war, they had sometimes bought in seconds to boost their stock, but people were eager to buy anything then. Since the stock was now readily available, Mrs Harper only put out damaged goods or lines that had for some reason not been popular on sale. Sometimes if a range had not sold, she would slash the price to below cost and there were several winter suits and coats at a fraction of their original price.

Kitty and the other two girls moved in their wake, looking at one another as an argument broke out between two young women.

'I want that – I was before you in the queue!' one red-haired woman cried, hanging on to the sleeve of a beautiful coat in the sale.

'Well, I got it first and I'm keeping it—'

'No, you're not—'

'Excuse me, madam,' Kitty said to the red-haired woman. 'That coat is a size 36. It won't fit you, but there is another similar just here that will.' She took a gorgeous blue coat from the rail and showed it to her. 'It will suit your colouring better than the brown.'

'I like that.' The redhead let go of the coat she'd been fighting over, grabbed a suit and the coat Kitty was holding. 'Where's the fitting room?'

'Just over here, madam,' Kitty said and signalled a junior to take her place as she followed her customer to the cloakroom. She did not wish to think ill of anyone, but when she'd been new to the department, one customer had tried to leave wearing a dress she'd tried on under her own coat, while handing over another garment and saying it didn't fit.

As it happened, the red-haired customer was honest and bought both items back to the counters and paid for them, before going off with a big smile on her face.

Kitty returned to the customers milling round the sales rails. She saw a youngish woman hunting desperately through the rails and watched her; it was obvious she was looking for something in particular. As she saw Kitty, she turned with a scowl of discontent.

'Are these *all* the sale rails?' she demanded rudely.

'Yes, madam. That is all that has been reduced this time.'

'Don't you have any silk blouses – or one of those fancy Miss Susie dresses?'

Kitty looked at her. She thought she might have seen her in the department some weeks ago, trying on clothes, but couldn't be certain, though the annoyance in her eyes was proof enough. She was looking for the items she'd smeared lipstick on – but she wouldn't find them.

'No, I am afraid we don't,' Kitty told her. 'I am so sorry, madam – is there anything I can show you? We have some nice coats at nearly half-price—'

'I wouldn't be seen dead in them,' the woman retorted rudely and walked off, clearly fuming inside.

Kitty smiled inwardly. That was one little mystery solved. If that particular young woman came into the department to try on clothes in future, Kitty would make sure she served her – and she would stick with her and watch that she didn't damage anything else.

'Miss, miss, can I try these on, please?' A young woman was trying to attract her attention. She had three items: a suit, a pretty dress and a coat.

'Yes, of course you can, but you can only take two into the changing room. I will come with you and keep one until you are ready to try it.'

'I wasn't sure if I could try them,' the young woman said shyly as Kitty led the way. 'I haven't shopped here before – but I heard things were cheap in the sale and your clothes are so beautiful. I've been saving up to buy something and Tel, my boyfriend, gave me a fiver to get something good... but there is so much and they are so pretty...'

'Well, I am sure we can find something to suit you,' Kitty told her. 'If these aren't right, we'll find some more to try.'

'Oh, you are nice,' the girl said. 'I'm Betty Lou – what's your name...? If you don't mind me askin'?'

'I am Kitty,' Kitty told her, and her name 'Wilson' was on a little badge on her shoulder.

'I'll remember you and come again one day, Kitty Wilson. I like this shop. It's friendlier than some. It's so exciting to be able to buy something here.'

Kitty smiled and agreed. She felt exactly as this young woman did. She would love to buy herself just one item, but for the moment she could not even think of it. Mariah had changed her life, giving her a warm and pleasant home, but Kitty still had debts and she must pay them before she could think of buying anything special for herself.

* * *

Kitty walked home at the end of a long day. It had been busy and she was tired but pleased. She had sold more than anyone else on the department – and she was almost sure she'd discovered the person who had damaged Harpers' goods. She'd told Miss Jones about it, but she hadn't seemed to want to know. Mrs Burrows would, though. Kitty would tell her when next she saw her.

She had reached the street just before Kettle's Yard when a van drew up beside her and a voice called to her. Turning her head, she smiled as she saw Larry.

'I could have saved you a walk and picked you up,' he said. 'I didn't know you were working late this evening?'

'It is because of the sale at Harpers,' Kitty said. 'Are you coming up to the house?'

'Yes.' He leaned across and opened the door for her to get in the passenger seat. Kitty slid in beside him and was driven the last few yards into the yard. 'Mariah wanted to see me,' he said as he switched off the engine. 'Besides, I have some money for you. I've sold most of the house contents for you.' He took a bundle of notes from his jacket pocket. 'There's forty-five pounds, Kitty. You can pay off your debt to Mrs Burrows now.'

Kitty stared at him in shock. 'There can't be so much,' she said. 'Those things were not worth all this, Larry. Please don't try to give me your money.'

He grinned at her. 'I knew you would say that – but a few pieces were silver and there was a nice vase that I got ten pounds for – Chinese. Good thing the old man knows as much as he does or I wouldn't have thought it was worth more than a few bob.'

Kitty kept looking at him, still half disbelieving. 'Are you certain? Was it that big vase with all the cherry blossom and figures on? That was my father's – from his grandmother.'

'I hope you didn't want to keep it?' Larry looked anxious, but she shook her head.

'I shall have to give Mum some of this,' Kitty said hesitantly. 'I only expected a few pounds – nothing like this.'

'She doesn't need it,' Larry said. 'She has a good home now – and, besides, she had a hundred pounds from your father's insurance.'

Kitty shook her head. 'Unfortunately, he let it lapse and there was nothing.'

'Is that what she told you?' Larry frowned. He reached into his pocket again and handed her a letter. 'I found that when I was clearing out... it had been thrown into a corner in the scullery, probably meant to go out in the dustbin, but it had fallen behind the mangle. I picked it up and looked at it in case it was important. It's a letter from your father's insurance broker asking if your mother had received the hundred pounds and saying that they considered the policy now paid and closed.'

Kitty took it and read it in silence. It was exactly what Larry had told her. Her mother had been paid one hundred pounds and yet she'd allowed Mr Miller to pay for the funeral – and Kitty to think she owed him a debt. She'd caused her so much misery and lost sleep over a debt they could easily have paid – need never have incurred since they could have arranged and paid for the funeral themselves. It was cruel and wicked.

'How could she?' Kitty said furiously. 'How could she do that to me – her own daughter?' She shook her head. 'To lie to me and keep that money for herself, forcing me to worry how I would ever pay...' She closed her eyes for a moment. 'I hope I never have to see her again!'

'She thought she could force you to wed him,' Larry replied, looking at her sadly. 'I'm sorry, Kitty. I thought it best you knew, but if it hurts you...'

'No, it just makes me angry,' Kitty said. She pushed the notes he'd given her into her jacket pocket. 'Well, I'll just keep the money you got for me. Mum's had her share. She could easily have paid for Dad's funeral, but she put me through all that pain and distress.' She felt the sting of tears but blinked them away. She wasn't going to cry!

Kitty had been regretting their quarrel and parting, but now she decided that it was best to put it all behind her. Her mother had behaved unkindly and deceived her and that both hurt her and made her angry. She didn't understand why her mother had been so hard and unkind. If she'd had the money for the funeral, why pretend they couldn't pay?

Well, it was over now. Annie Wilson had made it clear she didn't want to be bothered with her only daughter, so Kitty must stand on her own feet and make a life for herself. She had been lucky in finding good friends, and now she could pay off her debt to Mrs Burrows, which was a big relief.

Larry was looking at the anxiously, but she smiled at him. 'Don't worry. I'm all right,' she told him. 'You did me a favour by showing me the letter, Larry. And thank you for selling my things so well. It will make my life so much easier now I can pay what I owe.'

He grinned and nodded. 'I was glad to do it, Kitty. I hope it doesn't mean you'll be leaving Kettle's Yard too soon?'

'Oh no,' she said. 'If Mariah is happy for me to stay, I shall, because your home is much nicer than any room in a lodging house. I love being here and helping her – and your father knows so much. Besides, I like him and he makes me laugh.'

'Aye, he does know a lot,' Larry agreed. 'When I was a lad, I hated what he did and I hated living here – but I've learned a lot from him and it's stood me in good stead. I've my own business building up now – and one day I'll have a nice house with a garden, where children can grow and play away from the stink of this place.'

'It isn't too bad when you get used to it,' Kitty said as he locked his van and they went into the house. 'I quite like the smell of the horse now I am used to it and inside the house, you don't notice it at all.'

'You say that and mayhap you mean it,' Larry murmured wryly, 'but there's many a lass wouldn't have stepped through that door, as I've learned to my cost.'

Kitty didn't answer. Had he been hurt by a girl who had refused him because of who he was and where he came from? She moved on into the bright and warm kitchen. Kitty knew she had feelings for Larry Norton and they were not just gratitude for all his kindness. She'd hoped that special smile he sometimes gave her meant that he felt something more than friendship for her, but now she wasn't certain. Perhaps he had brought her here out of kindness but mostly for his sister's sake.

'Kitty, at last,' Mariah said as they entered. 'Are they slave drivers at that posh store then? Working until this late hour...'

'It was just because of the sale,' Kitty assured her. 'We did open an hour longer, to allow working girls the chance to come in and buy, and then there was all the tidying up to do. Things get all over the place on sale day.'

'Folks go a bit mad, do they?' Mariah asked, amused.

'Oh yes. Some of the early ones grab as much as they can from the rails – and two women were fighting over a coat at one point.'

'Daft as a brushes,' Alf said. 'I hope you would have more sense, Daughter.'

'You can be sure of that,' Mariah said. 'I make my own clothes by hand and always have. Besides, I don't like these short skirts the girls are wearing now.'

Mariah was wearing an ankle-length dress of some dark material that had seen better days. She always had a large white apron over her dress and Kitty had never taken much notice previously, but now realised that she had never seen Mariah in anything pretty, even on a Sunday when she sometimes went out for a walk. It was always the same plain dress, either in a rusty black or a dark brown.

'I can make clothes, too,' Kitty said. 'I could help you make a new dress, Mariah. Why don't you buy some nice blue – or a pretty green – material that we could make up into a Sunday dress for you.'

'Colours, is it?' Mariah looked thoughtful, but then shook her head. 'Where do I go to need a new dress?'

'You could go out with Arnie,' Larry told her. 'Didn't he ask you to the music hall on your birthday?'

Mariah sniffed. 'I refused. You know I did... His ma and me don't get on...'

'Doesn't stop you going out with him sometimes,' Larry persisted, but she shook her head.

'We could go out together for a little while on Sunday afternoons,' Kitty suggested, seeing Mariah was annoyed by her brother's teasing. 'Have tea together somewhere – now that I can pay my debt to Mrs Burrows, I could afford that sometimes.'

'You should let Kitty help you make something nice,' Larry said, joining in. 'I'll treat you to the material.'

'I've my own money if I want,' Mariah reminded him. She nodded and then smiled. 'Mebbe I will – blue, was it? Would you choose it for me, Kitty?'

'Yes, of course, I will,' Kitty said. 'I can buy it in Harpers and use my staff discount. I've seen some very pretty soft wool that has only just come in to the new haberdashery department.'

'Good grief, what is the world coming to?' Alf Norton exclaimed, and then as his children looked at him. 'Not Mariah's dress – there's to be a General Strike. Now we're in for it, mark my words. The Government won't just sit back and let them get away with it – there will be riots on the streets.' He shook his newspaper at them. 'Damned fools! What do they think they'll gain by it. They will break them, one way or the other...'

Larry took the newspaper and read the front-page headlines and article. 'It says there are contingency plans to keep things running, but that will lead to fighting and goodness knows what else.' He looked at Kitty. 'What will your employer do at Harpers – will they try to keep open or close their doors?'

14

'What are we going to do, Ben?' Sally asked when they discussed the news after dinner. 'I know all the tradesmen are going on strike, but what about the shops and small businesses? Will they have to close their doors, too?'

'It will vary, I expect,' Ben said, looking thoughtful. 'It depends on whether people support the strike or not. We shall try to keep Harpers open, the restaurant too, but if too many of our staff stay away, we shall have to close.'

Sally nodded. 'Yes, we can't open our doors if we haven't got enough staff to serve our customers.' She hesitated, then, 'Do you think there will be riots on the streets?'

'There's certain to be trouble when we break the picket lines, but I'm not sure there will be as much unrest as some members of the Government seem to think. The British people are even-tempered and peaceful as a rule. It will only be a few hotheads.'

'You have to have some sympathy for the miners, though,' Sally said. 'They don't earn sufficiently for the hard and dangerous work they do.'

'Yes, I can sympathise with them, but I don't agree with the TUC calling everyone out on strike. If they support the miners, then do something practical to help them, not try to hold the country to ransom.'

'Yes, that is exactly what they should do,' Sally said, but made up her mind that she would speak to a few of her friends about the situation of the miners and their families. Ben and many others thought them a hard-headed section of the British public who sought to get their way by bullying others, but she felt for the wives and children who would likely go hungry if the strike continued too long.

'So, are you prepared to man the canteen for us if need be?' Ben asked and Sally smiled. 'Yes, of course, I will. Maggie rang me earlier today. She is coming up to town tomorrow and she says if I need help, either in the canteen or the store, she is willing to help. Colin isn't coming. He thinks he would be more of a hindrance than a help to the strike breakers, but if he stays in the country with the children, it means Maggie can come. She wanted to buy new clothes for herself and the children, so thinks it is a good opportunity for a visit.'

'You will be glad to see her anyway,' Ben said and smiled.

'Maggie and Beth were my first friends at Harpers,' Sally told him, looking wistful. 'I didn't have many friends before I met them – not real friends. They are still my best friends, Ben. Maggie had such a terrible time in the war and I feared for her future when she married Colin, but they are so happy together.'

'Yes, I know,' Ben said and reached for her, drawing her into his arms. 'Are you happy, Sally?'

'You know I am,' she said and kissed him softly on the lips, then drew back to look at him, a twinkle in her eyes. 'So, tell me, what are you going to do while the strike is on, Ben? Or is it a secret?'

'Not from you,' he said with a smile. 'I am going to be driving a lorry to collect a cargo of food from the docks – the first day or so anyway.'

Sally felt a frisson of fear at her nape; it made her shiver, but she hid her anxiety. 'You will be in the thick of it then, Ben?'

'Yes, I might,' he agreed. 'Don't worry, Sally. There might be some fist fights, but I don't think the dockers will be out to harm anyone. They want to keep the British public onside if they can, because if they lose all sympathy, the strike will be over before it starts.'

'Do you think it will last long?' Sally asked, nerves fluttering. Harpers was just about back to pre-war levels of trade and a strike could only cause problems.

'No idea,' Ben replied. 'It depends how much support the TUC gets from the public – and how long their members are prepared to exist on strike pay for the sake of the miners.'

'I hope it is over quickly,' Sally said and suddenly gave him a quick fierce hug. 'Be careful, Ben. Don't take any risks.'

'I will do only as much as I have to,' he promised, but the gleam in his eyes told her that he was rather looking forward to it. Indeed, from what she'd gathered, others felt as he did and were eager to do their bit to keep the country going.

* * *

'Well, I think it is a crying shame,' Mrs Hills complained the next morning after the doctor had delivered their milk. 'He knocked at the door and handed it to me. Seemed to think it was a great joke to be driving the milk float – but he should be visiting sick folk, not wasting his time on milk rounds and so I told him.'

'He said that he'd got up two hours early to do it and would start his surgery just half an hour later than usual,' Sally said. 'I spoke to his wife last night, because Peter has a sore gum, and she said her husband was excited about it – seemed to think it was his patriotic duty.'

'Grown men who ought to know better!' Mrs Hills grumbled. 'Still, I suppose someone had to bring the milk. You wait until I see Reggie. I shall tell him what I think – he should have had more sense than to join the strike. If he thinks he's getting a tip next Christmas, he's got another thing coming!' Reggie was their regular milkman and often came in for a cup of tea and a bun with Mrs Hills on his morning rounds.

Sally laughed as her housekeeper went off, still grumbling to herself. Hopefully, for Reggie's sake – who was a pleasant young man – she would forget all about her annoyance by the time next Christmas came. It was still only May and much too soon to think about such things.

Mrs Hills was incensed by the very idea of a general strike. She thought it unpatriotic and foolish, to say the least. Quite a few of the British public were feeling the same way and they would become angry if it disrupted their way of life for too long.

'We had enough to put up with when there was a war on,' people were saying. 'It's ridiculous to cause all this trouble over the miners. If they want to strike let them, but why do all the other trades have to come out in support?'

Sally wasn't sure how she felt. It was wrong to hold the country to ransom, of course it was, but she had some sympathy for those men who daily risked their lives and their health to bring coal to the surface. Coal was so necessary for so many reasons. It was one of the main fuels that kept the country running and homes warm, but it was hard, grinding work and poorly paid. Also, the miners had not been well treated, suffering actual reductions in their pay more than once.

* * *

Sally drove herself into town that morning. The streets were much quieter than usual, scarcely any traffic about, and only a few buses. She saw the occasional lorry, driven by men who normally did other jobs, and a baker's van was making its rounds; it was possibly driven by the bakery proprietor who was not a member of the trade union.

Sally parked her car easily and went into Harpers. She was greeted cheerily by several members of her staff as she walked to the lift. Ernie, his scarred face beaming, took her up to the second floor.

'I am glad to see you here today, Ernie,' Sally told him.

'I couldn't let *you* down, Mrs Harper,' he replied. 'You gave me my first job and took me back after the war. Besides, I don't agree with it and I'm not a member of the union, so I didn't have to come out.'

'I suppose if you are a member you have to do as the union tells you,' Sally said.

'If not, they call you a blackleg and send you to Coventry,' Ernie told her, meaning they shut out those who didn't obey the union's call for strike action. 'Some of my friends and neighbours work on the railway and the docks and they are striking, because they daren't do otherwise – but they think it is daft. I don't reckon it will last long.'

Sally smiled and thanked him as she left the lift. She visited the dress department first and saw that most of the staff were there. Kitty Wilson came up to her.

'Good morning, Mrs Harper,' Kitty said. 'If you are looking for Miss Jones, she isn't here. Her father is a shop steward at the boot factory. He's taken all his workers out to support the miners – and he threatened her with eviction if she came to work.'

'Oh dear, poor Miss Jones,' Sally said. 'When did she tell you this?'

'I passed her house on my way in and she came running out to tell me,' Kitty said. 'She was in tears, Mrs Harper. Asked me to apologise to you if I saw you – but she dared not go against her father.'

'Well, of course not,' Sally said. She was thoughtful for a moment, then, 'Could you take charge of the department today, Miss Wilson?'

'Yes, of course, Mrs Harper,' Kitty smiled. 'The first rush of the sale is over now – we cleared most of the reduced stock yesterday.'

'Yes, the rail looks quite thin,' Sally agreed. 'In fact, we will probably put the remainder back in the stockroom tomorrow. I'm not sure whether we'll do much trade at present. It will be difficult for people to get into town.'

'I got up early and walked in,' Kitty said. 'But I often do. It saves the bus fare.'

Sally nodded, looking at her with interest. 'How are you managing now, Miss Wilson? I know it must have been difficult for you with your father passing.'

'It broke my heart,' Kitty admitted, 'but I am feeling better now. My— my mother has found herself work where she lives in, and I am living with good friends. I have been very lucky, Mrs Harper.'

'That is good to hear,' Sally said. 'Well, I must get on. Remember, you are in charge today.'

Sally left her and went through to the bags, hats, gloves and jewellery department. Everyone seemed to be present and the supervisor greeted her with a warm smile.

'Yes, all my girls have come in today, Mrs Harper,' she said. 'I spoke to them yesterday and asked if anyone would be supporting the strike and they all said no. Apparently, their fathers are all going to work – or helping with the volunteer force to keep things moving.'

'Thank you all so much,' Sally said, looking round at her staff with a smile. 'Your loyalty is appreciated – and will be rewarded. Everyone who comes in every day through the strike will receive a bonus in their pay. And for anyone who is sympathetic to the miners, I will just say that I feel for their families too. I spoke to a friend of mine last night and we are going to start a fund in aid of the wives and children.'

'I'd like to help with that,' one of the girls spoke from behind her counter. 'I have cousins in Wales and they have miners in their families. If I can do anything to help, I will.'

'Thank you, Miss Williams,' Sally said. 'I shall remember your offer. We might do a flag day and you could help with that, and packing parcels – but not until the general strike is over. We can't support the strike, but we shall support the families when it is done.'

Three of the girls clapped their hands and Sally blushed.

'No, no. It is what anyone would do,' she said. 'I'd best get up to my office – but, once again, thank you all for coming in today.'

Sally felt warmed by the attitude of her staff as she went back to the lift and was taken up to her office on the top floor. Her secretary was already at work and had placed the opened letters and catalogues on her desk. She smiled and nodded her thanks.

'Coffee when you have time, Pamela,' she said. 'I'm glad to see you weren't put off by the lack of buses.'

'I got a lift in with a friend,' Pamela replied with a smile. 'He is one of the volunteers, Mrs Harper. He is a builder and he gave his men two weeks' holiday so they didn't have to walk out or be called rude names. Some of them are joining him. He's driving trains of all things. Says he's always wanted to drive a train and how hard can it be?'

Sally laughed. 'Isn't that the dream of all small boys?'

'Yes, and Derek is still a kid at heart,' Pamela said with a laugh. 'I wouldn't change him for the world, though.'

Sally nodded and smiled as she began to go through her post. She had two appointments with travelling salesmen that day, but she had no idea whether or not they would turn up.

* * *

Both of the salesmen arrived on time. One had caught the milk train from Cambridgeshire, which had been driven by a volunteer. He laughed and told her it had been quite an experience.

'We had to cross a picket line at the station,' he said, 'and then, when the train started, it was a bit of a hairy journey. We had some false starts and went straight through a station at one point, but we got here in the end.'

'Well, it was very brave of you,' Sally said and smiled. She gave him a large order and he went off quite happily to see his other customers in town.

The second salesman had come a shorter journey and driven in. He told her the roads were very quiet. 'There is strong support for the strike today,' he said, 'but I don't think it will last. There isn't as much support for it as the TUC would like, because people had enough of going without during the war. This is the roaring twenties and they want to enjoy themselves.'

'Yes, I know – that's what my husband thinks,' Sally said. 'He is volunteering himself.'

The shop had several customers when Sally left just before one o'clock. It wasn't as busy as usual, but there were enough to warrant it being open. Sally heard someone saying how pleased she was that they hadn't closed their doors.

Sally found her car untouched outside. She had worried it might attract malicious damage, but none had occurred and she had neither seen nor heard any disturbance. It was more like a Sunday than anything, she thought as she drove home. She passed a couple of buses and there were a few lorries and vans about, but it was certainly much quieter than normal.

Mrs Hills fussed over her when she got in. 'Your mother was here a little while ago,' she said. 'She was worried you might have met some unpleasantness. She heard rumours about a bit of fighting...'

'Well, it wasn't near Harpers,' Sally said and smiled. 'How have the children been? Did Jenny and Peter get off to school?'

'Their school was open,' Mrs Hills said with a nod. 'But the seniors just down the road from it was closed. I suppose the teachers must have come out in sympathy.'

'What a nuisance for those children and their parents.'

'Oh, the kids were having a great day off,' Mrs Hills said. 'The parents might not have been so pleased – but if they were on strike, they would be at home anyway.'

The Harper children came rushing in then, followed by their dog Lulu, who was jumping and barking in excitement.

'Mummy, Mummy,' Peter cried. 'I'm hungry, can I have a biscuit please?'

'Hello, my darlings,' Sally said, pushing her worries to the back of her mind. 'Did you both have a good morning at school. Yes, Jenny?' She looked at her daughter who was bursting to tell her something.

'They let us play games because there weren't enough teachers,' Jenny said. 'I like painting, Mummy, and we did that all morning. Can I have a set of poster paints please?'

'Yes, I should think so,' Sally said and wiped a speck of red paint from Jenny's nose.

Peter pulled at her sleeve, repeating his request for biscuits.

'Yes, Peter, you can have one biscuit. Now, what shall we have for lunch?'

15

'You look real smart in that dress and coat, Betty Lou,' said the man lying on her bed, two pillows behind his head and his long, muscled legs stretched out in front of him. 'I'm glad I gave you a bit extra to get what you wanted from that sale at Harpers.'

'Oh, it was lovely,' Betty Lou replied with a smile and took off the coat and dress, under which she was wearing nothing. 'It was even better because there was such a nice girl serving. She made me feel like a proper lady instead of—'

'A whore?' Tel said and sat up. He was naked, but he proceeded to dress. 'You don't have to be, Betty Lou. I've told you I'll give you the money to find a little house.'

'But you won't marry me.' Betty Lou sighed. She'd been on the game – on the streets – when Tel had found her shivering and hungry, and brought her here to this safe house. She was now one of the 'girls' and protected from violence from her customers and from the sickness that was so easy to pick up if you worked the streets and had no one to look after you. All the girls were seen regularly by the doctors Tel paid and some of them had been given safe abortions when they'd fallen for an unwanted child. Had they sought the women who did cheap operations in filthy little backstreet rooms instead, they could easily have died, but they lived and were grateful. All the girls liked Tel and he could share the bed of any he chose, but he seldom did and it was usually to Betty Lou that he came. She liked to think of him as hers, but of course he wasn't – he was just the man who looked out for all the girls. It was a part of his job as the boss' right-hand man.

'I've told you before,' Tel said and looked at her sadly. 'One of these days I am going to get a knife in the back. You'd be a widow and worse off than you are now. Besides, I need freedom to come and go for my work – and it isn't just looking after you and the others. I just do that because I want to.'

'I know...' Betty Lou gave him her beautiful smile. 'Maybe one day you'll change your mind and we'll go off to the country and live happy ever after.'

Tel laughed, leaned in and kissed her. 'I think a lot of you, Betty Lou, you know that – and if I was the marrying kind I would choose you, and that's a promise.' He frowned as he saw the hurt in her eyes. 'You'd make me vulnerable,' he told her, a harsh note creeping into his voice. 'Put it out of your head, there's a good girl.'

'Yeah. I reckon you're right,' she said with an attempt to turn it into mockery, but the hurt was there. 'If I'd met you when I was fifteen, before I went on the game, you might have had me then.'

Tel reached out and grabbed her, pulling her into his arms. 'It ain't that, Betty Lou, and you know it. I'd kill the bugger what made yer do it if he weren't already dead – but I won't marry yer.' He sighed as she looked up at him longingly. 'Take my money, love. Get out of it while you can.'

'Maybe...' She gave him a little push. 'You've got work to do.'

'Yeah, yer right – and you wouldn't like some of the things I have to do, Betty Lou. It's my job. I was fourteen when I started to work for *him* – just an errand boy, pinchin' things and climbin' through windows no one else could – but now I'm his man. I run things for *him*, Betty Lou, and one day I'll be the boss – unless someone sticks a knife in me first.' He shrugged, careless of the danger that was ever present in his life. His boss was the man every crook in London feared. For years, he'd held them all in an iron fist, demanding his share of any profits they made and handing out ruthless punishment to any who defied him. Only Tel knew that that grip was slipping. Not much yet but enough that his rivals would be ready to move in if

Tel wasn't there to protect him. One day, the myth of his invincibility would start to fade and then Tel would have to act swiftly to take his place and put down the inevitable rebellion or he'd be dead himself.

'When will I see you again?' Betty Lou asked. 'You'll come again?'

'You know I will,' he said and kissed her softly. 'You're special, Betty Lou. To tell yer the truth, I ain't good enough fer yer.'

He pushed her away, grabbed his jacket and left her abruptly. Betty Lou stared after him. Should she have told him that she suspected she was carrying a child? She told herself it was his, because he was the only one she lay with and didn't use the stuff Doctor Dolly gave her to keep herself free of a kid. In her heart, she wanted Tel's child and she dreamed that when she did tell him, he would kiss her tenderly and tell her it was all different and that he would marry her and leave the work he did. He was so big and strong and clever. He could do anything – and he had money. Away from London and the influence of the man who ruled the criminal under-world, he would be the gentle loving husband she craved.

For a moment, Betty Lou allowed herself to dwell in her dreams, but then she pushed them aside. They were only dreams. Tel liked being the boss' number one man. He wouldn't give all that up for her. Why should he?

Shaking her head, she picked up her new dress and coat. They made her look like a real lady. That Kitty Wilson had picked them out for her and they suited Betty Lou down to the ground. Perhaps she ought to do as Tel suggested and leave the game while she could. She had a little money saved besides what she'd spent on her new clothes, and Tel would look after her. She wasn't sure what she could do instead. If she took lessons in something, she might be able to find a good job, especially now she was dressed the part. It would be nice to work in a shop like Harpers, but they would surely want references and ask where she'd worked before.

Betty Lou sighed. It was just another dream. The best job she could find would probably be behind the bar in a pub – but there she would attract the attention of men, just as before when she was a very young girl and her stepfather had sold her to a man she didn't know. She'd learned then how cruel the world could be to a young girl alone. No, it would never work. At least here, she was safe from the kind of men who liked to hurt women, and she got to see Tel most weeks, even though he didn't often share her bed.

She touched her lips, feeling that last kiss. He did care for her. She knew he did – but he was set in his ways. A smile lit her eyes. She was a pretty girl; it had been more of a curse than a benefit to her thus far, but she also knew how to please the man she loved. She would keep trying and if she really was carrying a child, she would tell him it was his.

16

The strike was now a few days old and Ben was late home. Sally began to worry as the time went on, but all she could do was wait. She wished he had phoned to let her know how late he would be, but she tried not to fret. When she heard him come in at past ten that evening, she jumped up in relief, going out into the hall to greet him.

'Ben, thank goodness,' she exclaimed. 'I was beginning to worry...' Her words drained away as she saw he had a bandage on his hand. 'What happened – have you been in a fight?'

'It was just a bit off a scuffle at the docks,' Ben told her with a wry look. 'They objected to us unloading the ship and we exchanged a few blows. I hurt my hand, nothing but a few bruises on the knuckles – but Dora insisted I have it looked at and it took a while at the hospital.'

'Oh, poor Ben,' Sally said. 'Does it hurt very much?'

'It stings a lot,' he admitted, looking a bit sheepish. 'I've got some bruises to my face and arms as well – but I think it's my pride that hurts the most.' He looked rueful. 'I thought I could hold my own in a fight, but those dockers are tough. I think they would've got the better of us had the police not arrived.'

'Good thing they did then. Did you get the food away?' Sally asked. Ben looked so sorry for himself. 'Shall I get you a drink, love?'

'Yes, to both,' he said with a rueful chuckle. 'I'm not as young as I was, Sally. Keep forgetting I shall be forty next year.'

'The years have flown since we first met,' Sally said, bringing him a glass of his best whisky. 'You don't look nearly forty, Ben. No one would guess if you didn't tell them.'

'Thank you, my love. I suppose I've gone soft. I have too good a life.' He patted his stomach, which was showing some signs of expansion. 'I think I shall have to take up some kind of sport to toughen me up.'

'Yes, you should,' she agreed. 'Swimming or cycling would be good exercise, Ben. You've got to keep fit so that you can look after me and the children.'

He gave a snort of derision. 'You don't need anyone to look after you! You seem to waltz through a charmed life.'

'Yes, I've been lucky since the children were born.' Sally had been very ill when Peter was on the way, but since then she'd recovered all her former health and energy.

'God, don't remind me,' he said with a shudder. 'I almost lost you then. Frankly, I don't know what I'd do without you, Sally.'

'Well, you don't have to,' she said and laughed. 'What are you doing tomorrow? Are you going back into the fray – or shall you leave it to the younger men?'

'Tomorrow I am driving a bus,' Ben said. 'We are rotating the jobs to give everyone a turn. I shan't let a few bruises deter me, Sally. Besides, the police were pretty good at putting a stop to the violence. I doubt we'll have too much trouble. The dockers are always the toughest – them and the miners. They do hard work and to be honest they probably deserve more than they get. It's just that the Government can't give in over this – if they do, they'll have all the trades demanding more and then you get a spiral of higher wages, higher costs, higher prices and no one wins in the end.'

'Yes, I understand,' Sally replied. 'I can't help thinking about the miners' families – the wives and children. They must have a hard time of it when their men are out on strike.' She hesitated, then, 'I was speaking to a friend of mine about it. She thinks we could start a little collection for them – but she says we have to wait until the strike is over. I know she is right—'

'But you want to help now?' Ben looked at her. She gave a little nod and he smiled and took her hand. 'Well, I don't see why you shouldn't begin the fund, Sally. I will give you a hundred pounds to start you off.'

'Oh, Ben, thank you,' she said, giving his hand a squeeze. 'I can raise money with a lot of people I know – but I was a bit unsure as to whether you would be cross if I did.'

'I'm glad you told me first,' he said. 'It may seem a conflict of interest as we have to break this strike, Sally, and I agree you can't actually give them any money, at least until the general strike is over, but after that— well, I don't like the idea of kids going without food any more than you do.'

'It is an awful thought,' Sally said and smiled. 'What about you? Have you eaten this evening? Are you hungry?'

'Dora made us all bacon rolls,' Ben said. 'I think I will just have another of these and get to bed.' He indicated his whisky glass. 'I have to be up at five in the morning to get to the bus terminal at six.'

'Oh dear, that is early,' Sally said. 'Who is Dora by the way?'

'Dora? Oh, one of the ladies at the canteen you helped to set up. She is in her fifties but full of energy and enjoying herself bossing us all about.' He laughed mischievously. 'Did you think I'd found myself a light o' love, Sally?'

She shook her head. 'No, I know you haven't, Ben. I just wondered who she was. Perhaps I could give them a hand for a couple of hours, though I have several salesmen to see this week.'

'Oh, good lord no,' Ben said. 'You helped organise buildings to set up temporary canteens and catering equipment for us, Sally – that's what you do well. We have loads of volunteers to serve cups of tea and make bacon rolls.'

'Yes, I am good at organising,' Sally said with a laugh. Ben was yawning. 'We'd better get you to bed, you're not used to all this hard work.'

'No, you're right there,' he said. 'I think I might buy myself a bicycle, Sally. It will do me far more good to cycle into work than to drive.'

17

'Good gracious,' Mariah exclaimed as her brother entered the kitchen the Sunday after the General Strike had begun. 'What happened to you?'

Kitty, who had been ironing a pile of shirts and tablecloths, looked at him in alarm. Larry's breeches were muddy, his shirt torn and he had a smear of blood on his mouth. 'You've been hurt,' she cried, putting the iron back on the range to heat and leaving her ironing to go to him. 'Shall I bathe that cut on your eyebrow?'

Larry put up his hand to touch the cut and winced. 'I didn't realise it was bleeding,' he said with a wry smile. 'I've been delivering food to the hospitals and someone took exception, called me a dirty blackleg, so we had a bit of a tiff.'

'I told you to stay out of it!' his father grunted from behind his newspaper. 'We're working folk. Daft though it is, you should support the workers or leave it alone.'

'The hospitals were short of certain supplies, including fresh food, so I volunteered,' Larry said. 'I've been doing all sorts of things, so have a lot of others round here. Your Arnie was helping unload at the docks, Mariah.'

Because of the strike, there were no newspapers. The BBC was broadcasting news of the strike every few hours, but, of course, many folk didn't have a wireless set. News was passed on the street and a lot of rumours were flying around, most of them untrue.

'He's not my Arnie...' Mariah muttered but looked interested.

'He sent you his regards and says he'll call to see you later today.' Larry frowned as his father snorted in disgust. 'I know you don't approve of the strike breakers, Father, but you'd be the first to complain if there was no milk for your tea. Besides, there's talk of the Government imposing martial law. Those of us who can are bound to help keep the country running.'

Kitty fetched a bowl of warm water and some cloths. Larry sat down at the kitchen table and allowed her to wipe away the blood. 'It is only a small cut,' she told him as she finished. 'It has stopped bleeding, so I don't think you need to go to the hospital.'

'Thank you, it feels fine,' he said and smiled at her. Kitty's heart skipped a beat. 'It's nice having you here...'

Kitty blushed at his words, but there was no doubting the warmth in his smile. 'I am lucky to have a home with your family. I am very grateful to Mariah for having me.'

'You're a big help to me,' Mariah informed her. 'I enjoy your company, Kitty – and I've never had such a pretty dress as the one you've made me.'

'Aye and she's done your hair different too.' Larry looked at his sister. 'Any chance that stew you're cooking will stretch to another one, Sister? I've got work to do this morning, but I'll be back for twelve-thirty if you could save me some.'

'Working on a Sunday,' his father grumbled. 'That's what comes of wasting yer time runnin' around after others.'

'Yes, I know it's not right, and I shan't make a habit of it,' Larry agreed. 'But this is something I promised I'd do – just a favour for a friend.'

'I'll hold lunch until then,' Mariah told him in a severe tone that belied the twinkle in her eye. 'But if you're late, it will be in the oven keeping warm and it's never as good then.'

'I'll be here,' Larry promised, threw Kitty a grin and went out, a jacket pulled on over his torn shirt.

'He's as daft as a brush,' Alf grumbled after his son had departed. 'If he had any sense, he'd be here courtin' you on a Sunday, Kitty – instead of rushing off all over the place.'

Kitty blushed crimson but said nothing.

Mariah saw her blush and shook her head at her father. 'You've embarrassed Kitty now, Father.'

'Well, anyone can see he's head over heels for her,' Alf muttered. 'Why doesn't he just ask her to marry him and get on with it?'

'Father! You don't even know how Kitty feels about that...'

Kitty laughed. 'Don't scold your father for me,' she begged. 'I like Larry very much. I am sure you both know that well enough.'

'Of course you do,' Alf said. 'Mebbe I should give him a hint...?'

'Please, don't!' Kitty exclaimed. 'If you did that, I would be very embarrassed.'

'Larry will ask her in his own good time if he's a mind to it,' Mariah said. 'Now leave it be, Father.'

'The girl knows I like her,' Alf muttered. 'I'd like to see my son married to her – before some other bright spark gets her first.'

Mariah shook her head in apology at Kitty, but she just smiled back. Living in this house, she had come to know Larry in a way that she might never have done if they'd just met now and then on the street. His kindness, good humour and care of his family had made her realise how much she liked him. She had begun to look for him and feel pleasure when she saw his tall figure approaching. In fact, of late, she had begun to think that if Larry did ask her to be his wife, she would like that very much.

* * *

On Monday morning, Kitty went to work as usual. When she arrived, she saw that one window had been splashed with red paint and the word:

Blacklegs

was scrawled over the glass. When she entered, Harpers was unusually quiet, as if the strike had begun to bite more, and some of the workers hadn't yet come in.

Kitty had walked into work, getting up early to make sure she arrived in time, and she hadn't seen many buses running. The milk seemed to be arriving on the early trains, driven by volunteers, but it was slow getting out to the depots and the milk floats were still delivering well into the morning. Normally, most would have done their work much earlier. Kitty had seen a couple of drivers she knew by sight, so it seemed that not everyone had answered the call to strike, but enough had to make it difficult for those who continued to work.

The headlines on the newspaper stands were all about the strike, of course, and Kitty saw some groups of working men standing about on the corners. They looked sullen as she passed them by. Inside Harpers, the girls were working as normal, but the usual chatter was missing. Going up to her department, Kitty saw that Mrs Burrows was already there.

'Good morning, Kitty,' she said. 'You managed to get in on time then.'

'Yes, I walked in and started out early. Are you working in this department today?'

'Oh no, you are in charge here,' Beth replied with a smile. 'I shall be helping out wherever I am needed. Mrs Harper is coming in, too. I think she may be working in the hat and bags department for a while. Mrs Jamieson telephoned her this morning to say that she was ill and wouldn't get in today...'

'I noticed some counters were not manned as I came through,' Kitty said. 'Do you think we can keep the doors open if they don't turn up?'

'We shall certainly try,' Beth said. 'It might be they are late because there aren't many buses running. Perhaps everyone isn't as conscientious as you and didn't get up early to walk in as you did, Kitty.'

'I do hope they get here. It would be a shame if we had to close.'

Mrs Burrows looked at her, hesitated, then, 'Has repaying your loan to me left you in financial difficulty, Kitty? I told you that you didn't need to pay it all at once.'

Kitty had given her the money she'd paid out for her the very next time they'd met after Larry had sold her possessions. She still had the remainder of it, as well as a few pounds she'd saved from the thirty shillings extra she now received in her wages from Harpers for acting as a supervisor. She had never had as much money in her life but was saving for the moment, because she was a careful girl and you never knew what might go wrong.

'I was glad to repay you,' Kitty said and smiled. 'It was so kind of you to help me as you did. Now that I am living with Mariah and Mr Norton senior, I am able to manage very well. Of course, I might find it difficult if Harpers closed for any length of time. I couldn't expect my friends to keep me for nothing. I don't pay rent, but I do take home food we all share sometimes.'

'You are happy there?'

'Very happy,' Kitty confirmed. 'To be honest, I cannot believe how good things are for me now.'

'I understand you are still helping Bella on your free afternoon and on Sunday.'

'I pop in several times a week and do small things for her,' Kitty said. 'Jerry wanted to pay me, but I told him I didn't need money now. I am just happy to help her – and pleased he is back home again.'

'Yes, he was lucky. Had the bullet entered closer to his chest, he could have died.'

'He was lucky *you* helped him,' Kitty replied. 'He thinks the world of you, Mrs Burrows – as I do, if you don't mind me saying so.'

Beth laughed. 'I think we are friends now, Kitty. It looks as if you are about to get your first customer, so I'd best be off and see where I can help. You have two of your girls in today, so it looks as if you will manage.'

Mrs Burrows went off and Kitty smiled as the customer approached.

'You are the young lady who helped me during the sale, aren't you?'

'Yes, I believe I did,' Kitty said; she'd helped a lot of women choose the things that suited them, but this redhead looked familiar. She was one of the women who had fought over the coats. 'What can I do for you today?'

A huge smile lit the young woman's face. 'I am getting married next week. It is just in the registrar's office – and my Derek, well, he has been married before. His wife deserted him when he was in the war and went off somewhere. He's managed to get a divorce and now he's asked me to wed him.'

'Do you want a new dress for the occasion?' Kitty asked, warmed by the young woman's obvious happiness.

'I thought I'd like a nice costume,' she said. 'I'll want a hat and shoes and gloves to go with it – oh and a silk blouse.' A smile lit her eyes. 'My

Derek has given me twenty pounds to buy new clothes. I think I can get all I want for that, can't I?' She gave Kitty an anxious look.

'Oh, you will have money left over,' Kitty told her. 'We have a lovely range of costumes – and they begin at just three pounds and ten shillings. A new hat, shoes and gloves will cost you perhaps five pounds if you want smart ones, but that will still leave enough for some pretty lingerie.'

'Oh, I knew you were the one to talk to,' the young woman cried. 'I wanted to shop here – because my new coat brought me luck. Derek said he'd never seen me look so lovely as I did in that and the blouse you sold me last time.'

'I am sure you will always look lovely,' Kitty replied. 'But we have a beautiful blue fine wool costume that I think would suit you. The skirt is straight with small pleats at the hem and the jacket fits into the waist. I think it is four pounds and five shillings...'

She led her customer to the appropriate rail and took out the suit she had in mind. 'Oh, that looks so smart,' she said. 'Yes, I would like to try that on please. Derek likes me in blue.'

'There is another blue costume at three pounds ten shillings,' Kitty said, taking it out to show her. 'It isn't quite as smart but very serviceable.'

'I won't need to worry about money so much in future,' the young woman said. 'My Derek has his own small business and he says nothing is too good for me.'

'Then I am sure he will approve of this one,' Kitty said, indicating the fine wool costume. 'Why don't you try them both and see for yourself?'

* * *

An hour or so later, Kitty watched her customer leave armed with several bags. She had sent one of her girls to the hat department for a pretty felt hat she'd seen there. It matched the suit perfectly. A pair of navy leather gloves and shoes completed a very smart ensemble and the customer was close to tears of gratitude when she left.

'You've been so kind and helpful,' she'd said to Kitty. 'I shall always do my shopping here.'

Kitty had smiled and assured her it was a pleasure. She was just instructing one of her juniors to return the other hats, shoes, and gloves back to their department, together with receipts for the money she had taken for the things she'd sold, and didn't notice that Mrs Harper was watching her.

'That was very well done, Kitty,' she said, making her start. 'What made you think of asking the other departments to send examples of shoes and hats?'

'Oh... it was just that my customer was unsure and asked for my advice. I remembered that there were hats in the department that would go well with the chosen costume – and it seemed to make sense to bring everything together so we could match it all for her. She thanked me for helping her choose.'

'As I noticed,' Sally said approvingly. 'That has given me food for thought. You are a clever young woman, Miss Wilson.'

Kitty blushed, but another customer had entered the department and she excused herself to Mrs Harper and went to look after her. Mrs Harper watched for a moment or two and then left the department as unobtrusively as she had come.

Kitty sold a skirt and blouse, but after that, it quietened and only two more customers came in that morning. Kitty took her lunch break at the normal time, but returned as soon as she had eaten. With one less assistant on the floor, she thought it best to be there just in case. She had just served the first of a little flurry of after-lunch customers when Mrs Burrows entered the department. She smiled as she came up to Kitty.

'I've come to relieve you,' she said. 'Mrs Harper would like to see you in her office, Miss Wilson.'

Kitty's heart caught. 'Have I done something wrong?' she asked.

'I shouldn't think so for an instant,' Mrs Burrows told her. 'Why don't you hurry along and see?'

Kitty did as she was told, but despite the reassurance from her friend, she could not help being anxious. Had Mrs Harper revised her opinion of Kitty's initiative that morning? Was she going to tell her never to do it again?

When she knocked at the office door, she was invited in. Mrs Harper was shuffling through some papers on her desk, but she looked up and smiled as Kitty entered.

'My secretary will bring coffee and biscuits in a few moments, Kitty. Please sit down. I wanted to talk to you because I have had an idea.'

Kitty did as she was asked, feeling a little bewildered. 'Yes, Mrs Harper. Can I help in some way?'

'I certainly hope so,' Mrs Harper replied. 'What you did this morning was very kind and also clever. A lot of customers buy a dress and then have to traipse from one department to another to match them – and I am sure sometimes they give up and go home. Then they might buy their accessories somewhere else. My idea is to appoint a personal assistant so that whenever someone comes in to buy a complete outfit or a wedding trousseau that assistant fetches – or sends for – whatever they need. For that, the assistant would need to have a good knowledge of all the departments.' She paused and looked at Kitty. 'For the moment, you are needed where you are, but when Miss Jones returns after the strike, I am proposing you for this job, Kitty. You will spend your time going from one department to the other, helping out on various counters – but whenever we have a customer in who wishes for help – or who intends to spend a lot of money – you will be asked to assist.'

'Me?' Kitty felt a tingle of excitement. 'I've never heard of anything like that before, Mrs Harper.'

'Some stores have department heads who try to help their customers purchase what they need, but usually only by recommendation. I think this is quite a novel idea – and it was yours to begin with.' Mrs Harper paused. 'You would receive the same wage as a supervisor for a start, as you have during the strike – but if this proves successful, I think you can expect to earn another two or three pounds as a bonus.'

'But that is almost twice as much as I normally earn...' Kitty stared at her in amazement.

'You will continue to receive a supervisor's wage for the time the strike continues,' Mrs Harper told her. 'You are doing Miss Jones' job for her and will be paid accordingly. However, I must return her job to her when she comes back to work. I will not punish her because her father would not allow her to work during the strike – but you have proved your worth, Miss

Wilson, and this is my way of rewarding you. Will you be happy to take on this challenge?'

'Oh, yes, please,' Kitty said, feeling a surge of joy. 'My customer was so pleased to be helped and I would like to do the same for others.'

Mrs Harper laughed. 'You will not find some of our wealthier clients quite as easy and may curse me when they have you running everywhere and then leave with nothing, but I hope the idea will catch on and be a success.'

'I think it will in time,' Kitty said. 'After all, who would not rather sit and be waited on than have to visit several departments to find what they need? And we have such wonderful designers for the hats. I am sure they could match some of the more expensive outfits if we asked them to come in and look at our new ranges—' She stopped as she saw Mrs Harper stare at her. 'Would that not work?'

'Of course it would,' Mrs Harper said and looked excited. 'I said you were a clever girl, Kitty. Why didn't I think of that? I could have gloves dyed to match hats or shoes too... we could display some of them in the clothes department...'

Kitty blushed and felt her eyes prick with unshed tears. No one had ever praised her like this before. Her father had loved her but he'd been set in his ways and her mother... well... she had not loved her at all. Ever. Kitty realised it was true at the same moment as she knew it no longer mattered. She was appreciated at work and cared for at home. What more could she want in her life?

* * *

Kitty decided to catch a bus at least part of the way home that evening. She was feeling happy and excited as she hurried through the yard, hardly noticing the smell now, and into the house. She opened the kitchen and went inside.

'Mariah, you will never guess—' she began and then stopped as she looked at her friend's face. 'What is it?' she asked, her heart catching. 'Has Larry been hurt?'

Mariah's face was streaked with tears as she looked at her. 'It's Father,' she said. 'He went out into the yard this morning and fell down – had a proper turn. Larry found him and carried him in, then fetched the doctor. He says he may be paralysed... that's if he recovers. At the moment, he's lying in his bed not sayin' a word or even flickering his eyes...' She gave a little sob. 'I don't want him to die...'

'Oh, Mariah, nor do I,' Kitty said. 'What can I do to help you? I can give up my job and help you nurse him...' It would mean the end of her exciting future, but Kitty genuinely wanted to help her friends.

'Larry has asked someone we know to come in for a few hours every day,' Mariah said. 'I shall nurse him – but I'll need help sometimes. I don't want you to give up your job, Kitty, but I shall ask you to sit with him when you can and to do all the jobs I can't manage, either before you go to work or in the evenings.'

'You know I will,' Kitty said and went to hug her. 'I am willing to give up my job if you need me, Mariah.'

'You love that job,' Mariah said. 'Nay, lass. Lily from down the road will help me – and so will Larry when he can. He's going to move back into his old room so that he can sit with Father while I sleep at night sometimes.'

Kitty nodded. 'Yes, that will be good. You will need help to lift your father if he can't move, but I shall help as much as I can.'

Mariah nodded and wiped her eyes. 'Thank you, Kitty. You're a comfort to me. Now, tell me why you were so excited when you came in then...'

'Oh, it was just a new job at work,' Kitty said. 'It will mean more money permanently, but it isn't important now.'

'Tell me. I'd like to hear,' Mariah insisted and so Kitty told her everything. Mariah looked at her in awe. 'And you were willing to give up all that to sit with Father?'

'Yes, of course,' Kitty replied. 'I care about him – I care about you all.'

'We care about you too, Kitty,' Mariah said and looked beyond her. 'Did you hear any of that, Brother?'

'Yes, every word,' Larry said and his eyes caressed Kitty. 'I always did know she was as lovely inside as out – that's why I love her and want her to wed me one day, if she will...'

Kitty stared at him, tears slipping down her cheeks. 'You know I will,' she said. 'I love you – I love you all...' They were her family now and she could not think of anything she would like more than to marry him and remain with these people forever.

'Bless your heart, Kitty. You're the sweetest girl I have ever met.' Larry smiled at her in a way that set her pulse racing. 'Father is awake at last. He heard you come in, Kitty, and wants you to go up for a while.'

'Yes, of course I will,' she said. 'How is he?'

'Not good. He can't move his left arm or leg and his face is a bit twisted. He is going to need a lot of care and love...' Larry put his hand on her arm as he passed him on the way to the stairs. 'I'll talk to you properly later, Kitty.' He gave her a rueful smile. 'It's a strange courtship you've had, Kitty. I've not even taken you out – but I'll make it up to you, lass. You know how much I care for you?'

'Yes,' she said softly. He might not have taken her dancing or to a concert or even for a walk on a Sunday afternoon, but in his way, he'd been courting her since they met. He was a shy man of few words, but he was kind and caring, and the feeling between them had built naturally. 'There's time enough for us, Larry. For now, we must think of your father.'

'Aye, we must,' he said and sighed, letting go of her arm.

18

'If it's true you're havin' a child, you'd best ask Doctor Dolly to get rid of it for you,' Tel said as he looked at Betty Lou's eager face. 'I told yer – I can't wed yer and you'd best forget it.'

Betty Lou gave a sniff. 'I suppose yer think the kid ain't yourn,' she said. 'I know it is. I've made sure of that, Tel. I ain't let anyone else do that since...' She blinked back her tears as she saw his stony face. 'I ain't goin' ter 'ave it killed, Tel. I know who the father is even if you don't believe me.'

Tel stared at her for a long minute and then sat down abruptly on the edge of the bed. 'Don't do this to me, Betty Lou,' he said. 'I can't 'ave a wife and a kid, not in my work.' He ran his long fingers through his wavy dark hair, his handsome face twisted with genuine regret. 'If I wed yer and let yer 'ave me kid, I'd be vulnerable. They would know how to get to me – and they would...' He swore softly as he saw the pleading in her eyes. 'I'm dealin' with a nasty customer right now, Betty love. He's a Yank and into all sorts of filth. If he muscles in on the old man's territory, he'll have you girls doin' things you'll hate. He'd think I was a soft bugger if he knew how I look after you lot. I 'ave ter be the hard man, girl. Yer know that, don't yer?'

'He wouldn't 'ave ter know,' Betty Lou said in a low voice that was caught with tears. 'Yer don't need ter put a ring on my finger, Tel. Just accept it's your kid and help me get on me feet – that's all I'm askin'.'

'Listen to me, love,' he said softly. 'My old man died when I was a youngster. Ma had another kid ter raise and no money. I went ter work fer the big boss and I worked my way up ter the top. I made enemies. If any of 'em found out about you, they would come after you. You wouldn't be safe.'

'It's too late ter get rid now,' she told him, crossing her fingers behind her back. 'Doctor Dolly says he won't do it, 'cos I'd die.' She'd seen the man the girls called Doctor Dolly because of his soft voice and gentle hands. He didn't use his professional name so he was Dolly to all of them.

Tel stared at her and gave a brief nod. 'I won't wed yer, because someone would find out, but I will look after yer and the kid, even if it ain't mine...'

Betty Lou's face lit up like a candle and he smiled. If he had time for love and softness in his life, he would have married her long since. 'Tell yer the truth, I don't like yer working the game, Betty Lou.'

'Oh, I won't, not if you'll look after me. I'll work in a shop when I can, but I need you ter stand by me until the kid is old enough ter go ter school.'

'I'll look after yer as if we were wed,' Tel told her. 'You keep it ter yerself, though. I ain't joking when I say they would get to me through you.'

'Oh, I shall,' Betty Lou said and smiled at him with love in her eyes.

'Mebbe one day...' he said, wanting to see her happy. She meant more to him than he cared to admit, but he didn't like it that she made him weak. He knew that he would be vulnerable from now on. If the truth leaked out, one of his enemies would use her – and Tel hated the way some men used women as pawns. The girls he looked after were all on the game because it was their choice. None of them were forced to work and they were looked after as much as was possible. Not all the girls who worked the streets were so lucky. He frowned as he remembered the girl who had been shot a while back. It was that low-life Yank who had enticed her away and then killed her. Maybe he'd discovered that she'd ratted on him and given important information to Tel.

'Are yer angry with me?' Betty Lou asked as he frowned.

He shook his head. 'Not you, love. I was just thinkin' of business...'

Betty Lou knew better than to ask. He rubbed the bridge of his nose as he pondered what he should do with the information he'd been given. He knew where the Yank the American government wanted could be found at most hours of the day and night. Should he make use of that knowledge?

The American was pushing the boundaries, testing the strength of the British, and, to put it mildly, the boss was annoyed. Once upon a time, he would have moved swiftly and decisively to put an end to his rival, but age had weakened him. He'd told Tel to do something about him, but he wasn't anxious for a turf war. The boss was feeling unwell, for perhaps the first time in his life, and his hold on his empire was in danger of slipping. Only Tel was holding it together for him.

The Yank had threatened someone else – someone Jerry thought a lot of. Tel's expression lightened as he thought of his younger brother and his mother. Jerry reported to him once a week. He was part of the eyes and ears all over London that kept Tel in control, kept him on top of things. Jerry seldom asked for favours. He paid his dues, same as all the other barrow boys, but he knew Tel was there for him if he asked.

Tel nodded to himself. It wasn't often he let himself enjoy the luxury of visiting his mother – and it wasn't because of her sharp tongue. She would undoubtedly tell him to clear orf and stay away, but she was his ma and he checked on her from time to time. Jerry looked after her and kept his nose clean, apart from a few small errands, but he was never asked to do anything the wrong side of the law. Tel often slipped him a couple of quid for their mother, knowing that she would refuse it from him, but what the eye didn't see the heart didn't grieve for. Not that he'd given up trying to persuade her to let him look after her.

'Yer laughin' now,' Betty Lou said and came to sit by him.

'Well, it ain't every day yer get told yer 'avin' a kid,' Tel said and squeezed her hand. 'I'll find yer a place ter live and I'll see yer all right – but yer got ter keep it ter yerself, Betty Lou. I ain't kiddin' yer – it might be a matter of life and death.'

'Yeah, I know,' she said and grinned. He laughed out loud. She'd got most of what she wanted, the little minx, and who knew – one day he might get out of this murky business and put a ring on her finger…

19

'Thank goodness the strike is over,' Sally exclaimed as she read the newspaper headlines that morning of 15 May 1926. Although most people had supported the General Strike on the first day, it had waned over the next few days and the TUC had asked the Government for terms, ending it in nine days, without making concessions. However, the miners had refused to return to work, even though the other trades had given in. 'You look worn out, Ben.'

He yawned over his coffee, giving her a sheepish grin. 'It has certainly given me a huge respect for the working man,' he told her. 'I thought I worked hard, but the average worker does far more than I've ever done – and it makes me realise how lucky I am.'

'Then imagine how the miners feel,' Sally said, pouring him more coffee. 'Their work is hard manual labour and their wages have been reduced almost by a half in the last few years. It is no wonder they refused and came out when they were told they would have to work longer hours for even less money.'

'Poor buggers,' Ben said, and, at Sally's raised eyebrows. 'I'm sorry for the language, but I've learned a few things since the strike began. I still support the Government; we can't have anarchy on the streets, but I feel for those miners and their families.'

'It says here that they are refusing to go back to work,' Sally said, looking at the paper, and then sighed as she put it to one side. 'I don't know the answer, Ben. I know the prices of coal have dropped a lot since before the war. We're not exporting anywhere near what we were – and you can't run a business if you can't make money... yet men can't be expected to keep taking less money for longer hours.'

'In my opinion, we should take over the mines,' Ben replied. 'The Government should be in charge of national assets like coal, because it is a primary source of fuel. Then they could pay the miners more and run it to benefit the nation rather than as privately owned industry.'

'Are you becoming a radical, Ben?' Sally teased with a smile. 'Why don't you stand for parliament?'

Ben looked at her for a few moments. 'You know, that isn't a bad idea,' he said. 'I sometimes think you could run Harpers entirely alone... Oh, I know you need managers and so on, but you don't really need my input that much.'

'Of course I do, Ben,' Sally replied, shocked. 'You make a lot of the decisions about growth and strategy – and look at the buying trip you just undertook. I couldn't possibly have done it alone.'

'We won't need to do that for a while,' Ben pointed out. 'We have lots of new contacts, and now things are starting to really pick up again, we'll have many more traders arriving at our door. I don't suppose being an MP would prevent me overseeing the future strategy for Harpers – but these past few days have taught me that I could do more.'

Sally was silent for a moment or two, then she nodded. 'I dare say we should still have time to discuss the direction we need to take – and we could employ a buyer for the men's department.' Ben had taken over that job after the war, but he was right in saying that most of what he did could be done by others. 'If you are sure it's what you want, I would support you.'

'Thank you,' he smiled at her. 'I think there's a few people I need to see today, but I will be thinking about it. I won't do it lightly but...' He shook his head. 'Sometimes I wish I could put the world to rights, or at least help make the right decisions. A lot to think about, though.'

'Yes, it is a big step,' Sally agreed. 'You will need to consider carefully. We would have to increase the number of buyers we employ. You've done the lion's share of that since the end of the war, but I will continue to oversee it.'

'You have a good eye for what is new and good rather than just new,' Ben said. 'I've always discussed everything with you. As I said, you could manage alone if you had to, for a while anyway. Sometimes I would need to spend long hours in the House, but at others – well, not every debate is vital. I dare say I would be around if you needed me. That's if I was elected, of course.'

'I would certainly hope you would be around for the children, Ben,' Sally looked him in the eyes. 'You have two children who want to see their father. Don't lose sight of all that truly matters.' He nodded and she looked at him thoughtfully. 'Which party will you try to become an MP for, if you do?'

'The Labour Party,' Ben replied. He smiled as he saw that she was taken aback. 'You think I should become a Tory? They are for the establishment and business, it's true – but I'm an American by birth. I think the Labour Party is young and thrusting. A trifle inexperienced in my opinion, but they will learn as they gain more experience of government. If I do take up politics, I want to help the working man and his family, Sally. I hope and believe they will do that, given time.'

'I'm not shocked,' Sally said. 'Just surprised. I thought you might try to bring change from inside the Tory Party rather than against them. I'm not certain the Labour Party will win the next election.'

'I suppose—' What he was about to say was lost as Mrs Hills came in.

'I am sorry to interrupt, Mrs Harper – but the police are here and want to see Mr Harper...'

'To see me?' Ben looked up in surprise. 'Where are they, Mrs Hills?'

'I asked them to wait in the morning room. I think it is bad news, sir...'

'I'll go immediately,' Ben said and left the breakfast room.

Sally looked at Mrs Hills, who had lingered. 'What did they say?' she asked, a shiver of apprehension at her nape. Was it something to do with what Ben had done in the strike or something more sinister?

'They looked so serious, Mrs Harper – and there's an inspector as well as a constable.'

'Yes, that does sound like bad news,' Sally said. 'I think I will go up to the children. Let me know if I am needed...'

* * *

It was Ben who came up to the nursery, where Sally had just finished getting the children dressed. She saw the look on his face and sent the children down to the kitchen for their breakfast.

'Tell Mrs Hills I will be down shortly please, Jenny.' She looked at Ben. 'Trouble? Is it the restaurant?'

'In a way...' Ben frowned. 'I didn't tell you, Sally, but Jack sacked that American agent after Beth was threatened...'

'Beth was threatened?!' Sally cried, shocked. No one had told her and it left her stunned and breathless. 'When did this happen? No one told me anything. Why wasn't I told?'

'Beth didn't want you told because she knew you would worry, but Jack informed me after he'd sacked Lucas...' Ben frowned. 'If he'd spoken to me first, I would have warned him not to do it, but he was angry and frightened for his family... Now Lucas is dead, shot through the head, so I've just been told.' Ben passed a shaking hand over his face. 'The moment Jack sacked that poor devil, he was a marked man.'

'What do you mean? Why should that have caused his murder?'

'They told Beth that Jack had to get rid of the stooge – American slang – or they would harm the children, and Jack thought that meant they knew who he was, but they didn't. They were aware someone was investigating them, but Lucas was careful not to be seen.'

'So when Jack did as he was ordered, it told them who he was,' Sally said, feeling sick and scared. 'That is awful, Ben. I am so sorry.'

'Yes, it is pretty rotten,' Ben agreed. 'I've had to explain what happened – and why – to my contacts and they weren't happy. They were going to warn him and pull him out, but it seems they were too late. The British police are involved now and pretty angry that they weren't informed about what was going on. I think they are going to arrest the man they believe to be guilty, but, as I told them, he won't have done it himself. He's sure to have a cast-iron alibi.'

'What happens now, Ben? Are Beth and the children safe – are *we* safe?' Sally gave him a look that sent shivers through him.

'My God, I hope so!' Ben exclaimed. He ran his fingers through his thick dark hair in agitation. 'I wish I'd never agreed the poor devil could work at the restaurant. Jack blames me for what happened to Beth – and we had a row. He threatened to pull out of the restaurant, said he wasn't prepared to put his family at risk.' Ben took an agitated turn about the room and then turned to look at her. 'I am to blame for all of it, Sally – a man's death, Beth's ordeal, and Jack's anger. I should never have agreed to it. I was a fool, but I never thought it would turn out this way.'

'You couldn't have known,' Sally replied. 'But you shouldn't have agreed to taking Lucas on without consulting Jack. He's a full partner in the restaurant and he had a right to know, to be consulted. As for the rest of it, Beth must be sick with worry.'

'Yes, I am sure she is. Jack – when we argued, well, I've never seen him look like that before. He told me Beth and the boys are his life. He is considering taking them away to the country, says he can't trust me and wants to sell his share of the restaurant, start over somewhere it is safer.'

'Oh no!' Sally looked at him in dismay. 'Surely he won't? He did what they told him...'

'I told Jack that made it worse,' Ben said. 'If they think they can force him to do what they want through his family, they can use him again, making the same threats.' Ben met her anxious look. 'You have to stand up to bullies, Sally. Give in and they take you over.'

'The police will arrest him surely?' Sally said, feeling fraught with anxiety. If Jack took his family to the country, she would lose her best friend; they would only see each other occasionally, and if there was a rift between Ben and Jack, it might mean they would lose touch completely. Worse than that was the thought that she – all of them – might be in some danger because of what had happened.

'Let's hope they can find the man responsible and that once they have him, they deport him. It's what the American Government wants, but, even if they do...' Ben shook his head. 'I don't know the answer, Sally. It's a mess and my fault for allowing Lucas to work for us.'

'Not entirely,' Sally said. 'These contacts of yours – American or British

Government – what are they doing about the situation? They got you involved. It must be up to them to sort this mess out.'

Ben sighed deeply. 'Even if they do, I'm not certain Jack will forgive me for my part in this...'

'I'll talk to Beth,' Sally said. 'She will calm Jack down, make him see reason.'

'No. I'd rather you didn't, Sally. I know you will want to, because you're worried about her – but don't get her involved. This is between Jack and me – and we have to sort it or— or go our own ways. I'm not sure if I can find the money to pay him out, unless I take on another bank loan.'

Sally hesitated and then nodded. Perhaps it was best to let the men settle their quarrel themselves. She felt unsettled and a little nervous herself, even though neither she nor their children had been threatened. What must Beth have been going through? She would be terrified because a man had been murdered and she would wonder if she, her children or even Jack would be next...

* * *

Despite her conversation with her husband, Sally drove herself to Beth's house later that morning. Beth opened the door to her, but her usual smile of welcome was a bit forced as she asked her in.

'Why didn't you let me know you were coming?' she said as she led the way into her sitting room. Both children were at home, playing with toys, even though it should have been a school day. They looked up and then came running to give Sally a hug. She'd brought fruit and sweets and after hugs and thanks, they returned to their games with a banana to munch each.

'Could we talk privately?' Sally asked once the boys had settled.

'Yes, perhaps we should,' Beth agreed and they went through to the kitchen. She looked at Sally and the fear was in her eyes. 'Jack told me what happened last night. That poor man. I feel responsible...'

'How could it be your fault?' Sally cried. 'I am so sorry, Beth. I wish you'd told me – Not that I could have done anything, but you've had to carry this alone, my dearest friend, and I know how angry and upset you must be. I am sorry Ben let that man work at the restaurant and didn't tell Jack until he had to. It wasn't right and he knows it – and he is sorry, but that doesn't help now.'

'No, unfortunately, it doesn't,' Beth said. 'Jack is so angry. We had yet another argument last night. He wants to take us down to the country, find a house for us to rent until he can sell his half of the restaurant.'

'Oh, Beth. I know he must be worried to death over all this and it is Ben's fault – but I should miss you so very much.'

'We quarrelled, because I told him I wouldn't go,' Beth said. 'I won't leave Vera when she has so much doubt hanging over her – the doctors want to take that lump out... and she's frightened, and then there's Dad, and all my friends, the children's friends... I've kept the boys off school today because of what happened last night, but I can't continue to let them stay home. I don't know what to do, Sally. I won't let Vera down and there's Bella too...' Beth gave a little cry of despair. 'But I am frightened, Sally. That man pointed a gun at me – or rather at Timmy – and if they can kill a man in cold blood...' Beth's face was white with tension as she breathed hard to steady herself.

'Yes, I know. It shocked me when Ben told me – that agent or police officer, whatever he was, knew the risks – but you and the boys are innocent.' Sally's voice rose slightly as the anger swept through her. 'If I knew who that devil was, I'd kill him myself for hurting you...'

Beth gave a shaky laugh at Sally's sudden fierceness. 'I believe you would,' she said. 'Let's have a cuppa, Sally. I could do with one. Perhaps you won't need to do anything drastic...'

Sally looked at her as she filled the kettle and moved it onto the range. 'What do you mean?'

'A friend told me something...' Beth said, lowering her voice. 'He visited me again this morning, shortly before you. He'd heard about the murder and he said the man behind it had had his cards marked. I asked him what he meant, but he shook his head and told me not to worry, because my troubles would soon be over.'

'What on earth does that mean?' Sally asked and shivered. 'That sounds a bit menacing to me. Who is this friend, Beth? I didn't know you had friends like that...'

'He isn't one of them, but he knows things that neither of us wants to know...' Beth made a wry face. 'He isn't truly a friend, though I've always liked him – but I dared not tell Jack what he told me. He would have us on the next train out of London.'

'It's that man – the one you helped when he was shot,' Sally exclaimed and saw the truth in Beth's eyes. 'Can you tell me what he said?'

Beth hesitated, then, 'Some of it... He says there are two rival gangs at war, Sally, both British and based in London. One of them has taken in this American and, apparently, he is trying to take over a lot of the other gang's business. The boss of the rival gang won't stand for it and they don't like it because he's pushing drugs and using guns far more than they ever have...' Beth laughed oddly. 'Apparently, the British way is gentle persuasion...'

'Or not so gentle,' Sally said grimly and nodded. 'I heard about something like that once before. Do you think the rival gang will kill this American?'

'I haven't been told in so many words but...' Beth nodded. 'Yes, I think they will. I've been told not to worry – that they... the American's gang – won't get near me again. I think I am being watched over, protected.' She gave a little shiver. 'I just can't tell Jack. He is sick of all this stuff – and he would think one gang as evil as the other, even if they have appointed themselves my guardians.'

'Yes, I see your point,' Sally replied thoughtfully. 'It's honour amongst thieves, I suppose, but they're all still thieves – or worse.'

'Something like that,' Beth said and poured their tea into china cups. 'If Jack thought that Jerry was even remotely involved with either gang, he would forbid me to go to his home and visit Bella. I like her and I'm due to take her to the clinic again.'

'I think you're very brave, Beth. I'm not sure I could be as calm as you in the circumstances.'

'I'm not calm in my head,' Beth replied. 'I don't want to be involved in any of it – and I hate the idea that others may die, but I know that whatever I say or do won't stop it. I don't belong in that world – none of us do, Sally – but we got caught up in it through no fault of our own. All we can do is keep our heads down and wait.'

'Don't feel sorry for that wretch who caused it all,' Sally said and laughed. 'I don't mean Ben. He didn't bring that gangster here – but perhaps the Americans will just grab him and take him back where he belongs. That's what they want. It would be the best way out of all this and they need him alive...'

'Then why don't they get on with it?' Beth said with a flash of anger. 'Unless they do, I think he will be killed and quite soon.' She shuddered at the thought of so much violence.

Sally looked at her anxiously. 'Do not feel guilty even if he is,' she said. 'I told you; I could cheerfully kill him myself – providing I could get away with it, of course.' She laughed and Beth laughed with her. 'It's the children I worry about. It makes you feel you dare not let them out of your sight.'

'Yes, I know – that's why we kept our two out of school.'

'I took ours in myself and I will fetch them back but...' Sally shook her head and sighed.

'What are we going to do about Jack and Ben?' Beth asked. 'They were such good friends before this, Sally. It seems a pity that their partnership should break up over it.'

'Yes, it is – and I don't want you to go and live in the country, Beth! I should hardly ever see you...'

'Then we'll just have to bang their heads together,' Beth said, smiling. 'I'm glad you came and we talked, Sally. I would hate it if we fell out over this...'

'We are not going to.' Sally set her face determinedly. 'Just keep your fingers crossed and hope it all works out somehow. I am sure that once the threat is removed, Jack will come round.' She gave Beth a brief hug. 'I have to go, love. I am meeting Maggie for lunch. She came up to town for a few days, but she's been so busy we've scarcely talked. I'll ask her to pop in and see you before she leaves tomorrow.'

'Yes. I'd love to see her...' Beth hesitated. 'You won't tell her anything?'

'No, of course not. The fewer people who know anything, the better.'

20

Kitty yawned as she sat on the bus to work. She was glad the strike was over so that she didn't have to walk back and forth every day. It was a little luxury now that she was earning more and could afford it and, besides, she was tired. Last evening, she'd done most of the chores Mariah couldn't manage the previous day. Larry had come in late at night and found her still ironing sheets. He'd banished her to bed and taken over in the bedroom with his father, sending his sister to get some rest.

It wasn't that Alf was a demanding patient, but he needed much of Mariah's time, because he couldn't do anything for himself. He'd had another slight stroke that first night and, so far, he'd woken a few times and smiled at her. Kitty had sat with him for a while, holding his hand and talking to him. She'd become so fond of him in the short time she'd known him and to see him so ill was like losing her father all over again. Kitty had helped Mariah turn him and clean him before she left for work, her heart catching at the tender way her friend cared for him. They often chided each other when he was fit and well, but the love Mariah felt for her father was obvious and touching.

Harpers was back to normal now the General Strike was over. The ground floor was already prepared for the day as Kitty passed through. She was working in the hat and bag department that day and looked forward to it. Mrs Harper had told her there was a new order of hats coming that morning and Kitty would be unpacking them so that she would be familiar with the stock. She had worked in the shoe department for two days, but shoes were much easier because most customers mostly went for a plain neat style of shoe when putting an outfit together. The fancy sandals came into their own in summer, of course.

'Good morning, Miss Wilson,' Mrs Jamieson, the supervisor of the hat and bag and jewellery department, greeted her with a smile. 'Nice and early. Perhaps you could help me set up my new jewellery display until the new hats come in?'

'Yes, you had some fresh stock in yesterday, didn't you?' Kitty said, interested at once. Jewellery wasn't part of her job, because, after all, most women did not buy their own – at least, not the expensive stuff. It was normally given as a gift and not always a consideration when an outfit was being selected. However, you never knew what you might be asked for as a personal advisor, so it was good to know what was new in stock.

'Mrs Burrows usually pops in to help me,' Mrs Jamieson said conversationally. 'However, she isn't coming in this week.'

'Oh? I do hope she and the children are well,' Kitty said, her attention caught.

'I think she has to take someone to the hospital – or that is what Mrs Harper said,' the supervisor told her. 'Now what do you think of these beautiful pendants? They are Art Deco in design and the enamelling is so delicate and pretty.'

'Beautiful,' Kitty agreed. 'Just right for a young bride – or bridesmaid...'

'Yes, that was what drew Mrs Harper to them. Now, how shall we display them to their advantage? Lying on velvet in the glass counter – or on a velvet stand in the wall cabinets?'

* * *

Kitty spent an hour helping with the jewellery display, then the consignment of new hats was brought up by the porter. She spent the rest of the morning unpacking and helping one of the counter assistants to price and list them. In the afternoon, she did the display for the new hats, because the salesgirls were all busy, and then someone came to tell her she was wanted in the dress department.

Kitty left at once and found three women waiting – an older woman and two young ladies. The younger women were eighteen and nineteen, and their aunt was about to take them on a trip around Europe, starting with Paris, before moving on to Italy and Austria, and they needed outfits to see them on the first stage of their journey at least.

'I like the Miss Susie range,' one of the girls, a tall, willowy blonde, said. 'I think they are the best Harpers do.'

'We shall see, Mary,' her aunt replied calmly. 'I believe they are the most expensive and we only have a hundred pounds for each of you today. We shall need shoes, hats, gloves...' The aunt looked at Kitty. 'I have been told you can assist with everything?'

'Yes, certainly, madam.' Kitty began and was fixed with a hawklike stare.

'I am Lady Rowbottom, and you will kindly address me as such. Now, my nieces have one hundred pounds each to spend today – but I expect good service and good value too. Sometimes, it is possible to ease the price a little, is it not? After all, you have sales and drop the price to nearly nothing...'

'Sometimes, but the garments reduced are normally flawed or damaged – and I am sure that would not do for these young ladies...' Kitty said. 'But we do have some very keenly priced clothes if you wish.'

'I want the Miss Susie range,' the taller of the two said again. 'I know Daddy told you we could have whatever we liked, providing it was suitable.'

'Your father is far too generous – and you will want to buy clothes in Paris,' her aunt reminded her, but the young woman set her mouth firmly.

'Why don't you show me the dresses you like?' Kitty asked her. 'I am sure we can find lots of lovely things for you within the limits your aunt has set.'

The girl nodded and led the way firmly towards the rail where the most expensive things were displayed. She went along it and picked out six dresses that she liked: two morning, two tea gowns and two evening dresses.

'May I try these please?' she asked.

'Certainly,' Kitty replied. 'If you would like to take two garments at a time into the changing room.' She turned and summoned a junior, who came running eagerly. 'Stay here and assist with buttons or zips if requested, Miss Earling. I will see if the other young lady has a preference.'

Kitty went back to Lady Rowbottom and discovered that the second niece was sitting patiently. Her hair was fair but straight and didn't have the sheen of her sister's blonde locks.

'What would you like to see, Miss?' Kitty asked her.

'Oh, anything suitable,' she said. 'I think I need clothes for all occasions. I saw quite a pretty one on the model, but someone is trying it on...'

'Ah yes, it is a day dress, suitable for most things – other than special occasions,' Kitty said. 'We also have it in pale blue – and yellow. I think the yellow might suit you. Shall I help you choose some dresses for a start?'

'Yes, please,' the girl said shyly and followed her to a rail of day dresses. 'I haven't long been out of the schoolroom. I'm Daisy. Mary is a year older. Daddy still thinks of us both as his little girls, but Aunt Eugenia insists that we go with her on her European tour. She wants to find us husbands, I think...' She gave a nervous giggle. 'Mary is so pretty and she wants to have some fun, but I'd just as soon stay home and look after Daddy...'

Kitty warmed to her. She was attractive but not pretty like her sister and obviously shy. There were a lot of beautiful dresses and suits in stock at reasonable prices that would suit this young lady and she could have a lot of nice things for a hundred pounds, which seemed a huge amount to Kitty to be allowed to spend on clothes.

* * *

Two and a half hours later, Daisy departed with a wardrobe that would surely see her around Europe and home again. She had eight new dresses, two suits, six hats, gloves, scarves and six pairs of shoes, including a very daring pair of high-heeled strappy sandals. After much trying on and pouting, Mary purchased four morning dresses, three tea gowns, two hats, some gloves and a pair of shoes.

Her aunt had refused to let her buy two very expensive evening gowns, declaring them too old for her and entirely unsuitable. Mary had refused to purchase some less expensive and more demure evening gowns and had sulked as she was taken off by her aunt to try elsewhere another day. In all, they had spent a hundred and thirty-five pounds and ten shillings.

Despite an exhausting afternoon, catering for the girls' every wish, Kitty felt she had failed. Mary had spent only thirty-seven pounds of her allowance, although Daisy had spent all but a few shillings of hers.

'You look tired,' Miss Jones said to her as she began to tidy up after the customers had departed. 'Do you think it was worth it? Our department took ninety pounds, but I am sure they would have spent that anyway...'

Kitty smothered a sigh. She was tired, but some of that was down to helping Mariah at home. Was that a faint hint of envy she'd heard in Miss Jones' voice? Did she resent Kitty's new job? Kitty hoped not, because they needed to work together in future if her job were to succeed.

'Yes, I am sure you are right,' Kitty said, 'but think what a help we were to them – and how pleased Miss Daisy was...'

'They are the daughters of a baronet,' Miss Jones said with a sniff. 'Not a lot of money from what their aunt said – she is the one with the money, I think – but they might have spent more had they wished.'

'Yes. I should have liked to sell Miss Mary more dresses,' Kitty said. 'She wanted them, but her aunt refused to allow her choice.'

'We shall have to see what Mrs Harper thinks,' Miss Jones said and walked off to harry the rest of the staff into tidying up as it was nearly closing time.

Kitty's heart sank. It was her first chance and she had failed to satisfy her customer. She could only hope Mrs Harper wouldn't change her mind about Kitty's role in the store.

* * *

'I told you some customers would be harder to please,' Sally Harper said when she spoke to Kitty the next morning. 'I think it worked well – you sold several hats and shoes, as well as the dresses. You can't win every time, Miss Wilson, but it wouldn't surprise me if they return and buy the evening gowns they refused. I have met a few stubborn young ladies in my time as a salesgirl, and unless Lady Rowbottom is prepared to put up with her niece's sulking, she will bring her back.'

Kitty was summoned back to the dress department that very afternoon. Lady Rowbottom was looking rather annoyed but forced herself to ask if Mary might have another look through the evening gowns.

'Yes, of course, my lady,' Kitty said and allowed the young woman to peruse the evening gowns. When she chose another four to try on and finally settled on the two she'd liked the first time, Lady Rowbottom looked resigned.

'If you wish to make a show of yourself,' she said in a tone of repressed annoyance. 'I suppose you may have them – though what your father will think, I don't know.'

'May I make a suggestion?' Kitty asked, causing them both to look at her. 'I think it is the very low back that is making you uneasy, Lady Rowbottom?' The older woman gave a slight nod and Kitty smiled. 'What might solve the problem is if we inserted a gauze panel. You would have the same superb styling but a little more modesty at the back...'

'Show me!' the beleaguered aunt demanded.

Kitty instantly produced the material she had earlier selected, just in case there was a need. There was a very fine blue gauze that exactly matched the blue gown and a silver tissue that would go with the dove-grey gown. She tucked them inside the gowns to show niece and aunt how well it looked.

'Very much better,' Lady Rowbottom pronounced, and after a moment her niece nodded in agreement. 'How soon can you do it?'

'I will have to ask our alterations department, but I believe they might be able to have both gowns ready by tomorrow evening – if that is suitable, my lady.' Kitty had already checked availability but knew that she could do them herself in Harpers' sewing room if necessary.

'Yes, perfectly.' The older woman's eyes gleamed with satisfaction. 'You are a clever young woman. Now you may provide my niece with shoes and gloves to match the dresses – and I shall need a new evening gown myself. Do you have anything suitable? I don't want any of this modern frippery – just a nice silk or a light velvet.'

'Yes, my lady. We have dresses to suit all ages and styles,' Kitty assured her. She smiled inwardly, because there were two gowns she thought perfect for the tall, but bony, figure of the austere lady, who had now very slightly unbent towards her – and if she could manage it, Lady Rowbottom would be leaving with both of them.

* * *

An hour later, the satisfied customers left the department and Miss Jones came over to Kitty. She gave her an oddly speculative look and then conceded, 'Well, you certainly know how to toady up to difficult old ladies. I didn't think you would manage to sell her anything.'

'Those dresses were perfect for her,' Kitty said. 'They might be a little conservative for our younger clients, but Mrs Harper tries to have something for everyone and I knew as soon as she asked that those gowns would be perfect.' Lady Rowbottom had purchased a heavy silk, ankle-length gown in silver-grey and another in a dark midnight-blue in fine silk-velvet, both with high necks and long sleeves, slender fitting but flaring out a little at the back into a train. Both were from the Miss Susie senior range and expensive. Indeed, Lady Rowbottom had spent nearly as much on her own gowns as on her nieces' gowns. She had also purchased three pairs of shoes and six hats, as well as gloves and scarves.

'I suppose you will be Mrs Harper's blue-eyed girl now,' Miss Jones remarked in a nasty tone as she went off to serve another customer.

Kitty sighed. She was loving her job and doing well, but it seemed the more she sold, the more Miss Jones resented her.

Leaving the junior to finish tidying up, Kitty left the department and went to have a cup of tea before returning to the hat and bag department.

Mrs Jamieson greeted her with a smile of welcome.

'Oh well done, Miss Wilson,' she said. 'Another six hats today – and all those evening gloves and scarves, too. You will put the sales figures up for our department if this keeps up – and you know we get a bonus if we do well.'

'I am glad you're pleased,' Kitty said quietly and Mrs Jamieson looked at her speculatively.

'Is everything all right?'

'Oh, it's nothing. I just can't seem to please Miss Jones...'

'Ah, Marion Jones,' Mrs Jamieson said and shook her head. 'Don't blame yourself for that, Miss Wilson. I know Marion and her family well – I recommended her for her first job here. She has a terrible time at home with that father of hers. He was angry because we kept open during the strike and I know he has been on at her to change her job, poor girl. I should think she hardly knows what to do with herself. He is a violent man and I think she is afraid of him.'

'Oh, poor Miss Jones,' Kitty exclaimed. 'Is there nothing anyone can do to help her? Could she not leave home and find lodgings elsewhere?' Kitty thought how much happier she was since finding herself a new home.

'I suggested that to her a long time ago, but she has a younger sister and brother and her mother struggles to cope. I think Marion helps her a lot in the evenings. She doesn't feel able to leave, even though her father is a brute – and it is Marion he picks on most of the time.'

'I am sorry she has such a rough time at home, but I don't know why she is so jealous of my little success.'

'Perhaps she thinks she will lose her department bonus if you sell the gowns rather than her,' Mrs Jamieson said and looked thoughtful. 'I'll have a word and explain that it won't change – in fact, the more you sell, the bigger the bonus her department will get.'

'Thank you,' Kitty said and smiled. 'We need to work together, not against each other.'

'Exactly,' Mrs Jamieson replied. 'Ah, I have a customer. This gentleman has come back for some things he looked at earlier and asked me to put by...'

* * *

Kitty left Mrs Jamieson to serve the gentleman, who was buying presents for his wife and two daughters. She went to the hat department and began to check through the stock, making notes on what they needed to replace. Navy straw hats were selling well and they had only a few left in stock. She would make a note of it and remind Mrs Jamieson to ask Mrs Harper to order more.

She was just about to check the gloves and scarves when a young man came up to her. 'Oh, miss,' he said hesitantly. 'I need to buy something nice for a young lady. I'm in her bad books at the moment...' His smile was charming. 'She isn't fond of jewellery but she does love pretty hats.'

'Oh, then you've come to the right place,' Kitty said with a smile. 'Tell me, what does your young lady look like?'

'She isn't my young lady; Marguerite is my sister – and she has dark hair with a hint of red, like yours. That's what made me ask you...' He hesitated and then gave her a shy smile. 'Would you mind awfully trying one or two on for me? If it suits you, it will her... she is very pretty.'

Kitty blushed, realising he was gently flirting with her. 'Well, it isn't really my counter...' She smiled at Shirley. 'You won't mind if I serve this gentleman?'

'I have another customer, thank you, Miss Wilson,' Shirley replied and gave her a wink as she moved to assist a young woman who was trying on some serviceable felts.

'Is there any particular hat you wished to see?' Kitty asked, and the gentleman indicated a blush straw and a blue. She obligingly tried them on for him and he decided on the blue, then changed his mind, and said he would take both. Kitty laughed. 'Your sister will forgive you now, I think...'

'I hope so,' he said. 'I did the unforgivable and forgot to fetch her home from a party and she had to ask for a lift with someone she doesn't much like.'

'Oh dear, that was unfortunate for her,' Kitty said and gave a little laugh. 'I am certain she will be pleased with these hats.'

She packed them in tissue and the distinctive black and gold boxes with Harpers emblazoned on the side and took the gentleman's money. He put his wallet away, picked up the boxes and then looked at her.

'I realise you don't know me, Miss Wilson – but is there any chance that you might be free to go out to tea with my sister and me on Sunday?'

Kitty blushed and caught her breath. She was certain it was a sincere and very thoughtful invitation, for with his sister included she might have gone had she chosen. 'How very kind,' she said. 'I am afraid I am unable to accept, sir – as you say, I don't know you, but I do have a gentleman friend of my own...'

She saw the disappointment in his eyes. 'Marguerite – or Daisy, as she likes to be called, told me how honest and lovely you were and I wanted to know you,' he said. 'You might recall that Daisy and Mary came with our aunt to buy a few clothes...?'

'Oh yes, I do remember. Daisy is such a pleasant young lady.'

'Yes, but very shy and you helped her. I wanted to thank you,' he said and offered his hand. She took it and he gave hers a gentle squeeze. 'I should have liked to know you better and I know Daisy would – but you have your own life. I perfectly understand. My name is Sylvester... James Sylvester.'

'Yes, I hope I may see Daisy again,' Kitty replied. 'One of the reasons I am not free is because someone I care about is ill and I help to look after him when I am at home. I do have a young man, Mr Sylvester – but perhaps one day I might have tea with Daisy if she wishes, when my friend is better.'

'You are kind,' he said and smiled. 'Daisy said you were.' He tipped his hat. 'Good afternoon, Miss Wilson.'

Kitty watched him leave. He was a polite man and clearly fond of his sister – but Kitty's heart was given and she would not deceive Mr Sylvester into thinking she might be free.

'Oh my,' Shirley said as she returned after selling a plain felt hat. 'He liked you, Miss Wilson. I could see the way he was staring at you before he asked you to try on the hats.'

'He asked me to tea with him and his sister. I helped her buy some clothes and he wanted to thank me for my kindness,' Kitty said. 'He was just being polite.'

Shirley shrugged. 'If a young man like that asked me to tea, I'd go, sister or no sister. And he didn't look as if he was just being polite. He looked as if he'd seen an angel...'

'Please, don't say such things,' Kitty said and blushed. 'Besides, I have someone—'

'Oooh! You never said,' Shirley exclaimed and Mrs Jamieson gave her a look of reproof. She lowered her voice, 'Tell me later, Kitty. I will walk with you to the bus stop.'

'Time to start tidying up, girls,' Mrs Jamieson reminded them and the girls immediately began to put their counters in order.

Kitty and Shirley covered the hat stands with fine gauze, and the cabinets with expensive bags and jewellery were locked, the keys given to Mrs Jamieson, who put them away in her drawer and locked it.

'You may leave now,' she told them. 'Kitty, please stay for a moment.'

'I'll wait for you outside,' Shirley hissed and went off with another wink.

'What was all that about?' Mrs Jamieson asked as Kitty went up to her.

'Oh, Miss Williams thought the gentleman I served was flirting with me... he is Daisy's brother. I suppose she is Miss Marguerite Sylvester. I just knew her as Daisy when I helped her buy her clothes. He came to buy some hats as a gift for her and to thank me for being kind.'

'It was more than that, I think,' Mrs Jamieson said. 'I heard him ask if you would go to tea and thought you handled it very well.'

'He was nice and I like Daisy – but I need to help my friends at the weekend. Their father is very ill. Besides, I do have someone. I believe we will marry one day but perhaps not for some time yet...'

'Oh, that is nice,' Mrs Jamieson said and smiled. 'I hope you won't leave us too soon, Miss Wilson.'

'Oh no. I should want to go on working for a while,' Kitty said, her cheeks blushing. 'Until I had a family...'

'Yes, of course – and you can always return later. I was on the counters until my children were at senior school and then I looked for another job – and Mrs Harper kindly gave me this one, as it had come vacant. Mrs O'Sullivan, who held the job before me, is expecting a child – she may have it by now. So I was very lucky...'

Kitty nodded and smiled, leaving as Mrs Jamieson did. She hoped Shirley would have got tired of waiting, but she was just outside the door. The evening was warm and it seemed she was in no hurry to get home.

'So, tell me everything,' she said, linking arms with Kitty. 'What is his name – and how long have you known him...?'

* * *

Kitty sensed the change as soon as she walked in that evening. Mariah was humming a little tune as she stirred the stew slowly cooking on the range. She looked at Kitty and smiled.

'Father is much better this evening,' she said. 'He managed to stand when I got him up and his leg is moving again. His arm is still awkward and he can't hold anything in that hand – but he was hungry. He asked for you to go up as soon as you got in.'

'Yes, I shall,' Kitty said and went up the stairs to the room above the kitchen. As she got nearer, she heard the sound of a man's laughter and knew it was Larry.

'So when are you going to ask her then?' Alf demanded, sounding very much like his old self. 'If you're not careful, she will be off with another young lad...'

'I'll ask her when I'm ready,' Larry replied in an even tone. 'Give her a chance to settle down and feel at home with us, Father.'

'Bah, you're wastin' time—' Alf broke off as Kitty entered the bedroom. 'Here she is like the breath of fresh air come to brighten us up...'

'Hello,' Kitty said and smiled at him. 'I hear you are feeling better?'

'Ah, I am that,' Alf agreed with a cheeky grin. 'Anyone who thought Alf Norton was on his last legs should think again. I'll be back down in the yard tellin' yer all what to do afore yer know it...'

'Good,' Kitty said and nodded. 'That's as it should be.'

Larry looked at her. 'Now that Father is better, I'm thinkin' that maybe we'll take a walk out on Sunday afternoon, Kitty. Perhaps have tea somewhere?'

'Oh yes, that would be nice,' Kitty said. She looked at Alf. 'That is the second invitation to tea on Sunday I've had today...' Her eyes met Larry's and she gave him a naughty smile. 'I said no to him, though.'

Alf went into a cackle of laughter and then choked. Kitty hurried to give him a glass of water and he winked at her. 'That's right, lass,' he said. 'You tell him – the slowcoach...'

'And who asked you then?' Larry said, looking a little peeved, even though he knew he was being teased.

'A customer,' Kitty told him. 'He came in to thank me for looking after his shy sister – and then asked me to tea with them both...'

'Why didn't you go?' Larry asked, his eyes watching her intently.

'If you don't know the answer to that, you're a daftie,' Alf chortled.

'I'll let you guess,' Kitty said and smiled. 'Now, I'm going down to help Mariah. I think that stew is almost ready...' She gave them both a cheeky look and went back down to the kitchen.

21

It was late that evening when Ben parked his car in his garage, then closed and locked the door. As he moved towards the house, he sensed a presence, but before he could look round, he felt something cold pressed into the back of his neck and knew it was a gun. A shudder of fear went through him, all kinds of horrific pictures rushing into his mind. 'Who are you?' he asked. 'What do you want?'

'You've nothing to fear as long as you don't look round,' the voice said, as whoever it was pressed the gun barrel deeper into Ben's neck. 'You made a mistake, Mr Harper, and now you need to put it right.'

'Yes, I know. What do you want?' Ben repeated; his mind flew to Sally and the children – were they safe or had something bad happened to them? 'My family—'

'Is safe,' the guttural voice rasped, the gun jabbing again. 'Shut up and listen. You know some people. Americans. They want someone and they want him alive...'

'Yes.' Ben's nerves tingled, his mind racing. Could he turn and overpower whoever was holding the gun or would it be foolish to try? 'You obviously know it all – tell me what I need to do.'

'Tell these friends of yours to go to the warehouse at the East India

Docks tomorrow at midnight – the one that is scheduled for demolition. They will find a package neatly trussed up for them.'

'Is— is he dead?' Ben croaked.

There was a harsh laugh. 'His death would cause a gang war. It suits us if he simply disappears, but it could be arranged if need be. Tell your friends that if they don't collect him, they will find a dead body when the warehouse is demolished.'

'Yes, I will tell them,' Ben said, suppressing a shudder. He took a deep breath. 'What about me and my family and friends when this is over?'

'We're not interested in them or you – and you have a *friend* looking out for you. Just don't interfere in our business again or that might change.'

'What do you mean – a friend looking out for me?' Ben asked, pushing his luck.

'Shut up! You've been told all you need to know. Walk towards your house and don't look back or you will wish you hadn't.'

'Right, understood.' Ben breathed deeply, trying to calm his nerves. Despite the reassurance that he wasn't at risk, he half expected the gun to fire as he walked away, but it didn't happen. Of course it wouldn't. They needed him to speak to his contacts.

At the back door of his house, he risked a glance towards the garage, but the light overhead showed there was no one there. He knew whoever it was had probably melted away into the night the moment he'd started to walk.

Unlocking the kitchen door with a hand that shook slightly, he went in and leaned against it for a moment before relocking it. Not that a locked door would keep a man like the one he'd just encountered out. He breathed deeply, his thoughts whirring.

Ben knew he needed to make some phone calls. The man who had held a gun to his neck was British. No doubt a hard man who worked for whoever ruled the powerful gang that controlled most of London's under-world. They wanted the American gone, back where he came from, but they didn't want a turf war. The American had allies and his brutal death might easily result in open warfare on the streets of London.

Ben shook his head to clear it. Had it really happened? It was the kind of thing you read about or watched in gangster movies. He would never have imagined it happening here in this quiet residential area –

except that he knew Beth had also been threatened. Beth and her children...

'Sally...?' Ben moved swiftly towards the sitting room she favoured, noticing with relief the light shining beneath it. 'Sally...?' His heart caught as he saw her leaning back in the chair and he moved swiftly towards her. She had fallen asleep waiting up for him. 'Oh, Sally, my love...' he choked as she opened her eyes and looked at him.

'Ben?' she said sleepily, and then as she came fully awake and saw the look in his eyes, 'What is wrong?'

'It's nothing...' he said, desperately concealing both his fear and his relief at finding her peacefully asleep. 'I'm sorry I am so late. I had a meeting that just dragged on and on...'

'A political meeting,' Sally said. 'If you're selected as a candidate, I expect there will be a lot of late-night meetings.'

'Yes, perhaps,' he said. 'I know it's late – but would you be a darling and make me some sandwiches and coffee? I have to make some phone calls—'

'And you want me out of the way,' Sally finished, looking at him anxiously. 'You're upset, Ben. I won't ask you until you've done what you need to do, but then I want to know.' She smiled. 'Smoked salmon and cream cheese all right?'

Ben nodded and she went off to the kitchen. He sat down, drew the phone towards him and started to dial. He'd been given a number he could dial at any time and he just hoped it worked...

* * *

'So,' Sally said as they sat eating sandwiches and drinking coffee some twenty minutes later, 'are you going to tell me what happened that made you look as if you'd seen a ghost?'

'If I do, I don't want you feeling scared—'

'Now you have to tell me,' she gasped. 'What happened?'

'A man put a gun to my head and gave me some instructions...' Ben saw the shock in her eyes. 'They want rid of the American who has been muscling in on their patch. Don't worry, they aren't interested in any of us...'

'Ben!' Sally stared at him in horror. 'Oh, my poor darling. How horrid for you. You must have been terrified something had happened to us.' She reached for his hand and kissed it.

'Yes, sick to my stomach,' he admitted. 'Thank God it was only the American gangster they wanted rid of... but he assures me we have a friend, though I have no idea what he meant.'

'Yes, that makes sense.'

'You don't sound surprised...?' Ben said, staring at her in bewilderment.

'I'm not actually,' Sally replied with a smile. 'Beth was told something similar. She hasn't dared to tell Jack, because he is still so angry, but she knows who the friend is – and so do I, though not as well as she does.'

'I might have known you would take it in your stride,' Ben said and laughed in relief, suddenly light-headed. 'Oh my God, Sally. I have never been as scared in my life – even during the war. I thought I was going to die and I was frightened you and the kids might already be dead – but they just wanted me to give a message to my contacts.'

'Which you have done,' Sally said and he nodded. 'It was a nasty experience for you and I'm glad I didn't know it was happening – but, hopefully, this will see the end of it as far as we're concerned.'

Ben reached for the glass of whisky beside him. 'I've been trying to cut down on this,' he said, 'but I need one tonight.'

'One won't hurt,' Sally said and squeezed his hand. Then, reflectively, 'I suppose they thought that to simply kill the American would cause a gang war. I think the people who spoke to you this evening run most of the crime in London's gangland, but there are others. One of them is a gentleman; he owns a gambling club and likes girls, if you know what I mean, but since he met the American, they've been planning to move in on another club. So the big boss decided they wanted him out of the way – and you were useful.'

'That is exactly right,' Ben said staring at her in amazement. 'I ask myself how you know such things – but then, you seem to know everything...' He raised his brows at her.

'Beth and I had a long chat,' Sally replied. 'Her friend told her an awful lot – far more than she actually related to me, I think, but I worked much of it out for myself. The friend isn't one of them, Ben – at least he isn't a criminal, but he knows them very well. He must have some influence because he asked for Beth to be protected and she has been ever since that incident. She was told that no one would be allowed to get near enough to harm her in future.'

'Handy to have friends in the right places,' Ben remarked drily. 'My God, Sally. I never expected to be so close to the criminal fraternity...' He frowned and rubbed at the bridge of his nose. 'The worst of it is I know I brought all this on us. I should never have agreed to let them place Lucas at the restaurant – poor devil.'

'Yes,' Sally said soberly and shivered. 'He never stood a chance once they knew who he was. I hope the people you contacted do their job and get this wretched American out of the country.'

'I've been told that if he is there in the warehouse, he will be on a government gunboat before morning and on his way back to face charges and imprisonment, unless he cooperates with them.'

'That's kidnapping, I suppose,' Sally reflected. 'Is it legal for them to do that, even if he is a criminal?'

'Probably not,' Ben said with a shrug, 'But that is their worry and I couldn't care less. I just want this over and done with.'

'Poor Ben,' Sally murmured with sympathy. 'I know you feel wretched about this whole thing – and I'm afraid Jack may not forgive us even if the danger is past. Beth says she has never known him to be so angry. She is upset, because she believes he is determined to leave London altogether.'

'I hope that he will forgive me once I am able to tell him that it is over. I shall give him my word that I shall never make decisions concerning the restaurant without his permission again.'

'Yes, I do think you must – and you must apologise, Ben.' Sally gave him a severe look and he inclined his head.

'I already tried, but he wouldn't listen.'

'He was worried to death about Beth and the children. Once he knows for sure it is all over, he will come round, I am certain.'

'I hope you're right.' Ben smiled and reached out to kiss her. 'I don't know what I would do without you, Sally. If Jack had endangered your life, I would have been ready to murder him – so I know he must hate me.'

'He is angry, but I doubt he hates you, not truly,' Sally said and held out her hand. 'Let's go to bed, my darling. It is late and you're tired.'

'Yes, I am,' he agreed. 'I don't think late meetings agree with me. Maybe I am not cut out to be a politician – it seemed to me this evening they all talked a load of drivel.'

Sally laughed. 'Think about it in the morning when you're not tired,' she said. 'It will all seem better then.'

* * *

'How do you expect me to believe that?' Jack said furiously as, the next morning, Ben explained what had happened. 'Why should I take *your* word for anything?'

'I know I made a mistake,' Ben replied, not letting himself get angry. Jack was entitled to let his feelings out. 'I thought it would all be fine – never imagined it could cause so much trouble or a man's death. But I've been assured that nothing will happen to your family or mine.'

'By a bloody criminal!' Jack exploded. 'Do you think I want to be beholden to that fraternity? My God, Ben. What the hell do you think you're playing at?'

Ben was silent for a moment, then, 'I had a gun stuck in the back of my neck as the message was delivered. He could have killed me – he could have killed the man they wanted out of the way – but he did neither. He seems to have his own code of honour. Believe me, I don't like it. If I could go back and do things differently, I would – but it might still have happened. We were looking for a new head waiter and you can't tell me you didn't approve of Lucas. He was efficient and polite, a good worker. You didn't even suspect he wasn't what he professed to be until I told you.'

'Damn you!' Jack suddenly punched Ben full in the face. Taken by surprise, the blow landed square and sent him flying. He fell hard, hitting his head against the edge of a table, and passed out. 'Oh my God! Ben...' Jack cried and bent over him, 'Speak to me. Please, don't be dead.' Jack felt sick as he looked down at his friend and partner, the anger draining out of him to be replaced by a dreadful fear that he might have killed him.

Ben didn't move, even though he spoke to him several times. Jack bent over him, pressing an ear to his chest. There was a heartbeat and his chest was rising and falling, but the colour was ebbing from his skin and his pulse was slow. Getting to his feet, Jack went swiftly to telephone for a doctor, his heart sinking. He'd acted out of anger, pushed beyond bearing, but he hadn't meant to kill Ben. If he died...

Jack shook his head. He didn't dare to think of the consequences. He already felt the guilt of Lucas' death deeply; it was a part of his anger, knowing that by acting so precipitately he had caused a man to die. Yet even that was nothing compared to what could happen now. Beth would never forgive him...

22

Beth heard the knock at her front door and went to answer it. She stared at Sally in surprise, seeing her strained, pale face. 'What is the matter?' she asked. 'Sally, dearest, come in...'

'I can't stay,' Sally said, stepping just inside the hall. 'I am on my way to the hospital, but I had to come. There has been an incident. Ben is unconscious and I need to get there, but I had to tell you... Jack knocked him to the floor and the police are involved...'

'Oh my God,' Beth said, her heart catching with fright. 'How could he? I can't believe he would do it... after Ben went to the restaurant to tell him it was all over and apologise. Why would he?' Her eyes filled with tears. 'I'm so sorry, Sally. I don't know what to say. I can't believe it! What if...?' But she couldn't finish. She couldn't speak the words, *if Ben dies...* though they were in her head.

'I know. It is too awful to think about,' Sally said with a catch in her voice. 'I am so sorry, Beth. I have to go – but I wanted you to hear it from me, because you are my dearest friend.' She caught back a sob. 'We will talk later – when I can...' With that, she was back out of the door and getting into her car.

Beth was too stunned to think clearly. Ben unconscious in hospital and her husband responsible. What had he done? What if Ben died? Jack could be arrested for murder...

Beth caught back her cry of distress as Timmy pulled at her arm. He'd been a little bit sick earlier that morning so she'd kept him away from school, though his elder brother had returned. She turned to scoop him up in her arms, hugging him to her as she tried to control her tears. The thought of what might happen filled her with dread. Sally could lose her husband and Beth could lose hers too.

What should she do next? Beth's thoughts whirled in confusion. Sally had told her the police were involved. Had Jack already been arrested? How could she find out?

She took Timmy back to the kitchen and gave him a Rich Tea biscuit while she tried to think what she ought to do. If she took Timmy to her father-in-law, she could go to— where? Was Jack at a police station or the hospital? He must be worried sick...

She had just decided that she would go to Bert and ask him for help when she heard her front door open and someone enter. She ran through to the hall and saw Jack standing there. He looked dreadful, his eyes meeting hers with a look that sent fear coursing through her.

'Is Ben...?' she whispered and he shook his head.

'No, but he is still unconscious. The police advised me to come home and stay away from the hospital. I have explained it was an accident, but they didn't believe half of what I told them. I've been warned that if he... if he dies, I could be facing a charge of either murder or manslaughter...'

Jack moved past her into the sitting room and sat down, burying his face in his hands. Beth went to him, putting her hands on his shoulders. She felt a deep sob of grief go through him and then he looked up at her.

'I've wrecked our lives,' he said brokenly. 'I've thrown it all away, Beth. I was so angry. Ben tried to explain, to tell me it was all over, but I wouldn't listen. I know he was right. It was my fault that man died but... I was so frightened of losing you and the kids and now I shall—'

'Don't!' Beth commanded. 'Stop right there, Jack. You didn't kill that man – a gangster did. Ben put him at risk by agreeing to the whole thing and you had a right to be angry with Ben, but you shouldn't have hit him.'

'Do you think I don't know that?' Jack riposted and then shook his head. 'Forgive me, Beth. I don't know what I'm saying or doing. I can't believe I was so damned stupid. I never meant to hurt him. It was gut reaction to something he said...' He choked back a sob. 'If I go to prison... if—' But he wasn't allowed to finish.

'No! It won't happen,' Beth said fiercely. 'We'll get the best lawyers. It was an accident. You didn't mean to hit him that hard...'

'He struck his head on a table as he fell...'

'Were there witnesses?' Beth asked, but he shook his head.

'It was early. The staff hadn't arrived. I left before they did... with the ambulance. The doctor had his own private ambulance and it was arranged quickly. I left the restaurant closed.'

'You went to the hospital with Ben... but the police...'

'Doctor Morgan said it was his duty to inform them. Someone came to the hospital and took the details.' Jack looked up at her. 'I told the constable that we'd argued over something to do with the restaurant and I struck him... that he hit his head as he fell... not the rest of it. It was too complicated...' He met her anxious gaze. 'I am sure they think I meant to kill him...'

'Why would you have got a doctor and gone with him to the hospital if you wanted him dead?' Beth said and stroked his head. Then she knelt down beside him, gazing up at him. 'I know you, Jack. You were angry, but Ben is your friend. I'm safe, the children are safe. I know you like and respect Ben in your heart.'

'Yes, I do,' Jack replied wretchedly. 'Will he ever forgive me? If he gets over this – I don't know what harm he may have suffered...'

'Please God he won't suffer permanent damage.'

'But if he does...' A severe blow to the head could be fatal or cause all kinds of problems.

Beth was silent for a moment, but she knew she had to stay strong. Jack couldn't think clearly; he was too overcome with remorse and fear. She straightened her shoulders, looking into his eyes. 'We will face that when we get to it,' Beth told him. 'I think you have to go back to work, Jack. You have customers and commitments – and when Ben recovers, he'll want his restaurant still running.'

Jack sat back, his gaze meeting hers. 'Yes, I know that's all I can do – for now. If the police arrest me, better it's there than here for the children to witness...' He looked up and saw Timmy was watching from the doorway and beckoned him forward, pulling the little boy into his arms for a hug, his agonised eyes meeting Beth's over the child's head. 'Will you forgive me?'

'Nothing to forgive,' she said and kissed his brow, then took Timmy from him, smiling into his wondering eyes. 'Daddy had a pain in his head, but he's all better now – aren't you, Daddy?' Her gaze met Jack's. 'You have to be for all our sakes, Jack.'

'Yes. Yes, I'll be all right now,' Jack said and smiled at his son. He fished in his pocket for a shilling. 'That's for you to buy sweets for you and your brother.'

Timmy's face lit up and he took the coin, looking at his mother. 'Can we buy sweeties now?'

'In a little while,' Beth said. 'We'll go and see Grandad and Grandma Vera, shall we? We can get some sweeties on the way there.'

Jack stood up. His face was still grave but she knew he had conquered his panic. He would face whatever came, as Beth would. She was praying hard inside that Ben would be all right. He had to be.

* * *

Beth spent the afternoon playing with her children at her father-in-law's home. She didn't tell him what had happened, because there was no point in distressing Bert unless she was forced to by further developments. He was worried enough over Vera.

'You still haven't heard the results of the tests then?' she said and he shook his head.

'Vera went to the doctor this morning,' he told her. 'Nothing has come in yet, so he is going to chase it up...' Bert frowned. 'Why can't they tell us one way or the other?'

'Perhaps it is good news that they haven't been in touch,' Beth suggested. 'I would have thought they would let you know quickly if the news was bad.'

'Yes, perhaps you're right,' he said and looked more cheerful.

Vera entered then, carrying a heavy tray of tea and cakes for the children. Bert rushed to take it from her, but she waved him away.

'I can still carry a tray, Bert,' she told him and smiled at Beth. 'It's lovely to see you all – but I thought you were going to see that friend of yours this afternoon?'

'Sally? Yes, I was... but she had to go out. She is always so busy...' Beth lied, avoiding the older woman's curious gaze.

'I suppose so,' Vera agreed and handed her a cup of tea. 'She does a lot of the buying for the store, doesn't she, as well as her charity work?'

'There are other buyers,' Beth said. 'But she oversees it all – and does all the buying for at least four departments herself. It is a lot of responsibility – especially with the children too.'

'I don't know how she does it,' Vera said. 'I suppose her husband helps with a lot of stuff?'

'Yes, I think Ben took over the general running of things after the war – but they have managers and supervisors, so he only makes the big decisions really.' Beth managed to keep her tone neutral but the thought flashed into her head that Sally would be devastated if Ben was no longer around to make those decisions.

'Is anything wrong, Beth love?' Vera looked at her oddly. 'You don't seem quite yourself...'

'Oh, just a slight headache,' Beth replied. 'It will go...'

'You should see a doctor if it persists,' Vera said kindly and Beth promised she would.

She took her leave after tea and walked to the Underground station, the children happily munching sweets they'd bought on the way. Jerry was nowhere to be seen when she got off some minutes later. It was unusual for him not to have his stall there and Beth wondered if he was all right. She would call to see Bella when she could. It just depended on what happened next...

* * *

Beth had finished putting the children to bed when the telephone rang. Her heart was thundering in her chest as she went to answer it. Her first breathy hello was answered by Sally.

'Beth, I wanted to tell you...' Beth's heart skipped a beat. 'Ben has recovered consciousness – but he can't remember what happened. He can't remember much...' Sally's voice was croaky with distress. 'He looked at me strangely. He knew I was his wife – but he thinks it is still wartime; he didn't know he has a son, just a daughter...'

'Oh, Sally...' Beth's eyes stung with tears of relief that Ben was alive. 'What did the doctors say? Will his memory return?'

'They seem to think it is temporary,' Sally replied. 'Yes, they say he was lucky and don't think there is any actual brain damage.'

'Oh thank God!' Beth exclaimed. 'I am so glad, Sally. I'm so sorry that it happened – and Jack is devastated by what he did. He didn't mean to hurt Ben so badly. He hit his head on a table as he went down.'

'Of course I know that. Jack would never have meant to harm him; it was just a stupid quarrel,' Sally said, but her voice caught on a sob. 'Oh, Beth, what a mess. I wish none of it had happened.'

'Yes, so do I,' Beth agreed. 'I wish I could help you.'

'I just have to be patient,' Sally replied. 'Ben was really odd – it was a bit frightening. He didn't seem like himself at all.'

'Oh, Sally. I am so sorry—' Beth's voice caught with emotion. 'I don't know what to say to you...'

'I don't blame you or Jack,' Sally said. 'Ben was in the wrong from the start. He knew it – but—' She gave a little sob. 'Sorry. I'll talk to you another time...'

Sally put the phone down and Beth felt herself sag against the wall. She was relieved that Ben hadn't died but worried that he might be permanently damaged or changed. One heard about that sort of thing, but it was just too awful to contemplate.

Walking into the sitting room, she sat in her chair and cried. Sometimes, life just wasn't fair.

23

'This is nice,' Kitty said, glancing round the small tea shop that Sunday afternoon. It was a pleasantly warm day in May, with just a slight breeze in the air. Situated in a quiet area not far from London Bridge, there were baskets of flowers hanging above the windows and tubs of pansies and irises by the door. Inside, it was a cosy room, the furniture all a pleasantly mellowed dark oak; blue and white china was set out on dressers at one end and each little table was dressed with a lace cloth and a tiny bowl of scented flowers. 'I've never been taken to tea like this before, Larry.' She gave an excited little giggle of pleasure, because she knew he'd chosen it carefully for her. 'Thank you for bringing me here.'

His cheeks tinged with pink as he met her smiling eyes. 'I wanted it to be nice,' he said, breaking off as the waitress arrived with their tea. There was a three-tiered stand with tiny sandwiches, scones with jam and cream and on the top tier slices of dark fruit cake. The teapot was white china patterned with roses to match the cups, saucers, plate, sugar bowl and milk jug.

'It's a change for the china to match,' he said, smiling wryly. 'Father never bothered with a set. Even when Ma was alive, we had a hotchpotch of china that didn't ever match but all had history and a quality about it.' He frowned but Kitty laughed.

'I love all the different cups and saucers in your house, and the way your dad can tell you what everything is,' she told him truthfully. 'They are all different, all precious pieces, and they all have a story to tell – or your dad does, about them.' Alf was recovering well, getting stronger each day, and he'd started to come downstairs again now that his leg had recovered its feeling, negotiating the stairs one at a time on his bottom. One hand still wasn't able to hold much, but he hadn't been permanently paralysed and they were all thankful for his steady recovery.

Larry nodded. 'Aye, I know. Father is a clever one in his own way...' he hesitated, then, 'You must know I think the world of you, Kitty, but...' His eyes met hers thoughtfully. 'I took you to Father's house because you were upset and didn't know what to do, but I know it's not fitting for you. It's not what I want for you, lass.' He shook his head ruefully. 'You've got a decent job now and you could find someone much better than me – a gentleman perhaps...'

'Oh, Larry, don't be daft,' she said. 'Just because my mother behaved as if she was Lady Muck doesn't mean your family isn't good enough for me. Surely you know I love Mariah and Alf? I have never been as happy as I am now.' He must know she loved him too, because she was sure he could see it in her eyes.

Larry's expression didn't change, his eyes holding hers. 'I've got my own little house – or I shall have once I've finished paying for it. I'd hoped to take you there, Kitty – if you thought you'd like to be my wife – but now, with Father ill...'

'I am happy to live where we are,' Kitty told him. Her heart did a little skip of joy. It wasn't the most romantic of proposals, but then, she hadn't expected him to go down on his knees. He was a quiet man, even shy, at least where she was concerned, and she liked that; she didn't want extravagant gestures. She just wanted to be loved. She reached her hand across the table to touch his. 'Are you asking me to be your wife, Larry? Only I'm not quite sure...' Her eyes twinkled at him naughtily as she tipped her head to one side. 'Are you saying you love me and want me to be yours forever and ever?'

'You know I am,' he said, a flash of humour in his eyes. 'I think you're wonderful – but I'm not much good with words, Kitty. I love you with all my heart and always will. I very much want you to be my wife, but I know you deserve better. I'm not good enough for you...' The look of adoration that accompanied his words was sufficient for her. Larry would never be the most romantic lover, but he would be constant, and to a girl who needed to be loved and protected that meant so much.

'I think I should be the judge of that,' Kitty said and gave a little gurgle of laughter. 'Don't you know I love you, Larry? Can't you see it in my eyes? Or are you as daft as Alf says?'

He was just sipping his tea and gave a snort of laughter; the tea went the wrong way and he choked and coughed, attracting raised eyebrows from an elderly couple two tables away.

Kitty giggled, a hint of mischief in her eyes. Larry shook his head at her and then reached for her hand, raised it to his lips and kissed it. He held it tightly, just smiling in a bemused way, seeming slightly dazed.

'Does that mean you will?' he asked when he could talk again.

'Will what?' she said promptly. 'You haven't asked me anything yet.'

'Marry me...' Larry blurted. 'Please say yes, Kitty, my dearest. It's killing me!'

'Yes, I think I'd better,' Kitty teased. 'Otherwise Alf will never give you a moment's peace.'

Larry laughed out loud. 'He'd have my guts for garters if I let you slip away,' he said. 'You're the best thing that has happened to me and my family. Mariah thinks the world of you, Kitty.'

'I love her too,' Kitty said and her smile dimmed. 'You offered me a home and I found a family. I'd never truly had that before, Larry. I loved my dad and my mother too, as much as she allowed. I don't think she ever wanted me, not really – and once Dad became ill and we had to move she seemed to withdraw completely.' She frowned. 'I'm not twenty-one until next year, Larry. We shall need her permission if we want to marry before then – and I'm not sure she will give it to us...'

'I will talk to her,' Larry promised. 'If she is stubborn and won't give it, we'll have to wait, but she can't stop you wearing this.' He reached into his jacket pocket and took out a small blue velvet box, which he opened to reveal a gold ring set with five small stones – three diamonds and two rubies, in a wide band. Taking it from the box, he slipped it onto the third finger of her left hand.

'Oh, that is beautiful. I have never seen anything like it,' Kitty exclaimed, turning her hand this way and that to admire the way the stones flashed, a little awed that he had given her such a precious thing. The ring fit her finger beautifully. 'Thank you so much. I love it.'

'It is a hundred years old and it's rubies and diamonds. I found it in a jewellers in Regent Street and I thought it would suit you. I would like to give you so much more,' Larry said, 'and I shall one day. The junkyard is Father's life and his home, and for the moment it must be ours too – but I intend to get on in the world, Kitty. One day we shall have a nice house with a garden for our children to play in.' He closed his big fist over her small hand and then lifted it to kiss her palm. 'I might not always say the right things, Kitty – but I'll work hard and I'll make a good life for us, I promise.'

'I know.' She smiled, a gentle sweet smile that spoke volumes. 'I hope my mother is reasonable. I want to be your wife as soon as possible, Larry.' She hesitated then, 'Will you mind if I keep working at Harpers – just until we start a family?'

'Nay, lass. Why should I?' His slow easy smile warmed her. 'You've a good job there – and I'm not one of these men who want to dictate how their wives live. It's only right you should enjoy your job for as long as you wish.'

'You are a wonderful, kind man.' Kitty looked at him lovingly. 'I didn't know what it was to be truly happy and free until you took me to live with your family.'

Larry nodded and popped a tiny cucumber sandwich in his mouth, swallowing it with one chew. He didn't look impressed and Kitty giggled, knowing that he liked a thick slice of Mariah's fresh-cooked bread with a hunk of cheese.

'They look nicer than they taste,' she said in a low voice.

Larry's eyes glowed with laughter. 'What taste?' he asked. 'Shall we pay the bill and go and tell the family the good news?'

'Yes, please,' Kitty said. She had eaten two sandwiches and a scone, but Larry had hardly touched the food. 'I am going to take the scones and cake home, though.' She took a clean paper serviette and wrapped the cakes and the second scone. 'I'll pop these into Bella on the way.'

Larry nodded. 'Aye she'd like that.' He summoned the waitress and paid their bill and they left.

Kitty tucked her arm through his. 'It was a nice place, Larry. I enjoyed being taken there.'

'Aye,' he said but didn't sound convinced. 'Mariah could put on a better tea with her eyes shut.'

'Yes, she probably could,' Kitty agreed. 'She is a wonderful cook.'

'I wish she would have her own husband and family to cook for one day...'

'If she wants, she can live with us...?' Kitty suggested, knowing that he worried for his sister if their father died.

'I know you wouldn't mind, but Mariah is too independent,' he replied with a shrug. 'I am hoping that she'll get together with Arnie. He hasn't given up hope of her, though she says she won't have him because she'd have to live with his mother. I dare say the real reason was that she'd never leave Father, but if anything happens to him... But we'll face that when we come to it...'

* * *

Larry dropped Kitty off outside Bella's house. She got out and went inside. She didn't knock and was surprised when she saw a man standing near the fireplace. Kitty had never seen the man before, though there was something familiar about him. He glared at her as though he thought her entry an intrusion.

'Oh, I am sorry, Bella,' she said apologetically. 'I should've knocked. I didn't know you had company. I just—'

'You don't ever need to knock at my door,' Bella said, interrupting her. 'No don't hurry away. This one is leaving.'

'Ma...' the man said, a note of annoyance in his voice. 'You haven't answered me. It's a lovely place and you'd be well looked after... I've plenty of money and I'll look after you if you let me.'

'You know my answer right enough. If I've told yer once, I've told yer a hundred times,' Bella replied. 'This is my home and its where I'm stopping until they carry me out in a box.'

'Be damned to you then!' the man said gruffly and glared at her and then Kitty. He took some money from his pocket, slammed it down on the table and then stomped off, shutting the door behind him with a bang.

'Come back, Tel. I don't want your money!' Bella cried, but the door remained closed. She shook her head, a strange look in her eyes. 'Put that money in the box on the mantel, Kitty, there's a love.'

Kitty gathered up what looked to be about twenty pounds in notes and coins and put it in the tin box on the mantel. There was already quite a bit of cash in there. She looked curiously at Bella. Why did she keep all this in a box when she could have spent it on good food for herself and Jerry?

'He's my eldest,' Bella said, answering her unspoken questions. 'He got into bad ways after his dad died. I told him to give up what he was doin' and get a proper job – but he wouldn't. So I told him not to come home while he was working for that lot...' Bella shook her head. 'Bad men, Kitty. I won't touch his money or go into the fancy place he wants me to, says they'd look after me, but I'm better off here with me friends. That money will stay in that tin until he takes it back – or they use it to bury me.' She gave a sniff of anger and then shook her head. 'So, what have you come for then?'

'Larry took me to tea – and I brought some of the cakes back for you.'

Bella's face lit up. 'That's a kind girl you are, Kitty love. Pop the kettle on the stove and make me a pot of tea, will yer? I'll 'ave them cakes now.'

Kitty did as she was asked and set the cake and scone on a plate, putting it beside Bella on an occasional table with a brass top. She brought a tray of tea through and set it down beside her.

Bella caught her left hand and looked at it, grinning at her in delight. 'So he found the courage to ask then?' she said with a little cackle of laughter. 'When is it to be?'

'That depends on whether my mother will sign for me to be married,' Kitty said with a sigh of regret. 'We didn't part on good terms and she despises Larry and his family.'

'Your ma is the daft one,' Bella said forcefully. 'A lovely lass like you – and she hadn't the sense to see how lucky she was.'

'I don't think she saw it that way,' Kitty replied sadly. 'I don't think she loves me, Bella. I'm not sure she ever did...'

'A mother always loves her children,' Bella said and there was sadness in her eyes now. 'Even when they don't deserve it...'

Kitty bit her lip. Bella had been upset by the visit of her eldest son, even though she'd tried to shrug it off. 'Perhaps some mothers are not as soft-hearted as you, Bella.'

'Me? I'm as tough as old boots,' Bella retorted, but the sadness was still in her eyes. Her sharp tongue hid a kind heart, Kitty already knew that, but until now she hadn't guessed how difficult Bella's life had been. She'd been left to bring up two boys alone after her husband had died – but while one son was devoted to making her life as easy as possible, the other one... Well, Kitty didn't really know anything about the mysterious Tel, so she couldn't judge.

'I'd best get back,' she said. 'Larry will wait until I get there to tell them about our engagement.'

'Good luck to yer, love,' Bella said and her smile was back in place. 'If anyone deserves it, you do.'

24

'Is there any change?' Beth asked when she rang Sally on Monday evening. 'Have you been to visit Ben today?'

'Yes, I spent most of the afternoon with him,' Sally said. 'He was pleased to see me and talks of coming home soon – but he thought we still lived at the flat. When I explain all the changes, he just stares at me so oddly...' She caught her breath. 'I don't know how to be with him, Beth. One minute he seems just the same as always and then the next he goes blank and stares into space as if he isn't quite with me. It... it frightens me...' She swallowed a sob of distress. 'What am I going to do if he never gets his memory back?'

'I wish I knew,' Beth told her. 'It must be so difficult for you, Sally. I am so very sorry...'

'It isn't your fault,' Sally said quickly. 'In a way, it is Ben's own fault, though I wish Jack hadn't hit him...'

'He shouldn't have lost his temper,' Beth agreed. 'He knows that and feels wretched over what happened. It was just a gut reaction, because he'd been so worried about me and the kids.'

'I know – and Ben understood that... At least he did after that terrifying incident the other night. When he felt that gun at his nape and thought that I might already be dead and the children, too. He told me he was so scared for us that he couldn't think straight.'

'Jack has been worrying like that for weeks,' Beth confirmed. 'I think something in his head just exploded when Ben spoke to him. It was such a stupid thing to do – and I feel terrible over it, Sally. We've always been such good friends...'

'We are still good friends,' Sally said firmly. 'I shan't blame you, whatever happens, Beth. Please don't let it affect our friendship. I would hate it if this came between us.'

'It won't, of course, it won't,' Beth promised, but, in her heart, she knew that it might. If Ben's change of personality continued for a long time, it must cause resentment. Sally might not blame Beth, but she would probably blame Jack, even if she refused to admit it.

They talked some more, both being careful with the other's feelings. As she replaced the receiver at the end of their chat, Beth knew it had already affected them both. Ben's illness was there, hovering like a dark shadow, and in the end, it might very well destroy the close friendship that they both valued so much.

* * *

The next morning, Beth went to visit Bella using the Underground. She looked for Jerry, but he wasn't in his usual spot. Wondering where he'd got to, she decided she would ask his mother when they'd been to the clinic. It wasn't like the cheerful barrow boy not to be on his pitch for several days running.

Bella was pleased to see her and Beth had employed a taxicab to take them to the clinic. Bella huffed and puffed about the expense, but she settled in the comfortable car and stopped grumbling once they were on their way.

'Don't know why you do this fer me,' she remarked to Beth. 'Ain't got no reason ter care about an old woman like me.'

'I promised Jerry I would look out for you,' Beth replied. 'Besides, I like you.'

Bella sniffed but said no more for a few minutes, then, 'Jerry's gone off on a bit of business,' she remarked. 'Don't ask me what 'cos I ain't got no idea. He just said he'd be away for a few days.'

'I wondered why he wasn't at his pitch,' Beth said. 'I hope he won't be gone too long. He might lose his pitch if he neglects it.'

'Nah, he'll be home ternight,' Bella said. 'Might be there when we get back.' She nodded as the taxi drew up outside the clinic. 'Hope they offer us a cup of tea and a biscuit this time. I'm hungry. I ain't 'ad a good meal since my Jerry went orf – except for a bit of cake Kitty give me. She's a good girl that one. She will make that young Larry a good wife...' She grinned as Beth looked at her in surprise. 'Didn't know, did yer? They got engaged on Sunday.'

'Well that is lovely,' Beth said, feeling pleased.

* * *

Bella's ulcerated leg was pronounced much better. She was given another jar of ointment and bandages and told that she need not come to the clinic for three months; although her toes were still sore and painful, they didn't seem to have got any worse and the doctor said she might not need the operation she'd been told she ought to have.

She sniffed as they left the clinic shortly afterwards. 'Bloomin' lot never give us so much as a sniff of a biscuit – and my leg still hurts, whatever they say...'

'It does look much better and I think the ulcer has almost cleared up,' Beth said and looked at her. 'How about we get some fish and chips on the way to your home.'

Bella's eyes lit up. 'Now yer talkin',' she said. 'I love a bit of cod and chips, plenty of salt and vinegar.'

'Oh yes, of course,' Beth agreed. 'We'll get a fresh loaf and you can have some bread and butter too.'

'Ain't got no butter until Jerry gets back...'

'I'll get some butter, too,' Beth said and smiled. 'Do you have any tea, Bella – or shall I buy a packet and some milk?'

'Thanks, but I've got them,' Bella said and gave a crack of laughter. 'You're too soft, missus. I could wheedle anythin' out of yer if I tried.'

'Only what I want to give, Bella,' Beth said and looked at her straight. Then they both laughed.

'Yer all right,' Bella said. 'I'm glad Jerry asked Tel ter look out fer yer – I told 'im 'e shouldn't, but 'e done right.'

'Who is Tel?' Beth asked, but Bella shook her head. 'Don't explain if you'd rather not – but Jerry assured me a friend was looking out for me.'

'I told 'im not ter 'ave anythin' ter do with that lot and he mostly minds me – but he said yer were a good friend that needed lookin' after and he was right. He says some bit of bother yer 'ad is over now and there ain't no need to worry – but I ain't got no idea what he meant.'

Beth had a good idea but simply nodded and said no more. She had her suspicions about who Tel was and what he did, but Bella and Jerry were entitled to their secrets...

* * *

Having delivered Bella safely to her house and seen her settled with a large plate of hot food and a cup of tea, Beth made her way home via the Underground. She was thoughtful as she entered her house and put the kettle on. Both of her children were at school and the house seemed empty without them.

She made herself a light lunch of cheese and tomato sandwiches and had just sat down with a cup of tea when someone knocked at her door. She got up to answer it just as her father-in-law opened it and came rushing in. One look at his face told her there was something badly wrong.

'Dad?' she questioned, heart thudding. 'Is it Vera?'

'Did you know – did she tell you?' he demanded and his face was ashen. 'I didn't know until she collapsed and the doctor said she should be in hospital – that lump she had tests done on... it's cancer and she kept the results to herself, pretended she hadn't heard anything.'

'Oh, Dad, no,' Beth said as he sank down into a chair at the table and slumped forward, his face in his hands. She could feel the emotion pulsing through him as she placed a gentle hand on his shoulders. 'I had no idea. She kept it all to herself. Poor Vera. How frightened she must have been and yet she didn't tell us.'

'Didn't want us to worry, that's what she told me when they rushed her off to the London hospital.' He looked up at her then through tear-drenched eyes. 'She needs an operation... but it might have gone too far now...' He shook his head. 'Why didn't she tell me? I'd have been with her, looked after her – but she just tried to carry on, pretending it was getting better.'

'I should have noticed,' Beth said regretfully. 'I'm sorry, Dad. I've had a lot on my mind. I thought she would've told us if...' A sigh escaped her. 'I should've seen the changes...'

'You've had enough to think about,' Bert said gruffly. 'Jack told me he was in a bit of bother at the restaurant... hit Ben Harper...' Bert frowned. 'Daft thing to do. Mr Harper has been good to him. I told him he shouldn't have lost his temper no matter what they argued over.'

Beth realised that Jack had kept most of the details from his father and nodded. 'He realises that now, Dad. It has caused a lot of stress and problems, but Jack wasn't thinking straight.'

'I hope things get sorted and that Mr Harper recovers back to full health – but at the moment, I can only think about Vera!'

'Yes, of course, and that's all you need to think about, Dad,' Beth told him. She looked at him. 'Have you eaten?' He shook his head and she pushed her sandwiches towards him. 'Have these and I'll make some more – and drink this.' She poured him a cup of tea. 'Don't say you aren't hungry. You need to eat. It won't help Vera if you fall ill, now, will it?'

'No, suppose not...' He picked up a sandwich and took a bite. His eyes sought hers anxiously as she prepared another round for herself. 'I feel so lost, Beth. Not sure what to do... helpless.' A little shudder went through him. 'I lost Jack's mother to a fever. Never thought I'd marry again. I can't bear to think of Vera suffering a lingering death.'

'What did the doctor say when they took her to the hospital?'

'Said she hadn't helped her chances by leaving it so long, but... they will operate. Just depends whether it has spread too far now.'

'We can only wait and pray,' Beth told him. She sat down next to him and ate her lunch, though the food was tasteless and she had to force it down, but, as she'd told him, it wasn't an option not to eat. Beth had to keep strong and keep the family together. 'We'll need to pack some things for her and take them to the hospital. We might be able to see her for a few minutes.'

'Yes, that's what we need to do,' Bert agreed. 'She went off without anything – and I was in such a panic that all I could think of was to tell you.' He looked at her sadly. 'It's a good thing you're as strong as you are, Beth. I don't know what we'd do without you.'

Beth smiled, hiding her own fears and anxiety. After the strain of the past weeks, being threatened by a gunman and Jack's anger erupting into that silly incident with Ben, it would be only too easy to give into the tears. Beth couldn't do that. She had Jack and the children to think of, as well as Bert and Vera – and Sally too.

25

Sally stood outside the store in Oxford Street and studied the windows. They were immaculately dressed with a summertime theme, featuring lightweight clothes for ladies, gentlemen and children. One window scene depicted a family watching a game of cricket, another was a family having a picnic, showing off linen, hampers, as well as clothes and toys, and a bicycle – one of Ben's latest ideas for the store. All very in keeping with the values Harpers liked to be known for and yet somehow the magic was missing.

Sally frowned. Would Mr Marco ever return from the leave of absence? He'd told Ben he was going to France to spend some time with the family who had sheltered him during his time there in the war. When she'd asked how long he would be away, both he and Ben had been very vague.

'He is taking Pierre to see his family,' Ben had told her. 'They may stay for some months. He has been training young Simon to take his place at Harpers, so it shouldn't matter too much.'

Pierre was Mr Marco's adopted son, the child of his late wife. Pierre's father had been killed during the war and Mr Marco had often talked of returning to see the family who had sheltered him. Sally hadn't expected him to be away so long and she was a little annoyed that he hadn't let them know when, if ever, he would return. Perhaps she was being over-fussy, but for her there was something lacking in Harpers' windows and she wondered if they should look for a more experienced window dresser.

If only she could ask Ben what he thought. A sigh left her as she went inside. The store itself had never looked better. There were wonderful displays everywhere: cut glass and silver, stationery and fountain pens, cameras, walking sticks and umbrellas, leather goods and trinket boxes, vases and lamp standards, and the smell of gorgeous perfumes and toiletries wafted through the entire ground floor. Sally had told the young woman who worked on the cosmetic counter to spray a little of the tester each morning and it ensured that there was always a beautiful fragrance when you entered Harpers.

She walked towards the lift, smiling at the young man who operated it. Ernie's scarred face had healed quite a bit in recent years. Sally had arranged for him to have some special treatment and it had improved the look of the skin where he'd been badly burned.

'How is Mr Harper?' he asked as he delivered her to her office floor.

'Doing well, thank you. He may be coming home this afternoon or tomorrow. We're waiting to see what the doctors think.'

'That's good, Mrs Harper,' he nodded to her as she left the lift and walked to her office.

Sally had two appointments with representatives that morning, one from a fashion firm who had some new winter lines to show her, and one from a small bag business that had just started up. She tried to keep the stock fresh and so gave her time to new firms because it was only by looking at samples and handling them that she could be sure the merchandise would fit into her store. Hers and Ben's... Sally mentally corrected herself. There were times when she thought of it as hers, but Harpers belonged to Ben – and although she had a free hand with the stock she purchased, there were many decisions that only he could make. In the past, they had mostly discussed them, especially since the war, Ben listening to her advice more often than not – but when she'd tried to discuss a couple of problems while visiting the hospital, Ben had dismissed her worries.

'Leave it to me, Sally,' he'd told her. 'There's nothing that desperately needs attention just yet. I will sort it out when I get back.'

Sally had sensed a reserve in him. She felt that he was holding back, avoiding talking to her about anything important. She felt a coldness at her nape. Ben seemed to have withdrawn from her – bringing back memories of when he'd shut her out in the early years of their relationship. She had been falling in love with him and he'd been so withdrawn at the start... hiding his secret from her. Sally had believed she was just another employee to him, but she hadn't known about the wife who lingered between life and death in a twilight world in a hospital over in America. Only when that wife had sadly passed did Ben reveal his feelings to Sally... and now she had the same kind of sensation again, as if he had shut her out or was hiding his thoughts from her. Why would he do that?

Sally shook her head. No, she mustn't let her imagination take over. Ben was struggling to remember his life, so if he seemed strange at times, she had to accept it was the loss of memory, nothing more. The doctors were hopeful his memory would return in time, so she just had to be patient.

* * *

'Is there any change in Ben?' Beth asked hopefully when she called round to see Sally. 'How are you, Sally? You look tired?'

'I haven't been sleeping well,' Sally admitted with a sigh. 'Ben seems physically to be recovering but still— well, acting strangely. I know he has amnesia but...' She shook her head. 'The doctors want to keep him in a bit longer. Don't let's talk of my problems, Beth. How is Vera? Have you heard anything since they took her in?'

'I know they did an operation almost immediately...'

'Any news as to whether it was successful yet?'

'Not yet. Dad was going to visit this afternoon,' Beth replied. 'He is worried to death over her, of course. I just wish she'd told us sooner, instead of letting it drag on. I don't think she ever would if she hadn't collapsed. The doctors said it was strain. She'd been keeping it all inside and fretting.'

'She must have been terrified,' Sally said, looking at her sadly. 'Why do things have to be so complicated, Beth? All we want is a nice quiet life we can enjoy with our friends and families and these things keep happening...'

'You must try not to worry,' Beth told her, touching her hand in sympathy. 'I am sure Ben's memory will come back in time and then everything will be all right again.'

'But will it?' Sally asked. 'Supposing that bang on the head has changed his personality and he isn't the man I love any more...?' She sighed. 'No, I mustn't be foolish. I just don't want to lose all we had, Beth. We were so lucky...'

'You will be again,' Beth reassured, but her stomach clenched with nerves. If Ben had changed, things might not be the same ever – and that would affect her and Jack, though not as much as Sally. Sally's life would be torn to shreds. 'We just have to keep positive, Sally dearest. Jack is all over the place. One minute he is being apologetic, walking on eggs around me, and the next he goes into a broody mood and just stares at me. I know how much he regrets punching Ben.'

'It was Ben's fault. He should never have got involved in such a smoky affair. I doubt if any of it was legal. These Americans, whoever they were – Ben said some kind of police but higher up – they really had no right to pursue their man over here. I'm damned sure it wasn't legal for them to kidnap him and take him back to America. Even if he was a criminal, he had rights...'

'No, that all sounds very dubious,' Beth agreed. 'I just hope it is all finished and there are no repercussions.'

'Ben won't do anything like that again. I think he'd begun to worry about the consequences and was wondering how to get out of the mess when this English gang leader decided to take a hand. Without his intervention, we would still be looking over our shoulder the whole time.' Sally looked thoughtful. 'Do you have any idea who he was – the one who delivered the message at gunpoint?'

'No, none at all,' Beth replied, even though she was pretty certain she did know exactly who had looked out for them. If it had been Bella's eldest son Tel, she certainly wouldn't – couldn't – tell Sally, or anyone else. She'd been trusted with a dangerous secret and she would keep it to herself. 'I know he must be mixed up in unsavoury stuff – but he can't be all that bad. He looked after us – and he sorted the mess out for the Americans too.'

'Yes, that's fair enough,' Sally conceded. 'I'm not agreeing with the things they do – extortion, robbery, whatever – but it seems that they have their own values and this American didn't respect them, so they got rid of him.'

'Yes, it seems that way,' Beth said. She stood up and Sally stood too. They kissed each other's cheeks and Beth squeezed her hand. 'Don't worry too much, Sally. Ben will be home soon and it will be all right – because you'll find a way to make it work.'

Sally smiled and nodded. 'Yes, I expect I shall. I may see you tomorrow at Harpers, but if Ben comes home, I shall take some time off...' She hesitated, then, 'Take a look at the windows, Beth. Tell me what you think. I shan't say anything more. I'll let you make up your own mind.'

Beth nodded. 'I know what you mean, Sally. There has been something missing and it's Mr Marco's magic touch. Have you heard nothing from him – no word of when he plans to return?'

'He may have written to Ben, but he hasn't told me...' Sally drew a sharp breath. 'I think we shall have to find someone to take his job if he doesn't return soon. The windows are immaculate but dull...'

'Yes...' Beth laughed. 'It is the little touches of fun that Mr Marco does that make them so individual. They are fine as they are – as good as most big stores – but they used to have something extra.'

Sally nodded. 'We had small crowds waiting every time a new window was revealed. It is a while since I've seen that.'

'Oh well, I dare say you'll find someone to replace him if you try – but it was strange the way he just went off.'

'He told Ben he owed it to his friends who had looked after him in France,' Sally said. 'He's never told me for certain but I am pretty sure he worked as a spy and a go-between for the British government and French resistance fighters...'

'He met Sadie there, too – and Pierre has relatives, I suppose...' Beth shrugged. 'I must go, love. I want to be there for Dad when he gets back from the hospital. I told him to have his tea with us.'

'Then I mustn't keep you. I'll be in touch soon.'

Beth was thoughtful as she walked the few streets to her own home. Sally was very anxious, though trying to hide it. Beth hoped Ben would be allowed home shortly and that he would be well again soon.

26

Kitty spent a whole afternoon with a small group of customers: a mother, two daughters in their late teens, and their grandmother. Mrs Constance Fairweather was a wealthy widow and she had decided to take her daughter's two girls to France for a holiday – in the hope of meeting the right contacts. Both girls were slender and fair, pretty but not considered beauties, and both had already had a season in London. Neither had found a husband and since their parents did not consider it proper for them to have jobs, they had decided on the holiday.

'It will do the girls a power of good to see something of the world. You've brought them up to think of nothing but their appearance, Mildred,' Mrs Fairweather announced to her daughter, not caring whether Kitty heard every word. 'They'll never catch husbands unless you open their minds to more than the next pretty dress. I will teach them about life – and I dare say they may both come back with greater understanding... or perhaps even a ring on their finger.'

'Oh, Mama,' her daughter replied, looking flustered. 'I'm not sure I want them married off to foreigners...'

'Rather have them tied to your apron strings?' Mrs Fairweather said drily, then, giving Kitty a hard look, 'Don't you have something more sophisticated for Erica? She is twenty and doesn't look well in those insipid pastels. She needs bright colours – deep blue, red or emerald...'

'Well, we do have the Miss Susie range,' Kitty said. She had hesitated to show them the gorgeous evening gowns, because they were rather daring and dramatic for young women. But now she brought three dress from the range and held them up for the critical lady to see. One was a deep French blue with crystal embroidery on the straps, another an emerald satin with a very deep dip at the back, the third a crimson velvet.

'Yes, they look more interesting – try them on, Erica, and stop sulking. You will enjoy this trip, I promise you.'

Erica gave a little sniff and took the dresses off to try on.

The younger girl looked timidly at her grandmother. 'Which should I try on, Granny Constance?'

'The yellow silk will suit you well, as will the pansy blue satin – and that deep pink. You may try all of them.' Mrs Fairweather turned her sharp gaze on Kitty. 'We'll need shoes, hats, scarves, gloves, all the rest – can you have them brought to us, young woman? I do not wish to traipse all over the shop in search of something that may match or tone...'

'Yes, of course, madam,' Kitty said. She made some notes on her pad and summoned one of the salesgirls, giving it to her and explaining what she needed to bring first. 'Alice, ask Shirley to help you with the hats. If she isn't serving. she might bring them herself while you go to the shoe department.'

Mrs Fairweather nodded her approval, then turned her attention to her eldest granddaughter as she returned, looking absolutely stunning in the emerald evening gown. 'Yes, very much better.' She turned a sour look on her daughter. 'See, Mildred. Had you dressed them in colours that didn't turn their skin sallow, Erica would have caught that earl you were so keen on her marrying.'

'I didn't like him, Granny,' Erica spoke up suddenly. 'He did like me, but I put him off – he was too old.'

Mrs Fairweather gave a cackle of laughter. 'So she does have some gumption, after all.' A pleased expression settled over her face and she nodded to Kitty. 'Yes, we'll take that one. See what else you can find. The girls need at least four evening gowns each, though we shall buy some in

Paris. However, that better range of yours has something special about it – almost as good as Worth one might think and a lot less money.'

'Oh, Mama,' her daughter said faintly. 'Really, one doesn't want to flaunt one's wealth... and I thought that gown made Erica look older...'

'Since it's my wealth and I'm paying, you need not concern yourself,' her mother replied coldly. She smiled at her younger granddaughter, who had dutifully tried on the yellow silk. 'Yes, dearest, very pretty. Give it to the salesgirl to keep for you and try on some more...' She nodded her satisfaction. 'Some hats are arriving and shoes, I believe...' She glanced at Kitty with approval. 'Very efficient, young woman. If you are ever in need of work, you may apply to me – as a companion...'

Kitty hid her smile as she turned away. She thought it might be easier to work in a factory than to be all day in the company of this overbearing lady, but she was clearly in the mood for spoiling her granddaughters that day and that could only be good for Harpers.

* * *

Mrs Fairweather spent an inordinately large amount of money with them, much of it on the Miss Susie evening range, but also on evening shoes, pretty hats for their daywear and so many scarves and gloves that Kitty wondered how they would ever need the half of them. It was a very busy afternoon and satisfying to know that her job was working out so well. Mrs Fairweather had been recommended to visit Harpers simply because of their new facility and also because they had a wonderful line of evening clothes that were exclusive to Harpers.

It was nearly seven when Kitty reached Kettle's Yard, because she had walked home, enjoying the pleasant sunshine. The yard smelled of the horse, as it often did in summer, but Kitty was used to it and took little notice. She entered the house and walked into the kitchen, excited to tell Mariah of her eventful afternoon, but when she did so, one look at her friend's face told her something was wrong.

'What's the matter?' she asked. 'Is Alf worse?'

Mariah gave a little gasp and shook her head. 'He's upstairs... It's bad news, Kitty. The worst. I don't know how to tell you...'

'What – my mother?' Kitty looked at her in bewilderment and then she felt an icy lump begin to form inside. Mariah wouldn't look at her that way if it was her mother. 'Larry – something has happened to Larry?'

Mariah inclined her head and the tears began to trickle down her cheeks. 'We got the news half an hour ago. I said it was best to wait until you got home, Kitty. Sit down, love...' She sniffed, cuffed her cheeks and then looked at Kitty. 'Larry's gone. There was an accident down on the docks. A crane was unloading and the chain snapped.' Mariah took a shaky breath. 'Larry saw that one of the workmen was in danger as the load fell. He shoved him out of the way, but then he tripped somehow and it fell on him...' A shudder went through her. 'They told me he died instantly... couldn't have felt much...' Mariah sat down, giving into the tears that were shaking her whole body.

Kitty stared at her. Her eyes felt gritty, but she was too stunned to cry. It was unreal. She couldn't believe it was happening. Larry was such a big cheerful man, full of life and caring for others. How could he be dead? They must have made a mistake. This couldn't be happening... it just couldn't... 'We were to have married as soon as we could,' she whispered, and her hand went to the beautiful ring Larry had given her that she wore on a chain underneath her dress for work. 'He can't be gone...' Her head was spinning and she felt faint. The shock was so sudden and so desperate, the death of a kind man she'd learned to love so final that she was stunned. 'I can't... I won't believe it...' She shook her head as she seemed to freeze all over. A great shudder went through her and she began to tremble and sway.

Mariah saw that she was in shock and she rushed to her as Kitty folded to her knees and then bent over, her arms wrapped around herself, keening in her grief as she rocked back and forth, but still no tears came. They had frozen, as she had, the cold emptiness stealing through her body, shutting off all feeling and thought.

'She's in shock,' Alf's voice spoke from behind them. 'I'll get her some brandy.' He limped over to the dresser, each step an effort for him, and poured a large glassful, bringing it back to them. His hands were trembling, spilling some of the liquid, as he urged, 'Come on, Kitty. Drink this. It will make yer feel better.'

Kitty shook her head, but Alf put the glass to her lips and pressed her to drink a mouthful of the fiery liquid. His intensity of purpose got through to her and she let him pour the brandy into her mouth. It stung her throat and made her choke. The brandy was burning a trail of heat through her, melting the ice as it went, and she suddenly went limp and collapsed against Mariah as the heavy sobs took over.

'Why him?' she whispered as the grief rushed in. 'Why Larry? He never harmed anyone...'

'Because he was a bloody hero,' Alf said harshly and suddenly all the fight went out of him and he stumbled and half fell into his chair by the range, his whole body shaking and trembling. 'Always thought of others...' His teeth were chattering and the words could barely be heard, his lips slathered with saliva. 'What will become of us without the damned fool?'

'Father...' Mariah left Kitty as she saw what was happening to her father. His face contorted and was drawn down at the side. 'Don't do this... we need you, Father. We need you more than ever...'

Kitty stared as she watched the agonising scene and saw Alf suddenly slump to one side. He'd made the effort to give her that brandy but his son's sudden death had been more than he could bear. She knew he was dying even before she saw the horror in Mariah's eyes.

'He's gone,' Kitty said as Mariah looked at her but couldn't speak. 'They've both gone. It's just you and me now...'

* * *

The next few hours were like a blur to Kitty. Afterwards, she could not remember what she'd done, but apparently some sixth sense had taken over. She'd made Mariah drink some of the brandy, sent the yard boy flying for the doctor and then made a pot of tea, which they both forced themselves to make a show of drinking.

People came to the door when the news filtered through Kettle's Yard, everyone stunned at the double tragedy. Alf had been respected, but Larry had been loved by the community. Stories of his kindness were told as women came asking if they could help. The doctor had to pass through a small crowd gathered in the yard before being ushered in by Mariah. Kitty answered and acknowledged the sorrow of others, but felt removed, her hurt too deep to be opened to public gaze. How could it be that her happiness had lasted such a short time? It was only a few days since they had pledged themselves and now it was all gone. Life seemed bleak and empty as she struggled to take it in. Larry had given her so much, but he'd been snatched away from her too soon. It was a cruel fate that could just take away the people she loved. And to lose Alf almost in the same minute was too much – for both Kitty and Mariah.

Alf's second stroke had been massive; it was a shock but not entirely unexpected. Stroke victims often suffered another, but he'd seemed to be getting better. But the terrible shock of his son's death had brought on such a massive seizure that the end had been inevitable, though nonetheless shocking.

Hours passed. People came and went. Kitty and Mariah moved as if they were in a dream, hardly hearing all the well wishes and the tears. Cups of tea were made but not drunk. The murmurs of condolence were hidden behind a mist of pain and grief.

After Alf was officially declared dead and his body taken upstairs to be prepared for his funeral and their friends and neighbours had gone, the two women sat together in silence for a time. It was late now, past midnight, and the silence was painful.

'We must have them buried on the same day so that they lie side by side,' Kitty said at last. 'It will be best that way, Mariah.' Her hands trembled in her lap as she looked at her friend. 'What do you want to do now? You always said you would sell this place – will you do so?'

'It might not be up to me,' Mariah replied, surprising her. 'Father left everything between Larry and me – and Larry left a will, leaving everything to you. He did it even before you promised to wed him.' Mariah's voice caught as she looked at Kitty. 'He wanted you to be secure for the future after the way your mother treated you.'

'Oh, Mariah...' Kitty's throat was tight and the tears trickled down her cheeks again. 'I loved him so much. It just isn't fair. I don't want his property, I want him.'

'Aye, I know that.' A watery smile touched Mariah's face. 'I never thought Larry would find someone he could love the way he did you, Kitty. He helped others if they were in trouble, but was always one for keeping his feelings to himself.' She raised her head, recovering her normal calm. 'We shall mourn them both, but then we have to go on, because it is what they would want and you'll get your share of everything, no matter what the law is. Father thought a lot of you, Kitty. And Larry adored you.'

'Don't, please don't,' she begged. She couldn't bear to think of things like that when Larry was no longer with them. Yet she knew they had to face the future and Mariah was as lost as she felt. All her strength and energy seemed to have deserted her, her eyes hollow and her face grey with pain. 'What do you want to do?' Kitty asked. 'I will agree with whatever suits you, Mariah. I know you said you wanted a nice little house with a garden...'

'I suppose we could keep this place going if we tried, get a man in to look after the heavy stuff...'

'You know that awful man – Joshua Miller – will be after you to sell the place to him,' Kitty said. 'He was afraid of Larry, but he won't be of us – two women alone. He will try to bully us into selling all your father's property to him.'

'Over my dead body!' Mariah said fiercely. 'I might sell, if you don't mind, Kitty, but not to him.'

'Supposing he is the only one to offer?'

'I've no fear of that,' Mariah said, sighed and got up. She went over to the large oak dresser and took a letter from behind a large blue and white jug. 'Read that and tell me if it means what I think it does.'

Kitty opened the letter and frowned as she read it through twice. 'This is from the council. They are going to redevelop this area over the next few years and they will give us twenty-four months' notice when they are ready to start purchasing the land and property.'

'Father had another letter with a valuation for the property – nearly twice as much as Joshua Miller offered. It would be enough to buy us both a nice little house.'

'Do you want to buy two properties?' Kitty asked. 'I was hoping we might continue to live together as family and friends...'

Mariah looked at her and her face lit up from within. 'Bless you, dearest Kitty. I wasn't sure if that was what you would want – now that Larry and

Father have gone.' She brushed a hand over her cheek and gulped back her sorrow.

'Of course it is,' Kitty said. 'You are my family, Mariah. If you ever want to marry, I can move out then.'

Mariah gave a sharp crack of laughter. 'You'll be the one to marry, Kitty. A pretty girl like you and with a little money in the bank...'

'I shall never marry,' Kitty told her and her eyes were bleak. 'I could never hope to find another Larry – and I don't want second best.' They had had the briefest of courtships, but every second was precious to her. Larry had loved her and she would never, ever forget him. She reached towards Mariah and took her hand. 'If you are willing, we'll live together as we do now. I'll go to work and you will keep house... unless you have other plans?'

'I do have an idea for the future,' Mariah said. 'We'll talk about it when the time is right, Kitty. First, we have to get through the next few days and weeks. It will take several weeks to clear the house, let alone the yard – though I know someone who would take it over until the council are ready to do whatever they intend here.' She stood up and arched her back. 'I'm tired, Kitty. I need my bed, though I probably won't sleep. It will seem strange without Father to look after...'

The sadness in her then made Kitty's heart ache. 'I must try to sleep, too,' she said. 'In the morning, I will ring Harpers and let them know I shan't be in for two weeks. I am due a holiday and I shall take it now. We have a lot of decisions to make, Mariah – and I think we need to be together until we can start to make something of our lives again.'

They kissed each other's cheek and Mariah went to check all the doors as she always did last thing. Kitty took an oil lamp, lit it and carried it up to her room. She sat on the edge of the bed, listening as Mariah followed her up and went to her own room.

Kitty's tears were falling again. She had controlled her grief while she and Mariah spoke of their future, but now they fell, thick and fast. The sense of disbelief was still there at the back of her mind, but she knew that Larry was lying in a hospital mortuary, his body waiting to be collected by the undertaker who would also look after Alf. She would visit him then, when they had dressed him in his coffin, to say her last farewell...

The double tragedy had numbed them both, but Kitty knew in the days to come it would hit hard as they realised that the men they had loved were no longer around. It was almost impossible to think of life going on here without Alf and Larry. Kitty had spoken with conviction when she said she would never marry. Even though she had never been Larry's wife and had kissed him only a few times, he was her husband in her heart. She would never replace him.

Lying down on the bed fully dressed, Kitty let her thoughts wander over the past few months, remembering the way Larry had come into her life, always there when she'd needed him – how he'd come to her rescue when she was close to despair and then his shy proposal of love and marriage. He'd told her he'd loved her from the first time they'd spoken together, though he might never have dared to tell her if her mother had not deserted her.

The pain that struck her heart then was almost unbearable. She buried her face in her pillow and wished that she might die, but even as she did so, a small voice told her that she must think of Mariah. Without her, Mariah would be alone.

Kitty sat up, brushing her cheek with the back of her hand. She had to go on for her friend's sake – and because Larry would want her to.

'I want you to have a good life, my Kitty. Live and be happy. Live for me...'

Perhaps the words were only in her head, but she felt that they came from him and a little sad smile touched her lips. It was what he would say if he could.

She got up, went to the washstand and poured cold water from the jug into the bowl, splashing her face to cool it and take away the sting of salt. Life went on and Kitty must go on. She had a good job at Harpers and she would make that her life. It was what Larry would want for her and it was the only way forward now.

27

'Kitty's fiancé and his father – both of them?' Beth was stunned by the news when she reached Harpers that morning. 'That is terrible. What happened?' She listened to Sally's account and then shook her head. 'It is unbelievable – so very sad. Kitty looked so happy when she showed me her ring and told me she was intending to marry as soon as she could. Larry was going to speak to her mother and ask if she would give her permission. Otherwise they would wait and marry when she reached twenty-one.'

'When she rang, she asked to take two weeks' holiday,' Sally told her. 'Naturally, I agreed that she could take the time off and return when she was ready. She doesn't have to take it as her holiday, but she says she hopes to be back in two weeks, after she has helped Mariah do whatever they need to do.'

'I'm shocked and upset for her,' Beth said. 'I have come to know Kitty well and she is an intelligent and sensible girl, Sally.'

'Yes, I know and she is making a difference for Harpers.' Sally looked thoughtful. 'Will you visit her at her home?'

'Yes, I shall,' Beth confirmed. 'I shall go later this afternoon and ask if there is anything I can do to help... I wouldn't put it past that mother of hers to make trouble for Kitty.'

'Surely not?' Sally said. 'Well, tell her that if she needs anything that I could help with, she has only to ask. I could get a lawyer for Kitty if her mother does try to make things difficult for her.'

Beth nodded thoughtfully. 'I don't mind saying I don't trust her mother – or that man she was trying to make Kitty marry. I'm not sure how Kitty will go on now... if she can continue to live where she is...'

'We have a spare room if she needs it for a while,' Sally offered. 'But I think she gets on well with Mariah. She says they help each other. I believe she will stay there for the time being anyway.'

'I am glad if that is so,' Beth replied. 'It is such a shocking thing, Sally – to become engaged and then, only a few days later, the man you love dies a violent death.'

'He saved the life of a working man who had a wife and three children to support. The man has been round to thank them and ask if he can do anything for them. I imagine his wife must be thanking God for his life – but that it should be at the cost of his...' Sally shook her head. 'Such a brave thing to do. Larry Norton did not deserve to die.'

'No. It is such a waste,' Beth agreed. 'He was a considerate man and I know he truly loved Kitty. I spoke to him only a short time ago, soon after I visited that awful Mr Miller and paid him off. Larry told me something in confidence then, something quite shocking that he'd discovered, and the way he spoke to me then as a trusted friend of Kitty's showed me how much he cared for her.'

'Well, we shall both help her if she needs it,' Sally said. 'And now I really must get on. I have to be home by two, because Ben is coming out of hospital this afternoon.'

'At last. You will be glad to get him back,' Beth said, looking at her. 'You thought he would be home before this, didn't you?'

'Yes, I did. He seems to be fine in himself, but the hospital staff were reluctant to let him come until his memory returned fully.'

'Has it done so?'

Sally shook her head. 'I don't think so... Sometimes he says things that make me think he remembers, but he has been acting so oddly that I just don't know what to think.'

Beth went back to work and Sally got on with the mountain of paperwork that seemed to have been piling up recently. She could have dealt with it long ago had it not needed Ben's approval and she frowned over an order that needed to be attended to for the men's department. It was Ben's job, but it had been waiting for his signature for three weeks now. Sighing, she signed it herself. If it was left any longer, the new suits for the autumn and winter would not arrive in time.

At least the sales figures had held steady for the past three weeks. Perhaps the persistent drop in the first few months of the year had been just a glitch. They were down slightly on the figures for the previous year, but as long as the trend did not continue, Sally hoped it might reverse again now – and yet if one read the papers, it did seem that the boom of the years following the war might be over. If the current prosperity were to disappear and a more testing time follow, Harpers might need to make changes. There would be no spare cash for further expansion...

Sally sighed. Ben really needed to be back at his desk or allow her to deal with everything in his absence, but he hadn't wanted to talk about Harpers, especially the restaurant. Each time she'd brought something up, he had given her a blank stare that made her feel guilty. She'd asked if his head ached, but he'd just looked away. Sally hoped that he would leave hospital that afternoon, because she needed to talk to him. Something was wrong and she would be uneasy until she could speak to him in private. In the hospital, there had always been a nurse or a doctor around.

* * *

After some hours at her desk, Sally left her office and made a little tour of the store before leaving. It was busy and the assistants seemed to be selling well. All was as it should be, despite the windows that both she and Beth had felt lacked inspiration of late. Once Ben was home and she could talk to him they might be able to come up with a plan for the windows. Ben wouldn't like the idea of looking for a new window dresser, but perhaps they ought to if his friend didn't intend to return soon.

Sally drove herself home. She'd considered visiting Kitty but decided that it might be a bit daunting for the grieving women if Kitty's employer arrived at such a time and she knew that Beth planned to call in. The two women had enough to cope with for the moment. Sally would talk to Kitty about her future plans – and plans she had herself for Harpers – when the girl felt able to return to work. At the moment, she must be devastated. Sally could not imagine how she would feel if anything like that happened to Ben. His accident had been worrying enough and his manner since made her uneasy and anxious for him.

A bang on the head could cause all kinds of problems and Sally wondered what they would do if he had changed in his feelings towards her and the children. He'd seemed so distant since he'd been in hospital, refusing to talk about the children or Harpers – it was almost as if he'd cut himself off from them...

Sally parked her car outside the garage and walked up to the back door. Entering the kitchen, she saw Mrs Hills making a tray of coffee with cups and a plate of biscuits.

'Oh, Mrs Harper, you're back,' Mrs Hills smiled at her. 'Mr Harper is in the sitting room. Your mother fetched the children from school, but she left them with Mr Harper. I am just taking him a tray...'

'Oh, thank you, Mrs Hills. I can take it now,' Sally said. She picked it up and walked towards the large sunny sitting room overlooking the garden where they liked to sit on fine days. It had long French windows and opened out on to a smooth lawn surrounded by flower beds. The sun was playing across the room in a rainbow of colours as she walked in and set the tray down on the table. Ben was on his knees playing with a train set with Peter and Jenny.

'Daddy, can I have that new bicycle you promised me?' Peter asked. 'The red one we saw in the shop...'

'I only said we would think about it, Peter. I told you; we must ask Mummy if she thinks you should have it.'

'I want some red shoes,' Jenny said. 'Please, Daddy – you said I could...'

'But Mummy said they were not suitable,' Ben replied, then seeming to become conscious that someone had entered, 'Thank you, Mrs Hills. I hope you've brought us all some of your special almond biscuits...' he said without looking round and Jenny went into a delighted peal of laughter.

'Silly Daddy, it's Mummy,' she said in her high childish voice.

Ben swung round to look, still on his knees. Sally watched the smile drain from his eyes and then he got to his feet as he saw her baffled expression because, listening to his answers to the children's requests, Sally knew he'd been lying to her.

'Why don't you two go and play in the garden for a little while,' he said, giving Peter a little push towards the open door. 'Go and see what Lulu is up to...'

The little brown dog was sniffing at something on the lawn. Peter scampered off to discover what she was doing and Jenny followed reluctantly, giving her father a long look before she went.

'Sally...' Ben stood up, looking at her awkwardly. 'I am so sorry. I know you're going to be angry with me, but I thought it for the best...'

Sally stared at him, then nodded as the truth sunk in. 'You didn't lose your memory at all, did you?'

'No, I didn't,' he admitted ruefully.

Sally just kept looking at him, feeling a little bewildered. 'Why did you lie to me and the doctors, Ben? I don't understand—'

'Because, when I first came round, I couldn't remember much – then I did and I wasn't sure what to tell the police. I pretended that I couldn't remember anything.' He sighed and ran his long fingers through his shorn hair, which had been shaved in the hospital and was now growing rather spikily. There was still a pink mark on his scalp where he'd cut his head open, but no lasting injury. 'I didn't want to get Jack into trouble – and the tale I would have had to tell if I'd gone for the whole story would have sounded ridiculous. Gangsters and guns in the back of my neck and a man being kidnapped and shipped off back to America sounds almost too crazy to be true. Besides, I was warned not to tell anyone about that... I couldn't tell the Inspector who came to see me at the hospital. He was the officious sort and it might have caused all kinds of trouble – for the American government and the man who arranged for him to be trussed up like a chicken in that abandoned warehouse... He may be a criminal but he did us a good turn.'

'So instead you lied to me, you were so strange, so remote...' Sally gave him a long hard look. 'I've been worried to death, Ben.'

A look of contrition flashed into his eyes. 'I know, but I daren't get into any discussions in case I made a slip-up in front of others.' He threw her an anxious look. 'Are you furious with me, Sally?'

'Perhaps I ought to be,' she said and sank down in a large armchair as the relief swept over her. 'I'm not. I'm just glad you're back, Ben. I was afraid I might have lost you – that you had stopped loving me and the children.'

'Never! I just wanted a chance to get things straight before I tell the police my story. I don't want to get Jack into trouble when this is all my fault. What did Jack actually say to them, do you know?'

'He didn't tell them much,' Sally assured him. 'Just that you'd had a disagreement and he'd hit you. He never meant to harm you, Ben, not really. He'd just been so tightly strung, worrying about Beth and the boys...'

The tension left Ben's face. 'I'll speak to Jack, tomorrow before he leaves for work, and then I'll go to the police station and tell them my memory came back when I got home and it was just a small disagreement. They don't need a long, involved story they probably wouldn't believe anyway.' He gave a rueful laugh. 'If they did happen to believe me about being protected, they'd think I had connections to the criminal element in London and that we were mixed up in nefarious things. I don't have connections and I don't want to come in to contact with any of them again – even if they were supposedly looking out for us.'

'I quite agree,' Sally said. She looked at him and then started to laugh.

'What?' Ben said but Peter came running back, Lulu in his arms, and Jenny running behind them with a long earthworm in her hand. 'Jenny – what are you doing with that?'

'Lulu was trying to eat it,' Jenny said. 'I wanted to show you...'

'Bad dog, Lulu,' Ben said and grinned at Sally. 'Put the worm back where it belongs, Jenny, and wash your hands before we have our biscuits and cake.'

* * *

Later that evening, when the children were in bed, dinner was over and Mrs Hills had gone home for the night, they sat in the cosy small sitting room, soft music playing on the radio.

'This is what I've missed stuck in that place,' Ben said. 'I thought they would never let me come home.'

'Why didn't you just ask me about what Jack had said sooner?' Sally said, and then, before he could answer, 'I suppose you could never be sure who would come in. What a tangle, Ben. Poor Jack has been suffering terrible guilt over what he did and Beth has been upset. You must sort things out with him, Ben. I'm not sure what he will want to do. He was talking of selling his share of the restaurant and moving away from London.'

'I do hope he will reconsider,' Ben said. 'He is a good friend and I regret that I acted without thought for him... but I never expected things to go the way they did. I thought it my duty as a good citizen to help them corner a dangerous criminal.'

'You've learned your lesson,' Sally agreed. 'Even though you were trying to help the Americans in their search for a wanted criminal, you risked too much. It is best to keep your distance from that element of society – and I know the restaurant was already being used by some of them, but you can't dictate who uses your premises.'

'Yes, we can,' Ben said determinedly. 'Next time one of them wants to book a table – we're full.'

Sally laughed. 'Don't think you can stop them that easily. If they want to come, they will – and, surely, they have the right to eat where they choose, but not to use it for their unpleasant business. Next time if Jack tells you something like that is happening, let him go to the police.'

'Yes, I shall,' Ben agreed. 'It's nice to see you smiling, Sally. Why did you laugh when the children came in with that worm?'

'I was just thinking of your face when you told me of your little encounter with our protector. I wonder who he was and why they chose to intervene as they did.'

'I have no idea and what's more I don't want to know. I just hope I never have cause to find out...'

'Oh, I believe it is over,' Sally said with a smile. 'I suppose it is simple enough when you think about it. The American gangster was trying to muscle in on their patch so they arranged for him to be parcelled up and sent home.'

Ben gave a snort of laughter. 'You make it all sound so reasonable, almost normal,' he said, highly amused. 'Do you take everything in your stride, Sally?'

'No point in having hysterics over it now,' she said. 'I was pretty worried about you for a while, Ben. How am I supposed to run Harpers without you?'

He met her eyes and smiled. 'Oh, I think that is the least of your problems, my darling. You could do it with your eyes half-open if you didn't have to refer back to me – but I don't want you to have the whole load on your shoulders, Sally. I want you to have time to enjoy yourself, to play with the children and go shopping with your mum when you feel like it.'

'Yes – and it has been rather a lot to do,' she agreed. 'I am thinking of taking on a personal assistant to help me with some of it, but I'm not sure yet...'

'You must do as you wish,' he told her, 'but I'm back now, Sally. Next year, we'll make sure we have enough staff to look after things while we go on a long holiday.'

'Talking about staff – have you any idea when Mr Marco is coming back? We need to think about the windows and getting someone new if he's gone for good.'

Ben nodded. 'As a matter of fact, I had a letter from him. He should be returning to work next month. He is bringing someone he met with him – a young man he thinks has a talent for window dressing – and he asked if we would take him on as an apprentice—'

'Ben Harper!' Sally exclaimed indignant now. 'You are the limit! Here was I worrying about the lack of inspiration in our window displays and wondering where we could get someone to take over Mr Marco's job...'

Ben laughed as she jumped to her feet. He got up and pulled her into his arms, kissing her fiercely. 'Forgive me. His letter came the morning I went to the restaurant to speak to Jack, before my hospital stay... but I didn't get a chance to tell you, and in the hospital, I couldn't tell you when I wasn't supposed to remember anything...'

'Damn you, Ben,' Sally said, but then laughed as he pulled her back close. 'I do love you, but sometimes—'

'I know. I am very irritating,' he murmured and nuzzled her ear. 'Shall we go to bed and I can show you how very sorry I am...'

Sally melted into his chest. 'Yes, please,' she murmured. 'I've missed you so much, Ben. Please don't go away again...'

28

'Oh, this is lovely,' Betty Lou said when Tel showed her the house he'd bought for her. It was an end of terrace on the corner of Dressmakers' Alley and Silver Lane. 'I can make this a real home.'

'You know I won't be here most of the time,' Tel said, trying and failing to conceal the fact that her delight made him feel good. 'I'll come when I can – but it is still our secret.'

'Yes, I know,' she replied and smiled at him. 'When I'm able, I'll work and repay you...'

Tel cut her off with a bruising kiss on the mouth. 'Don't be bloody daft, girl. You've got yer way and I'll be lookin' after yer from now on. Yer off the game and if I catch yer at it, I'll make yer sorry.'

Betty Lou pealed with laughter. 'I didn't mean that kind of work. There's a dressmaking place just round the corner. I wouldn't mind working there when the boy is old enough.'

'It might be a girl,' Tel said gruffly.

'Nah, it will be a boy,' she said, 'because he's yours.' She smiled at him. 'Thank yer for lookin' after me, Tel. Yer a good man...'

'You have no idea of the things I do, Betty Lou,' he said harshly now.

'I think I do,' she said and the smile left her eyes. 'Some folks are so wicked, Tel. I heard somethin' when I went ter see Doctor Dolly to have me check-up... he told me he'd agreed to do somethin' and now he regrets it. He wants you to tell him what ter do...'

Tel gave a sigh of exasperation. 'If one of the girls had a late abortion and died because of it, he can do time for it. I've warned him to take no risks...'

'It ain't that, Tel,' Betty Lou said. 'There's a girl – I know her, because she served me at Harpers. Lovely, she is...' She drew a deep breath. 'These people are plannin' ter do somethin' wicked, Tel. Just because she's come into some property...'

Tel sat down on the edge of the bed and began to unbutton his shirt. 'Why don't yer get in 'ere with me and tell me all about it?' he invited with a quizzing smile. 'Then mebbe I'll do something about it...'

Betty Lou giggled and began to slip out of her dress. She snuggled up to him as he kissed her and caressed her, his large hands lingering on the bump that was their child. Tel said he was a hard man and she knew he did bad things, but she was sure he would help that girl. She was such a nice girl and Tel could do anything if he set his mind to it. Betty Lou didn't often think about what Tel did when he wasn't with her; she didn't want to know about his business – but she knew he was one of the most powerful men in London. More than the Prime Minister perhaps and the King... and now he was hers.

She smiled as she began to kiss his firm chest and tell him about the wicked thing that Joshua Miller had paid Doctor Dolly to do. Doctor Dolly had changed his mind and said he wasn't going to be involved, but there were always others who would. Some folk would do anything for money, but her Tel wouldn't let it happen.

* * *

Tel frowned as he left the house in the early hours. Betty Lou was still sleeping. He'd watched her for a few minutes before he walked away; she had the face of an innocent angel. For a moment, anger flared against the stepfather who had put her on the game. That man was dead and not by Tel's hand. He was lucky the bus had knocked him down and he'd died almost instantly. Had Tel got him, he would have died slowly and painfully.

A scowl marred his handsome features as he looked each way, making sure that he wasn't being watched. It was habit, but he'd have to be more careful in future. Tel had too many enemies and some of them wouldn't hesitate to take their revenge on an innocent woman.

There were some evil buggers about. Tel had done his share of nasty stuff when he'd had to, but Betty Lou's story had filled him with real revulsion. He knew Joshua Miller by reputation. Outwardly, a respectable property owner, he was disliked by the girls who worked the streets. He was cruel and demanding and one girl had been in the hospital for months after he'd done with her. Now he was planning something so vile that it turned Tel's stomach.

Well, he wouldn't get away with it. By chance, Joshua Miller had asked Doctor Dolly to be one of the doctors needed for the filthy business he had in mind; he'd probably heard that he looked after the street girls and believed he would do anything for money, but he hadn't known that Doctor Dolly had a soft heart and owed Tel a lot. Tel grinned suddenly. He would pay his mother and brother a little visit...

29

'Sally rang me at the restaurant this evening,' Jack told Beth when he got home later that night. 'She said Ben wants to see me – so I'll go round to their house in the morning. Apparently, he is feeling much better and there is nothing to worry about, but he wants to talk about the future.'

'That is wonderful, Jack. I am so pleased,' Beth replied. 'The bad blood between you needs sorting out – but how do you feel about things now? Do you still want to sell your share of the restaurant and leave London?'

Jack looked at her for a few minutes in silence. 'To be honest, I don't,' he said. 'I've thought about it a lot – and I know we could buy a small restaurant on the coast and have a nice quiet life there, but it isn't what we'd planned.'

'No, it isn't. You and Ben had big plans. Jack, do you think you can forgive him and make it all right again? I would rather not leave London – especially now that Vera is so ill. She had the operation but isn't doing well. If she doesn't come out of hospital, I'm not sure what your dad will do. I really don't want him to have to live alone.'

'No...' Jack sighed. 'I mentioned that I'd thought of perhaps leaving London and asked if he and Vera would consider moving with us, but he said no. He would visit us for holidays, but he says he belongs here in London.'

'We all do,' Beth said. 'If you really needed to make the move I'd do as you asked, but it's not what I want.'

'Then I'll do my best to make things right with Ben – but he may not wish to continue the partnership.'

'Fingers crossed he will,' Beth said and kissed him. 'We shall manage whatever happens, because we're lucky. We have each other.'

Jack nodded, gazing into her eyes. 'I know I am lucky to have you, Beth.'

* * *

Beth was thoughtful the next morning after Jack had left to meet with Ben. She knew that Sally believed Ben was ready to take the blame for their quarrel since he'd behaved in a high-handed manner. The restaurant was a partnership and yet he'd taken important decisions alone, without consulting Jack – indeed, he'd kept it to himself for some time. It wasn't right and it could have led to serious consequences. They were lucky that 'someone' had been looking after them.

Beth was pretty certain that she knew who that 'someone' had been. It must surely have been Jerry's elder brother Tel. He had connections to whoever was at the heart of the gang that controlled most of London's crime, and because Beth had befriended Jerry when he was wounded, she and her family – and her friends, the Harpers – had been protected from the threats of another very dangerous man.

It was a secret Beth knew she must keep. Bella had trusted her, but Beth doubted she knew much about what had been going on. Neither brother would tell their mother such things. Beth wondered how deeply Jerry was involved with the murky underground life of the criminal element. She wouldn't ask him, because it was best not to know, but she was glad that he'd been her friend.

* * *

Bert called in to see Beth just before lunch. He was on his way to the hospital and Beth had some magazines for Vera and some grapes.

'I'm not sure she will be up to eating or reading much,' Bert told her.

'They were going to do another procedure on her this morning to get rid of some fluid. She might not even be awake, but I'll be there when she wakes if I can.'

Beth reached for his hand and squeezed it. 'Are you sure you don't want me to come with you?'

'I'll be all right, Beth love,' he replied. 'I'm glad you're not too far away. I'd miss you if I couldn't pop round when I wanted to.'

'I'm waiting to see how Jack got on. He was meeting Ben this morning to discuss the future – but I doubt we'll move away whatever happens. Jack doesn't really want to now that he's calmed down. I am sure he could find a good job here in London, though I don't think he could afford to start his own restaurant here.'

'He'd find a good job anywhere,' Bert said stalwartly. 'I might have a few bob put by if he needs it.'

'You should keep that to enjoy yourselves,' Beth said. 'When Vera is over all this, you should take her somewhere special – perhaps to Cornwall or even to Scotland.'

'She might like to go on a train up to Scotland and then on a bus tour round the Highlands. She's spoken of how beautiful it must be up there...' Bert's anxiety was plain to see. 'I just pray she will get over it, Beth.'

Beth hugged him. 'She was silly to hide from the truth so long. Had she gone to the hospital sooner, it might not have been quite so serious, but hopefully she will recover now; they did say it hadn't spread too far, didn't they?'

'Yes, that's what they told me,' Bert agreed. 'Can't help worrying though.'

'Yes, I know,' Beth replied. 'Just keep your chin up. Vera is pretty tough and she will get through this.'

'Yes, of course, she will.' Bert hugged her, took the bits and pieces for Vera and left.

* * *

Beth glanced at the clock. Only another hour before she needed to collect the boys. She wished that Jack had telephoned her to let her know the result of his meeting with Ben but tried not to worry about it.

Deciding to make herself a cup of tea and then leave for Timmy's school, she had just put the kettle on when there was a knock at her back door. She jumped and hesitated. Whoever was there had scrambled over her back wall, because the gate was locked and bolted.

'It's me, Mrs Burrows. Jerry. It's all right...'

Beth opened the door, half expecting him to be covered in blood, but he was grinning at her. 'Jerry – what's wrong with the front door?' she asked. 'You gave me a fright.'

'Didn't want to be seen,' Jerry told her as she stood back, inviting him in. 'No, I ain't in trouble wiv the cops or them other lot – I just didn't want anyone to know I'd brought you a message.' He hesitated, then, 'It's from Tel. Ma said you saw him at the house. She don't like him to go there, but sometimes he pops in to make sure she is OK. He ain't bad, Mrs Burrows, not like some – though you might not approve of things he gets up to...'

'I am quite sure I wouldn't,' Beth said crossly. 'What does this brother of yours want from me?'

'Nuthin'. He heard somethin', that's all, and thought you were the one to sort it – it's about Kitty Wilson...'

'Kitty?' Beth looked at him sharply. 'Is she in some trouble?' Beth had had an uneasy feeling about the girl ever since she'd learned that Larry had died and his father too, leaving the two women together and unprotected. The secret Larry had told her in confidence had worried her since his death.

'She ain't yet, but she might be,' Jerry said. 'Tel heard it – that bloke her mother moved in with is a bad one, Mrs Burrows. He's planning to have her locked away in an asylum for bad girls so that he can get his hands on the yard and property the old man left her and Mariah...'

'Surely not!' Beth stared at him in horror. Yet she knew it would be easy enough for Joshua Miller and Annie Wilson to have Kitty confined in an asylum. She wouldn't be the first *wilful* girl it had happened to. Her mother had only to tell the doctors that she was concerned for her daughter's physical and mental health and she could be incarcerated for years, even her whole life. 'They must not be allowed to do that, Jerry. It's wicked.' Beth's thoughts were racing wildly. How could she intervene? Kitty was still under the age of twenty-one, still under her mother's control. 'I knew they were unpleasant people, but to do something so evil... just to get their hands on her property.' She frowned. 'Surely Mariah must own most of it? They can't force her to sell...'

'No, but the threat would be enough to force her hand. They will probably lock Kitty up and say that she will be released once the property is theirs or some such thing. Tel don't know all the details, just what they plan to do to Kitty.'

'That mustn't be allowed to happen,' Beth said. 'Once Kitty was locked away, we might never get her back.'

'That's why Tel told me to come to you,' Jerry said. 'He knows somethin' important – but he's not sure how to prove it. He ain't in a position to go to the law, so he thought you should know... that Annie Wilson... she ain't Kitty's mother...'

'What?' Beth stared at him in shock. For a moment, she couldn't take it in and then she nodded. 'Yes, of course. That makes sense. I wondered how she could treat her own daughter the way she did – so whose daughter is she then?' It made sense of the way Annie Wilson had acted when Larry had asked her for permission to allow them to wed. He hadn't told Kitty or Mariah, because Mrs Wilson had sworn at him, yelling and shouting abuse.

'She told me she'd see Kitty dead first,' Larry had confided to Beth. He'd come to her house when he'd been in the area delivering goods, because he'd known she was Kitty's true friend and he'd been troubled. 'I can't tell Kitty that, because it would distress her, but it's made me glad I've protected her. If anythin' happened to me, Kitty will have money. I told her mother so – told her I had property in a decent street, but it made no difference. She just repeated that she would see Kitty dead before she saw her wed to me.'

Beth had advised him to tell Kitty, but she didn't think he'd got around to it. Beth knew he was protecting Kitty's feelings, but she ought to know the truth.

Jerry was speaking again, and Beth's thoughts returned to what he was telling her.

'Her father was killed on the docks before she was born and her mother went into premature labour and died havin' her,' Jerry said. 'Mr Wilson was a friend of Kitty's father and he took the baby home to his wife. He loved her as if she were his own child, but maybe his wife resented what he'd done. She could never have children of her own so she took the babe as hers... but it weren't done legal.'

'So Kitty was brought up as their daughter and never knew the truth,' Beth said thoughtfully. 'That means Annie Wilson has no rights over her and neither does Joshua Miller.'

'That's the size of it,' Jerry nodded, looking pleased with himself. 'Tel says you can take out an injunction or some such thing, making Kitty your ward and protect her from them.'

'Yes, I've heard of something like that, but I'm not sure...' Beth said. 'I'll speak to Sally Harper. She will know how to do it – or she will have a friend who does.'

'I reckon she might be able to do it as Kitty's her employee,' Jerry said, lifting his head to scratch his head. 'I ain't got much book learnin', Mrs Burrows, but I hear all sorts. In the old days, employers often had the charge of young lads what was sold to them. It ain't the same, but there may be some law or somethin' – anyways, it's down to you now. Tel can't get involved, though he knows a few good lawyers!' Jerry grinned. 'Not the sort you want, missus, but that Mrs Harper sounds a smart one. She will know...'

'Yes, she will. We will get a lawyer for Kitty immediately, but she has to be warned to be careful. She ought not to go out alone, just in case they try to snatch her.'

'You can leave that to me,' Jerry said. 'I'll put the word out that she's to be watched over. They won't snatch her on my patch, but I can't stop them taking doctors there and whisking 'er orf somewhere secret. Until the truth comes out, they have the upper hand...'

'I am going to see Sally now.' Beth took her coat from the back of the kitchen door, 'and then I'll collect my children and pop round to tell Kitty what is going on.'

30

'I've had a reply from the council,' Mariah told Kitty as she came in from the yard, where she had been helping to sort out some old furniture. A man who dealt in second-hand furniture had brought a cart and cleared out one of the sheds, paying her twenty pounds for the privilege. 'They are pleased we're selling to them and we have at least a year before we need to move out, so plenty of time to find a new home for ourselves.' She waved the letter at Kitty. 'It came while I was clearing out that shed and the postman gave it to me. There's a letter for you, too.'

'Oh... thank you,' Kitty replied and frowned. She had been sorting through some of the boxes in the big living room. The family had seldom gone in there and it was used mainly as a store for Alf's bits and pieces. She tucked the letter into her pocket. 'I'll read it after tea.'

Mariah looked at her. 'You've been crying again, lass. I thought you'd be all right if I gave you a job to do. It will be better once we've laid them to rest and can think of moving away from this place.'

'Yes, perhaps,' Kitty said. 'It was just seeing all the pretty things Alf had put by, Mariah. A lot of the china bits are not perfect; they have cracks or chips, but they are delicate and unusual. I know they are something special or he wouldn't have kept them.'

'Father knew what they all were,' Mariah told her. 'Some of that china stored in the dining room is Chinese and very old. I remember Father telling me that they would be very valuable if they were perfect. One piece he reckoned was something like "Ming"... hundreds of years old and price-less if it didn't have a crack in it.'

'I love it that he kept things like that even though they were damaged. You won't throw them away, Mariah?'

'We can't keep everything...' Mariah looked at her and smiled. 'You're as daft over the old things as Father was, Kitty. We'll keep as much as we can, but I've been thinking. We might open a little junk shop and sell a lot of it – it won't fetch huge amounts, but I reckon it could fetch a bit and we'd have enough stock to last for years.' She chuckled. 'I wanted Father to open a little shop for me years ago, but he said I didn't need to work. I thought I might open for a few hours every day – or perhaps three days a week. I'd enjoy that and we'd get more for it than we will selling job lots. That furni-ture I've just cleared would have fetched twice as much if I'd sold it to the public. Mind, I kept the best stuff. Only let Mr Nosey see in the one shed. He badgered me to get in the others, but I said no. I reckon we'll sort the best out for our shop – if you agree.'

'Of course I do, whatever you want,' Kitty said and smiled at her. 'I can't help crying for them, Mariah, but I am happy to know that I'll be living with you and I think your shop is a wonderful idea.'

'Good. You sit there and read your letter while I pop the kettle on.'

'Thank you.' Kitty brushed a cobweb from her cheek and sat down in Alf's chair. She opened her letter and gave a little cry of surprise. 'Oh, it is from my mother.' Kitty read the few paragraphs swiftly. 'It is a nice letter, Mariah. She says she is sorry for my loss and she has invited me for tea. Oh, she says can I come today as she is going away for a while and would like to see me before she leaves...' She looked at Mariah, feeling puzzled. 'What do you think she wants to tell me? She says there is something important I should know...'

'I've no idea,' Mariah frowned. 'Do you trust her? Shall you go?'

'I'm not sure...' Kitty sighed. Her mother had hurt her badly, but she was still her mother. 'I suppose if she wants to make friends, I should try... but it is already nearly tea time and I've been working all day...'

'You could have a quick wash,' Mariah suggested just as someone knocked at the door. 'Drink your tea while I see who this is.' Mariah went to the door and gave a little cry of surprise. 'Bella – come in, please. We were just going to have a cup of tea.'

'Thank you, I shall,' Bella said and hobbled into the kitchen with the aid of a walking stick and stood looking around the large kitchen. 'Well, this is nicer than I expected. That yard puts yer off a bit, but this is pleasant – a lovely big room.'

'Bella, whatever made you walk here?' Kitty asked in concern. 'I would have come to you if you'd sent word.'

'I know, lass, I know, but it's important...' She walked heavily to the nearest chair and sat down with a little wheeze and a wince. 'I thought I'd best come and tell you, lass. Don't trust that mother of yours, 'cos she ain't yer ma...'

'What do you mean?' Kitty stared at her in astonishment. 'I've just had a letter from her asking me to tea today.'

'Well, of all the connivin' wretches!' Bella exclaimed indignantly. 'So that's how they planned it. Good job I came as soon as Jerry told me what they was after...'

'I don't understand,' Kitty said and stared at her, a cold shiver at her neck. 'What are you talking about, Bella? What did Jerry tell you?'

'It's that Joshua Miller what's behind it,' Bella said and Kitty's hand trembled as she saw the look in her friend's eyes. 'Plannin' ter kidnap yer they were and pack yer orf to some asylum for bad girls – tell everyone yer was in mortal danger, no doubt. Then they were goin' ter make yer sell yer property to 'im at his price, Mariah,' Bella finished grimly. 'The wickedness of it is what makes me angry.'

The colour had washed from Kitty's face.

'There, there, my lovey. No need ter worry, Kitty. My Tel knows most of what goes on around 'ere and he got the word. Joshua Miller had paid two doctors ter say yer weren't in yer right mind and needed puttin' away fer yer own good, but one of 'em got cold feet. Tel told my Jerry and he's been ter see Mrs Burrows; says she will sort them devils fer yer...'

'How can she do that?' Kitty asked, her mind whirling in confusion. She was trembling because the future her mother and Mr Miller had planned for her was a fate worse than death. She glanced at Mariah in fear. 'What can I do? I won't let you sell to them, but if they lock me up...'

'They know I'd do it for you,' Mariah told her. She too was pale and shaken. 'And there I was encouragin' you to get ready and go to your ma for tea...'

'If they come here...' Kitty looked from one to the other in fear. 'How can I avoid them? They will take me... force me to go; she has the power over me until I am twenty-one.' It wouldn't be the first time a rebellious girl had been locked in an asylum, simply because she'd run away from home or become involved with a man her parents did not approve.

'Nah, she don't,' Bella said a look of satisfaction in her eyes. 'She ain't yer mother – never was. Yer ma died givin' birth to yer and Mr Wilson took yer in, 'cos yer didn't have no one else. He loved yer, girl, ain't no doubt about that – but she never wanted yer. Yer real dad was killed on the docks the day afore yer were born.'

'How do you know all this?' Kitty said, staring in disbelief. She was pale and shaking, bewildered by all she had just heard. 'Why didn't you didn't tell me before...?'

'I'd forgotten all about it,' Bella admitted. 'Tel remembered – yer real father was a good friend of my 'usband, 'elped us after he died, so 'e wasn't likely to forget. My old man said at the time that he thought of asking me to take Kitty, but then Mr Wilson just did it and no one bothered to ask or check where you'd gone. There was no other family and Mr Wilson arranged the funerals and that was an end to it... otherwise you'd probably have been given away to another family or put in one of them orphanages. I dare say no one thought you would live long at the time with yer mother gone and you only a suckling babe.'

Kitty stared at her, a little colour returning to her cheeks. 'I wondered why she never loved me. Father was kind and good to me...'

'He was a good man,' Bella said. 'He did what others just thought of doin' and he did care for yer, love. I suppose he just had to be careful because of yer ma's bitter tongue. If he'd shown you too much affection, lord knows what she might have made of it...'

Kitty nodded. 'So they really would have me locked away if they could – my so-called mother and Mr Miller.'

'We shan't let them,' Mariah said determinedly. 'They won't take you out of my house. I'd shoot them first! I've got Father's pistol and I'd use it afore I'd let them take you, Kitty.'

'We'll none of us let them,' Bella said and her eyes sparked with determination. 'My Tel has folk lookin' out fer yer, Kitty love – and Jerry says Mrs Burrows and Mrs Harper will fix them pair good.'

'What can they do?' Kitty said doubtfully.

'Something a smart lawyer will think up,' Bella said cheerfully and shifted reluctantly in her chair. 'Well, I suppose I ought ter be gettin' back 'ome fer me tea...'

'You stay and have your tea with us,' Mariah said. There was a militant look about her. 'You may as well know, Bella. We've already arranged to sell our yard and property to the council. All we need to do is to keep Kitty safe until this gets sorted.'

'There is the funeral the day after tomorrow,' Kitty said and gave a little sniff. 'I am going to that, Mariah. I won't hide behind a locked door and I want to say prayers in church for those I loved.'

'You'll go to the funeral,' Mariah said. 'I've got a few friends of my own, Kitty love. They will make sure you're safe – and let's hope this Mrs Burrows knows what to do to make sure you stay that way.'

* * *

Kitty spent the next day on tenterhooks, expecting her mother and Mr Miller to come knocking on her door, but it didn't happen. She received a note from Beth, explaining all that Bella had already told her and telling her not to worry as she and Sally Harper were speaking to a lawyer to make her safe and she would call on her soon. She still had no idea what that meant and was anxious lest an attempt was made to abduct her. Mariah had kept Alf's pistol nearby and swore she would use it if they tried to get at Kitty, but the day passed without incident.

On the morning of the funerals, Kitty and Mariah dressed in black from head to toe. Mariah had found some black felt hats for them to wear; they were nearly new and looked smart. Not that either of them truly noticed.

They just wanted to look proper to pay their respects to the men they had loved.

They were both pale as they left the house together, getting into the black car that followed the hearse, which was pulled by four black horses. They were a fine sight with their great plumes of feathers on their heads. Outside in the square that formed Kettle's Yard, several men and women had gathered to watch them leave, heads bent and hats off in respect.

'Alf would have liked this,' Kitty murmured as she saw how many of their neighbours had turned out to follow the funeral cortege.

Mariah nodded and squeezed her hand. Kitty swallowed hard and fought the desire to cry. She'd cried so much, but it didn't help. The pain of losing Larry was still sharp and fresh inside her. She hadn't known him long, but their love had been a quiet, gentle thing, but none the less for that and his loss had left an emptiness inside her.

The church was packed and there were people standing outside. Larry had been popular and his act of bravery in saving the life of another man meant everyone who lived and worked locally wanted to be there to show their respect. When the hymns were sung, the male voices were strong and filled the church, soaring to the rafters high above.

The prayers and the tributes followed – more than one person stood up and spoke for Larry, including the wife of the man he'd saved, who made an emotional speech thanking Larry for the life of her husband and father of her three children.

Kitty felt the prayers and the music helped her to get through something that had seemed almost unbearable, but the internment in the graves, side by side, broke her and the tears trickled down her cheeks once more. Mariah reached for her hand and held it and they stood together, heads bowed for some minutes after the vicar had said his last prayer.

Why? Kitty wanted to ask as she threw a single red rose into Larry's grave, but she'd asked herself that a dozen times and there was no answer. It was unfair and cruel that she should lose him so suddenly and so soon after they had promised to wed, but nothing would bring him back and, somehow, they must find the will to go on and make the most of their lives.

'We should go,' Kitty said as everyone else began to move away.

'Yes. I've asked a few of Father's friends back to the house for a cup of tea, Kitty, just like we agreed.'

Kitty nodded. There was no one she wanted to ask, other than those people Mariah had spoken to. However, as she turned back from the grave-side and began to walk back to the church, she saw Mrs Burrows and Mrs Harper. They moved towards her, murmuring words of sympathy.

'Thank you. It was so kind of you to come,' Kitty said, a little surprised. 'Will you come to the house for refreshments?'

'Yes, we will, Kitty, thank you,' Mrs Burrows said and smiled at her. 'We have some news for you. I know Bella warned you of what we'd learned and you had my note, but there has been progress.'

'You must tell me when we get home—' Kitty broke off as she became aware that someone was staring at her hard. She turned her head to look and a cold shiver went down her spine as she saw Mr Miller watching her from a distance. For a moment, she met his eyes defiantly and then he turned and walked away.

* * *

Back at the house, Kitty and Mariah were busy for a while greeting people and serving them hot tea and tasty sandwiches that had been kept cool and moist in the large pantry. Mariah had made sausage rolls, scones and a sponge cake with jam and buttercream. Kitty was introduced to lots of people she'd never met who had known Alf or Larry and everyone was kind to her. She was asked what she intended to do and replied that she and Mariah would continue to live together but didn't say anything about their future plans.

After an hour or so, most of the guests had departed and Kitty was able to talk privately to Mrs Burrows and Mrs Harper.

'I wasn't sure you would come,' she told Beth. 'And you, Mrs Harper. I know how busy you are. It was so kind of you...'

'We wanted to – and we wanted to give you this...' Mrs Harper opened her handbag and handed Kitty a letter in an envelope. It was long and thick and felt important.

'What is it?' Kitty asked, unsure as she looked from one to the other.

'You have been told of the plot against you?' Mrs Harper asked and she nodded uncertainly. 'We went to my husband's lawyer and he told us what to do – you are under the age of twenty-one so you need a legal guardian and we requested that he make out this document. It says that Mariah and I have joint guardianship of you until you are twenty-one. I have sworn an affidavit that in my opinion you are of sound mind and high moral standards and Mrs Burrows also signed to confirm my opinion...' She laughed as Kitty looked baffled. 'Yes, I know. It sounds like a lot of rigmarole, but it protects you in law. With this document registered with the courts no one can say that you are in danger of being morally corrupted or that you are of unsound mind. If this evil man and woman were to try to have you locked away in an asylum, they would be in contempt of court and liable to arrest.'

'Oh, that is wonderful, thank you,' Kitty said and threw her arms about her and kissed her cheek. 'Oh, forgive me, but you are so kind – both of you.'

'I do not want to lose a valued employee,' Mrs Harper said. 'I was very angry when I learned what they had in mind for you, Kitty. I believe that is one of the worst things anyone can do to another person and I was determined to make sure it couldn't happen.'

Mariah had come over to listen and she nodded her approval. 'That was very kind, Mrs Harper. They are wicked folk to even think of such a thing – and we were lucky that Bella's son heard what they'd planned.'

'Yes, indeed,' Mrs Harper said. 'Had he not done so and acted on it they might very easily have taken her somewhere it would have been hard to find. We should still have done all we could to discover her whereabouts – but it is not an experience I would like her to suffer, even if only for a short time.'

'It was extremely lucky,' Mrs Burrows said, smiling at Kitty. 'I've been told in confidence that one of the doctors got cold feet over it after he'd agreed to sign for you to be put away and decided to tell someone he trusted and that happened to be a friend. Had he not done that, the chances of their plans being discovered were almost nil.'

Mrs Harper looked at her and there was a decided twinkle in her eye. 'You didn't tell me that bit, Beth...'

Beth Burrows laughed. 'No, I didn't, did I?' she said and looked at Kitty.

'We must go now. We both have work and children to see to – but we wanted to be here today. If that awful man should attempt anything despite the precautions we've all taken, please let us know. We are here to help you, Kitty, whenever you need us.'

'They tried to lure Kitty to have tea with her mother and she'd have gone too, had Bella not turned up and told us what she knew,' Mariah said. 'I was all for her making it up with her mother, for I thought Mrs Wilson her mother then – but let her try somethin' now and she'll be sorry.'

'Yes, I am sure she will,' Sally Harper said and impulsively hugged Kitty and then Mariah. 'We must go, as Beth says, but please do let us know if there is any trouble.'

'With that document we can see them off,' Mariah told her, smiling broadly. 'My fear was they would come to the house and take her and I wouldn't be able to stop them – because her mother had the right, but now she doesn't. Kitty has you and me to look out for her. Now their only chance would be to snatch her and we've friends who will make sure that doesn't happen.'

'I think it might be an idea to invite Annie Wilson to tea here,' Sally Harper suggested. 'Show her the document, tell her that this is your copy and there are others – and let her know she has no authority over Kitty at all.'

'Yes, that should put an end to it once and for all,' Beth said and kissed Kitty on the cheek and then Mariah. 'I am sorry for your grief. This is a sad time for you both. You know that should either of you need further help you need only say.'

With that, they took their leave and the kitchen seemed unnaturally silent for a moment, until Mariah spoke. 'That Mrs Harper is a clever woman,' she told Kitty. 'I would never have thought of anything like that, Kitty. I think she is right – we should ask Annie Wilson to tea. If we confront her with this document and tell her the property is already sold to the council, it should see an end to this nonsense – and then we can get on with our lives.'

'Yes, I suppose that might be best. Get it over with,' Kitty agreed. 'I don't want to keep looking over my shoulder for months on end. I hate the idea of having to speak to her, but at least it would be over then…'

'That's what we'll do then,' Mariah said. 'I thought she might have tried to talk to you at the funeral but she didn't – too many folk around, I suppose.'

'Was she there? I saw him but I didn't see her...'

'She tried to keep herself hidden, but I saw her watching you, Kitty.' Mariah frowned. 'They haven't given up their ideas, Kitty. She was there in case an opportunity to lure you away arose, believe me. I doubt either of them realised how many folk would turn out for the funerals.' She nodded to herself. 'We'll ask her for Saturday tea – and we'll make sure we have a little surprise waiting for her if she tries any tricks.'

31

'You didn't tell me our mysterious friend was Bella's eldest son,' Sally said with a note of slightly amused accusation in her voice as she drove away from Kettle's Yard. 'It makes sense, of course. He is Jerry's brother and you saved Jerry's life when he was shot – so they looked after us. Even if they are criminals, they care about family and friends, it seems.'

'I didn't actually know for sure until Mariah said it,' Beth replied, glancing at Sally's face. 'Besides, I thought it best not to mention it – and I don't think you should tell Ben. I haven't told Jack and I shan't.'

'Oh, certainly not.' Sally's laughter tinkled delightfully. 'My poor Ben has had quite enough of the criminal element. He knows nothing of our little trip to the solicitor and, as far as I am concerned, it will stay that way. He knows we came to the funeral, but Kitty is an employee – and one I value, too.'

'She is a lovely girl,' Beth agreed. 'I shudder to think what could have happened to her had that doctor not got cold feet and got word of it to Tel, because even if he'd refused to go through with it, others could have been found. Unscrupulous people will do anything for money.'

'Had they got her and we'd known nothing, she would probably never have been found. They wouldn't have dared to let her go...' Sally frowned. 'It has been done before now and is perfectly legal if two doctors agree that she is mentally incapable and in danger of moral corruption. They could have made a good case for it, because the junkyard isn't exactly a pleasant location – all that scrap metal, rags and the stables too.'

'No, although the house itself is nice,' Beth said. 'I wonder if they will choose to stay there.'

'Kitty spoke of them moving when they are ready,' Sally said. 'I am hoping she will continue to work at Harpers. I think she could do well in the future.'

'Now what bee do you have in your bonnet?' Beth asked with a laugh.

'Oh, plans, you know,' Sally said airily. 'I like Kitty. She is honest and intelligent and we need people like her at Harpers.'

'And you have plans for her future?' Beth laughed. 'Don't worry. I shan't ask for details. That is for you and Kitty to decide. I am just glad you came up with that idea...' She laughed again. 'The look on your solicitor's face when you told him what you wanted. He was full of objections, said it couldn't be done just like that and there were procedures that took time, but you just kept smiling at him and saying you were sure he could find a way, so he did.'

'He knew I wouldn't let him get off to his lunch meeting if he didn't,' Sally replied. 'As you know, he wasn't quite sure how that document would stand up in court, but it will never be needed. It is enough to make that pair of rascals stop and think – and that is all that is necessary. Mariah says she has as good as sold the property to the council and that is the only reason Mr Miller would be interested in shutting Kitty away. He will see that it is a waste of time and so it will be all right.'

'Providing they don't just go ahead and do something out of sheer spite,' Beth said. 'I can't understand how a woman who had called herself Kitty's mother for years could even think of agreeing to such a wicked plan!'

'Perhaps she resented the way her husband just brought Kitty into their home,' Sally said. 'We shall probably never know – but the sooner she and that paramour of hers understand they've nothing to gain, the better.'

'Yes, indeed,' Beth agreed. 'It is so sad for Kitty to be told that her true parents died and she never knew them – and that the woman she believed her mother always resented her.'

'Yes.' Sally nodded thoughtfully. 'But she has Mariah and she has us,

Beth. It is my belief that Kitty will find her own way to live and be happy – and I intend to do all I can to help her.'

* * *

'Did the funeral go off all right?' Ben asked when he came in later that evening. Sally nodded. She was sitting with a glass of orange juice, leafing through some fashion catalogues as the children played with their toys. They came rushing to greet him and Sally's answer was lost and forgotten until some minutes later when Mrs Hills had taken them off to bed.

'Was your political meeting interesting?' Sally asked as he poured himself a small whisky. 'No, not for me, darling, thank you.'

'Yes, it was interesting. I was asked if I would stand in the next safe seat election, but I turned them down.'

'What?' Sally looked at him. 'I thought you had all sort of ideas for setting the country to rights?'

Ben laughed. 'Yes, I did, and I shall probably bore you about what is wrong with the politics of this country many times in the future – but if these past weeks have taught me anything, Sally, it is that my family and friends are all that matters to me. I did consider entering politics, but I've changed my mind. We have Harpers to run and a family – and we need time together, to enjoy life. If I became a member of the House, I would be out until all hours of the night, leaving you far too much work at Harpers.'

'Don't let that bit of it worry you, Ben. I intend to find myself a personal assistant in the near future and she will take on some of the buying.'

'A woman? So you already have someone in mind.' Ben smiled. 'It makes no difference, Sally. I shall be glad if someone takes on some of your load – we need to get out together more as a family. Just enjoy life.'

'We shall,' Sally replied. 'If you're sure you don't want to be an MP, then I shall say I am glad. It would mean very long hours and I would rather we spent more time as a family, too... especially as it is going to increase in the not-too-distant future.'

Ben was about to take a sip of his drink, but he spluttered and coughed, his eyes shooting towards her in shock. 'Sally! You're not— This is a joke— It isn't...' He looked at her incredulously. 'You are quite certain?'

She nodded; her eyes bright with laughter as she saw him struggling to take it in.

'But I thought... you couldn't have another child?' His face clouded with sudden anxiety. 'Sally, the doctor said you mustn't have another baby. You were so ill last time.'

'It's all right, Ben,' Sally told him. 'I've spoken to my doctor and he thinks I shall be fine. I know I was told that it was unlikely I would conceive again – and that it might be best not to try for a third child – but my body has completely recovered and the doctor says I am fine.'

'Sally, are you sure that it won't be too much for you?' He hesitated, then, 'I don't want to lose you, my darling. We could enquire about terminating...'

'No, Ben. I won't even consider it. Besides, I've never felt better in my life. When I was carrying Peter, I was often faint and ill, but this time I am fine. I've hardly even been sick and I didn't realise I was pregnant until I suddenly realised that I hadn't had my monthlies,' Sally said and held her hand out to him. He came to her at once and knelt beside her chair, holding her hand tightly. 'Please, tell me you're happy about our news...'

'Of course I am – you know I love children, but you... I couldn't bear it if I lost you, Sally.'

'I promise you won't,' she said and lifted her face for his kiss, which was gentle and tender. 'I am carrying this one perfectly well, Ben. I'm already three months gone, so it is too late for a safe termination anyway; even if a doctor said it was necessary to save my life, there would be a huge risk. I didn't want to tell you until I was sure everything was as it should be and it is.'

'Oh, Sally,' Ben said and caught her to him, holding her close as his lips touched her neck. 'I love you so much. You and the children are my world.'

Sally sat back and looked at him. 'I shall be fine. You'll see – but now you understand why I need a personal assistant as well as your help. I may have to rest more, though at the moment, I am bursting with energy!'

'As long as it stays that way,' Ben said and smiled. 'You must promise me you won't overdo things, my darling.'

'Yes, I promise I will take care of myself and the little one. Do you want another son or a daughter?'

'I don't mind,' Ben said. 'We've already got one of each and they are perfect. What does Beth think and your mother?'

'I haven't told anyone else yet,' she said. 'I wanted you to be the first to know, Ben. It does mean we may not be able to travel abroad together for a while. I know you were looking forward to taking me to America, but I don't think I will be going for a couple of years...'

Ben laughed and shook his head. 'It doesn't matter. None of that matters. Just as long as you are well and happy... *You* are happy to be having another child?'

'Yes, Ben,' she said. 'I am happy.' She smiled at him as he stood up. 'It has been a difficult few months – the strike and your quarrel with Jack and the threats to Beth – but it is over now. We can look forward to the birth of our third child and the future.'

32

'That must be them,' Kitty said as the front doorbell rang that Saturday afternoon. She swallowed nervously. 'It will be all right?' She looked to Mariah for reassurance.

'You know it will,' Mariah said. 'Just stick to our plan and nothing can go wrong.'

Kitty nodded, licking her suddenly dry lips. 'I'll let them in then.' She went through to the hall; it smelled of the rose petals that Mariah kept in large porcelain jars. Her stomach was fluttering nervously, even though she knew that she must be safe enough here in this house, but it made her feel sick to think that a woman she'd known all her life could agree to the plot to shut her away in an asylum simply to get the property she'd inherited.

Painting a look of welcome on her face, she opened the door to the man and woman who stood there. 'Mother. Mr Miller,' she said and stood back. 'Won't you come in, please?'

Annie Wilson sniffed the air and nodded. 'The roses disguise it, but I don't know how you can stand to live here, Kitty. You were brought up to know better.'

'Was I, Mother?' They had decided she should call Annie Wilson her mother so as to lull her into a sense of security. It would not do to confront them with the truth too soon.

'I should have thought you would know that,' Annie Wilson said as she followed her down the hall to the spotless kitchen. It smelled of baking and herbs and lavender polish. Mariah's dresser shone from the extra polishing Kitty had given it that morning. 'Well, I suppose this is comfortable enough... it is bigger than I expected.' Annie Wilson's eyes darted everywhere, dwelling on the dresser that was set out with attractive porcelain and trinkets.

'Please sit down,' Mariah said. 'Annie Wilson – and you, too, Mr Miller. I know Father said you would enter this house over his dead body, but he's gone now so I don't suppose one quick visit will make much difference.'

'Ah, Miss Norton,' Annie Wilson said, looking at her for the first time. 'Yes, it will be a quick visit as I've come to take my daughter home. Kitty, get your things. It is time you were under my care once more.'

'Annie...' Joshua Miller said a little uneasily. 'No need for rudeness. I am sure Kitty will be glad to come now that she knows you're sorry for the breach between you.'

'No,' Kitty said. 'I will not be glad to come – in fact I refuse to come with you now or ever.'

'I told you what a wilful girl she is!' Annie Wilson exclaimed. 'She deserves what is coming to her – and you will come, Kitty. You are my daughter and I have the right to demand that this woman releases you into my care immediately.'

'No, you don't have the right,' Mariah said and took an envelope from her apron pocket and placed it on the sparklingly white tablecloth. 'The document in here says that I am joint guardian of Kitty until she is twenty-one. Mrs Harper – Kitty's employer – is the other guardian.'

'What are you talking about?' Annie Wilson spluttered, her face turning pink as she gave Mariah an indignant glare. 'She is my daughter...'

'I think you know that is a lie,' Mariah said calmly. 'You were unable to give your husband a child so he brought an orphaned girl home to you and asked you to bring her up as your own, which you did to a certain extent – but Kitty was never adopted legally.'

'How do you know?' Annie Wilson exploded with fury, spittle on her lips. 'You can't know... it was a secret—'

'Idiot!' Mr Miller hissed at her. He smiled at Kitty. 'I am sure you're very grateful to the woman who loved and cared for you, looked after you all your life. I know Annie has been very upset by what has happened between you. She is sorry she was harsh to you after your father died and she wants the chance to make it up to you – don't you, Annie?'

Annie Wilson glared at him but nodded. 'Yes, I do,' she said between gritted teeth. 'You will have a decent life with us, Kitty. Besides, you owe me for all *I* did for you. You must come with us now.'

'Kitty, I forbid you to go with these people,' Mariah said. 'I don't know them and I don't like them. I think they should leave my house.'

'I will do as you tell me, Mariah,' Kitty said. She looked at Annie Wilson and then at Mr Miller. 'I shall stay here with my legal guardian, because she is also my friend and she loves me. You never loved me, Annie Wilson, even though you took me in. Your husband was a good man – but you were a cold woman.'

'Kitty, think very carefully about what you are doing,' Mr Miller said. 'This property will soon be mine and then you will be on the streets...'

'I wouldn't sell to you if you were the only one who wanted it,' Mariah told him then. 'I'd burn the place down first – and, besides, I've already sold it to someone else.'

'Your father owed me money...' Mr Miller blustered, taken by surprise at her announcement, 'and I intend to be paid.'

'Prove it in court,' Mariah said, her eyes meeting his fearlessly. He was lying and they both knew it. 'Your little schemes won't work – so just go away and leave us in peace.'

His eyes darted about the kitchen and then lighted on a pistol lying on top of a chest of drawers. He picked it up and pointed it at Kitty. 'Either she comes with us now or I shoot her – and then you...'

Mariah reached for a small bell on the table and rang it once. 'I don't think you will, Mr Miller,' she said and smiled as four large burly men entered the room from the door at the back of the kitchen. 'As it happens, that pistol isn't loaded, but this one is...' She raised her apron and showed them the pistol she had hidden there. 'Arnie, will you and your friends show Mr Miller out. He has just expressed his intention to kill Kitty and me – and I think you know how to deal with a man like that.'

'You won't get away with this,' Annie Wilson screeched at them, her face contorting with fury. 'He promised me money if we got your property. All those years I looked after you and you were *his* little pet. You stole my husband's love from me. When we get you locked up, you little wretch, I'll make sure they never let you out.'

'Oh, we know all about your kind plans for Kitty,' Mariah told them. 'You thought you would snatch Kitty and force me to sell to you, didn't you, Mr Miller? It might have worked, but people talk and we have a lot of friends. If anything happens to Kitty now or in the future – both of you will be arrested, and if she can't be found, you will be charged with murder.'

'I'll kill her...' Beside herself with rage at the way they had been outwitted, Annie Wilson launched herself at Kitty but was caught by one of the rather large men and thrown, struggling and spitting venom, over his shoulder.

'You are making a show of yourself,' Mr Miller said, disgust on his face. He threw the pistol onto the kitchen table. 'We've lost and that's the end of it.' He inclined his head to Kitty and then to Mariah. 'I give you my best on this occasion, ladies – but don't get in my way ever again. I won't hesitate to make your lives a misery.' He shrugged as one of the men moved towards him. 'I'm going. No need to get violent, just remember I've a good memory for faces.'

The man grinned and pushed his face to within inches of his. 'Take a good look, Mr Miller. I might be around to see you one day. Tel don't like folk what threaten innocent young ladies...'

The colour drained from Mr Miller's face and he turned and almost ran from the kitchen. Annie Wilson continued to shriek as she was carried unceremoniously out into the yard and then dumped.

Mariah turned to look at Kitty and smiled as the front door was shut firmly behind them. 'I don't think they will give us any trouble in the future. It is good to have the right friends sometimes.'

Kitty laughed and sat down. 'Thank goodness that is over. It is over, isn't it, Mariah?'

'Oh yes. She may not know it yet, but he does and she can't do anything unless he agrees.' Mariah shook her head. 'She is a nasty piece of work, Kitty. I knew she'd been unkind to you, but I couldn't believe she would be so very bitter towards you until I saw it with my own eyes.'

'No...' Kitty looked sad. 'I wonder what I did to deserve it.'

'I dare say she was jealous because your father loved you, Kitty. Everyone liked him, but she was never popular – thought herself above the rest of us.'

Kitty smiled and looked at her fondly. 'You were so brave and strong standing up to them like that, Mariah. Just think what would have happened to me if we hadn't been warned of their wicked intentions.'

'It worked perfectly, so we can forget about it – and that awful woman. She is the one that needs locking up in an asylum and I wouldn't put it past him to do it either.'

'I think she has got worse since she went to live with him,' Kitty said. 'I don't think he treats her quite as she expected. I know she hoped he might marry her.'

'Don't you go feeling sorry for her,' Mariah said. 'She deserves whatever she gets in my opinion for what she tried to do to you – but now we must forget them both and start planning the rest of our lives. I've been told about two nice little terraced houses that would suit us down to the ground, Kitty. We can knock through a wall and make the kitchen bigger so we can get Father's dresser in and the collection. Then we could use the parlour of one as the shop and there will be spare bedrooms to store the extra stuff until we decide what to do with it.'

'Oh, they sound ideal,' Kitty said. 'Whereabouts are they?'

'Just around the corner from Dressmakers' Alley and not too far from Commercial Road. It should be a busy enough area for the trade I'm planning.'

'I don't know that area,' Kitty said. 'It sounds as if I could catch a bus to Harpers in Oxford Street easily enough.'

'You'll be closer to work than you are now,' Mariah said. 'I told Arnie we'd take a look at them next week. He reckons they need a fair bit of work inside, but he can do that for us.' She laughed, her eyes sparkling. 'Good thing Mr Miller didn't know all them muscles come from hauling bricks not boxing. He's as soft as butter inside...'

'He likes you a lot,' Kitty said. 'Are you sure you don't want to marry him, Mariah? I could find somewhere to live nearby if—'

Mariah shook her head. 'Mebbe one day I'll change my mind, but Arnie will wait. He's a nice lad and he looks after his mother. Her and me don't get on, never have and never could – she's the true reason I won't wed him, Kitty. One day, if we still like each other, then I might reconsider – but she's still going strong and good luck to her. I don't wish her gone. Arnie comes to see me when he feels like it and we're happy that way. We might start to fight if we were married.'

'I don't think anyone would want to quarrel with you, Mariah,' Kitty told her, 'but I am happy you want to live with me, at least for a while. If you do change your mind, we can talk about it when the time comes.'

Mariah chuckled. 'I can't see it happening anytime soon, but we'll wait and see – and now I think we should have our tea...'

Kitty nodded and went to fill the kettle. 'You made some lovely sandwiches and cakes, Mariah. Should I call the men in so that they can join us. We don't want all this delicious food to go to waste.'

'They deserve a nice tea,' Mariah agreed.

Kitty smiled as she made the tea in the large brown pot. 'I feel a lot better now. I'm never going to forget Larry or your father – but I think I am ready to go back to work, Mariah. I'll take some time off when we move, but that won't be for a while – and Mrs Harper says I can still take my holiday when I'm ready.'

'Aye, Kitty love, you do that,' Mariah told her. 'What Father and Larry would want is for us both to be happy. We shan't forget them, which is as it should be, but we'll go on living and we'll have good lives.'

'Yes, we shall,' Kitty replied. 'I shall start work on Monday then, Mariah. Perhaps we could go and have a look at the houses tomorrow – if that is possible?'

'Arnie will take us and bring us back,' Mariah said confidently. 'He has the first option on them to renovate, so he'll be happy to do them as we want...' She brought a bottle of sherry to the table. 'I don't often drink but Father and Larry liked a drop of sherry now and then. We'll have a small glass each, Kitty, to celebrate our victory here today and to toast the future.'

33

Everyone was kind to Kitty on her return to Harpers that day in June, including Marion Jones, who said she was sorry for her loss but pleased to see her back.

'We've noticed a difference on the sales floor without you,' she said and smiled at her. 'I am sure you don't want to talk about what happened – but if you'd like to go out one day, to the cinema or just for a walk in the park...' Marion blushed. 'You know where I live, Kitty.'

Kitty thanked her and smiled, fighting a rush of emotion. The pain was still raw but life had to go on and she was lucky to have such a good job to come back to. She spent the first couple of hours tidying displays in the dress department, paid a visit to the hat department and then the shoes, making a few notes about new stock. It was as she was on her way for a tea break that someone called her name and she saw Pamela, Mrs Harper's secretary, beckoning her.

'Mrs Harper requests that you take coffee with her this morning, Miss Wilson,' she said and smiled but made no reference to Kitty's loss, which was a relief. People were kind, but their sympathetic words only brought back the sorrow.

She followed Pamela into the lift and out again on the top floor, and was told to go straight into the office. When she did so, she saw a man sitting in the chair opposite Mrs Harper and halted uncertainly.

'Forgive me. I was told to come in, Mrs Harper.'

Sally Harper turned and smiled, 'Yes, do come in and take a seat.' The man had risen to his feet and was offering her his chair. 'This is Mr Marco – our window dresser. He has been away for some months, so I doubt you'll have met him. Mr Marco this is Kitty Wilson.'

'I am pleased to meet you,' Mr Marco said. He smiled and turned from her to Sally Harper. 'I have work to do and your windows will soon be sparkling with fresh ideas again. I saw that they needed a little lift here and there as I came in, but that can soon be rectified.'

'We have missed your magical inspiration,' Sally said. 'I had begun to think you would never return.'

'I had things to arrange,' he said vaguely. 'Jules has become a special friend, you see, but he wasn't certain he wished to leave France. Happily, in the end, he was persuaded to come.' He winked at Sally Harper. 'I am pleased to say that we are arranging our lives to suit us both... Jules is a cousin of Pierre's father, but, somehow, we did not meet when I was in France during the war. That was unfortunate but has now been resolved very satisfactorily – my only fear is that he may take over my job. He is a talented artist, as you will soon discover.'

Sally Harper motioned to Kitty to take the seat he had vacated as he left the office. 'Mr Marco likes to tease, which you will discover if you work together,' she said. 'It will be a part of the new job I want to offer you...'

Kitty was taken off guard. 'Is my present job not working well, Mrs Harper?'

'Very well,' Sally said and smiled at her. 'Please, in future, when we are in my office, do call me Sally. Beth always does and we shall have regular meetings the three of us – if you wish to take the position of my personal assistant...'

'Your personal assistant?' Kitty was astounded. 'I'm not quite sure what that means, Mrs Harper.'

'It means that you will learn to do my job,' Sally told her frankly. 'I shall train you to buy for various departments, to advise on others, and, on occasion, help Mr Marco with ideas for the windows. It means keeping an eye on the store in general, learning to spot where there is a potential problem, being able to weed out dead stock that is never going to move, as well as all the tedious paperwork.'

'Good gracious...' Kitty stared at her in amazement. She was stunned by the very idea of it. 'Do you really think I can do all that, Mrs Harper?'

'Yes, I believe so, but you will have years to learn. I don't expect you to take over everything tomorrow.' Sally laughed. 'You may as well know, though only close friends and family have been told as yet, but I am having another child. It means I may be unable to come into the store for weeks or even months after the birth. I shall need you to bring me reports on stock and sales to my home and we will discuss what needs to be done. We will go through the new lines together and you will gradually learn what will fit in with Harpers and what won't – though I believe you have a fairly good grasp of that already. You know the stock situation in certain departments almost better than I do. We have several buyers at Harpers, most of whom report to my husband – but the clothes, bags, hats, jewellery, lingerie and all the things ladies love are my particular concern. This is where I shall need help.'

'It sounds wonderful,' Kitty said. 'I would love to try – if you think I could do it, Mrs Harper – I mean Sally...' She said the name shyly. 'But what about the job I do now? Will you continue the idea? Has it been a success?'

'Oh yes.' Sally looked at her quizzically. 'For the moment, I'm afraid you have to do that, too, while you learn. However, I want you to choose two members of staff to train to take your place. We can employ other girls to serve on the counters; there are always young women keen to work at Harpers, but I prefer to promote girls we already employ if there is a vacancy and more money involved. It gives everyone an incentive to know that they can progress.'

'It hardly ever happens to young women,' Kitty replied. 'Most can never hope to become a supervisor. Those posts are often reserved for men and the women who do hold them seldom leave as they are dedicated to their jobs.'

'Yes, perfectly true,' Sally agreed. 'It has never been my policy, though. I started out on the counters and thought myself fortunate to get the job. Beth started at the same time. We have both done well in our lives and there is no reason why other women should not do something similar.'

Kitty nodded. For a moment, she was silent, then, 'I think Shirley Williams from the hat department could do my present job – and there is a young woman who works in stationery. I think her name is Phillipa Hastings – she always tries hard to find what her customer wants.'

'Oh, I couldn't agree more,' Sally cried, delighted with her insight. 'Shirley was due for promotion a long time ago, but she didn't want to be a supervisor. I think she might like your job, Kitty – and I've noticed Miss Hastings, too. I will ask them to come to the office and discuss it.'

'Thank you,' Kitty replied, still a little stunned by what was happening. 'How do I begin, Mrs Harper?'

Sally laughed as Pamela brought in their coffee. 'Will you bring the latest sales and stock figures in, Pamela? Thank you, those biscuits look delicious. If my son was here, we wouldn't get any. He would eat them all!'

'Coffee icing,' Kitty remarked. 'They do look good.'

'Oh, they are,' Sally said as her secretary left once more. 'For a start, you will continue as you are, helping certain customers, familiarising yourself with the stock and generally keeping an eye out for anything that isn't quite right. Beth helps me with that, as you know. She walks the store twice a week and tells me if she thinks something is wrong – but Beth has two small children and a family to look after and I need someone who can work full-time, overtime if needed...' She caught her breath. 'I apologise if that sounds harsh, Kitty. I know what you've lost, but from what you've said to me on previous occasions, I believe you want to make your life here at Harpers, at least for the time being?'

'It is what I want,' Kitty confirmed. 'I've cried until I can't cry any more, Sally. There is an empty place inside me and I believe there always will be. I do not think I shall ever marry... I know that it is possible I might one day change my mind, but that day is not now nor for a long time. No one can ever say that something is forever...'

'That is so wise and true,' Sally murmured. 'I knew you were a young woman who thought deeply and I had it in mind to promote you, but now I think you may well dedicate your life to a career. I know that if I lost my husband, I could not even contemplate another marriage. Harpers and my children would be my life – but *you* are young, Kitty, and may find love again.'

Kitty inclined her head. 'I have Mariah. She is like a sister to me and I love her dearly. We have found a new home and it will be renovated and made right for us. We shall have friends and our work – Mariah is to open a little curiosity shop with her father's stuff – and I shall have my work here. I believe it is what Larry would want for me, to see me happy and busy. The job you have offered me will stretch me and I shall not have time to look back, only forward.'

'Oh Kitty, my dear.' Sally stood up and went round the desk to embrace her. They hugged, both emotional. 'Now, we shall have regular meetings on the days I come in – and one of the first things I want to show you is a list of my best suppliers, backing those assertions up with sales figures and profit margins.' She laughed as Kitty looked daunted. 'Don't worry. It is all beautifully prepared and presented by the office girls. All we have to do is to look and compare.'

Kitty nodded. For the moment, she was breathless, still unable to take it all in, but she knew it was exactly what she needed. Sally Harper had become a friend to her. She had shown trust in her and given her a chance to learn and make something of a life that could have crumbled in the ashes of a bitter loss.

It would not happen to her, Kitty vowed. The woman she had thought of as her mother had turned sour with jealousy. Had she clung to Kitty at their time of sorrow she could have shared Kitty's good fortune, but she had let herself sink into her own private hell of bitter resentment. Kitty would take the opportunity that had been given her. She would seize it with both hands and make it work, for herself, for Mariah and for Harpers.

She could never forget Larry, who had loved her and changed her world, but she would learn to live without him and she would live in a way that he would have approved of. Kitty's fortunes were rising, but she knew others who were not as fortunate. She would not cease her visits to Bella, and she would reach out to Marion Jones, because she knew her former supervisor needed a friend. She had an uneasy home life, much as Kitty once had. Kitty would help her as she'd been helped.

Life would not be easy, but she wanted to work hard and to learn. Through work and helping others would come her own salvation and the future had a rosy glow about it that beckoned her on...

ABOUT THE AUTHOR

Rosie Clarke is a #1 bestselling saga writer whose books include Welcome to Harpers Emporium and The Mulberry Lane series. She has written over 100 novels under different pseudonyms and is a RNA Award winner. She lives in Cambridgeshire.

Sign up to Rosie Clarke's mailing list for news, competitions and updates on future books.

Visit Rosie's website: www.rosieclarke.co.uk

Follow Rosie on social media here:

facebook.com/Rosie-clarke-119457351778432

x.com/AnneHerries

bookbub.com/authors/rosie-clarke

ALSO BY ROSIE CLARKE

Welcome to Harpers Emporium Series

The Shop Girls of Harpers

Love and Marriage at Harpers

Rainy Days for the Harpers Girls

Harpers Heroes

Wartime Blues for the Harpers Girls

Victory Bells For The Harpers Girls

Changing Times at Harpers

Heartbreak at Harpers

The Mulberry Lane Series

A Reunion at Mulberry Lane

Stormy Days On Mulberry Lane

A New Dawn Over Mulberry Lane

Life and Love at Mulberry Lane

Last Orders at Mulberry Lane

Blackberry Farm Series

War Clouds Over Blackberry Farm

Heartache at Blackberry Farm

Love and Duty at Blackberry Farm

The Trenwith Collection Series

Sarah's Choice

Louise's War

Standalones

Nellie's Heartbreak

A Mother's Shame

A Sister's Destiny

Dangerous Times on Dressmakers' Alley

Sixpence Stories

Boldwood

Boldwood Books is an award-winning fiction publishing company seeking out the best stories from around the world.

Find out more at www.boldwoodbooks.com

Join our reader community for brilliant books, competitions and offers!

Follow us
@BoldwoodBooks
@TheBoldBookClub

Sign up to our weekly deals newsletter

https://bit.ly/BoldwoodBNewsletter

Milton Keynes UK
Ingram Content Group UK Ltd.
UKHW041117200624
444314UK00002B/10